To H
thank
(nt

Paul

THE
GODSONS
INHERITANCE

Paul Gait

by

PAUL GAIT

Grosvenor House
Publishing Limited

This book is published by
Grosvenor House Publishing Ltd
28-30 High Street, Guildford, Surrey, GU1 3EL.
www.grosvenorhousepublishing.co.uk

This novel is entirely a work of fiction. The names, characters and
incidents portrayed in it are the work of the author's imagination. Any
resemblance to actual persons, living or dead, events or localities
is entirely coincidental.

A CIP record for this book
is available from the British Library

ISBN 978-1-78148-878-2

Thanks

To my wife Helen, for allowing me to spend countless
hours continuing to develop the Godsons stories;

To family and friends, for continued support
and encouragement.

To Janet for again spending many hours
proof reading my manuscript.

To the readers of the prequels, 'Godsons-Counting
Sunsets' and 'The Godsons Legacy', for their positive
comments and ongoing interest in the Godson's story.

To the Gloucestershire Young Carers charity for
valuable assistance during my research.

Foreword

The prequels 'Godsons Counting Sunsets' and 'The Godsons Legacy' have created a demand for this the third novel in the Godsons series.

Their relationships are well established, their personal problems recognised so surely obtaining their legacy should be a straight forward event - but not for Geoffery Foster's Godsons.

We rejoin their exploits as they prepare to comply with the terms of their Godfather's will and hopefully get their hands on their inheritances?

But as they quickly find out, first they have to make personal sacrifices and become 'team' players. Are they ALL prepared to pay the price?

They encounter many obstacles on their journey and perhaps when the megalomaniacal Sue's case finally comes to court it will be one that disappears?'

PART ONE

Justice at last?

CHAPTER ONE

The desert bleached camouflage netting twitched in the sand laden breeze as Carrie maintained her lone vigil. She had lain under the baking hot sun, in her clandestine hide, for six long, sweat soaked hours.

Moving in under the cover of darkness she had silently dug the shallow hole near a rain parched bush whose skeletal branches gave her little protection as the sun rose higher.

After setting up her equipment, the only thing she had moved since was her eyes. The wait seemed like an eternity.

She had trained herself to control her metabolism in order to endure the range of extreme desert temperatures, the fifty degree furnace like day time heat and the freezing mind numbing night time cold.

In order to keep herself hydrated she sucked tepid water through a foul tasting tube connected to a water bladder by her side.

Unable to move for fear of being spotted she urinated where she lay, the specially designed high absorbent incontinence pants preventing tell-tale moisture escaping, more importantly stopping any smell emanating that would attract curious dogs to her.

At last there was movement. With mild excitement she heard faint voices. She strained to hear what they were saying, her communications headset restricting the clarity. Then she saw them. Two men, in long flowing robes, carrying digging implements passed through her field of vision into a slight depression.

Her patience had paid off. The intelligence was correct. Soon she heard the sound of digging. The stakeout was going to be fruitful after all.

Immediately she called it in. Talking very quietly into her headset microphone, she passed on the information complete with precise coordinates.

Within minutes she spotted the drone circling silently overhead like an eagle menacingly sizing up its prey.

Through her earpiece she heard the strangely familiar voice of the pilot sitting thousands of miles away in his air conditioned control room back in the UK.

She imagined him moving the remote controlled aeroplane with a games like control console, watching the TV pictures, zooming in to the targets as they prepared the IED trap.

'Targets acquired,' she heard him say. The voice so familiar but who was it? The radio transmission distorted by the Doppler effect hindered her identification.

'I have two targets, permission to strike.'

Carrie knew the procedure well. Back in the control room senior officers would be looking at the pictures and analysing the situation. After a few minutes another voice said, 'Permission granted.'

She knew that the death sentence had been agreed. Any minute now the hellfire missiles would be on their way. The insurgents wouldn't know anything about it until it was too late.

Her clandestine operation would possibly save the lives of many of her colleagues who would never know of her involvement.

She heard the calm countdown, 'Roger strike authority confirmed. Missile release in three, two…

And then she saw the child. It was a little girl. She was walking towards the men. She was carrying something in her arms. 'Oh my God, they've got a child to carry the explosives!'

Carrie immediately went back on the radio and shouted 'Abort, abort,' at the same time as the drone Pilot spotted the child.

'Third target joining the other two, third target is carrying something.' He waited a few seconds and started the countdown again. 'Three…'

Carrie called again. 'Abort! Abort launch.'

'Two…'

'No stop. Abort, abort, abort.'

'One… firing.'

She saw the white trails of the missiles leaving the drone.

Breaking all the rules of covert operation, she shouted in Pashtu to warn the child and at the same time trying to get up out of her hide. But after six hours of immobility, she couldn't get her legs to work.

She watched the billowing white smoke trails getting closer.

The child, frightened by the voice from 'nowhere', was running towards the men. Towards certain death.

Frantically she pulled herself out of the hide and started a fast crawl on her elbows, dragging her useless legs behind her.

In her ear she could hear the pilot calmly describing the estimated time until the 'kill'. The voice was so familiar. But who the hell was it?

She had dragged herself to the top of the depression and watched helplessly as the missiles struck.

Automatically she pushed her face into the sand as the massive explosions occurred throwing body parts, sand and missile debris high into the air.

As the smoke cleared the Pilot said calmly, 'Kill confirmed.' Then it dawned on her the voice was her boyfriend, Tim.

'Tim you've killed them. Why didn't you stop?' she shouted holding her mouthpiece to her lips.

As she scanned the scene of devastation she could see next to the body of the child there were no explosives, only the body of a dog partially wrapped in a blanket. 'Oh my god, they were only burying a dead dog.' She realised. 'You've killed a child. You stupid bastard. Why didn't you abort?' Sobbing she pounded the sand with her fists. 'Why didn't you stop?' she demanded.

'Jesus Carrie! Now what the bloody hell are you dreaming about? Christ I'm black and blue.'

Carrie awoke with a start. She was trembling and drenched with sweat.

'What did he say? It was only a dream, a dreadful nightmarish dream. Oh thank God,' she said trying to regain her composure.

'The sooner you start this assessment for your PTSD the better,' he grunted, rubbing his arm.

'Oh Tim it was horrible. I was on a covert mission and it all went terribly wrong. There was this child,' she wailed.

'It was a dream. A nightmare. It didn't happen. It was all in your imagination,' Tim repeated wearily.

'But it could have...all those missions I did.'

'Yes but it didn't, did it? Now stop beating yourself up for a sodding dream.'

Tim put her arms around Carrie's trembling body and kissed her hair.

'It's alright. There's nothing to be frightened of. I'll protect you.'

At the same time he was wondering if he had the mental strength to put up with her continuing unpredictable and weird outbursts.

CHAPTER TWO

Unusually Andy was home when the postman made his morning delivery. He saw the official looking brown envelope on the mat and picked it up hoping the tax man hadn't heard about his windfall from Geoffery's generosity.

He ran his forefinger under the flap and pulled out the letter. It was a heart stopping moment as he examined it.

He had been summoned as a witness for Sue Williams-Screen's trial.

Suddenly his world collapsed. His past indiscretion would come back to haunt him. His reputation was going to be denigrated in open court.

He slumped heavily on to the kitchen chair and stared at the demand to present himself at Gloucester Crown Court.

He blamed the Policeman, the Detective Sergeant, Graham Fredericks for getting him embroiled in the court case.

Against his better judgement he had taken the policeman's advice to make the complaint. *'Unless you stand up to these people they will carry on with their evil ways. Blackmail and extortion would be a significant addition to the charges against her,'* he'd said.

But the Police wanted to 'nail' her and so Andy had agreed to make the complaint. Was it too late now to retract it?

If only he hadn't been filmed by that evil woman. None of this would have happened.

True he had got himself in to the compromising situation with a scantily clad woman in a hotel corridor during the early hours. Admittedly he had been in her room for two hours. But it was all innocent. It was just a platonic parting kiss. A peck on the lips. Nothing sexual had happened

The repercussions from this sensual episode with Nadine in the Monaco hotel several months previously had nearly broken up his family and ended his marriage.

But he had been able to convince his wife of the platonic nature of the kiss and things had calmed down since. After the initial disclosure of the incident their marital relationship, although turbulent, had survived.

But when it's brought up in court it would open up the whole 'can of worms' again and worse it would be in the public domain. He feared for their future.

He would now need to convince other, sceptical people of the innocence of the episode as well.

The newspapers were going to have a field day. He could imagine the headlines *'Scout Leader in midnight romp'* or similar sensationalised 'tacky' headline.

When Helen became aware of the incident she'd seized the 'bull by the horns' and much to his surprise had telephoned Nadine demanding to know 'what the hell was going on'.

Nadine had told her the truth that Andy had got drunk and had fallen asleep on the sofa. There were no romantic incidents.

In fact, his ego was badly bruised when Nadine had told Helen he wasn't her type anyway.

Helen was sceptical about Nadine's explanation, but said she'd give him one more chance.

Everything was slowly improving and getting back to normal. However the arrival of the letter was bound to 'upset the apple cart' and re-open newly healed marital wounds.

How would his claim of innocence be received by the court? Would they then side with that evil woman Sue? Had his apparent adultery undermined his credibility in their eyes? Would the jury believe his word against that woman's?

It was a mess, a terrible mess.

What if they dragged up the tensions in his marriage? Helen's post natal depression? Would they find out about them not resuming normal marital relationships following Molly's birth?

Would they suggest his sexual frustrations led him into moral infidelity?

Hell. He was after all a private man and now all his dirty washing was going to be aired publicly.

Perhaps he could speak to her lawyers and strike a deal? Was it too late?

Andy looked at his watch. 'Shit! I'll be late for work.'

He had continued to work at the hospice where he had nursed Geoffery Foster until the end.

His reluctant involvement with his former patient's personal life had pitched him into a miscellany of hassle that had turned his quiet life into a series of 'challenging' incidents.

Unfortunately even after Geoffery Foster had died, the fallout from his life continued. Andy had been thrust into the politics of someone else's family problems.

Geoffery's three godsons all had significant issues and their personal baggage had disrupted Andy's already busy life.

He had become embroiled with Tim, the self-centred and petulant childhood meningitis amputee; Rupert the quiet individual battered by his violent wife Sue and James the former childhood millionaire then living on the streets of London, a homeless, well-educated drunken vagrant whom Andy had helped to rescue.

Andy's personal legacy from his former patient included ensuring the three Godsons did something useful with their lives and were prudent with their anticipated huge financial legacies.

Andy gazed at the letter again and cursed Geoffery Foster for making his life so complicated? When it used to be so straightforward.

CHAPTER THREE

The secondary school was erupting pupils at the end of the school day.

Some children ran quickly to their parental or grandparental taxis to take them home, often just a short walkable journey away.

Others filled the streets and surrounding roads, a mass of teenagers, a lava flow of young people arrogantly devoid of road sense or courtesy for other pedestrians caught going the wrong way during the schools exodus.

Ben was leaning on his bike deep in conversation with one of his Scouting friends when the tide reached them.

He heard the first derogatory comment about his role looking after his alcoholic mother which, as usual, he dismissed.

'Look there's Bird, the weirdo who puts his mother to bed.'

'Too strange! Hey Bird show us your six fingers.'

'Oi Bird is that right your Mothers a pill head?'

The others laughed and pointed.

Ben had been taunted like this all throughout his childhood, but today it really got to him and he reacted – badly.

Irrespective that his taunters were two years older than he was, he nevertheless, went against his own judgement and engaged in some backchat.

'Why don't you bully the little kids, that's more your style, isn't it?'

'Feeling brave aren't we?' The tall, leader of the gang said advancing towards him.

'So, what of it?' Ben's nervous voice betrayed his discomfort.

'What of it? You need to learn some manners kid.' The gang leader threatened.

'Oh why don't you go play with yourself.' Ben said, bravely.

Other members of the small gang surrounded Ben as he realised too late that he had overstepped the mark.

'What did you say,' demanded a pimply faced adolescent.

'Nothing,' Ben said, lowering his gaze, realising he had carelessly stepped into the danger zone.

'Oh not so brave now are we?' The acne faced one growled, towering over Ben and pushed him heavily in the shoulder.

Ben rode the shove and stood his ground.

The other pushed him again. 'Want a fight do ya?'

Ben said nothing.

'Don't you think its weird putting your mother to bed?' he demanded, glaring at Ben.

'Yeah what do they call it?' One of the others asked.

'Incest,' added the one confronting Ben. 'Are you doing it with your moth…'

Ben saw red and before the yob could finish off the inquisition, Ben's knuckle smashed into his mouth.

The surprised reaction of the others delayed the all-out assault on Ben by only a fraction of a second.

Too late Ben realised he had 'bitten off more than he could chew' and as he went down under a rein of blows he rolled into a foetal position protecting his head with his hands as they kicked at his prostrate form.

Other homeward bound pupils quickly surrounded the fight and the onlookers started chanting 'Fight, fight, fight.'

Fortunately Ben was saved any more serious punishment by the arrival of one of his teachers who was cycling home and attracted by the chant of the crowd.

'What the hell's going on here?' he demanded as the crowd peeled back to let him through.

'Nothing Sir, Bird just fell over.' The instigator, nursing a fat lip, replied.

'Yeah a likely story. Now clear off the lot of you before you get into any more trouble.' The teacher directed.

The gang stepped back from the figure on the ground but not before the fat lipped one gave Ben another kick in the ribs.

'Move now, before I call the Police,' the teacher threatened.

They moved off slowly, muttering. Ben painfully picked himself up.

'You alright Bird?' asked the teacher, looking into his face.

'Yes Sir, thanks.'

'What was that all about?'

'Nothing Sir.' Ben wasn't going to elaborate that he had been defending his mother's honour.

'Nothing! That appears to be a pretty dangerous thing that 'nothing'! Ok. Are you sure you're alright then?'

'Yes Sir,' Ben replied, vainly trying to dust himself down at the same time picking his bike up.

'I suggest you wait a bit until they've cleared the area before you go home.'

'Yes Sir.'

The teacher cycled off shaking his head, 'Kids,' he muttered.

Ben was more concerned about his precious bike than himself.

One of his attackers had stood on the front wheel in his attempts to get at Ben and had buckled the wheel and broken several spokes. As the bike was un-rideable he put it over his shoulder and carried it the half mile to his home.

By the time he reached his gate, he was in pain. The bruises from the violent kicking started to hurt as the adrenalin wore off.

Ben never knew what to expect when he opened the front door of his house, for although his mother had been in a 'drying out' clinic, she was far from over her addiction to the bottle.

What was even worse was the strange men she brought home when drunk. He rarely felt safe entering his own home.

Beth, his mother, was pregnant at the age of sixteen with Ben. Over the past fourteen years she had been trying to regain her lost youth and had virtually relinquished her parental duties.

Today she was sober and as she wandered into the hall she saw his dishevelled appearance and demanded, 'What have you been up to?'

'Nothing.'

'Your blazers filthy and you've got cuts over your face. Have you been fighting again? What about this time?'

Ben never told her that all the fights he had endured were because he was defending her honour. Otherwise he knew she would be reaching for the bottle again.

'No wonder I need to drink, I never know what you'll be up to next.' Beth ranted. 'You're heading for prison if you keep on like this. No wonder I'm a nervous wreck. Now get upstairs and sort yourself out. I don't know. You never used to be like this. What has come over you?'

But Ben had been her very young carer since he was only four years old. When she was drunk and incapable of looking after herself, he used to get bowls for her to be sick in, help her get undressed and tuck her into bed. By the age of five he was making cups of coffee and giving her headache tablets running errands down to the local shops.

She had instilled in him fear of the 'evil' social worker who would come and take him away if they knew about their 'little secret' that occasionally he had to look after her while she was poorly.

This threat had reinforced his determination to look after his mother and it was that special bond that was now getting him in to fights. But being his mother's 'champion' had done little for his self-confidence or self-esteem.

Everybody on the estate knew about her alcohol problem and Ben's role looking after her, but there was a conspiracy of silence that prevented Social workers becoming aware of the situation.

Ben went upstairs and gingerly undressed, he studied himself in the mirror. He was covered in bruises. He carefully lied back on his bed, put his hands behind his head and gazed at the ceiling. 'It won't always be like this, will it?' he wondered.

CHAPTER FOUR

It was nearly four months after Sue was initially charged with causing death by dangerous driving, manslaughter, actual bodily harm and extortion, that her case finally came to Gloucester Crown court.

Andy arrived in plenty of time, his stomach filled with frantic butterflies. Helen's 'good luck' wish had done little to allay his apprehension.

Although he had never been into the building before, he had seen the unattractive arched stone entrance with its large antique wall lamp on TV news during some infamous trials.

He stopped on the pavement, the anticipation of what was about to happen making his feet leaden. In case anybody was watching he pretended to be admiring the imposing building and tried to look as if he was studying its ancient symmetry.

He knew that the 19th century grade two listed building had two large court rooms housed either end of the large lozenge shaped structure.

Around the first floor frontage of the octagonal court house he could see six large arch shaped windows. The architects original design had been modified some time in its lifetime so that every other window aperture was bricked up and now only served as an ornamental feature.

Galvanising himself into action Andy overcame his inertia and bounded up the short flight of concrete steps, past groups of nervous witnesses, defendants and relatives getting their final nicotine fix before going into the austere building.

He made his way through the sturdy oak panelled external doors into a large porch area. Before him more stone steps led him to a first floor inner door at which stood a uniformed security guard.

'Can I ask what your business is here today?'

'Yes, I'm a witness for the Prosecution,' Andy said, getting out the letter summoning him to court.

'Ok Sir, if you'd like to advise my colleague at the table there that you're here,' he said pointing to another uniformed security official seated nearby.

'But first I'll ask you to empty your pockets into the grey plastic mail tray, if you wouldn't mind. It's just like normal airport security procedures. If the machine goes off I will have to conduct a search of your person. Is that OK?'

Andy did as he was directed and satisfied that he had emptied everything out of his pockets he stepped through the airport style metal detector.

He hated the thought that the alarm would sound because he'd overlooked a coin in the bottom of a pocket. It was embarrassing. He felt like a criminal being 'patted down' with other people smugly watching.

Unfortunately as he stepped through the sensors he was greeted by a warning bleep and a line of red lights.

'Step this way. Put your arms out please Sir.' The guard's friendly greeting now changed to a terse instruction.

Andy did as directed and the guard 'swept him over' front and back with a handheld detector.

Finding nothing suspicious the Security guard said, 'That's OK, carry on. Don't forget to pick your stuff up from the tray and please turn off your mobile phone.'

Andy approached the second guard and informed him that he was there for the trial of Sue Williams-Screen. The guard checked the list and after turning over a few pages ticked against his name.

'If you'd like to take a seat somebody will come and see you shortly,' he said.

As Andy left the guard he followed the wide circular corridor which hugged the periphery of each court.

Suspended signs pointed to side rooms off the circular corridor to the Probation office, interview rooms, CPS and Witness Room.

A large number of people were already sitting on the line of benches that swept around the long curved outside wall which served as an open waiting room.

Some were watching a TV screen mounted at head height on the inside wall. Andy thought it was an odd addition to the courts until he realised it was displaying lists of the cases in court that day. The lists seemed endless, almost hypnotic as it constantly scrolled through the names again and again.

Overwhelmed with the sheer volume of cases, the court's schedules had already slipped.

He wondered whether a devious judicial mind had organised the chaos and the interminable waiting as part of some undeclared punishment regime.

Some bailed defendants sat nervously waiting to see their name appear, while others on remand, like Sue, would be waiting in the cells under the court.

Remand prisoners would have been transferred from prison in the mobile cells constrained within a security van that Andy had noticed waiting in the car park.

The corridor was a hubbub of people constantly coming and going. Authoritarian Court ushers, strutted through the waiting throng calling out names from a list. Like grammar school teachers, their black scholastic gowns billowing behind them like bat wings.

White wigged Barristers bustled through the crowd and disappeared into private anterooms to seek ordered seclusion for case discussions with colleagues.

There was a cosmopolitan cross section of 'civilian' people amidst the pompous judiciary, waiting for the wheels of justice to turn for them.

Their faces, a mirror on their soul; some gloomy, most concerned, some scared and some even scarred, bearing the record of some violent incident.

Most people were sitting, just patiently waiting, reading or chatting quietly, while a few others wandered nervously back and forth.

Some people clearly experienced at the judicial waiting game had come prepared with bags containing books, food and drink to sustain them.

Shortly after Andy had found a seat someone from the Witness team came and led him to another waiting area. He was relieved to see Rupert already there.

Andy and Rupert sat nervously together, making small talk, waiting their turn to give evidence.

'How're you bearing up Rupert?'

'I shall be glad when this is over. I'm not sure what's going to be worse being grilled by her defence barrister or the thought of seeing my missus Sue again.' Rupert said, licking his fear dried lips.

'I've never been to court before, but I gather it can be quite daunting. I'm concerned that they might embellish the incident in Monaco.' Andy said, fidgeting in his seat.

'What'd you mean? The photos of you and Nadine?' Rupert asked, puzzled.

'Yes.'

'I shouldn't think so. It's got nothing to do with her being charged with dangerous driving has it?'

'I know, but there's the extortion charge as well. These lawyers tend to rake up the muck.'

'You mean when she tried to blackmail you?'

'Yes.'

'Hopefully the jury will see through it.'

At that moment the Usher came out from the court and approached them.

'Mr Andrew Spider?'

'Yes that's me,' Andy said, standing.

'Would you like to follow me?' she invited. 'It's time. Are you OK?'

'Yes, I think so. A bit nervous.'

'That's perfectly understandable. You'll do fine I'm sure.'

As Andy followed the black gowned usher back along the corridor, Rupert called 'Good luck, see you later.'

'Thanks.'

CHAPTER FIVE

While Rupert and Andy had been nervously awaiting their turn to give evidence at Sue's trial, across the other side of the city Tim and Carrie were also waiting apprehensively.

James had arranged for them to be interviewed on local Radio to publicise their walking company. Unfortunately, as much as they wanted to support the others this was the only slot that he could negotiate with the radio station.

They had been met at reception by the show's producer and while James had been shown into the visitor's area, Tim and Carrie had been taken quietly to the studio where the presenter was broadcasting live on air, but he nevertheless greeted them with a smile and a wave as they entered.

'If you'd like to take a seat, Simon will be with you shortly,' the producer informed them in a whisper as she left the studio.

Neither had been on radio before and felt self-conscious sitting in the goldfish bowl of the studio with a microphone in front of them.

They looked in awe at the paraphernalia of the studio. It was crammed full with a bewildering array of panels, knobs, lights and controls in the small cubicle.

A foam covered microphone held by an angle poised arm partially hid the presenter's face. In front of him two thin LCD monitor screens displayed various details of the record currently being played and the radio station's Facebook page. On the desk all the associated detritus of an internet linked computer, keyboard, mouse etc.

After he'd cued up the record he had chosen to introduce their interview, Simon closed his microphone down and turned to them.

'Welcome to my 'office'. Thanks for coming. Have you been on radio before?'

'No.' Tim and Carrie chorused.

'Well there's nothing to be frightened of, just forget you're on the radio and think of it as a just a normal chat between us. OK?'

'Yes, thanks.'

However in spite of his reassurances, they sat anxiously waiting for the record to finish.

Meanwhile James had taken a seat in the visitor's area so that he could watch them through the glass partitions of the studio.

It was a modestly decorated room, fitted with several long, comfortable settees separated by glass topped tables. On the walls hung large framed promotional posters of events that the station had covered in previous years. He noted that the live broadcast was playing quietly in the background.

James and Tim had a common bond. They were both Godsons of the late Geoffery Foster. Geoffery brought the previous strangers together after a quest to track them down from his hospice bed.

As their friendship developed James had volunteered to use his business expertise to help the pair set up a walking company.

Simon was monitoring the progress of the recording on the screen in front of him, his hands deftly moving over the faders and as it finally came to an end, he announced, 'and that was Nancy Sinatra with *'These boots are made for walking'* composed by Lee Hazlewood. Would you believe that was written and recorded by Nancy Sinatra in February 1966? It went on to be a number one hit in the States and UK Pop charts. Well they don't make them like that anymore.

Perhaps it's not the most subtle introduction to my next guests on today's show but welcome Tim and Carrie.'

'Hello.'

'Hi.'

'Thanks for joining me on the show.'

'OK. Thanks for having us.' Carrie said, clearing her throat.

'Now I gather you're here to talk about your walking company, is that right?'

'Yes.' Tim said, nervously.

'I understand there is something special about it?'

'Special? Oh yes, ah, that's reet.' Carrie replied, her Geordie accent exaggerated by her nerves.

'I can see you're not from around here.'

'Nay, Newcastle is, was my home.'

'Well I know you have some stunning scenery and picturesque walks in Northumberland. So what brings a Geordie down here to set up a walking company?'

'Well we're only based here. But we'll be organising walks all over the country for our clients, including in and around my old stomping ground.'

'How come the two of you are together?' Simon asked quickly looking at the crib sheet prepared from James' communique with the station.

'Tim and I have a special bond. We are both double leg amputees. Tim's through childhood Meningitis and mine during my service career.'

'Double amputees! Some people might say that owning a walking company is a bit ambitious for somebody with your physical challenges. How do you answer that? Or do you have other people to lead the walks and you do all the administration in the office?'

'No chance. Disability is a state of mind,' Carrie said firmly. 'We are as fully mobile as any able bodied person.'

'We even did the 'Three Peaks Challenge' last year. You know, Snowdon, Scafell and Ben Nevis,' Tim boasted.

'And put in a good time too,' Carrie added.

'Yes, we even had snow on top of Ben Nevis,' Tim said feeling less nervous as the interview progressed.

'So what's so special about the company, apart from you two of course, Tim?'

'We're going to provide a hiking experience for people who are physically challenged.'

'Do you mean amputees?'

'Yes, but by no means excluding anybody else who has other health issues.'

'And we're also offering the service to people who suffer from PTSD,' Carrie added.

'Sorry, you'll have to explain to our listeners. What do you mean by PTSD?'

'PTSD stands for Post-Traumatic Stress Disorder. It can be a devastating limitation on people's lives. Many service personnel suffer from it following active service. They are often haunted by the horrors of conflict and become depressed and introvert.'

'Yes, so I believe. But I also understand that non service people can be tormented by it as well.'

'Yes, that's right. People get affected by all manner of trauma,' Carrie added. 'The trouble with PTSD is there's nothing to see, unlike the loss of a limb. So people think sufferers are exaggerating their condition.'

'Yes, we've heard the same claim by other guests I've interviewed about mental illnesses generally.' Simon agreed sympathetically.

'Many people end up with severe depression and… Well the suicide rate is very high for sufferers.'

'Yes, it's very sad, so we're trying to do something to help these less fortunate people to get their lives back,' Tim chirped in.

'Well, I take my hat off to you for trying to do that.' Simon said genuinely.

'Thanks.'

'I gather you have quite an interesting story behind the formation of the company too?'

'Yes…umm. It's umm. It's a condition of my Godfather's will.' Tim explained.

'Godfather! Are we talking Mafia involvement here?' Simon said flippantly, trying to make the conversation a bit more upbeat.

'No. Just a normal Christian Godfather,' Tim responded naively. 'You know, christenings and all that stuff.'

'Well that went right over your head, Tim. So is there anything out of the ordinary with your Godfather then?'

'Sorry! Tim said, puzzled at the presenter's attempt to lighten things. 'Well, yes. He was a millionaire.'

'Well that's got to be good news.'

'Well it was, because when he died he left three of us, his Godsons, a legacy.'

'So do you need to work at all then?'

'Yes. Because the conditions were that we had to do something worthwhile with the money, before it was released to us.'

'I see.'

'So...I...we...decided to set up a walking company for less able people,' Tim continued.

'It's believed that less able people benefit from exposure to the challenges of the outdoors,' Carrie added.

'Carrie, I believe your involvement is even more personal than Tim's, is that right?'

'Yes. I suffer...am suffering from PTSD.'

'You mentioned you were in the services. Is that when it started?'

'Yes. The horrors of war, I'm afraid. But I'd rather not elaborate about it if you don't mind.

'Right, OK, I'll respect your privacy and we won't dig any further.'

'Thanks. Suffice to say I can empathise with all my colleagues who suffer with this terrible affliction.' Carrie added.

'OK, so tell me more about the Walking Company. What's the name and how do people book?'

'Right the name of the company is 'Just Do It Walking' and people can find all the information, including brochures online at our website 'Just Do It Walking Company.Com'

'Well it all sounds most fascinating. Thank you for coming in and telling us about your story. I sincerely wish you all the success for the company and we'll dedicate the next record to you both.

I think it's very appropriate for you. It's the 1961 hit for Helen Shapiro, *Walkin' Back To Happiness.*'

As the music built Simon shut down his microphone.

'Thanks once again for coming in. When you're up and running please pop in some time and give us a progress report.'

'Yeah OK, we'd be delighted.'

'Thanks for the publicity, much appreciated, Carrie added, shaking the presenter's hand.'

They were then shown out of the studio and back to where James had been listening in the visitor's waiting area.

'Congratulations. Well done,' he said, giving them both a hug. 'That wasn't too bad was it?'

'No. I suppose not.'

'Well let's see where the sales go from there. We have a hit counter on the website. Let's just hope we can bring in the punters.'

CHAPTER SIX

Andy's heart was 'hammering' as he followed the Usher into the Court room.

The short walk from the entrance door to the witness box, gave him the opportunity to quickly take in his surroundings and he was impressed with the majesty of it all.

The large, high ceiled, court room was neatly partitioned into judicial 'corrals', beautifully constructed enclosures in polished oak panelling. It was a showpiece of the cabinet maker's meticulous craftsmanship.

The semi-circular design ensured that the elevated Judge's 'bench' was always the central focus of all of the court's occupants.

The uniform of the bewigged and colourfully gowned Crown court Judge further reinforcing his authority.

The ancient court room was be-decked with the paraphernalia of the twenty first century for recording, broadcasting and videoing proceedings now common place in British courts. All enclosures were equipped with flexible height microphones.

Video conferencing equipment, consisting of a large TV screen and camera, was mounted on a wall to the Judges right for conducting video links with prisoners at their prisons. Although there was no current video link established, the TV manufacturer's logo bouncing around the screen briefly distracted Andy.

On the Judges desk, a microphone and laptop computer lay amidst the piles of paperwork to which he was referring as Andy entered.

Immediately in front of the Judge's bench facing into the court room was the black gowned clerk of the court. Her desk furnished with a computer and telephone, and an equally large pile of paperwork. By her side the 'stenographer' was busy typing at a keyboard.

The prosecution and defence barristers sat next to one another looking directly at the judge with reams of paper and bulging clip files in front of them. Behind them in another judicial enclosure sat the barristers support teams.

The twelve members of the jury watched him as he entered. Their red upholstered seats arranged in two tiered rows, one in front of each other giving them a clear view of witnesses.

Sue had been brought up from the cells under the court and was sitting in the dock next to a white shirted guard. She gave him an icy stare as he looked around.

The press box was occupied by two journalists who were busily making notes on laptops.

On the far side of the court a large group of law students were seated, clearly studying the case.

In front of him and at the judge's left hand side, were two witness boxes. One had a curtain attached to the side which, when necessary, would hide the face of the witness from the defendant.

Andy followed the usher's invitation and climbed nervously into the un-curtained witness box.

He felt the eyes of everybody in court looking at him.

Although Sue was charged with a multiplicity of offences, the Judge decided to initially focus on the most serious charge of causing death by dangerous driving, where she could be looking at a maximum fourteen years in prison.

The barristers had already made their opening speeches to position their opposing views with the Jury.

After taking the oath, the prosecution lawyer ran through Andy's witness statement.

'Mr Spider, on the night of 23rd December last, I believe you were one of the last to see Mr Screen and Miss Carr before the fatal multivehicle accident on the M5 motorway?'

'Probably.'

'Is it correct that you saw them leave the Green Leaf Hotel where the wake for Mr Geoffery Foster was being held?'

'Yes.'

'Did you see anyone else get into the car with Mr Screen and Miss Carr?'

'No.'

Did you see a black VW Polo follow Mr Screens car out of the car park?'

'Yes.'

'The very same black Polo that later caused the fatal crash on the motorway?'

'I assume so.'

'Objection! The witness is speculating.'

'Sustained! Please stick to the facts.'

'Yes my Lord.'

What frame of mind was Mr Screen in when he left the hotel?'

'He was upset.'

'Because?'

'I had told him his wife was out of jail and he was frightened she would attack him, again.'

'Objection! Mr Screen and his wife's domestic relationships is not relevant to this charge.'

'On the contrary, I believe it is very relevant.'

'Objection overruled.'

'So would you say their relationship had irrevocably broken down?'

'Yes.'

'Can you expand on the reasons?'

'Rupert, Mr Screen, was a victim of domestic violence.'

'Objection!'

Overruled. The defendant is also charged with Actually Bodily Harm for a series of attacks on her husband.'

'Can you tell the court how you know about this dreadful record of domestic violence.'

'The late Mr Geoffery Foster and myself witnessed it on several occasions.'

'You mean you saw the results, rather than the actual assaults?'

'Yes, but Rupert...Mr Screen, was obviously petrified of his wife. He was in fear for his life should he upset her. The strain was causing him to have psychological problems.'

'Objection, the witness is not a qualified psychiatrist.'

'On what do you base your comments?'

'I am a fully qualified nurse. I work at a hospice and I have received special training in psychology and stress related illnesses.'

'Overruled.'

'Your witness.'

Sue's defence barrister, be-gowned and white wigged Amelia Purdown, rose and addressed the jury ignoring Andy who felt a bit awkward.

'M'lud, members of the jury, the dispute we have here is whether my client was driving the stolen black Volkswagen Polo that caused the fatal crash. The car is assumed to have been stolen earlier that evening from a nearby churchyard. There is no dispute that the black Volkswagen Polo was the trigger for the horrendous multi-vehicle road traffic collision.

My contention is that my client was not the driver. Instead, she was actually a rear seat passenger in her husband's car which was subsequently caught up in the accident.

Indeed, she therefore does not deny being at the scene of the accident where the Police found a broken heel from her boot.'

Turning back to face Andy she said, 'Mr Spider, you say you were one of the last to see Mr Screen and Miss Carr before the accident?'

'I believe so, yes.'

'Could you actually see the passengers as the car left the car park?'

'No.'

'Why was that?'

'Because it was dark.'

'So Mrs Williams-Screen could have been in the back seat of the car, as she claims, and you wouldn't necessarily have seen her. Is that correct?'

'Well I...err...suppose.'

'You say Mrs Williams Screen had been in prison. Why was that?'

'She had been accused of the attempted murder of Mr Geoffery Foster.'

'And why was she released?'

'Because I took a CCTV video recording of the alleged incident in the hospice to the Police.'

'And what made you take it to the Police?'

'It showed that she didn't actually attempt to murder Mr Foster.'

'So is it right that Mr Foster had ensnared her to help him, so say, commit suicide and she had been, to use the vernacular, set up.'

'Yes,' Andy revealed, fidgeting uncomfortably.

'So perhaps having failed to get her incarcerated by one means there is a conspiracy to get her imprisoned by another trumped up charge.'

'No, it wasn't like that.'

'I submit that together with your former benefactor, Mr Foster, that you waged a vendetta against my client and therefore you have a bias against her.'

'No.'

'Your credibility as a reliable witness is therefore suspect. Your evidence, I submit, must therefore be discounted.'

'No, that's not right.' Andy denied, gripping the edge of the witness box.

'Is it true that you initiated an assault on my client?'

'No. When?' Andy said, desperately trying to think what she was talking about.

'I see you have a convenient memory. Let me remind you. My client was testing out a video function on her new mobile phone whilst staying at a hotel in Monaco when she quite innocently recorded you during the test,'

At the mention of Monaco Andy's heart stopped.' His worst nightmare had become reality. He wished now that he had withdrawn his complaint so they wouldn't pursue the extortion charges against Sue. It was too late now. His early morning indiscretion with Nadine was now going to be exposed to the 'world'.

Sue smirked at his discomfort as he fidgeted in the witness box.

'Can you say what you were doing in the corridor?'

'I was saying goodbye to someone.'

'And what time would that be?'

'I'm not sure.'

'Let me remind you. It was 0535 AM. Just after half past five in the morning.'

'Probably, I didn't check my watch.'

'Would that be because you were distracted by the lady who was only wearing a negligee?'

'I...err,' Andy stuttered.

'Was the lady in question your wife?'

'Err...no,' Andy said quietly, colouring up.

'Sorry, Mr Spider, could you repeat that louder so the jury can hear it,' she demanded.

'No,' Andy repeated, his head spinning from the embarrassment of his own admission.

Out the corner of his eye Andy noted one of the journalists in the press box frantically typing into his laptop.

'So having been unfortunately caught in a compromising situation with a scantily clad young lady, you then sent someone to assault my client and to steal her mobile phone.'

'Well umm...no, it wasn't like that.'

'Objection. My Lud, this is not relevant to the charges against the accused,' the Prosecuting Counsel interjected.

'Yes, what is your point in pursuing this line of questioning?' demanded the Judge.

'Purely to show that Mr Spider, far from being a reliable witness, is hostile to my client. His evidence, that he didn't see my client in the back of her husband's car that night is therefore suspect.

As previously stated, there is no dispute that the VW Polo was the trigger for the fatal Road Traffic Collision. However, I contest that my client was not driving it. She was, as stated, the rear seat passenger in her husband's car. No further questions.'

The Prosecutor stood up again and addressed the Judge.

'Milord as my learned colleague has brought up the matter of the filming. I would like to question Mr Spider concerning the Extortion charge facing the defendant.'

'Yes. Carry on,' the Judge said sifting through the paperwork in front of him.

'Thank you. Mr Spider, we have heard of the embarrassing incident when you were filmed saying goodbye to somebody. Can you tell me how you knew about the filming?'

'She...'

'She? Can you be more specific,' the Judge directed.

'Yes. Sorry. Mrs Williams-Screen told me and threatened to publish the photos. I subsequently received a letter and photo at work.'

'What was the picture?'

'It was taken when I was saying goodbye to the young lady mentioned previously,' Andy explained quietly.

'What did the letter say?'

'Just two words. Legacy or Exposure.'

'And the Police found files on the defendant's computer.'

'Yes, I believe so.'

'No further questions.'

Milord, this is hardly blackmail. My client sent them as a joke. No further questions.'

'You may step down Mr Spider,' the Judge directed.

Andy did as he was instructed and left the court feeling that his reputation was in tatters.. He had been unfairly labelled as a liar and a gigolo. He had to warn Helen that the papers would probably sensationalise the incident.

Sue smiled at his discomfort as he left the court.

CHAPTER SEVEN

'Aunty Kay do you like my drawling?' Five year old Amy said, thrusting a spider drawing under her nose.

'Oh yes that's lovely darling, aren't you clever?' Kay said generously.

'Go and do some more drawings for Aunty Kay in the lounge, that's a good girl,' Helen encouraged. 'We're having a chat at the moment.'

Amy ran off excited by her artistic compliment.

Kay had agreed to be with Helen while Andy was at Crown Court as Helen was still emotionally sensitive from her bout of postnatal depression following the birth of baby Molly.

'What do you think will happen when they start questioning him?' Helen asked.

'Well hopefully they won't talk about Monaco,' Kay said, optimistically.

'No. But if they do...The possible repercussions could be ...'

'Don't worry yourself. He'll be alright,' Kay said cheerfully. 'Worrying won't help.'

'No you're right, of course.'

'Anyway my Tim and Carrie are on the radio talking about their Walking Company this morning, let's listen to them. But first a nice cuppa is called for.'

'I'll put the kettle on. It'll take my mind off things,' Helen said, going into the kitchen. Kay followed.

'It's no good I need to talk about it.' Helen volunteered, 'I've been having terrible nightmares about it all. The thought of Andy's... involvement with that Nadine becoming public knowledge is awful and the implications on us and the kids. Not to mention his Scouting. Then there's the shame of having it all exposed to our neighbours. Can you imagine the school gate gossip?' Helen asked.

'You poor thing,' Kay said, desperately thinking of a way to divert her thoughts.

'In my dreams I've been tarred, feathered and paraded through the streets naked.' Helen described her nightmare. 'And that Nadine and that Sue woman are looking at me and laughing. Oh it's horrible. I shall be glad when it's all over.'

'Well it won't be long now.' Kay said sympathetically. 'What time does the case start?'

'Ten thirty I think. They reckon it'll take a couple of days. Depends on how long the jury take to come up with a verdict.'

'Oh I do hope they find her guilty. She is such a horrible woman and that poor Rupert. He has really been through it recently.'

'Yes, you're right. What with the accident, the baby being born pre-term and the little one going back and forth to the hospital, he must be exhausted.'

'And there's poor Jo stuck in a wheelchair. No. He isn't exactly having an easy time of it is he?'

'Andy has been agitated too. What with this court case and the administration of Geoffery's will. I wish he'd never got involved with that Geoffery Foster.

They told him at the hospice to steer away from getting personally involved with his patients' lives, but oh no! He knew better didn't he?' Helen divulged.

'But it wasn't all bad was it? I mean, the Scouts got a new hut bought by Geoffery and I believe you have a new car and a few pounds in the bank now too.'

'Yes I suppose there is that.'

'And well Geoffery was such a nice man. I mean, had it not been for him, my Tim would still be sat in that chair playing computer games, feeling sorry for himself.'

'Yes I suppose I was a bit harsh criticising him. Didn't you and he have a thing going some years ago?'

Yes, but unfortunately it was before he had his millions. He went off to Europe and I ended up staying here and marrying George. Marrying him was a mistake too. He soon buggered off and literally left me holding the baby, our Tim.'

'Although I gather, even after all those years, Geoffery still had a soft spot for you. Is that right he left you money in his will for a cruise?' Helen asked, smiling.

'Yes. Enough for a world cruise too. It's something I always wanted to do too. Isn't that exciting?'

'Have you started shopping for the trip yet?'

'Yes, of course. I've got to look posh at the Captains reception and the formal evenings, haven't I?'

'Oh!' Helen gasped, suddenly looking at the kitchen clock. 'What time did you say Tim was going to be on the radio?'

'Damn, I think we might have missed them.'

'I'll switch it on now,' Helen said, going to the radio.

'And so don't forget. If you want to go for a walk with some very special people I'm sure Tim and Carrie

will welcome you with open arms at Just Do It walking.' The radio presenter said cueing up the next record.

'Oh blast, we missed it. I was supposed to record it too. Tim will go ape.'

'I think they do an iPlayer version. You'll be able to listen again, I'm sure.'

Just then the phone rang and Helen dashed to pick it up.

'Hi, it's me,' Andy said sounding tense. 'I've just given my evidence and I'm going to go back in to listen to Rupert.'

'How did it go?'

'Not good.'

'Oh…did they bring up the Monaco thing?'

'Yes. There were journalists there too. I'm sorry love.'

'Yeah me too.' Helen whispered distantly, trying to control her emotions. 'Well what's done is done. We'll just have to make the best of it. Won't we?'

'I really am sorry. I must dash and get back to hear Rupert. Give him some moral support.' Andy ended the call.

Kay had been listening to Helen's responses and guessed what had gone on.

'It doesn't sound very encouraging,' Kay conceded, walking towards Helen, ready to give her a hug.

'No it isn't.' said Helen, filling up.

'Another cuppa?'

'Yes please,' Helen sighed, looking for a tissue.

'I wonder how poor Rupert will get on. If Andy was a bag of nerves he must be close to a nervous breakdown.'

CHAPTER EIGHT

After the brief call to Helen, Andy checked that it was OK for him to watch Rupert give his evidence and being given permission, he made his way up to the public gallery.

He smiled to himself as he climbed the carpeted stairs, for each step had black and yellow hazard tape stuck to the edge.

Clearly the court had employed the services of an over-zealous Health and Safety inspector to avoid litigation if anybody slipped. 'Ironic really,' he thought.

As he reached the top of the stairs he re-entered the court through a plain wooden door into the back of the public gallery.

The tiered gallery consisted of three rows of hard wooden benches in a complete semicircle looking down into the court.

The Judge saw the sudden movement out of the corner of his eye and was momentarily distracted by Andy's reappearance. Self-conscious, Andy sat down quickly.

The prosecuting barrister stood up and said, 'I should like to call Mr Screen to the witness box.'

The court Usher duly shepherded Rupert into the court room.

Rupert was shaking, his hands clammy as he took the stand. He saw Sue for the first time since her intimidating visit to the hospital many months previously. The sight of her smirking face froze his heart.

It was her threats to harm Jo and their unborn child that caused him to initially lie to the police and give her an alibi.

Rupert's voice exposed his nervousness as he took the oath. *'I swear by almighty God that my evidence to the court and the jury on this trial shall be the truth the whole truth and nothing but the truth.'*

'Mr Screen, how would you describe your relationship with your wife?' The Prosecutor demanded.

'Pardon, I don't understand what you mean.' Rupert coloured, embarrassed that he'd failed at the first hurdle.

'Well, would you say you were happily married?' The QC guided him.

'No... We are separated.'

'Why would that be?'

'M'lud, is that relevant to the charge?' questioned the defence barrister.

'M'lud, I am only seeking to demonstrate the control that the defendant has over the witness.'

'Objection overruled. Carry on.'

'I ask you again. Why are you separated?'

'We are no longer living together because...my wife used to beat me up,' he related quietly, embarrassed by discussing his personal life in front of a group of strangers.

'Sorry, I didn't hear that.'

'Yes please try to speak up,' the Judge instructed.

'I'm ashamed to admit that my wife beat me up on several occasions.' Rupert repeated, his voice still tremulous.

'I assume by that you mean your wife used to physically assault you?'

'Yes.'

'There is nothing to be ashamed of. Violence can happen to anyone. The assailant, whether male or female, can still inflict the same amount of actual bodily harm,' the QC said encouragingly. 'Did you report it to the Police?'

'No. I...I couldn't. She'd have killed me.'

'Objection, the witness is exaggerating an imagined outcome.'

'No, I'm not,' Rupert blurted, suddenly finding his voice and courage. 'You should have been there to have received the brunt of her anger and seen her manic face. Have you ever had your arm broken deliberately by somebody? Or to have been thrown down the stairs? To be forced to wear an electronic dog collar and receive several thousand volts when you displeased her?'

'Objection, the witness is overdramatizing alleged events,' the defence barrister protested.

'M'lud we have medical records to substantiate his story.'

'Do you have any proof he is lying?' the Judge demanded.

'No, M'lud,' the defence conceded.

'Overruled! If records exist then we should not dismiss it out of hand.' The Judge directed.

'M'lud, indeed we have a Police statement confirming the use of an electronic dog collar.'

'Objection. There is no disputing the injuries. But I contend that what we are hearing is a catalogue of wounds caused by a mentally unstable person, self-harming.'

'The damage stated do not form any known pattern used by people to self-harm.' The Prosecutor was quick to state.

'Overruled.' Please continue.

'Your Witness.' The prosecutor said, sitting down.

'If you have broken off relationships with your wife, where do you now live?' The Defence barrister asked staring at her notes.

'I live with my girlfriend. That was, I lived with her before the accident. She is still in and out of hospital.'

'I'm sorry to hear that. I understand that both of you were hurt in the motorway crash on December 23rd?' She said sympathetically, softening her voice.

'Yes we were.' Rupert's mind flashed back to the frightening events of that night and the worrisome and unpredictable outcome of Jo's paralysis during her late stage pregnancy.

'What was the extent of your injuries?'

'I sustained head injuries, a broken collar bone and...'

'Head injuries?' The barrister seized on the words interrupting Rupert's list.

'Yes.'

'Head injuries can cause memory loss. So is it possible that you could have forgotten that your wife was also in the car with you?' she coaxed.

'No. She wasn't there. The reason we left...'

'Just answer the question.' She ordered firmly. 'Is it true that Mr Spider visited you in hospital and persuaded you to change your statement to the Police?'

'Well yes he did come and...'

'Just answer the question. As we've already established Mr Spider was in cahoots with Mr Foster trying to falsely implicate my client in a non-existent crime.'

'No it wasn't like that,' Rupert shouted, frustrated by her allegation.

'Your witness,' the defence Barrister said sitting down.

The prosecution Barrister rose again and quickly picked up Rupert's point. 'So what was it like Mr Screen?'

'She threatened to kill my girlfriend and our unborn child by switching off her life support machine if I didn't say she was in the car with me.' Rupert said firmly.'

There was a gasp from the jury at this revelation.

'She has bullied me all the way through our marriage. Well, no longer. I'm standing up to her,' he announced looking contemptuously at Sue to reinforce his determination.

'Objection M'lud, we have heard no evidence that my client has threatened anyone.'

'M'lud I am seeking to show that the accused is a person well used to getting her own way by virtue of her aggressive nature.' The Prosecutor responded in their game of legal point scoring.

'Overruled, please continue.'

'May I say something, Judge?' Rupert asked, looking towards the bench.

'If it's relevant, otherwise I will stop you.'

Summoning up all his courage Rupert spoke to the court, 'If you are emotionally strong you probably can't understand how sensitive people can allow themselves to become so susceptible to the threats of bullies.

I was ashamed at myself for allowing this to happen to me. After all I am a man. I am supposed to be the warrior, the hunter.

But God made gentle people too. I am not a wimp as some people might believe. I didn't want these things happen to me.

Perhaps they think that I'm a masochist and welcomed this sort of punishment, or perhaps that somehow I deserved to be abused.'

The prosecution lawyer, surprised by Rupert's eloquent delivery, looked at the Jury and pleased with their positive reaction sat down. 'Your Witness.'

The defence lawyer was at Rupert straight away. 'Perhaps masochistic is correct. I put it to you, that rather than the alleged domestic violence by the defendant, you were in fact self-harming. My client was merely trying to protect you from yourself but instead is now implicated as an abuser.'

'No, that's not right.' Rupert argued forcefully.

'So in truth you actually hurt yourself. Isn't that right?'

'No…that's simply not true.' Rupert became flustered that anybody could think that's what had happened to him.

'Look at the physical difference between you both. Clearly you are stronger than her. You are what, six foot? My client is only five foot three.

'Objection! My learned colleague is bullying the witness. He is NOT on trial here.'

'Sustained. Because we have a difference in stature, it does not designate who is abused or who is the abuser. Strike that remark,' the Judge directed.

'Your Witness.'

'The Prosecution barrister addressed the jury. 'As you will have heard, the defendant has many charges on her charge sheet, including extortion. The extortion charge, you have heard, is based upon a 'blackmail' letter sent to Mr Spider. I put it to you that this is a woman who bullies her way through life.'

'Objection! The letter sent by my client to Mr Spider was a joke, which backfired.

'The Prosecutor continued,' Mr Screen is a battered husband. The fact that he didn't report the abuse shows the evil and controlling nature of the defendant. No further questions.'

'You may step down.'

Rupert left the court as directed and deliberately gave a defiant stare at Sue as he stepped down from the witness box.

She in turn gave him a dismissive smile. 'You'll regret that, see if you don't,' she thought, mentally logging it.

Andy left the public gallery at the same time.

After battling his way through the throng of people in the still crowded corridor, Andy was amazed to see Rupert smiling.

'Well done Rupert, you did well.'

'That will surprise the bitch,' Rupert smirked. 'She wouldn't have expected me to stand up to her. I have to say that after the initial bit I felt quite good. But I'm glad it's over.'

'Yeah, me too.'

'How did you get on Andy?' Rupert asked, sensing the tension in Andy's response.

'Not too good. They brought up the Monaco incident. The press are going to have a field day.' Andy said, looking pained.

'Oh dear, sorry to hear that,' Rupert replied sympathetically. 'Perhaps it will be overshadowed by another bigger story.'

'We can but hope.' Andy said, unconvinced that he would be that lucky.

CHAPTER NINE

Andy and Rupert made their way up to the public gallery and listened as several other witnesses were called including the Crash investigation team, the Forensic analyst who conducted the tests on the muddy heel, the fingerprint expert and the arresting Police Officers, Graham Fredericks and John Sparrow.

And finally, the defendant Sue Williams-Screen herself who gave a distorted, but very confident version of the incidents surrounding that very tragic night.

The Defence team briefly exposed her story that Ben had been seen by Geoffery's grave that night and that Sue had got in an argument with the gravedigger about it, but she strongly denied the manslaughter charge.

Ben was not called to court because of his age and the Defence team's nervousness of using him as a witness.

Finally, the Prosecutor began summoning up. 'Members of the Jury, my learned colleague recognises that the broken heel found at the scene of the accident did belong to one of the boots that the defendant was wearing the night of the fatal crash.

As you have heard, forensic tests prove that the mud on the heel was the same type that came from the grave of Mr Foster.

Thus the defendant was at the hillside burial ground that evening. Not only was she on the hill, but I contest, that she got into an altercation with the gravedigger, Mr Criscroski, and after knocking him unconscious she then stole his car, the black VW Polo.

The weather that night was bitterly cold. Temperatures in the area were recorded as low as minus six degrees; In rendering Mr Criscroski unconscious, she left him vulnerable to the extreme weather conditions and as a consequence of which he froze to death.

She then drove his car, the black VW Polo, to the hotel where the wake for Mr Foster was being held. She waited until she saw Mr Screen leave and then followed her distressed husband out of the car park and on to the motorway.

For some reason, known only to herself, she inexplicably pulled on to the hard shoulder, an illegal manoeuvre by itself and then, without looking, she re-joined the busy motorway. Her careless manoeuvre then caused a fatal multiple vehicle collision.

Accident investigators proved categorically that the VW Polo was directly responsible for causing the death of one of the drivers caught up in the mayhem.

Members of the jury, can there be any doubt about her character? This is the same person who threatened to kill an injured woman and her unborn child. This is the same woman who tried to blackmail one of the witnesses by sending him a photo taken covertly.

This is a callous person that would obviously lie and threaten witnesses to save her neck.

Her years of domestic abuse have as yet gone unpunished. I believe it is now time for her to pay for her misdeeds.' He sat down confident that the case against Sue was water tight.

The defence barrister rose and addressed the jury. 'My client does not dispute getting into an argument with Mr Criscroski following a misunderstanding about damage to Mr Foster's grave.

However, she assures me that it was already damaged before she arrived. You will recall that she did see a young boy known to Mr Spider in the area. This boy somehow had gained possession of Mr Criscroski's mobile phone. You need to take this in to account when reaching your verdict.

You'll recall that she only defended herself against Mr Criscroski's aggressive approach and he was the author of his own demise when, unfortunately, he ran into a tree whilst running back to his car, knocking himself out.

Understandably she did not stop to see if he was OK due to his antagonistic nature.

There were significant physical differences between the defendant and Mr Criscroski. As you can see my client is five foot three tall and weighs ten stone; Mr Criscroski was over six foot tall and weighed over fifteen stone.

Surely there can be no doubt about who was the aggressor. If there was any conflict at all it would have been self-defence not manslaughter.'

My client denies stealing the car. There is no evidence to link her with the car or its use. Rather, as she claims, she was in the back of her husband's car.

Remember, Mr Screen suffered from a head injury and was clearly confused. Therefore it is obvious that if she was in her husband's car, she could not have caused the accident. She is therefore innocent of the very serious charge of causing death by dangerous driving.

Mr Screen's claims that he was forced to give his wife a false alibi because of fears of domestic violence is a serious allegation. But you have to wonder why he had never reported any incidents to the Police until recently.

Remember, it was Mr Spider who convinced Mr Screen to change his statement to the police.

As to the charge of extortion and blackmail, my client assures me that the picture found on her computer showing Mr Spider and a scantily clad lady was sent purely as a joke with no intention to blackmail him.'

Therefore members of the Jury there can only be one verdict, innocent on all charges.' Amelia Purdown sat down convinced in her own mind that the case was lost.

The Judge addressed the Jury and directed them to give verdicts on each of the various charges. He reminded them not to discuss the case with anyone or to consult the internet for additional information to assist with their verdict. They had to base their judgement on the evidence that had been presented in court.

He then discharged them for the night.

The following day, after several hours of deliberation the jury returned to the court.

Andy and Rupert had been hanging around in the crowded corridor waiting for the Jury to reach their verdict and went to the public gallery to see what they had decided.

The clerk of the court asked the foreman of the Jury to stand.

'Have you reached your verdict?'

'Yes.'

'On the charge of causing death by dangerous driving how do you find the defendant?'

The foreman of the Jury read from his piece of paper. 'Guilty.'

Sue struggled to contain her anger. Her defence lawyer looked across at her and shook her head to warn her.

'On the charge of Manslaughter, how do you find the defendant?

'Not guilty.'

It was a verdict that the Prosecutor was expecting. The difference in stature had swayed the jury after all. Sue allowed herself an indulgent smile.

'On the charge of Actual Bodily Harm for domestic violence?'

'Guilty.'

Sue's rage built inside her. The colour drained away from her face. She wanted to scream at the fools who had come up with the verdict but bit her tongue.

'On the charge of Extortion, how do you find the defendant?

'Guilty.'

The charge of stealing a car without the owner's permission was dropped because, although Sue was driving it and had caused the fatal collision, there was no proof that, although highly unlikely, she hadn't previously obtained the owner's permission.

The judge directed that he wanted to see reports before he sentenced her and discharged the Jury. 'Take her down,' he told the guard.

Sue was furious with her Barrister's failure to secure an acquittal.

As she left the dock she looked up at the smiling Rupert and Andy in the public gallery and glared at them. 'They'll regret giving evidence against me,' she thought, 'just you see.'

Andy and Rupert shook hands and beamed with delight.

'At last they've got her. Let's hope the judge sends her down for several years,' Rupert, said feeling as if a ton weight had been lifted off his shoulders.

CHAPTER TEN

'Where are you going?' Helen asked as Andy made his way to the door.

'Foster Lodge,' he said pulling on his coat.

'Where? I can't hear you above this noisy old washing machine.'

'The Scout hut, Foster Lodge,' he shouted.

I might have guessed,' Helen acknowledged, coming into the hallway.

Andy strode back and gave her a peck on the cheek.

'Well, now the court case is out of the way I can start getting back to normal,' he said picking up his bag.

'Nearly normal!' Helen reminded him. 'We haven't seen what the press are going to do about you yet.'

'Don't remind me. I was trying to put that to the back of my mind. See you later.'

'Yeah bye. Don't get involved with anything complicated. Don't forget you've got to go to work later.'

'Don't I know it. Two to Ten,' he said giving her another unresponsive 'peck on the cheek'.

Andy loved his job at the hospice but it was always a wrench to leave some of his Scout Leader jobs half done.

'Perhaps I should cut down my working hours and supplement my income with the money that Geoffery paid me for helping to track down his Godsons. Perhaps working on a permanent day job would be even better,' he thought.

But he loved being involved with his patients. He felt good about making sure that they had the dignity and support that would ensure their final days were peaceful.

'See you later.' Andy strode off purposefully.

The Scout hut was within walking distance, so he left his beautiful white Mercedes AMG that Geoffery had bequeathed him parked outside his home.

On his way to the Scout HQ he reflected on how he had become embroiled in Geoffery Foster's personal life.

The old hut which had burnt down by a mysterious electrical fault and Geoffery's tantalising offer of buying them a new one had persuaded him to get involved.

Andy was always suspicious about the timing of the fire. It came shortly after he'd rejected Geoffery's request to help him trace his Godsons. He felt he had been coerced. But he had no proof. And he had to admit, the new hut was a million times better than the old one anyway.

As Andy arrived at the lodge he could see that someone had removed the anti-vandal metal shutters that normally lived permanently over the entrance door. 'Another break-in,' he wondered, as he approached the entrance cautiously.

He tried the door. It was unlocked. Andy opened it quietly, full of apprehension about what he would find.

Pop music was coming from the kitchen. He crept stealthily along the short corridor. He could hear someone moving inside.

Wondering if he should confront the person, he reached for his mobile ready to dial the Police. The floor creaked under his weight.

Inside the kitchen somebody stood. A drawer opened and he heard the sound of clinking cutlery as someone grovelled in it.

'Who's there?' Don't come any closer. I've got a knife,' the voice said.

Andy recognised the voice straightaway. 'Ben, what the hell are you doing here?' as, reassured, he walked into the kitchen.

Ben was holding a knife and seeing Andy he quickly put it back into the drawer.

'Thank heavens it's you. You made me jump.' Ben said relieved.

'Well it serves you right. I've told you before about locking yourself in. Anyway, why aren't you at school?'

'Mum's got that bloke back again. He got her drunk and... I've had it with her Andy. Geoffery spent all that money to get her 'dried out' and she's gone straight back on it.

'Oh Ben, I'm sorry.'

'I don't want to end up in care, Andy.' Ben said disconsolately.

'I know,' Andy replied sympathetically. 'I know.'

'It's just as well Geoffery gave me a key for here.'

'It's a pity you have to use it though isn't it? Andy said putting the kettle on. 'Let's have a cuppa. Do you want me to ring the school?'

'Yes please.'

'There's no reason why you shouldn't go in this afternoon though is there?'

'Oh it's double English. The teacher is crap. She doesn't know how to control the class. It's just chaos. We don't learn anything,' he moaned.

'You need to keep your attendances up otherwise they will start making enquiries about you again.' Andy advised him, getting the cups out from the well-stocked cupboard.

They both jumped as they heard the outside door slam.

''You didn't lock it either then?' Ben said, cynically. 'Don't do as I do, eh?'

'Ben. Ben are you in here?'

'It's Mum.'

'Yes Mrs Bird, we're here in the kitchen.'

Beth appeared at the kitchen door.

She was looking uncharacteristically dishevelled. Her normal, glamorous look missing. With no makeup on Andy thought she looked 'rough'.

Her face was pale and blotchy. Her normally perfect coiffured hair was greasy and piled into an untidy bun on the top of her head. Her eyes were still blackened by last night's smudged eyeliner, black bags under them making her look like a cage fighter who had come off worse.

'Ben I've had a call from the school. Why aren't you there?' she demanded.

'Because of you,' Ben shouted angrily.

'What do you mean? I didn't stop you.'

'I wasn't staying in our house with that...that bastard abusing you.'

'He wasn't abusing me...' Beth said, touching her hair clearly uncomfortable at having to explain herself. 'We were just...you know...having a bit of...adult fun. That's all.'

'You were drunk too. All Geoffery's money sending you to that clinic was a waste of time,' Ben ranted, putting on his blazer.

'No it wasn't. I know how to give it up. I was just having fun and testing myself that's all.'

'Well it's no fun for me Mum,' Ben said, walking towards the door.

'Where are you going?'

'To look for my Father. You obviously don't care about me. Perhaps he might.' Ben turned on his heel and left with Beth wobbling after him, clearly still under the influence.

'Ben, come back,' she called 'Ben!'

Andy shook his head, 'Poor kid doesn't stand a chance of ever growing up normally.'

CHAPTER ELEVEN

Helen picked up the local newspaper where Kay had tried to hide it behind the sofa.

It was two days since Andy had given his evidence in court. And she had been mentally preparing herself for the newspaper's slant on Andy and Nadine's late night liaison.

In spite of trying to put it to the back of her mind the shame and embarrassment of becoming public knowledge kept thrusting itself into her foremost thoughts. The apprehension of any possible exposé made her feel constantly sick.

The front page banner headlines read; '*Motorway death driver found guilty*'.

She read the story, the knot of concern tightening in her stomach.

'*The driver of the car which caused the inferno on the M5 motorway last Christmas has been found guilty of causing death by dangerous driving.*

The multi-vehicle crash which resulted in the death of a 35 year old salesman from the Stoke on Trent area, closed the motorway for several days causing gridlock for Christmas shoppers.

Sue Williams-Screen denied driving a black Volkswagen Polo identified as the cause of the horrendous crash.

Rupert Screen told the court that his estranged wife had threatened him with violence unless he lied to say that she was a passenger in his car at the time of the accident.

Mr Screen explained to the court that the reason for their marital separation was that he had suffered years of domestic violence at his wife's hands. The jury were given graphic details of several incidents.

A fingerprint expert gave evidence that there were no fingerprints belonging to Mrs Williams- Screens on the inside of Mr Screen's car, which failed to support her insistence that she was a rear seat passenger in her estranged husband's car.

The prosecution QC further discredited her version of events when he pointed out her apparent remarkable luck at being uninjured when both her husband and his new partner were so badly hurt.

In addition, crash scene investigators examining the wreckage of Mr Screen's car stated that they would have expected the rear seat passenger to have been trapped with potentially life threatening injuries.

Forensic evidence was also used to link her to the death of the gravedigger Jan Criscroski in the prevailing freezing temperatures.

The defendant was found not guilty of the manslaughter charge because cause of death was due to hypothermia.

Sentencing is expected within the next few weeks.

Under the story was a smaller article headlined 'Local Scout Leader in hotel incident.'

Helen nervously read the article with growing apprehension; the newspaper shaking.

'During the trial of the driver, who caused the fatal M5 crash, local Scout Leader, Andy Spider, was accused

of arranging an assault and theft of the mobile phone belonging to Mrs Williams-Screen.

The incident was alleged to have occurred after Mrs Williams-Screen filmed him in a late night liaison with a scantily clad woman in a hotel corridor.

However, it is believed that Mr Spider's wife was not on the trip with him.

No charges are expected to be made as the incident, which occurred in Monaco, was not reported to the police.'

Helen was absorbed in her thoughts as Kay returned from the kitchen carrying two cups of tea on a tray.

'Oh, you've found it? I'm sorry, I tried to keep the paper out of your way,' Kay said, putting the tray down.

'It's alright Kay. It would have been a miracle if they hadn't reported it. At least I was expecting it.'

'It's not that bad though is it? Kay asked, trying to sound optimistic.

'No, but it's bad enough,' Helen replied, reflectively.

'So what happens now the 'cat is out the bag?'

'I don't know. There's his work at the hospice and his Scouts which could both be impacted.'

'Heavens, I hadn't even thought about that.' Kay admitted.

'The worst case scenario is that Andy might have to give up Scouts I suppose. That'll break his heart. He loves working with the kids.'

'What about you two?' Kay asked, looking into Helen's sad eyes.

'Who knows? I hope we can survive whatever comes along. Call me naive, but I still believe that nothing happened with her.'

'Unfortunately the paper tends to make it look pretty seedy though, doesn't it?'

'Yes. It doesn't look good. But I tell you what. If he's got to go back to Monaco to finalise sorting out of this, 'flaming' will, then I shall insist on going with him. And, I'll make sure there are no overnight stays either.' Helen declared.

'Well if you want a babysitter, you know who to call.'

'Thanks Kay, that's very kind of you.'

'What about her? That Nadine.'

'As much as I'd like to throttle the tart, if she's there, I'll just ignore her.'

'How's Andy coping with it?'

'He's trying to put a brave face on it. But I don't think the newspaper article will help. As you'd expect, he's 'down in the dumps'.

'Is he still at work?'

'Yes, but I gather the hospice has told him to sort himself out because they don't want his personal problems impacting on his patients. I don't know what they'll say when they see the newspaper report.'

'But it's reported as allegations. They haven't proved anything.'

'Yeah, but as he was telling me, 'mud sticks'.'

'Well, I suppose it's all of his own doing. He's only got himself to blame.'

'Yes, I know, but it doesn't help.'

'Time's a great healer,' Kay threw in optimistically.

'I hope you're right,' Helen added, picking up a tissue. 'I hope you're right.'

CHAPTER TWELVE

It was the end of the troop meeting at the Scout hut and Andy was tidying up the paperwork from the evening's programme.

Ben was helping him but could see that Andy was distant, not his usual positive self. 'What's up Andy? You don't look very happy.'

'Sorry Ben, I'm just preoccupied at the moment.'

'Is it because of that court case?'

'Yes, that and the newspaper report.'

'Oh! Well that stuff that happened in Monaco was a long time ago...and as you'd tell me, 'it's all water under the bridge'.'

'Unfortunately not everybody will see it like that. Newspapers sometimes continue to dig around looking for more things. If they can't find any real facts they sometimes exaggerate things or even make them up completely.

Some daily papers occasionally sensationalise stories with big banner headlines just to sell papers.'

'In other words they lie. Well that's just not fair.' Ben concluded.

'I wouldn't go so far as saying that. They would probably say 'it's in the public interest and the public have a right to know'. I mean, they made it look as though I had an affair with Nadine because of the time of night.' Andy complained. 'It's all that Sue's fault. She was just waiting to catch us, I reckon.'

'But you never had an affair with that Nadine, though, did you? You told me,' Ben asked, seeking further reassurance of Andy's innocence.

'No I didn't. But I should have known better to have put myself into that stupid situation. So now, understandably, people will question what really happened.'

'Yeah but why? It's got nothing to do with anybody else. I mean it's not as though you hurt anybody, is it?'

'Apart from Helen that is,' Andy admitted.

'Yeah but you didn't thump anybody did you?' Ben countered.

'No, but unfortunately, when Carrie took that woman's mobile phone from her, to retrieve the 'damning' photos of me and Nadine, I got the blame. Although I wasn't charged with anything, they suggested in court that I was responsible for arranging the assault and subsequent theft.'

'So what will happen now?'

'It's possible now that the story is out the Scout Association will ask me to resign.'

'What! Give up Scouts? No, they can't do that. I mean, look what you've done with us lot,' Ben pointed out.

'Unfortunately they have a responsibility to safeguard the good name of Scouting and well...'

'I'll get a petition up to stop them,' Ben asserted, getting animated. 'I mean you were...'

'Thanks Ben, but I don't think it would help. The newspaper article has made me out to be a villain and a gigolo.'

'A what?'

'A gigolo. A person who chases women.'

'Well, I can tell them the truth.'

'Thank you Ben, but remember at one stage even you thought I was being unfaithful to Helen and the children, didn't you? So people who read the papers who don't know me or the background behind it will believe the newspaper reports. Unfortunately 'mud sticks.'

'What do you mean?'

'In spite of my denials, some people will still believe that there is no smoke without fire. Some of it must be true because the paper said so.'

'Oh, it's so unfair.'

'I'll go to the Commissioner when he comes back from holiday and discuss it with him. But I have to face it. I might have to give up.' Andy declared.

Several days later, a very anxious Andy had the meeting with the 'top brass' and was pleased to receive a sympathetic understanding.

'Well Andy, I'm pleased you initiated the meeting,' the Commissioner advised. 'Please relax, I'm not going to interrogate you.'

'Thanks,' he said, taking a deep breath. I felt I needed to let you know as soon as possible before HQ was on your neck,' Andy confided.

'I've read the newspaper report. But what's the truth behind it? You don't have to tell me unless you want to,' the other conceded.

'No, I'm quite happy to let you know. I have nothing to hide. I stayed out late with Geoffery Foster's former partner at the Casino in Monaco. She was showing me the sights. Somebody took a photograph of me and her in the early hours as we were saying goodbye. But it was all innocent. You know what the French are like, very tactile. All 'kissy kissy'.'

'Not that it's any of my business, but how is Helen with all this?'

'Yes, alright. Obviously it was a bit tense for a while but I explained what happened and…yeah we're OK now.'

'What about the alleged assault and theft of the ladies mobile phone?

The question wrong footed Andy.

'I…this was all a bit of misunderstanding by one of my friends. She took matters in to her own hands. This thoroughly objectionable woman, you know the one that has just been sent down for dangerous driving, was going to blackmail me and …'

'Andy, you don't need to convince me,' the Commissioner said, cutting him short. 'I'm sure you're telling the truth.'

'Thank you,' said Andy relieved.

'Anyway, that doesn't sound like anything that would undermine your role as a Scout Leader. Have you had any complaints from the parents?'

'No.'

'No I haven't either. Well let's 'let sleeping dogs lie'. If we get any complaints we might have to review it. Until then carry on. Keep up the good work. But try not to get involved with anything else contentious.'

'Oh thank you. Thank you so much.' Andy beamed, grabbing the others hand and pumping it excitedly. 'The kids will be delighted.'

By the way, tell Ben, his petition worked.'

CHAPTER THIRTEEN

Beth looked at Ben, concerned. 'But why do you want to look for your father?'

'Because I do,' Ben said, slumping down onto the tired sofa.

'That's no answer,' she said anxiously, fearing the consequences of Ben's quest.

'I want to know who he is. I want to know why, according to you, he doesn't want to see me. I want to ask him face to face,' Ben declared.

'Best of luck. If you can track him down,' Beth said, sceptically.

'But you must know where he lives? You can tell me.'

'No Ben, just keep away from him. Leave it as it is. I still don't understand why you want to find him.'

'I want to know what it's like to be a normal family. To have a Mum and Dad living together in the same house.'

'Well that isn't going to happen, is it? You can forget that for a start.'

'Why? You told me to dream. You said dreams sometimes come true.'

'This wouldn't be a dream son. This would be a nightmare, believe me. Just give it up. It's an impossible dream. Don't waste your time.'

'Why?' Ben demanded, firmly slapping the arm of the sofa in frustration, sending up a cloud of dust.

'I don't want to see you hurt. You'll be heading for a big disappointment. If you don't find him you can still live with your dreams. If you see him are you prepared to be disappointed when he dismisses you out of hand?'

'Why would he? Are you protecting me or yourself?' Ben screeched. 'How do you know he will reject me? He might not.'

'Believe me son it will be a case of when he rejects you, not IF. As you know, I tried for years, when you were a baby, to get him interested in you. He wasn't, believe me. You're better off leaving things as they are.' Beth said quietly, looking out of the window.

'OK, but do you want to know the real reason I want to see him?'

'Yes, of course.'

'It's because I don't want to go into Care. And you keep letting me down by going back on the booze.'

'But...I'm getting there,' she pleaded.

'Mum, I can't wait any longer. At least if I have a Father and a Mother they can't take me can they? I've heard the social services people are in the area asking questions. I've had enough.' Ben stood next to her and emphasised his point of view, 'I've given you lots of chances and what happens in the end? You get pissed out of your head and I have to look after you again.' Ben pointed out and threw himself back on the sofa again.

'But this is different,' she implored.

'How is it different?'

'Yes it is because now I know how to cope with it,' she explained and knelt in front of him to emphasise her commitment.

'No Mum, you don't. There is no 'coping' with it. If it involves the bottle, you have to finish. Stop. Give it up completely. James can do it. Why can't you?' Ben ranted.

'It's because…because I can't face life without it. It takes away…the…umm…'

'The pain? Yes, that's what James used to say…his escape from reality. But what about me? What about my reality? I'm your son, your child. Don't you realise your messing up my life as well?' He stood up and walked away from her.

'I'm not. That's a horrible thing to say.' Beth yelled, hurt.

'It's true Mum. When did you take me anywhere? To the pictures or for a birthday meal. Or anywhere?'

'Well, I…I never had the money to…'

'But you found the money to buy booze,' he countered, pointing an accusing finger at her.

'Ben you don't understand, you're only a kid. I am not as strong as you. I…I need help. The booze gives me confidence. But I am trying. Honestly I am.'

'I'm sorry Mum, I've given you enough chances.'

Just then there was a knock on the door.

'Who's that likely to be?' Beth asked looking anxiously at Ben.

'I don't know, open the door and find out. If it's one of your boyfriends, I'm off out.'

Beth made her way apprehensively to the door. She opened it cautiously, just wide enough to see through the small gap, hoping it wasn't going to be Ben's father. She was reassured to see Andy on the door step.

'Oh hello Andy, nice to see you,' she said, relieved.

'Hello Mrs Bird. Is Ben in?

'Yes.'

'In that case can I come in?'

'Yes of course,' she said, opening the door wide.

Beth led Andy through the cluttered hallway side-stepping Ben's mountain bikes and he followed her in.

'Ben, it's Andy. You'll have to excuse the mess,' Beth apologised, leading Andy into the lounge.

'Andy, thanks for coming over,' Ben said.

'Hi Ben. I got your message. I've done some digging,' he said sitting on the sagging sofa.

'Digging?' said Beth naively. 'I didn't know you were into gardening.'

'Not that sort of digging Mum. I asked Andy to help me cope with your problem.'

'We don't need any help,' Beth insisted indignantly, sitting down on the edge of the equally shabby easy chair. 'We're sorting our problems out ourselves. Isn't that right Ben?'

'No Mum, we aren't. I need some...some real help.'

'Mrs Bird...'

'Please call me Beth.'

'Beth, I've found about an organisation called 'Young Carers' that might be able to help you both. I phoned them and they were very helpful. I told them about my involvement with Ben after he had been thrown out of your house in the early hours.'

'What! When was that? I'd never do that to him,' she said indignantly

'No I believe it was one of your boyfriends.'

'Yes, well. That's not likely to happen again. I don't see him anymore after I learnt what he'd done,' Beth countered defensively.

'Well, apparently, Ben's experience is quite common. They tell me that most young people who have joined

Young Carers have been subjected to or have witnessed domestic violence.'

'I've never hurt you Ben have I?'

'Not physically. No.'

'What do you mean by that?' Beth demanded.

'You know what I mean...we were talking about it before Andy arrived.'

Beth twiddled her fingers and looked at the floor, hurt.

'Anyway,' Andy continued feeling slightly awkward. 'They are going to send me a form so that I can refer Ben to them.'

'Refer! What do you mean by refer? Beth asked, frowning.

'It's just a way of recording why Ben might need their help.'

'Oh!' she said, sitting back in her chair. 'Not sure I like the idea of that. We don't need help from the likes of them officials.'

''I do Mum. I want help to deal with it.'

'You've never had help before. You've always coped before.'

'Well not anymore. I'm tired of your false promises. I'm fed up with having to put you to bed and getting up in the middle of the night to make sure you're still breathing. I'm scared you'll choke on your own sick... I've had enough of coping with this on my own.'

'But I'm stopping. It will get better I promise.'

'I've heard you say that so many times before. It doesn't mean anything. The clinic people must be tearing their hair out. You have let them down, as well as yourself and me.' Ben said strongly.

'Ben, I'm trying.' Beth said desperately and started sobbing.

'I know you are Mum,' Ben said going over to her and putting his arm around her shoulder. 'But this is for me. Please give it a try.'

'Well I suppose…if it helps you,' she sobbed.

Andy felt uncomfortable at being the instigator of her distress.

'Look these people are experts. Why don't you give it a try as Ben suggests, if it doesn't work out then you can always stop it,' Andy suggested, throwing her a lifeline.

'So what happens next Andy?' Ben asked, still hugging his Mother.

'They want to see you together and they will create a plan for you both.'

'A plan! What kind of a plan?' Beth said, wiping her tears with the back of her hand.

'Well once they get my referral, my filled in form, they'll contact you and arrange a meeting appointment.'

'Oh, I'm not sure. I mean look at this place.' Beth said, looking around the untidy lounge with its shabby paintwork and faded wallpaper.

'If you'd prefer, we could meet at the scout hut and James and I could be there too to offer you moral support.'

'What if they contact Social Services?' Ben asked, concerned that increasing the profile of his problems would actually bring about the very thing he feared.

'Don't worry Ben, I asked them about that specifically and they assured me they wouldn't do anything without consulting you first.'

'Ok, so long as they keep their word,' Ben said.

'Will it be a man or woman?' Beth asked, gingerly.

'I think it will be a woman. They apparently have a woman expert who deals with people with alcohol and other substances problems.'

'Other substances!' Ben said. 'Like what?'

'Drugs,' Andy replied. 'Substance abuse they call it. I've seen a few unfortunate people at the hospice who have abused themselves and overdone it on drugs.'

'Oh I'm not sure,' Beth said having second thoughts. 'I hate seeing these officials, they scare me.'

'Please Mum, do it for me,' Ben pleaded.

Beth looked into Ben's sad eyes and relented. 'Ok for you my son, I'll do it.'

Ben felt elated. At last he didn't have to cope alone anymore.

CHAPTER FOURTEEN

Andy completed the 'Young Carers' referral form for Ben and subsequently returned it to the charity as he'd promised.

Consequently, a family advocate from the organisation came to see Ben and Beth at the Scout hut and, as agreed, James and Andy were there too to lend moral support for the nervous pair.

They had arranged to go to Foster Lodge, because of Beth's concern about the shabby nature of her house.

The group sat in an informal circle in the well-appointed kitchen area clutching steaming mugs of tea.

Andy led a round of introductions to advise the visitor who everybody was and their role at the meeting.

The woman advocate was a naturally charming person who gave some background about herself and the charity; the aims of which Andy thought paralleled that of Scouting, which was 'to support a society where children and young people reach their potential and achieve transition to adulthood regardless of family circumstances.'

She put Beth at ease straight away. She was not the officious person with whom Beth usually felt intimidated.

Lacking in self-esteem, Beth normally retreated into herself in the presence of officialdom and ended up agreeing to whatever 'they' said without actually engaging in a meaningful dialogue.

But the lady from 'Young Carers' made her feel that her input was valued. She felt able to put her point view and engaged fully in the discussion.

More importantly, the advocate listened to what Beth had to say and didn't dismiss her nervous self-conscious explanations of their domestic situation out of hand.

Ben, too, was pleased to hear that she understood his worries and his hollow feeling of isolation because of his Mum's problems.

She explained that she understood if he didn't feel able to talk about his Mother's issues to his mates and further explained that children saw caring responsibilities in a different way to adults.

The visitor said that they believed in putting the 'young' back into 'young carer', ensuring that children were never expected to take on adult responsibilities.

It was as if a weight had been lifted off his shoulders. At last somebody understood what he was going through. There was some light at the end of the tunnel after all. He felt happy enough to smile. Something he hadn't done for a long time.

'Beth, I'm pleased to hear that you have at least recognised that you are an alcoholic and have been treated at a suitable clinic,' the advocate said smiling. 'But the hard bit is for you to stop continually testing the success of the treatment by going back and indulging again.

We have found that the best way to prove you have conquered your demon is never to drink alcohol again.'

'What never?'

'Never. One drink is one too many as a lot of people have found. One drink leads to another and...'

'But I need it. It is part of my social life. My friends will laugh at me if I start drinking soft drinks.'

'Then perhaps it's time to look for some new friends.'

'Oh, I couldn't. I don't make friends easily.'

'I think if you want to, you'll find it easier than you think. Do your friends respect you now when you become paralytic?'

'No, I don't think so. They think it's funny.'

'What about the impact on Ben?'

'I know I've let Ben down,' Beth said grabbing hold of his hand and giving it a squeeze.

'And by the look of it you have friends here who will help you too, I'm sure,' she suggested, looking for confirmation from James and Andy, who chorused,

'Yes of course.'

'Beth, you know I've been on the same path as yourself...look at me,' James said. 'My liver is 'shot'. In the worst case scenario I might well die because of my own stupidity. You have Ben to think of, as well as yourself. You have a chance to pull back from the brink. Don't go the same way as me,' James implored.

'OK, I'll try.'

'Thank you Mum,' Ben said, uncharacteristically giving her a peck on the cheek.

Through the rest of the evening they made a plan which Beth and Ben signed up to.

First on the list, Beth had to empty the house of her hidden caches of alcohol and she promised to attend local substance abuse discussion groups. By sharing her problems and the temptations with others the sessions aimed to improve her self-esteem and self-worth.

James agreed to attend the same meetings which made her feel happier. She also promised to look for a new social group of friends recognising that remaining with the same 'boozy' crowd would be to expose herself to continuing temptation.

Most importantly, she recognised that Ben too should have some help. 'Young Carers' seemed to be the right thing for him so that he too could meet with other children who were having their childhood destroyed by parental problems and issues.

'Beth, you must be under no illusions. It won't be easy. But I'm sure your friends here will keep you on the straight and narrow.'

'Nothing worth having is,' Beth said, reflectively.

'We will support you as much as we can and put you in touch with other organisations that can help.'

'You can count on me Beth,' James said, giving her a shoulder hug.

'Well, I think we've made a good start,' the advocate said. 'Ben I've given you the details for the next meeting of the local Young Carers group, haven't I?'

'Yes thanks.'

With that the meeting broke up in a flurry of smiles and good intentions.

So in spite of Beth's initial reluctance, Ben joined the local 'Young Carers' group and a few days later went, with great apprehension, to his first meeting.

At one stage he almost turned around and went back home but he felt if he did so he'd be letting his Mum and Andy down.

'After all it was me that started this. If Mum can do it, so can I.' he said under his breath opening the large glass entrance door.

The meeting was in a local church hall, so he didn't have far to travel. The leader of the group was expecting him and went straight across as he entered and warmly welcomed him.

'Hello, my name is Penny. Welcome to our group. Don't be shy. You will find that all the young people here have challenges in their lives, so please feel free, if you wish, to share your own to whomever you want.

We offer you support, a voice and fellowship with other young people who share similar circumstances to yourself.'

She introduced him to several people including a skinny 14 year old girl called Janie.

'Hi, so what goes on here then?' Ben asked, looking around at the group

'Hi, I'm Janie. Oh we do lots of things. We have people coming to see us and talk to us about various things. And we do games and stuff.

Last week we had somebody from the local Round Table who set up some Wiis and we played games all evening. It was great. He even brought his family along too and they joined in the games. I think the Round Table also make donations to 'Young Carers' because we are a charity, apparently.'

'Oh, I see.'

During the evening Ben discovered that Janie was the principle carer for her Mother who was suffering from MS and who, like Ben, came from a single parent family.

'The 'Young Carers' also organise weekends in April and October where people on camp are invited to tell everybody about their personal problems.'

'I go camping with the Scouts.' Ben said, dismissively.

'This isn't in tents. They got proper cabins that sleep four people.'

'Different.' Ben admitted.

'You meet kids in similar circumstances. They talk about developing coping skills and stuff.' Janie added.

'I've had to develop my own,' Ben informed her. 'Sounds pretty dreary if you ask me.'

But Janie persisted. 'They have experts from other organisations who come and chat about problems with drugs and alcohol, you know. Substance misuse...'

'There's nothing they can't tell me about that, I've seen it all with my Mum. If that's all, I think I'll give it a miss, thanks.'

'No that's not it. They put on lots of fun activities.'

'Such as?'

'Well, although it's not really an activity weekend, they make sure it's fun. There's archery, raft building, games in the lake and kayaking of course, African drumming...'

'Oh I've never done that before.'

'Karaoke...'

'I always fancied myself as a singer in a boy band,' Ben admitted, a hint of enthusiasm creeping in to his voice.

'And lots of team build stuff.'

'Oh, we do that in our patrols at scouts too.'

'Workshops in the morning and evening,' Janie continued, reeling off the list.

'What like carpentry and stuff?'

'No! It's talking about things,' she amplified.

'Anyway, I don't think I'd like sharing my family problems with strangers,' Ben reiterated.

'Why not? Everybody knows what problems I have looking after my Mum. Anyway I bet within a couple of hours you'll unwind and tell them everything. You don't have to worry. Nobody judges you,' she sought to reassure him.

'Yeah but your problems different to mine and anyway you're a girl and...'

'And what do you mean by that?' Janie's hackles rose.

'Well you girls talk about things that us 'guys' wouldn't dream of sharing.'

'Perhaps that's why you 'guys' are so uptight and aggressive all the time. You need to get it off your chest. You'll feel better for it I promise you,' she argued.

'No I don't think so,' Ben decided, he had learnt that the old adage- 'least said, soonest mended', was much better.

'Please yourself, but if you want to just talk to me about them I promise not to tell anybody else,' Janie offered.

'I don't know. I don't know you,' Ben said sceptically.

'That's OK, when you're ready.'

Ben thought about the things he would love to offload. His wish list included his uneasy relationship with the Police; his Mothers unpredictable behaviour and drinking problem; the strange men she brought into their house, the hunt for his Dad; the fear of being taken in to Care; the death of his friend Geoffery Foster and the desecration of his grave and finally the threats from Rupert's missus, Sue. She really was a scary lady. At least she was now locked up in prison.

The more he thought about it the better it sounded to talk to somebody about it all and get it off his chest.

'I ride a bike too,' Janie said, breaking into Ben's thoughts.'

'Do you? What, a pink one with painted flowers on the frame?' he teased.

'No, cheeky sod,' she screeched indignantly. 'I've done Mountain Bike races,' she elaborated.

Ben's ears pricked up. Here was a girl after his own heart. A bike racer. Perhaps things were going to be alright after all.

CHAPTER FIFTEEN

'Quick, get down Tim,' Carrie instructed, urgently pulling him to the ground.

'What?'

'Over there, behind the trees.' She said pointing.

'What?' Tim asked, peering in the direction of her gaze.

'Sniper.' Carrie whispered, continuing to stare.

'Carrie. Effing hell! A sniper? For Chrissake there's no bleeding sniper.' He ranted, pushing himself up. 'We're in the Cotswolds not Afghanistan.'

'Get down you fool,' Carrie shouted, grabbing his sleeve.

Tim shrugged her hand off aggressively. 'Will you stop this crap?'

Carrie looked up at him frantically, 'Get down before he gets a bead on you,' she implored, expecting any moment to see his head explode as the sniper found his mark.

'Carrie. You're in England now,' he ranted, reaching down and pulling her up.

'England? Carrie repeated, puzzled, looking around vacantly.

'That's it. I've had enough. Either you get yourself sorted or I'm off.'

Carrie looked around her and suddenly recognised her surroundings.

'Oh God', she said eyes brimming. 'I saw a flash from over by the trees. I thought it was a trap. Oh Tim, I'm sorry,' she sobbed, falling into his arms.

'You...we can't go on like this Carrie. You need to see somebody. Get it sorted for good,' he begged her.

'No, I can do this myself...with your help.' She said, sobbing.

'You keep saying that but you're getting worse, not better.' He pulled her tight to his chest. Frightened at what she would do next.

'I mustn't give in...who dares...'

'Not in this case. Forget the bleeding SAS motto. You need professional help. Get help or I'm off,' he threatened.

'Tim...'

'I tell you I've had enough. What with your violent nightmares. You're bleeding well kicking me black and blue.'

'I'm sorry, I can't help it,' she wailed.

'I know,' he said holding her. 'You can't see it, but you've changed. Your demeanour...it's frigging scary.'

'If I do, what will happen about the walking company? We've worked so hard to create it,' she whimpered. 'All our hard work...will be for nothing.'

'Don't worry about that. You get yourself sorted and I'll do what I can to keep things ticking over until you're fit again,' Tim reassured.

'It might take a long time,' Carrie predicted.

'That's OK. I'll be here for you,' he reassured, hugging her tighter.

'What about the conditions of the will?' she asked, suddenly realising, the future of the walking company depended on fulfilling certain criteria before Tim's legacy would be released.

'I'll worry about that. You concentrate on getting better.'

The next day, after several aborted attempts, Carrie contacted the veteran's organisation 'Combat Stress'. She was greeted with kindly understanding as she explained her problem.

'I can fit you in tomorrow for an appointment, if you can make it?' The receptionist informed her.

'Yes I'll be there,' Carrie confirmed, looking at Tim for reassurance.

'See, that wasn't difficult, was it? he said, giving her a light kiss.

'No. But that's just the start.'

'You'll be OK. I'm sure,' he encouraged, more in hope than judgement.

The initial appointment led on to a five day assessment, where Post Traumatic Stress Disorder was confirmed by a psychiatrist.

'Well what happens next?' Carrie asked.

'We have a place available on a course which will help to start the healing process.

It consists of another ten day assessment – group therapy and one to one sessions with a lead nurse worker.

After that we usually find that it is beneficial to attend a PTSD Intensive Treatment programme along with six other veterans.'

At first Carrie was sceptical that anyone could help her but slowly things started to improve.

The sessions were full on. Supervised by a psychologist, she found herself working with a group of others who had similar flashbacks and experienced bizarre incidents.

Most importantly the sessions helped her understand that the guilt she suffered as a survivor was perfectly normal. Survivor's syndrome often caused nightmares and mood swings.

The staff reinforced the reality that fate had played a hand in the fortunes of her less fortunate colleagues who didn't come home. And nothing that she could have done would have changed that.

They told her, what she already knew, but didn't believe that in spite of 'beating herself up'; she could have done nothing to have saved them.

It was a teary and very emotionally painful period. But slowly she felt herself getting better each day. Her mood swings reduced considerably.

She had also been advised of a technique to help her to control her terrible memories. It entailed imagining that she was putting her nightmarish dreams and bad recollections into a box and locking them away.

'You just post all your nightmares and bad thoughts in there,' the psychologist explained.

'How? Do you need an actual box?' she queried.

'Some people find seeing a physical box is easier than imagining one. It's up to you what you feel will work for you.'

'You mean you don't physically write something and post it in?'

'You can do that as well if you want. Or you can psychologically post your nightmares in there. Whatever you decide, believe in your choice.'

'But how do you keep them in there?'

'Imagine there's a flap in the top, like a letterbox.'

'But how do you stop the bad thoughts escaping when you open the flap to put another in?'

'You mentally put a one way valve in it. What's in - stays in.'

'Do people really feel better after they've posted their bad thoughts?'

'Yes. Most people who try it find it works. But it takes some time to learn the technique.'

'How do you mean?'

'You've got to be strong and really want to get rid of your bad thoughts. Otherwise you'll find that you can't put them in there. They will just continue to haunt you.'

'What's to stop the bad thoughts reoccurring?'

'You.'

'What do you mean?'

'You have to be convinced that you really want to get rid of them from messing with your head.'

'Oh! But surely that's difficult to control.'

'Yes, it is. But unless you do your nightmares will probably continue.'

'I can see that. But...what if they all escape at the same time?'

'Conceivably you could be overwhelmed by all your bad thoughts and you could be in serious trouble...It might lead to a breakdown.'

'Bloody hell!'

'But don't think of the bad things. Think of the good things, it's a positive way forward. And once you start, you will feel better. Keeping the bad thoughts in the box becomes easier and easier as you regain your confidence.'

Although sceptical at first, she gave it a go. Without really noticing any major step change, she, however, found that her flashbacks had reduced considerably.

Tim noticed the difference in her and he too felt a lot happier, more relaxed.

As a bonus, the course also enabled Carrie to 'sell' the services of the 'Just Do It Walking' company to the clinic.

The task was made easier because the doctors were already strong believers that regular contact with the natural environment was a good medicine for people recovering from PTSD and other ailments. Medically proven research showed that endorphins released during the exercise created a 'feel good' factor thus improving people's general demeanour.

It was a 'win- win' situation Carrie was getting to grips with controlling her PTSD episodes and felt good that she'd made up for her short absence by bringing business in to the Walking Company. And the other Service people suffering from depression got a special tailored deal too.

Tim was happy that their relationship was back on track.

CHAPTER SIXTEEN

Beth had been deeply hurt by Ben's accusation that she did nothing for him. True, they didn't go anywhere together, but she felt that they had a good relationship. Not so much Mother and Son but more akin to being good friends.

However, she was determined to prove that she was a good Mother and asked Andy if they could hold a 'surprise' birthday party for Ben at the Scout Hut.

Andy gladly agreed and made an arrangement with Ben to come to the hut after school on the pretext that he wanted help to move some kit into the store.

As the time approached for Ben to arrive at the Scout hut Andy peeped out through a crack in the door and spotted Ben arriving on his bike.

He rushed back into the kitchen and got everyone except Beth to hide.

Ben walked into the kitchen where he was greeted by Beth holding a birthday cake with fifteen lighted candles.

'Happy Birthday son,' she said, smiling.

'Mum!' he said in surprise.

Beth was 'dressed up to the nine's'. Her hair and makeup perfect. However her night clubbing clothes of tight, sparkly sequined skirt, ruffled white blouse and high heels were totally out of place in the Scout hut. But at least she'd made the effort for Ben's special day.

People emerged from their hiding places and sang a chorus of 'happy birthday' to him.

Ben was shocked. This sort of thing had never happened to him before. It was an even greater pleasure because when he'd left for school that morning Beth didn't even wish him a happy birthday, let alone give him a card.

Consequently he'd spent the day bemoaning the fact that she had forgotten altogether.

'You've got to blow the candles out all in one,' she said smiling. 'Don't forget to make a wish.'

Ben took a huge breath and succeeded in his task, he wished that all his birthdays would be like this, surrounded by friends and family.

He was the centre of attraction and he beamed at the smiling crowd which, as well as his Mum and Andy, included Helen, Amy and baby Molly, James, Ben's Grandad Harold and some of his Scouting mates.

'Happy birthday Ben, we've bought you a little present,' Andy said, giving Amy a small brightly coloured package to give to him.

'Thank you Amy,' Ben said, kneeling down to take it from the equally excited little girl.

'I helped my Mummy with the wrapping paper,' she informed him.

'Did you? Well I think you did very well,' he praised.

Unused to receiving birthday presents, he felt obliged to study the label it read. '*Happy birthday from Helen, Andy, Amy, Molly and cousin Rose*'.

'Thank you folks.'

And then he hastily demolished the carefully crafted wrapping, paper flying everywhere as he excitedly ripped into it.

'A mobile phone!' he exclaimed in astonished amazement. 'Mum, I've got a mobile. Wow! A Samsung Galaxy! Brilliant.' Ben yelled, taking it out of the box.

'I thought as you'd showed great dexterity using somebody else's...'

'Don't remind me,' Ben answered, guiltily.

'...it was about time you had one of your own.'

'Is it OK if I give you a hug?' Ben asked, looking at Andy.

'Of course,' Andy confirmed.

Ben moved to him and they hugged.

'Happy birthday Ben,' Andy whispered. 'Let's hope you enjoy using it. I thought that at fifteen, you're old enough to have one. By the way it's PAYG and your Grandad has put thirty pounds on it. So it should last for a day or two.'

'Thank you Grandad,' Ben acknowledged, enthusiastically hugging him too.

'My pleasure son.'

'I've bought you a little something too,' James added, handing over a large squidgy feeling parcel.

'This is great. I've never had so many presents. Thanks. How exciting is this?' Ben's fingers eagerly ripped open the wrapping paper to reveal a yellow cycling jersey and a pair of black cycling shorts.

'Thank you, thank you very much,' Ben said hugging James as well.

Ben spotted his Mother looking crestfallen and gave her a hug too.

'Sorry Ben, I couldn't afford much,' she said, giving him a small package. 'By the time I'd bought the nibbles...'

'It's OK Mum, don't worry,' he interrupted. 'I'm sure it'll be great. Anyway your main present to me is this party. And that you're here and...sober. I know how difficult it is for you.'

Beth put her arm around his shoulders as he demolished the wrapping around the small gift to reveal a Sports bracelet.

'Just what I wanted,' he said putting it on his wrist and admiring it. 'Thank you.' And he gave her another hug and a kiss on the cheek.

'I've laid on some food for your party too,' Beth said, leading him over to a table populated with plates of sausage rolls, sandwiches, crisps, cheese and pineapples on sticks and tea cakes.

Andy put some music on and Ben invited everybody to 'tuck in'.

Ben felt happier than he had been for a long time. If only his Dad would walk in now, it would really make his day.

CHAPTER SEVENTEEN

Sorry I missed your birthday,' Janie said as they left the Young Carers meeting wheeling their bikes.

'That's OK. It was a small surprise party. I didn't know anything about it until I got to the Scout hut myself.'

'What did you get?'

'A mobile. My first.'

'Oh, I've had one since I was ten, because of my Mum,' she told him.

'And a new cycling top and a pair of shorts,' Ben continued

'What did your Mum get you?'

'Well...she couldn't afford much...you know, after she bought stuff for my party, so she bought me this sports bracelet.' He said, lifting his arm to show her.

'Great.' Janie said, admiring it. 'I always fancied one of those.'

'I got a birthday cake from her too.'

'Was she...you know?' Janie probed.

'What?'

'Tiddly?' she added, delicately.

'No. That was probably the best thing. She hadn't been on the bottle. Where are we going anyway?'

'I thought we could go to the bus shelter and celebrate your birthday.'

'What do you mean? Celebrate,' Ben asked suspiciously, leading her along the pavement bordering the main road.

'You know...' she said digging into a carrier bag she had been guarding all evening. '...like adults do.'

'What you got in that bag?' Ben asked, already suspecting the answer.

'Vodka. Want some?' she said happily pulling the small bottle out to show him.

'What the hell are you doing with that?' he demanded in disbelief.

'I thought you'd be pleased,' she said, deflated by his reaction.

'You're only fourteen. You idiot.' He hissed.

'Don't get like that. I'm nearly fifteen anyway. I thought you'd be happy that I was thinking about you,' Janie murmured, hurt.

'We don't need booze.' Ben fumed angrily, grabbing the bottle from her and leant his bike against the church railings.

'Why not?' she demanded, putting her bike next to his.

'It'll ruin your life. That's why not.' He informed her. 'I should know.'

'Oh get off your 'soap box'. Just cos your Mother can't cope with booze. It doesn't mean that everybody has the same problem.' Janie said angrily.

'You what?' Ben demanded.

'Sorry, that was a mean thing to say,' Janie apologised, feeling awkward. 'I didn't mean...you know...that...to be hurtful.'

'My mum was sixteen when she started drinking and she's been messed up ever since. Once you start...I mean it's like a drug she takes to escape the real world. And when she's sober again it's still the same world. Probably worse than when she tried to escape from it.'

'Yeah well that's why I drink…to have a little escape from having to deal with my Mother's illness.' Janie confessed.

'You're an idiot.'

'Come on, I'm a kid. I need to be enjoying myself. Although I love my Mum, being a nurse to her is hard. The kids at school can be cruel too, once they found out about me looking after Mum. There's some who taunt me all the time. It makes me so angry.'

'Tell me about it,' Ben said reflecting on his own miserable experiences.

'Sometimes I wish something would happen to their parents so that they would know how hard it is.'

'That's pretty harsh but I know what you mean,' Ben admitted.

'That's why I joined Young Carers. Anyway, its good fun getting drunk. You lose all your…inhibitions and well, you can end up doing some exciting things that you wouldn't normally do,' she said moving coquettishly towards him.

'You stupid, stupid…idiot. So you've already got a habit? Don't you see what a crazy thing you're doing? You're playing with fire.' Ben admonished.

Janie stepped back, surprised at his reaction. 'Anyway, it's my life,' she countered.

'Yes, my Mother thought the same and ended up being laid by a married man who got her pregnant. So what happened? She drank to forget him and now she's ruined both our lives. Now we're struggling to get her off the booze.'

'It won't happen to me. I can control it.' Janie said confidently.

'You think you can. The trouble is it becomes an addiction and you can't give it up. I've seen it with my Mum and my friend James. At least they've got some help now.'

'What sort of help are they doing for her?'

'Well she's been in a clinic, but that didn't work for long. The substance abuse lady from Young Carers is on the case now and we've got a plan to try and sort herself out.'

'I'm sorry…I didn't mean to upset you,' Janie said, touching his arm.

'If the plan doesn't work, I might end up in care soon if the Social Services get involved.' Ben said, enjoying the warmth of her touch.

'I'm sorry. Oh god that would be terrible. You might have to move away from here.' Janie said removing her hand.

'Yeah, I know. That's one of the things I'm afraid of. Anyway this isn't about me this is about you…drinking will mess up your life. Worse still it will mess up your performance on the bike.'

'It hasn't affected me so far.' Janie pleaded.

'It will. You'll start putting on weight and…'

'What do you mean?' Janie queried, suddenly more focussed.

'You've seen men with beer guts.' Ben said, gesticulating as if he had a pot belly.

'Yeah but that's through drinking beer, isn't it?'

'The alcohol starts it.' He informed her.

'Oh I didn't know that,' she said, subconsciously feeling her waist.

'Listen, I've been around enough drunks to know how it ruins your life. My friend James has destroyed his liver. He took to the booze to escape from some emotional problems and all it's done is messed up his health. It might even kill him yet.'

'Yeah, but come on. I ain't drinking that much.' Janie rationalised.

'No. Not yet. But if you carry on, you will. Believe me.'

'Everybody goes on about social drinking and drinking responsibly…'

'Yeah and for some people, that's where it stays. But if you start drinking now, you'll end up as one of those tarts in the gutter every Friday night who are pissed out of their heads. Men will take advantage of you. Nobody will respect you.' Ben said passionately.

'Ok then 'clever clogs' how do I cope with my Mum's illness?' Janie asked, turning away.

'I know it's hard, but you got to find some…some inner strength.'

'Inner strength! You sound like a bleeding teacher.' She said dismissively.

'I escape by riding my bike. It's one of the ways I cope with my Mum and her drinking. Getting out in the countryside on my bike…well, I can get my head together. Things seem different somehow. It's good training, improves my race performance too.' Ben explained zealously.

'Yeah, well I do training rides too, but, I never thought of it sorting my head out.' Janie confessed.

'You could always come out training with me…if you want to?' Ben offered.

'Nah! You'd ride faster than me.' Janie dismissed his offer.

'I'll do some easy routes.'

'Well,' she pondered.

'Want to give it a try?' he continued.

'Ok. So long as you promise not to bomb off and leave me,' she dictated.

'No, I won't. Right, so now you won't need this then,' Ben said, taking the top off the Vodka bottle.

'No don't pour it away. Please.' Janie pleaded, reaching for it.

Ben held the bottle at arm's length and was about to pour it down the drain as a Police car drove by.

'Oh shit,' he said. 'Why does that always happen?'

The Police car pulled up in a screech of tyres, followed by the sound of it reversing at high speed.

'Quick, let's go,' he shouted, as he climbed on his bike, putting the open bottle in his coat pocket.

Inside the car the two Police officers decided not to get out. Instead they watched as Ben and Janie rode off at top speed.

They knew Ben from a series of recent incidents including the missing mobile phone belonging to the deceased gravedigger.

'Might have known that Master Bird would be up to no good,' the female officer said. 'Drinking under age and I doubt the girl he was with is eighteen either.'

'We going to go after him?' the driver asked, checking his rear view mirror as the two cycled away on the pavement.

'No. He knows what he's done and seeing us will probably put the shits up him anyway. Perhaps we might mention it to that Scout Leader bloke. He'll probably get more sense out of him than we can.'

'Is it this kid that's got the 'alky' Mother?'

'Yeah.'

'Well, looks like he's going to follow in her footsteps.'

'Poor sod doesn't stand a chance of having a normal life, though does he? In a way I feel sorry for him.'

'Yeah, if he carries on the way he's going. He'll be locked up for the majority of it too, I should guess. Sad really, just another wasted life!'

'Come on it's time for a break.'

They blended back into the traffic and drove off in the direction that they were originally heading.

CHAPTER EIGHTEEN

'Where we going?' Janie shouted at Ben's back as they high-tailed it up the road.

'Umm...not sure... I know, we'll go up the Scout hut. There shouldn't be anybody there tonight and I've got my keys.'

'Are you sure?' she asked, breathing heavily.

'Yeah, we'll be OK there, trust me.'

The pair cycled up to the Scout hut and was relieved to see nobody there. Ben quickly opened the door and they took their bikes inside. He locked the door again, remembering the earlier berating from Andy.

They went into the kitchen area.

'God, I smell of booze,' Ben said, taking the half empty bottle of vodka out of his pocket. 'I'm going to pour this away,' he said taking it to the sink.

'No please don't, that cost me a lot of money.' She pleaded.

'Look, I've already told you....' But he stopped scolding her as they heard a key turning in the lock followed by the door opening and Andy stepped in.

Andy was surprised to see Ben's bike in the hallway and made straight for the kitchen area.

'Ben, what the hell...?' he called, stopping in his tracks as he saw Janie and the bottle in Ben's hand.

'OK, what's been going on here? Can I smell alcohol? Have you two been drinking?'

'No.' Ben said quickly. 'Honest we haven't.'

Andy walked towards Ben. 'God Ben, don't lie to me, I can smell it on you.'

'I didn't. It must have spilled in my pocket.' Ben explained innocently.

'A likely story!' Andy was brusque in his condemnation. 'Did you buy this?' he demanded, taking the half empty bottle from Ben.

Janie and Ben answered together 'Yes.'

'Well it sounds like one of you is lying,' Andy said, looking at each of them in turn.

'Ben, I thought you would have had more sense than to start drinking. Especially as you have seen what a devastating effect it has had on both your Mother and James.

'Yeah, well blame them.' Ben retorted. 'I might as well join the club. Perhaps if they see me drinking it might stop them. Especially when they see what other lives they've ruined.

'No. That's not right.' Janie said coming forward. 'Ben didn't buy the bottle. I did. He was trying to protect me.'

'And who might you be?' Andy asked, giving her an icy stare.

'My name is Janie. Ben and I met at Young Carers.'

'Oh I see. Perhaps I shouldn't have referred Ben there after all if this is going to be the result.' Andy suggested angrily.

'Come off it Andy. You can't blame the organisation for what we did.' Ben said, logically.

'No you're right of course.' Andy agreed. 'But I think you two might be trouble for each other. And why are you both here anyway? Or is that a stupid question?' He looked at each one in turn. 'Ben you had the key to this place on the understanding that you would sleep in here, only if there was trouble at home. Not for any other purposes.'

'Come on Andy. What are you suggesting?' Ben probed.

'Don't come the innocent with me.' Andy said sceptically. 'You know very well what I mean.'

'We weren't doing anything Mister...' Janie interrupted.

'Call me Andy,' Andy directed.

'Andy. We came here to...' Janie looked at Ben for reassurance for what she was about to say. He shook his head, but she carried on anyway.

'We came here to hide from the Police,' she continued.

'The Police! Oh no,' Andy said shaking his head in disbelief. 'I don't believe it. Ben are you in trouble again?' He demanded.

'No it was just that...' Ben stuttered. 'Well I was holding this bottle when they drove past.'

'So you were drinking?' Andy concluded.

'No. Ben had taken the bottle from me and was telling me off.' Janie looked at the floor embarrassed.

'Don't say anything else,' Ben told her, suddenly holding her hand. 'If Andy doesn't believe me that's his problem.'

Ben started to leave and had to walk past Andy to get to his bike. He dug in to his pocket and threw the hut keys on the kitchen table. 'I guess I won't be using these anymore.' He said resignedly.

'That's typical of you Ben isn't it?' Andy rebuked him.

'What?' Ben responded.

'Running away…again.' Andy berated him. 'How many times do I have to tell you? If you really didn't do it, you need to state your case.' Andy counselled. 'Running away is no answer to anything, as you ought to know by now. You need to stand your ground. If you didn't do it, be confident and say so.'

'Yeah well it's alright for you. You're an adult. People believe you. Nobody believes a kid.' Ben said vehemently. 'We're bound to be lying aren't we? Well you taught me better than that and I ain't lying. Come on Janie.' Ben grabbed Janie's hand and made to push past Andy again, but Andy put his hand on his shoulder.

'OK. I'm sorry I doubted you.' Andy said calmly. 'But why does it always happen to you?'

'Don't know,' Ben said, shrugging his shoulders. 'You tell me.'

'Go on then, take your keys but leave the bottle, I'll dispose of it.'

'But…' Janie said imploringly.

'I'm afraid not, young lady. This goes down the drain.' And he proceeded to do exactly that. 'And Ben…'

'Yeah?'

'Try to keep out of trouble.'

'I always do. But it comes looking for me. Come on Janie.' Ben said leading her to the entrance. With that, they pushed their bikes out of the hut and cycled off.

Andy shook his head in despair as he watched the pair depart.

'The kid doesn't stand a chance does he?' he thought to himself.

CHAPTER NINETEEN

The stranger knocked loudly on the front door. Beth opened it expecting to see the cheerful face of the Postman.

But the face that greeted her was not the Postman. It was a face from the past. Although she didn't recognise him at first, the eyes gave him away. The face was fifteen years older than when she'd last seen him. It made her blood run cold.

'Oh my god! Mike, what are you doing here?' she demanded, stepping away from the door, frightened by the unexpected and unwanted visitor.

'I've come to see my son. Ben,' the other replied.

'You must be joking,' she gasped, overcoming her initial shock. 'What, after all these years?'

'Yes. And what's wrong with that?' The visitor asked.

'Why?' she demanded, unnerved by the presence of her former lover.

'Because I realise that a boy needs a father…'

'Bullshit!' Beth hissed.

'…and,' he continued ignoring her comment, 'from what I hear you haven't been much of a mother to him.' Mike accused.

'How would you know what has gone on in this house. You've never shown any interest before.' Beth had overcome her initial shock and was becoming increasingly angry at the nerve of her son's father to arrive unannounced on her door step and demand to see Ben after rejecting him for so many years.

'Well I am now. So where is he?' he insisted.

'He isn't here. So you might as well leave.' Beth directed going to close the door on this spectre from her past.

'Aren't you going to invite me in?' He asked arrogantly moving towards the doorstep.

'You must be kidding, she said firmly. 'No chance.'

'So we'll let the neighbours hear our dirty washing then shall we?' he observed leaning against the door jamb.

'I don't care. You're not coming in.' Beth said, jamming the bottom of the door with her foot in case he tried to barge his way in.

'Rumour has it that even without me being around you've fallen on your feet anyway.' He announced.

'What do you mean?' she asked curious as to where the conversation was going.

'Got lots of wealthy friends, so I hear.' He said with an unnerving smirk. 'Bought the boy some expensive bikes I gather.'

'I thought there'd be more to it than just wanting to see Ben,' Beth exploded. 'You think he's got money. That's why you've re-appeared now isn't it?' She moved to close the door but he put his hand against it and stopped it midway.

'I thought he might like to help his brothers and sisters financially as I've been made redundant and the kids don't have a lot.' Mike explained.

'He hasn't got any money. Get that into your thick skull.' Beth shouted.

'You always were a selfish cow,' Mike bellowed viciously.

Beth again started closing the door, but he quickly jammed his foot against the jamb and stopped it.

'I've come to see my son. That's all. No harm in that is there?' He said wincing as she leant against the door squashing his foot.

'As I said, he's not here and I don't know when he's likely to be back.' She repeated, panting at her efforts to close the door.

'I gather you haven't been doing a proper job bringing him up?' He jibbed viciously, 'what with your boozing and that.'

'Yeah! Is that right? Well at least I've done some-thing for him. Which you haven't,' she argued, keeping the pressure on the door. 'Why then didn't you want anything to do with him when he was a baby, a toddler? When I tried to get you interested in him?'

'Circumstances weren't right.' he replied dismissively. 'I had my family to think of… the other kids, Ben's step brothers and sisters.'

'Yeah. So what's changed? Why the sudden interest? As if I can't guess,' she added cynically.

'I want to be a part of his life,' Mike continued, through the small gap between door and frame.

'Part of his life?' Beth said cynically. 'What are you really after Mike?'

'Yeah well, that's it, I want to be there for him,' he responded still pushing the door to ease the pressure on his trapped foot.

'Why?' she demanded, leaning all her weight against the door, stalling for time.

'They grow up so quickly. Will you stop squashing my foot and let's have a decent conversation?' Now getting angry at the ridiculous game they were playing.

'As if you'd care. You've never thought about anybody else but yourself.'

'Well I am now, while he's still a kid.'

'I was just a kid when you…you made me pregnant with him.'

'It takes two to tango Beth. You led me on, remember? You nearly got me divorced by throwing yourself at me.'

'Bullshit,' Beth shouted. 'You were trying to get your way with as many girls as you could. I found out that I wasn't the only one you were cheating on your wife with. I don't know how she put up with your lecherous ways for so long.'

'Because she loved me.' He said glibly.

'Ha! Right!' Beth exclaimed, belittling his claim.

'We had an understanding, a special relationship. A special love.'

'Love? Love? The only person that you ever loved was yourself. It was probably fear. Not love.' She said disparagingly.

'I'm number one with a lot of the ladies still,' he boasted.

'You haven't changed have you? You're still the same self-centred arrogant pig as you ever were. I don't know why I ever got involved with you in the first place.'

'Cause I'm irresistible to women, that's why.' he oozed, neatening his hair with his fingers. 'You ladies don't stand a chance when I'm around.'

'You arrogant bastard.' Beth shouted. 'All you wanted was another conquest to boast about wasn't it?

My Mother warned me about you. But I thought I knew better. It's your fault that I'm an alcoholic. I drank to get over you. You ruined my life.' She declared.

'I'm not sure whether I ought to be flattered or what. In reality, you drank because you're a weak pathetic excuse of a woman, that's why. Nothing to do with me,' he suggested cruelly.

'I've had enough of your rubbish,' Beth said finally kicking his foot out and closing the door.

'Tell Ben I called and I'll be back to see him soon.' He shouted through the closed door.

'Like hell I will.' Beth said relieved to have shut him out from her house, but not out of her mind. The spectre of her innocent years was back. How would she cope?

'I'll be back,' he said, in a badly impersonated Arnold Schwarzenegger voice and laughed.

Beth leant against the closed door and wept. Her worst nightmare had come to haunt her. She made her way to her hidden alcoholic comforter to ease the mental anguish of seeing Mike. The implications of his appearance after all those years frightened her.

CHAPTER TWENTY

James had deliberately kept himself busy. He found that by focussing on work activities, like writing business procedures for Tim and Carrie's walking company and on researching and preparing for his own project for teenage runaways, the endless longing for alcohol was at least pushed to the back of his mind.

It was a roller coaster ride of temptation.

The desire for the alcoholic buzz was constantly waiting to ensnare him again; to trap him in the endless loop of self-abuse. He might have been able to fool the others that he'd cracked it. But he couldn't fool himself.

His Achilles heel was the continuing pain and anguish of his former broken love life. He had run away from the pain of rejection and ended up living in an alcoholic haze of regret on the streets of London.

If only he could time travel…if only he could have prevented Sebastian falling for someone else or may be even just being there to save his life after the desertion by James' love rival.

If only, if only…But there was no going back.

His downward spiral of self-destruction following Sebastian's death had bankrupt him and pitched him on to the streets of the capital as a drunken vagrant…these things could not be erased.

It had happened and he had to deal with the consequences of his bad choices.

There was no doubt Geoffery's intervention to track him down and get him off the streets had saved his life.

Although, he found adapting to his new social status challenging, for suddenly, from being derided as an undesirable drunken bum, here he was back in a 'normal' social circle, being treated like a normal human being again.

Furthermore, he rediscovered that people liked him. They sought his advice. He was wanted.

He felt good about getting back into a business frame of mind too. It was a long forgotten 'comfort zone' which he enjoyed. The whole ethos excited him.

The vocabulary of the business world made him feel comfortable. The 'strange' business speak, the meetings, the power of decision making, the governance, PC applications, business processes, documentation, project plans.

He started to feel alive again.

Until inexplicably, he suddenly succumbed to moments of self-doubt, the highs were repressed by waves of emotional lows where self-pity overwhelmed him. His body reminded that the endless street drinking had permanently damaged his health.

He had mutilated himself with reckless boozing, his abused body punished him constantly.

He painfully reflected on a large part of his life that he had thrown away. There was no going back. The damage was done. It was too late to cry. The milk was well and truly spilt.

He knew he had to remain strong and keep off alcohol permanently, but the signs weren't looking good. He was starting to get cravings again. He noticed he had developed a habit of subconsciously licking his lips and endlessly running the back of his trembling hand across his mouth.

Did this mean his will was weakening or was it another symptom of further deterioration of the health of his liver?

Prior to James' bankruptcy and breakdown, he'd had a financially rewarding, albeit glamorous, career as a Stockbroker cum Banker.

His public school education had given him a head start into the world of business through the 'old boys' network.

His ability to buy himself into firms with his late father's inheritance had also helped considerably.

But he was no fool. He had an agile business brain that quickly gained him respect with his colleagues.

Now he was getting himself back together, the memories of those exhilarating days resurfaced.

But he missed the camaraderie, the banter, the buzz of the office, hearing other people's views.

He recalled the 'no expense spared' corporate hospitality meetings and the 'crazy' team build events. He had enjoyed driving tank like vehicles or taking part in laser shotgun competitions or even hunting and defusing dummy bombs hidden in the middle of a forest.

However he was sceptical about whether it ever achieved the goal of galvanising a team's 'togetherness'.

It was very contentious as to whether they actually achieved their prime aim of cementing the team together as the various groups continued with their own agendas back at the work place.

PAUL GAIT

Managers who were not of the same 'team build' mind-set called them expensive 'Jollies' and pointed out that the real work was backlogged while the other teams were out enjoying themselves.

James had come away from the work place with lots of 'saleable' business qualifications as a Business Analyst and Project Manager in Process development. He could also add Change and Business Management to his CV.

He was therefore well qualified to help Tim and Carrie set up the business side of their Walking Company.

So when it came to developing his own business project to help young runaways, James had come to the same conclusion as Rupert.

It would be more beneficial to support existing charities, rather than going in with misguided 'missionary zeal' and 'reinventing the wheel'.'

After all, existing charities had experienced professionals already looking after teenage runaways, addressing their needs and offering them shelter.

So, after doing 'due diligence' on several charities, all of whom were doing great jobs and making a difference. He decided that his part of Geoffery's legacy would go to the charity 'Railway Children'.

The aim of his contribution would be to enhance or supplement the number of safe houses that were already in place.

The charity's website echoed his own observations:- *'The dangers faced by children once they are on the streets are often even worse than those they were desperate to escape from at home. They are highly vulnerable and an easy target for abusers. Violence and sexual exploitation often become a way of life. Frequently they're even necessary for survival.*

Children living on the streets often become involved in drug use as their only escape from the horrors of reality.

With no support or protection, children live with constant fear, loneliness and hopelessness. They can see no way out; no opportunity to escape the relentless poverty, violence, hunger and abuse.'

James particularly empathised with the final statement.

'We fight for children living on the streets, to provide protection and opportunity for children with nowhere else to go and nobody to turn to.'

James had witnessed the exploitation of runaways himself and warned Ben about the dangers when he too was looking for a better life. Fortunately Ben had eventually listened to him before it was too late.

James had thought long and hard about cause and effect of children running away from home before he made his decision to support the existing charity.

Perhaps one of the answers to this age old problem would be to improve the environment in which children lived, to stop them feeling the need to run away. But he realised this was a utopian dream.

First you have to resolve the social issues created in thousands of dysfunctional families and pacify individuals who have anger management problems to cut domestic violence.

No, he concluded. As logical as it was to stop the cause rather than address the consequences, his proposal was more of a manageable alternative than 'boiling the ocean'.

He duly documented his proposals and along with the others he submitted them to Andy.

A sudden deep pain in his abdomen reminded him that the sands of time were running out for him. The prognosis for his longevity was not good. He recalled the consultant's assessment of his condition, '*Liver failure WILL happen. Your liver can't possibly recover from this amount of scarring damage.*'

What a fool he had been, mistreating his body. It was only now in the cold light of day, where his mind wasn't fogged by alcohol, that he appreciated what a precious gift life was.

In a way he envied Ben, for in spite of the obvious challenges with his mother's alcoholism, he was starting to develop as a person.

It seemed that he had found a girlfriend. He had a great love of biking and more importantly, he had his health; indeed he had a lot to live for.

James decided that the transplant couldn't come soon enough. But he was still amazed that the selfish, pig-headed Tim would have agreed to donate a part of his liver.

He wondered whether, when it was time for the operation, he would suddenly change his mind.

CHAPTER TWENTY ONE

Ben pushed the door open and wheeled his bike into its usual place in the hall. He had been out training with Janie and was hot and sweaty from his exertions.

Beth came out of the lounge to greet him.

'Have a good ride?' she asked brusquely.

'Yes thanks,' he said, taking his helmet off and hanging it over his handlebars.

'Ben.'

'That's my name, 'he said flippantly, bending over his bike and checking the suspension.

'Your Dad came here today.'

'What?' Ben stood up and looked at her in shock.

'Your father came. He wants to see you.'

'Great. See I told you I'd find him.' Ben beamed.

'I don't want you to see him.' Beth said earnestly.

'What!'

'No. I don't want you to see him,' Beth repeated.

'Well tough luck. You know why I want to see him,' Ben answered firmly.

'Yes and...'

'I warned you,' he asserted.

'I know but...'

'You can't keep off the booze for one minute can you? I can smell it on you even now,' Ben said, walking away from her dismissively.

'Yes I know. But I needed it. It was a shock seeing him. You wouldn't understand what I've been through because of him,' Beth pleaded.

'Yes I do. You keep going on about it.'

'Ben, please listen.'

Ben turned and looked at her. 'Mum, I'm fed up with your excuses. I need to think of me.'

'Yes OK, I have a problem,' Beth said returning his look and putting her hand on his sweat soaked shoulder. 'I admit it. But...'

'But what about me Mum? What about what I've been through with you?' He reminded her. 'In spite of what you promised me and the substance abuse lady, you're constantly getting drunk and bringing those... those men into our house?'

'I'm trying to stop, you know that.' She whined.

'Yes I do. But it'll be too late.' He said moving into the lounge. 'They'll take me away.'

'Please Ben I beg you.' Beth pleaded tearfully following him. 'Don't get involved with him.'

'Did he leave a message? A telephone number?' Ben demanded.

'No.' Beth said, looking for a tissue to wipe her eyes.

'Are you lying to me?' He questioned.

'No.' she said dabbing her eyes. 'He said he'd be back.'

'When?'

'He didn't say.'

'What's he like?'

'He hasn't changed. I can't think what I saw in him.'

'Stop it. Don't rubbish my dream,' Ben yelled.

'It's not going to be the dream you are looking for Ben. I'm sorry,' Beth sobbed.

'No. You're just saying that because you don't want me to see him,' Ben said angrily. 'Mum, I've given you a million chances to sort yourself out and nothing has changed. I don't want to be taken into care. Do you understand?'

'Yes I...'

'So why do you carry on drinking?' Ben was angry and shouting at his mother.

'Because I'm an alcoholic...I'm addicted. I can't stop.' She sobbed.

'You've been to the clinic.' Ben said agitatedly walking around the room. 'They have helped you. James has helped you. I've helped you. Why can't you help yourself?'

'Please Ben give me one last chance.' She begged.

'For what Mum?' He stopped and glowered at her. 'To show yourself up again?'

'I won't. It'll be different this time.' She wailed helplessly.

'Why didn't you ring me on my new phone? 'He demanded, remembering his birthday present. 'I could have come home.'

'I can't remember your number.' She confessed.

'No, that would have been too much to ask for, wouldn't it?' Ben said talking over the top of his Mother.

Ben turned on his heel and stormed off to his bedroom upstairs and slammed the door.

Beth went back into lounge and fished out the bottle she kept hidden in the base of the sofa. Her hands shook as she unscrewed the top. She looked at its contents, wanting so much to drink the elixir and to feel the liquid spreading through her that would give her release from her heartbreak.

Instead, she collapsed back on the sofa and gazed at the ceiling where Ben's bedroom was and joined him in a mournful melody of tears.

CHAPTER TWENTY TWO

Things were really buzzing for Carrie and Tim at the Walking Company.

With the initial setup money they had rented a small industrial unit on a business park. It had office space big enough for two office desks and filing cabinets, a small kitchen and a 'one trap' toilet.

The large community car park also provided secure parking for the Walking Company's minibus.

In anticipation of both of them leading walks they had already hired a part time driver to assist with the various transport arrangements.

They had also enlisted assistance from the other two Godsons, James and Rupert, to provide a professional input to the setup of the business; which also met Geoffery's condition in his will to ensure that they helped each other out.

James had been doing all the business administration, documentation and procedures.

Whereas Rupert had done a great job designing and building the 'Just Do It Walking Company' website.

He had researched other walking company websites and combined the best ideas and functionality from all of them.

The menus were colourful and easy to follow. There were photos of happy smiling walkers taken with fantastic scenic backdrops.

The site was fully interactive. People could actually book online and pay via PayPal.

He had even created a rolling year calendar with a scheduled list of walks, some already falsely showing that they were fully subscribed. Most of these were reserved for their armed services clients. For although they intended to open the walks to the general public, their prime customer base was their special needs groups of amputees and those suffering from PTSD.

The site also carried endorsements from the three military services, army, navy and air force with links to other relevant veteran sites including Combat Stress.

He had also set up Facebook and Twitter feeds.

Carrie's personal sales campaign, whilst being treated for her own PTSD problem, brought in the first set of walkers for the inaugural hike.

The ramble was an easy circular route of about four miles. The main aim was intended to shakedown all the various procedures and logistics.

It traversed the edge of the stunning Cotswold escarpment, with views to the distant Gloucester cathedral, Churchup Hill, Robinswood Hill, May Hill, the Forest of Dean and distant welsh mountains.

Starting from the viewpoint called Barrow Wake, it followed local footpaths, minor roads and part of the Cotswold Way long distance footpath before returning via the picturesque Crickley Hill Country park.

En route they called in at the Star Bistro, run by the National Star College, for a coffee and piece of cake.

The college is an exciting and innovative educational establishment, working with young people with a wide range of disabilities.

Carrie's support was therefore empathetic to the college's vision for *'providing a world in which people with disabilities are able to realise their potential as equal and active citizens in control of their lives'.*

Tim and Carrie had been actively running group hikes for a couple of weeks when they received a curious Facebook posting:-

SWS;

There was no photo of the sender just an image of a pair of imploring hands.

The message read:-

I understand from your website that you organise walks for Service Veterans. I am suffering from PTSD having served in Iraq and Afghanistan. I have agoraphobia and wondered if you do one to one hikes? Please note there might be some delay in my replies because I am living in a tent in a wood and rarely travel into the Internet Café.

'Have you seen this Tim? What do you reckon?'

Tim gazed over Carrie's shoulder at the screen.

'No we can't do hikes for individuals. It will take both of us out to do it. Whoever it is won't want to cover the cost of our normal group of eight, will they?'

'No, but I feel sorry for them,' Carrie said sympathetically. 'They probably need a bit of TLC, that's all.'

'You can't bank pity. It's a currency that won't pay our bills.'

'But you'll be getting your money from the will soon.'

'Soon! Yeah but how soon is soon? We haven't sent our stuff to Andy yet and he's then got to send it, along with the others stuff, to the Lawyers in Monaco.

You know what these legal people are like. Frigging long winded. We're stretched enough with our overdraft.'

'Ok. I'll put them off for the time being then,' she capitulated reluctantly.

Carrie replied:-

Carrie JDIW;

We don't usually do 'one to one' hikes because we feel that walking in a group is good therapy. People relax and start talking, off - loading their problems. So I would encourage you to check the website and select a suitable date. Sorry.

'Well I hope they do select a hike. I guess we'll never know.'

'Not unless they introduce themselves to us if they join one. But we don't want to throw money down the drain do we?' Tim pointed out.

'No, I guess not. I'll get back to finalising that project documentation. The sooner Andy gets it, the quicker he'll send it to Monaco and we'll get the money from the will.'

'How much do you think I'll get?'

'Umm, I don't know.'

'Geoffery was a multimillionaire wasn't he? Just imagine, I could be a multi-millionaire before long. Exciting isn't it?' Tim exclaimed, grabbing Carrie from behind and planting a kiss on the soft white flesh of her neck. 'Then you'll have to be especially nice to me.'

'Aren't I always?' she said, gently leaning her head against his and putting her hand up to cradle his head closer.

'Wouldn't it be terrible if, after all this, we find out he hasn't got any money after all?' Tim speculated.

'I'll still love you even if you're not a millionaire.' Carrie said, huskily.

CHAPTER TWENTY THREE

Rupert carefully pushed Joanne's wheelchair from the scanning suite.

'You OK love?'

'Yes. But I'm glad that's over. I hate being in a confined space.'

'The consultant said he'd have the images pretty quick. It's all computer generated files these days.'

'You'd know about that wouldn't you, in your job?'

'Well at the end of the day, it's only data of some sort or other he added knowledgeably.'

They had just arrived back in the waiting room when the consultant called them into his office.

Apprehensively they entered the small office.

'Please take a seat Mr Screen.'

Rupert did as directed and positioned himself next to Joanne's wheelchair.

'After examining the latest MRI scan, I can see the cause of the problem. The scar tissue is pressing further on the spinal cord. Look,' he directed, pointing at an area on the screen

'Is that why I still can't walk?' Jo asked, gazing at the image on the monitor.

'Yes. I'm sorry to put this bluntly. But it is my belief that unless this is treated surgically it is unlikely that you will regain the ability to stand, let alone walk.'

'Is it something that you can do, here?' Rupert asked, squeezing Jo's hand.

'No, I'm afraid not. It's a very specialist operation. I don't know of any UK surgeons who have performed it either.'

'So what do we do? Are you saying that's it? Joanne said close to tears. 'Am I going to be in a wheelchair for the rest of my life?'

'No. Our next step is to refer you to an American neurological surgeon for his assessment. He has performed several successful operations in the USA. He's world renowned for his pioneering work in spinal injuries.'

'USA! So we're talking big bucks then?' Rupert observed.

'Yes, I'm afraid so. However, as the injury was caused in a road traffic accident I presume you will get compensation from the insurance company?'

'Well, unfortunately, not in this case. The trigger for the accident was a car driven without insurance by my estranged wife.'

'Oh dear. That is awkward then,' the Consultant replied, stroking his chin, thoughtfully. 'Well, the surgeon will need paying 'up front' for even looking at the MRI scan, let alone performing an operation. That's if he thinks he can successfully operate to resolve the problem.'

'Hopefully the money situation will be resolved soon. I am shortly due to receive a large legacy from my Godfather's estate.'

'Ok. So do I leave it with you then? And you'll let me know when you have adequate financial resources.'

'No, please go ahead and get him to look at the scans. Hopefully I have sufficient money to pay for that.

From what you said, I don't think we can afford to wait for any further delays can we?'

'No, you're right. The longer it is left without surgical intervention, the less likely that the spinal surgery could be performed let alone be successful.'

This latest visit to Jo's consultant had therefore refocused Rupert's plans.

The stark reality dawned on him that without the operation soon, Jo would never be able to walk again.

So he desperately needed Geoffery's legacy as soon as possible to pay for the operation, if it was possible.

Like Tim and James, in order to get his legacy he had to fulfil the pre-requisites of the will. He had to come up with a worthwhile project and convince Andy and then Geoffery's lawyers that his project was going to help others before the money could be released.

However he was behind schedule compared to Tim and James.

He had found little time to research his own project because of looking after the wheelchair bound Jo and addressing the needs of pre-term baby Jeffery.

In addition, setting up Tim and Carrie's walking company website had also taken a considerable amount of time.

Identifying an appropriate project was the easy part. He had chosen to help the victims of domestic violence.

It was a subject close to his heart from his own dreadfully abused experiences during his disastrous marriage to Sue.

As he started his research he soon discovered that there were a lot of new initiatives already being implemented and others being planned to tackle the, apparently, unrelenting tide of domestic abuse.

These included plans to teach school children about the rights and wrongs within relationships and the evils of 'control and domination'.

He also found parliamentary strategies to change the definition of abuse to further strengthen the criminalisation of domestic violence. The ultimate aim of which was to give perpetrators lengthy prison sentences coupled with anger management treatment.

He planned to write to his MP to provide information about his own wretched experiences in support of the parliamentary initiative

He was surprised to discover the list of things now categorised as abuse included physical, mental, sexual, psychological, financial and emotional abuses.

He had suffered many of these cruelties during his own turbulent marriage.

Most charities were concerned about the effects of Government funding cuts on some vital services which had been relegated to 'nice to have' because of these budgetary constraints.

So he decided to sound out several existing domestic violence charities to identify something that he could contribute to using Geoffery's money, possibly the opening of a new shelter.

He discovered that the principle aim of most charities appeared to be the same, namely to ease the effects of traumatic relationships and protecting children from the mental scarring of abuse.

The list of their services and support network was already quite comprehensive and included providing a sanctuary, safety net and legal advice for people to escape from violent partners.

Sadly this knowledge had come too late for him, when he, personally, needed their help. Like many victims, he was unable to break away from the dreadful circle of violence and seek help.

As his research progressed, he came to the conclusion that to set up, staff and maintain a new shelter long term was inappropriate and an inefficient use of Geoffery's Legacy. Whatever his inheritance was likely to be.

Therefore he started arranging meetings with various existing charities.

He was heartened to hear of the fantastic dedication of their staff who, knowingly, faced daily aggravation whilst supporting and protecting victims. Some organisations ran shelters for specific groupings of victims, some for female and child, others male only, others both sexes.

Rupert read copious papers from the various charities and other sources, often working into the early hours to create his project report.

Used to putting business cases together at short notice, he soon created a project plan, associated documentation and proposals which he felt would stand up to scrutiny.

Finally, feeling drained by the long late hours, he emailed it all to Andy for his comments.

In his covering note he emphasised the need to expedite the submission to Monaco because of Jo's surgical needs.

In spite of his fatigue, psychologically he was already feeling stronger within himself.

The pivotal psychological tipping point had come whilst giving evidence against Sue.

He felt better able to stand up against her and break the domination and control which she had exerted over him during their marriage.

The project would demonstrate his resolve to help combat the effects of domestic violence.

CHAPTER TWENTY FOUR

'How's the school gate gossip now? Is it getting any better?' Andy asked, finishing loading the dishwasher.

'What do you think? What they don't know they make up. The last I heard was that you were organising drug fuelled orgies for the mafia in Monaco,' Helen said flatly.

'Oh. As bad as that?'

'What with the new car as well. They add up one and one and make seven.'

'Well it won't be for much longer.' Andy reassured her.

'I'm glad about that. It's getting me down. How much more have you got to do with these Godsons and the will?'

'I'm still waiting for one more project and then I can send them off to Monaco.'

'Right, listen to me. Whenever you organise going back to Monaco, I am coming with you, OK?' Helen said firmly.

'What about the kids?' Andy said surprised at her intention.

'Kay has already volunteered to look after them for a day.' She informed him.

'It could take longer than a day.' Andy added.

'For a day. No overnight temptations. A day, hear me?' She dictated firmly.

'What if the lawyers need more time…?' Andy hypothesised.

'Then we go back.' She replied quickly.

'But you'll miss out on staying in a luxurious five star hotel.' Andy exclaimed trying to sway her.

'That's OK. We can do that some other time with the kids.' Helen rebuffed his observation.

'Yeah, OK,' he capitulated unenthusiastically. 'Good idea.'

'How many are going?' Helen asked.

'I was thinking of cutting down the numbers.' Andy said, thinking. 'Just the three Godsons and Carrie. Oh plus you and I, that is if you're coming.'

'What about Joanne?' Helen enquired.

'I doubt that she would want to travel, what with the baby and being confined to a wheelchair.' Andy surmised.

'You should at least give her the opportunity to say no.' Helen instructed.

'I'll send Rupert an email.' He said putting the last cup into the machine. 'Where's the dishwasher tablets?'

'In the usual place, under your nose. Whatever happened to just a simple phone call?' Helen observed.

'Well, it's easier on email. He can access it when it's convenient.'

'Please yourself.'

Andy placed his laptop on the table and logged on to his email. 'At last,' he said opening it. 'The final project, it's from Rupert. Ah yes, there's an attachment of several files with it too. Oh that's interesting.' He added.

'Are you talking to yourself or me?' Helen asked.

'Well Rupert wants to move things forward quickly because Joanne might have to have an operation in the 'states'. Andy informed her.

'Well that's good news. Let's hope they can do something for her.' Helen said feeding the washing machine with dirty baby clothes.

Andy sent a reply email confirming that he would expedite it as quickly as possible and asked if he thought Joanne would like to come to Monaco when they went to finalise the will.

Although he had no business knowledge to really vet the submissions from the three Godsons, he decided that all he would do was quickly check the proposed projects and pass them on to ICE, the Law firm in Monaco.

He decided that they all looked feasible; James and Tim's had a very similar layout.

'So what have we got?' He said to himself. 'A walking company for less able customers. Support for a charity for runaways and support for a domestic violence charity. It all sounds very charitable. Let's hope the lawyers think so.'

'What happens next then?' Helen asked looking forlornly at the huge basket of ironing she was about to tackle.

'My understanding is that ICE will conduct an appraisal and 'due diligence' on each project ensuring that they would comply with the conditions of the will.' Andy informed her.

'Oh that's good then. So the trip might not be too far away then?'

'No, that's right. Did I tell you that Tim had got wind of James' and Rupert's intention to support existing charities rather than starting from square one as he and Carrie had done with the walking company.'

'So, is that a problem?'

'No I don't think so. James had done the majority of the project plan for the Walking company submission anyway'.

'Sounds like he's a bit of a whinger.' Helen observed, plugging the iron in.

'You can say that again.' Andy mimicked Tim, 'Oh it's not fair. They're not playing according to the rules of the will.'

'He sounds worse than the kids.' Helen added.

'Where there's money, they start squabbling like kids,' Andy concluded.

'What did you tell him?

'Sorry Tim. That's not my decision. The lawyers will advise me on that.

If they say it's OK and that it meets the spirit of Geoffery's will, then so be it. Remember though, you all get your legacies together or none of you get it. So be careful what you wish for.'

'What did he say to that?' Helen said, deciding to have a cup of tea to summon up interest in the ironing.

'Oh he went off muttering to himself. Anyway I'm fed up with the whole Godsons thing.'

'So you keep saying, do you want a cup of tea?' Helen asked, reaching for a mug.

'Yes please, well you know I was reluctant to get involved with it in the first place. However, Geoffery's persuasive talents had got me embroiled in the whole painful saga. It's brought me nothing but additional angst and grief.'

'And a quarter of a million pounds in the bank.' Helen reminded him, 'and the almost brand new Mercedes car.'

'Yes I suppose you're right,' Andy agreed, 'and the Scouts had benefitted with a new hut too.'

However on the down side, Andy thought, there was the unfortunate incident with Nadine and Sue filming it, which had almost destroyed his marriage and undermined his standing in the community when it had become public knowledge. The gossip was still rattling round the neighbourhood even now.

Anyway, he cheered himself up with the thought that it was nearly over.

As to whether the Legacy for the Godsons would be released or not, the Law firm would be the final arbiters, not him.

He didn't know how long the lawyers would take to check the submissions or whether they would want clarification on certain parts, but once they gave the thumbs up, he would be organising the trip back to Monaco for the final bit and the Godsons would come back as wealthy men, possibly millionaires.

But two of them would still have to get their projects underway. He hoped he wouldn't be dragged into that as well. He'd had enough.

He composed an email to ICE and attached all the various project files and smiling to himself, 'clicked' on the send button.

'Here's to the beginning of the end,' he said, and rewarded himself with a celebratory glass of port, a Christmas present from his Scouts.

PART TWO

The Inheritance

CHAPTER TWENTY FIVE

Clearly the Lawyers had noted Andy's request to fast track the 'due diligence' because two weeks after submitting the projects he received notification from them that everything was in order.

He duly arranged with the Godsons to make a return trip to Monaco.

This time, however, at Helen's insistence, it was going to be a day trip and she would be going with him.

He was more than happy with this suggestion as he assumed that Nadine would be there too.

He did not want to be compromised by any possible suspicion of a repeat of the overnight liaison with her.

Joanne had taken up Andy's invitation to join them and insisted on bringing baby Jeffery as well.

So the group size comprised of just eight passengers with Andy, Helen, Tim, Carrie, James, Rupert and Joanne, plus baby Jeffery.

Andy had ensured that special arrangements were made to lift Jo and wheelchair into and off the chartered Hawker 800 jet.

The Godsons and partners were all in a buoyant mood. They were like excited children at Christmas waiting for Santa's visit. Soon they would know the value of their inheritances. This was going to be like winning the lottery without buying a ticket.

At Andy's direction the stewardess had uncorked a bottle of champagne before they'd even cleared the county border. James was provided with an elderflower cordial.

'Here's to fame and fortune,' Tim said, raising his glass.

The others echoed his toast.

After an uneventful flight from Gloucestershire airport, where the baby slept most of the way, the jet touched down at the sun drenched Nice Cote d'Azur airport. And, as before, the happy group were led to the waiting stretch limousine by Monique, from the law firm ICE.

The trip from the airport over the spectacular mountain road was quickly completed and they soon arrived at the plush offices of ICE in the heart of Monaco.

After the usual identity checks, passes were issued and they were shepherded in to a small, but delightfully decorated reception room and provided with coffee and a variety of delicate French pastries.

Centre of the refreshment table was a stack of croquembouche, high-piled cones of chocolate, cream-filled profiteroles all bound together with threads of caramel. Around the side, were a variety of croissants and Bichon au citron, lemon and Bavarian cream filled puff pastry encapsulated in an outer layer of partially caramelized sugar.

'Oh my word,' Joanne exclaimed, gazing at the spread, 'Look at that lot. I could quite happily put on a few pounds sampling those.'

After doing a good demolition job on the pastries, the group split up.

The ladies were planning on a sightseeing trip around Monaco, while the men were going to the conference room that they had used on their previous trip.

'Hope it all goes well,' Helen said, giving Andy a peck on the cheek. 'Let's hope that Nadine woman isn't there. If she is…keep away from her,' she warned.

Carrie, Helen and Jo re-boarded the stretch limo and were chauffeur driven around the tourist spots of the fairy tale principality.

Meanwhile, in the conference room, the Law Practice Manager welcomed them again. Andy was relieved that Nadine was not there, but he was apprehensive in case she showed up.

The Manager explained the agenda for the session, 'I am satisfied with what you have submitted in your project reports. However I would like confirmation that you have done the work yourselves. I would therefore like to invite each of you to do a short presentation of your project.'

Tim immediately started panicking, for although he had collaborated with James during the creation of the project, he had allowed him to complete it and had failed to look at the final version.

More concerning was that he'd never given a presentation to anyone, ever.

'God, James, what shall I do?' I'll cock it up. I won't get the money.' Tim whined.

'Don't panic. It'll be alright. You know what it's all about without looking at the paperwork. Just tell him what you told me. I'll help where I can. Don't worry.'

In spite of James' words of common sense, Tim became very nervous as he watched the others do their presentations.

Andy started the round of presentations. 'I believe all the three projects meet Geoffery's criteria.

I have thought long and hard about this, but I believe his legacy is not only about the money. It is also about the journey that each one of you, his Godsons, has taken.

Remember Geoffery's reference to the Wizard of Oz characters, Rupert's new won courage; Tim's humanity and thoughtfulness using his heart rather than his head and James using his brain again to become 'tea total'.

I reckon, if you looked inside yourselves, you would probably identify the changes.

Until Geoffery came along you were strangers to each other. Look what you have achieved. You have not only become friends but you have actively engaged and supported each other.

Especially James and Rupert, who in addition to coping with health problems, had been working to help Tim establish his walking company.'

Tim wasn't sure whether to be relieved or annoyed that Andy had spilled the beans to the Lawyer.

Andy continued, 'thank you for making my job relatively easy.' He sat down to a ripple of applause.

James stood up and addressed the meeting. 'The progress of my project of assisting the charity '*Railway Children*' for runaways is on target. The charity is currently closing a deal on buying another suitable property in London and I need the release of Geoffery's Legacy to finalise the contract exchange.

The earlier financial advance has only allowed basic property searches. I am concerned that every minute of every day another child falls into the clutches of bad people. Any further delay in providing additional accommodation is jeopardising young lives. Thank you.'

Rupert stood up next and explained. 'My plans to form a partnership with the charity 'Refuge', which is a sanctuary for victims of domestic abuse, is in a similar situation to James' plans for purchasing a property.

I have also helped Tim with his walking company website and I'm in discussions with James about a suitable 'street cred' website for young runaways.'

'I have a question,' the lawyer interrupted. 'If the young people are on the street surely they won't be accessing the website.'

'We have researched this and you'll be surprised to know that most of them usually retain their mobile phones, sometimes even forgoing a meal to fund it.'

'Thank you for that clarification. Please continue.'

'In addition to being a fulltime father and carer for my wife Joanne, I have had limited time to implement any more ambitious plans.'

Tim stood up nervously as Rupert sat down. 'I...err have never done a presentation before, so you'll have to forgive me if I 'cock it up'.

But..err... basically we have already set up our Walking Company, from scratch, I must add. And we did get a lot of help from James and Rupert.

Our company aims to give people with disabilities the chance to take part in organised walks. The scheme is working well and we aim to expand it across the country...and that's it really.'

'I believe there are only two of you in the company at the moment?' The manager quizzed.

''Yeah, that's right. We got a bloke that works part time though.'

'What about the sustainability of the firm in the event of either Carrie or yourself being indisposed for some reason?

'Well, our plans are to employ more people when we have more money to invest of course,' Tim said, giving the Senior partner of the Law firm a quizzical look.

'Thank you, you may sit down now.'

Tim sat down, feeling he had acquitted himself well.

'Well done. See, I told you you'd be OK didn't I?' James said, patting him on the shoulder.

The Manager stood up and after checking his notes said, 'I am satisfied that you are actually fulfilling Monsieur Foster's wishes.

I would now like to move on to the final step of the process,' thus saying he operated a switch on the control console in front of him and the video wall 'fired up'.

Everyone held their breath anticipating Geoffery's reappearance on the screen. The opening shots showed a sunset and then dissolved in to a close up of Geoffery sitting by the hospice pergola that he'd constructed as a young builder.

In spite of their mental preparation, it was still a shock to see his pale face again months after his funeral.

'Hello again and congratulations Gentlemen.'

As he looked at the image, Andy had forgotten how frail Geoffery had become before his death.

'I said I'd be back. Well, I anticipate that this will be the last time I shall confront you with my fading image. I have no idea how long it has taken you to get to this stage but I know my friends at the Law firm and Andy wouldn't let you get away without fulfilling the spirit, if not the letter of my challenge to you all.

You've obviously met the strict criteria that I put into my will, otherwise you wouldn't be watching this video.

I hope the process you have gone through has helped you become better people and you now appreciate the things you have in your life.

My challenge for you to do something for other people is an important key to this as well as having a windfall yourselves.

I wish I could have been there to see what you are planning to do. However, without droning on any longer, here is the news that you have all been waiting for.'

Tim crossed his fingers, butterflies filled his stomach. He was going to be rich. From today on, people would treat him differently. Money brought respect. He was going to be a millionaire, maybe a multimillionaire.

By his side, Rupert sat sweaty palmed just wishing it was over. The anticipation was unbearable. All he really wanted was to get to see Jo and the baby, although she was only on a sightseeing trip around Monaco and in safe hands with Carrie and Helen, every moment apart from her seemed an age.

He had an irrational fear that without him by her side something awful might happen to her. He nearly lost her once in the crash. To lose her again would be too much to bear.

James had been frustrated by the delay in releasing the money because he knew that every minute of every day runaway kids were being lost to the Pimps and Drug runners.

He knew his money could save a few from effectively losing their freedom as well as their childhood. He had put the thought of his own operation to the back of his mind.

'*My estate is to be broken into quarters. My Godsons Tim, Rupert and James will each receive one quarter.*

The final quarter will be used to pay off any outstanding debts and the residual I have bequeathed to the Dorothy and Tom hospice, where I received the most wonderful care. Hopefully, the money will allow them to continue to provide the high standard of care that I myself received during the final phase of my wonderful life.'

I am therefore pleased to advise you that you will each receive approximately five million pounds.

There were gasps of amazement from all around the room.

Andy immediately thought. 'Thank goodness for that. The money has at last been released. I've discharged my responsibilities.' He sat back and relaxed, smugly smiling to himself.

He was looking forward to getting some normality back in to his life. His initial reluctant involvement with Geoffery Foster had now being going on for too long. Hopefully his dealings with them all were finally at an end.

Geoffery's voice broke into his thoughts.

'*A word of caution. I have made you put some efforts into qualifying for this money. However, I recognise that a sudden windfall like this can make people go off the rails. You will be thrust into an unknown world of wealth and extravagance. It can destroy your ability to make sensible judgements.*

Ask James. He has been there once before. I have therefore ring fenced some of the money for the exclusive use of your projects. The rest is open for your own personal use.

I entrust the overview of the use of the project money to my very good friend and hospice nurse, Andy.

Andy couldn't believe his ears. 'Damn it!' he thought. His plans of stepping away from the Godsons and their projects were derailed already.

'I hope in some way I have made up for lost time. I enjoyed meeting you all and sincerely hope that my brief involvement in your lives has helped you to a better future.'

And with an obvious 'lump in his throat', realising the finality of his words, he added.

'Goodbye to you all. Don't forget to make the money work for your chosen projects. Remember, it's never too late to be who you could have been.'

Geoffery's face faded into a glorious view of a sunset over the Cotswold Hills. The room remained quiet and still for a few minutes while they contemplated the good news of their fortune.

'Well gentlemen, I think that concludes our business for today,' the Law firm Manager said finally. 'You will find that the money has already been transferred to the bank accounts in which your advances were placed.

May I, on behalf of my Law firm, wish you all the best in pursing your plans for helping others.'

Tim couldn't contain himself any longer. 'Five million...five bleeding million quid! Jesus that's more than I was expecting. I really am mega rich now,' he said to no-one in particular. 'And so are we all.

Look out casino, here I come,' he shrieked, punching the air. 'Yes', he said triumphantly. 'Yes...yes...yes.'

Rupert sat in stunned silence, thinking about his order of priorities. Number one had to be getting Jo the urgent surgery in the US to sort out her spinal damage.

James was nonplussed. He had been a millionaire before when he was only eight, but now he would be doing something constructive with his money.

So long as his health held up he would do his best to prevent gullible, emotionally fragile young runaways becoming victims of the drug and prostitute gangs.

Andy's thoughts of losing close involvement with the three Godsons had been scuppered by Geoffery's continuing requirement for him to 'keep an eye' on things.

The Law firm Manager approached him, thanked him for organising the Godson's visit and gave him an envelope. Andy recognised the spider scrawl on it. Geoffery hadn't finished with him yet.

Andy opened it nervously, wondering what else his former patient was going to embroil him in. Quickly he read it.

'Dear Andy, thank you so much for so many different things.

Since the first day we met I knew you'd be a good man to have on my side. I have observed you at work and you have a special humanitarian quality that restored my faith in the human race.

As you can imagine in the process of amassing a large fortune you have to be a bit ruthless and sometimes end up unfortunately destroying people. Your role in the hospice is quite the antithesis of the life I've led.

It was a privilege to know you and I have to make a confession here. Yes you've guessed it, to go with a clear conscience, the usual death bed confession.

I am ashamed to say that I arranged for your old Scout hut to be burnt down to get you on to my side. I felt that buying you a new one would make you feel morally obliged to help me out. And of course it worked, didn't it?

Whereas I regret endangering young Ben's life (I didn't know about your arrangement for him to sleep there) and destroying all your records, I am pleased that I got you on my side.'

'Why, you conniving old man,' Andy said at the letter. 'I suspected as much.'

The letter continued, *'I know I will have had a good death, thanks to you. It was the only thing that I really feared, but you helped me more than you will ever know.*

Perhaps we'll meet somewhere in the future. I look forward to that day, but hope for you and the rest of your family's sake it's a long, long time away.

Keep up the good work, as I know you will.

Kindest Regards, your friend Geoffery

PS: Please take the cheque to the Dorothy and Tom Hospice and see that it is used properly.'

'Good bye Geoffery,' he said, his eyes brimming. 'It was a pleasure.'

Andy folded the letter and pocketed it.

CHAPTER TWENTY SIX

The three ladies had been driven around Monaco on a lightning tour looking at the Old Town, the famous rock, the Royal Palace and the Cathedral.

They were relaxing with a coffee near the famous Rascasse café on the quay. Their table overlooked a flotilla of expensive yachts bouncing around at their moorings in the azure blue Mediterranean.

Helen had assumed a temporary maternal role and was bottle feeding Jeffery, when Jo's phone rang.

'Oh, I wonder if this is Rupert?' she wondered, removing the mobile from her handbag.

'Hi, this is Jo.'

'Miss Carr?'

'Yes, who is this?'

'Mr Staples, your orthopaedic consultant.'

'Oh hello.'

'I have some good news for you.'

'Yes?'

'Mr Jepponski, the American neurosurgeon, has studied your scans.'

'Yes! What did he say?' Joanne asked apprehensively, crossing her fingers.

'His initial assessment is that there is a high chance that he might be able to do something for you.

But he needs to do various other tests and checks before he can say categorically what the likely prognosis will be.'

'But he thinks there's a chance. Yes?' she repeated eagerly.

'Yes. That is his preliminary observation.'

'Oh this is brilliant news,' she beamed. 'Thank you... thank you so much. When... when can he see me?' she continued breathlessly.

'As this now becomes a private transaction between you and him, you will need to make those arrangements directly with him. I will get my secretary to post all the various details to your home address. Is that OK?'

'Yes, that's wonderful. Thank you so much.'

'I hope he will be able to help. Goodbye.'

'Bye and thanks again.'

Joanne was beaming as she put her mobile back into her handbag.

'I gather it's good news,' Helen said, gently patting Jeffery's back to wind him.

'Yes. The American surgeon thinks he might be able to do something for me. Isn't that great?'

'Oh that is marvellous news.' Helen agreed.

'Rupert will be over the moon.' Carrie added. 'Are you going to call him?'

'No, I'll wait until they've finished their meeting.' Jo said, buzzing with excitement.

Shortly after, Carrie's phone rang. She briefly looked at the screen as she removed it from her trouser pocket. She could see it was Tim.

'Tim, I thought we agreed not to use the mobiles while we are over here because the charges are so expensive,' she berated.

'Forget that,' he said dismissively. 'They've just given us the statements for our share of the will. We're rich girl. RICH!'

Helen and Jo looked at Carrie in anticipation of sharing the news.

'Go on, guess how much,' the jubilant Tim teased.

'No I can't,' Carrie replied, getting excited by Tim's infectious exhilaration. 'Don't be such a tease and just tell me.'

'Five,' he said, dramatically.

'Five, Five what? Hundred? Thousand! What? Tell me,' she squealed.

'Five...MILLION...pounds,' Tim said slowly, luxuriating in the words.

'Five million!' Carrie shrieked, repeating it loudly so the others could hear.

Jo put her hand to her mouth in disbelief. 'Oh my God, Five Million pounds,' she said quietly. Then a wave of emotion hit her. 'I can have my operation, at last. I'll be able to walk again.' Then the tears flowed, as the enormity of Rupert's inheritance dawned on her.

'We're going to celebrate in style girl,' Tim continued. 'I think a trip to the Casino is called for.'

Carrie could see that Jo was getting her mobile out.

'Hang on Jo, use my phone. Tim, Jo wants a word with Rupert. Hang on, I'll see you later. Love you.'

Carrie could hear him whooping as he handed the phone to Rupert. She handed her phone to Jo.

'Jo, Jo are you there?' he said his voice full of emotion.

'Yes love. I'm here.' They both started to speak at the same time.

'You first,' he said, 'you sound excited.'

'I am. I've just heard from the consultant. The American specialist thinks he can do something for me. Isn't that great?'

'Oh Jo, that's wonderful news. I expect you've heard my news already. Geoffery has left us five million pounds each. Isn't that great? Some of it can only to be spent on the project. But it means we can go ahead and travel over to the USA and see the specialist.'

'Yes,' Jo said eyes brimming with tears.

'Jeffery can have a house full of toys. We can move house too, so that bitch will never know where we are,' he added, emotionally.

'Even better.'

'When can I see you? Are you on your way back? I just want to hold you both.' Rupert continued emotionally.

'I'm not sure where we are at the moment. But the car is here. So we'll start back straight away and see you soon.'

'Hurry,' Rupert urged, 'I just want to hug you.'

Rupert handed the phone back to Tim.

'Andy, want to speak to your Missus?' Tim asked.

'Yes if you don't mind,' he said, taking the phone.

'Hi, could I speak to Helen, please?'

Jo handed the phone over to an anxious Helen. Who, in turn, passed the baby back to his mother.

'Hi, Andy, is everything alright? Is it all over now?'

'Hi, yes nearly.'

With that Helen's tone changed. 'Oh Andy. Now what does he want you to do?'

'It's OK. He just wants me to take his donation to the hospice, that's all,' he lied

'And then is it over? Can we pick up our lives again?' she asked cautiously.

'Yes,' he said, a knot of anguish already building in his stomach.

'Oh thank God for that. Was that...that woman there?'

'Nadine? No. There was nothing for her this time. Apparently she's already had her small inheritance.'

'Oh good,' Helen said triumphantly. 'So are we celebrating with a posh meal before we fly back?'

'It would be rude not too, wouldn't it? I'll ask the others and see you back here at reception.'

The ladies were duly driven back to the offices of the Law firm and were greeted by a trio of jubilant partners waiting in the reception area.

Feeling slightly out of it James stood and smiled as the couples embraced. Andy, vigilant as ever, spotted him and invited him in for a group hug.

They decided to celebrate their windfalls at the same Michelin star restaurant where they had stayed previously. James volunteered to organise things and duly asked the Law firm's receptionist to make a reservation for them all.

'Tonight the champagne will flow to celebrate our good fortune and to thank Andy and Helen for helping us get our inheritance,' James said. 'However, I will be toasting you with the finest spa water that money can buy.' he added.

They all laughed disproportionately, intoxicated by the thought of their new millionaire status.

CHAPTER TWENTY SEVEN

It was a lovely balmy evening as the small group congregated on the terrace of the exotic Hôtel de Paris Monte-Carlo to celebrate their good fortune.

From their vantage point they could hear the distant waves of the captivating Mediterranean and rustling palm trees creating a lullaby of tranquillity.

To add to the magic of the moment the famous Rock of Monaco lay before them effused in an orange glow from the evening sunset. It felt like paradise.

James had persuaded the hotel to provide the normally exclusive Le Louis XV-Alain Ducasse restaurant menu to them, out on the terrace.

For their starter they ordered - *Shellfish and seafood, squids and octopus sautéed together 'romano' brocoletti.*

Followed by a *Mona Lisa potato gnochi red squash black truffle condiment*

Then came a *Mediterranean sea bass with fennel raddichio and citrus fruit*

Finally they were served with a *Breast of squab grilled duck foie gras with polenta, tasty jus thickened with giblets*

The meal was washed down with a 480 Euro bottle of Dom Perignon vintage champagne and James' drink of pure Evian water at 8 Euro.

Already feeling satiated, they were then served with a selection of tasty cheeses and a sweet consisting of a heavenly creation combining *Grand Marnier, vanilla, chocolate, strawberry, and raspberry.*

Eventually they had an after dinner *coffee accompanied by home-made delicacies and chocolates.*

Andy felt bloated and excused himself to go to the toilet.

All through the meal Tim continued to insist that they should visit the Casino to bring a great day to a happy climax. However, the others were not in agreement and wanted to leave for home after the meal.

'James will help me won't you my friend?' he slurred. 'You used to gamble here didn't you? After all, I'm giving you a bit of my liver. Surely you can give me some of your time?'

'Yes, I will and as I've said before, I'm extremely grateful to you for promising to donate part of your liver...but perhaps we could...umm come back another time? he suggested anxiously, not wishing to upset the very man who was potentially going to save his life. 'I believe Andy and Helen want to get home for their children,' he added

Meanwhile Andy was on his way back to the table when he felt a hand on his shoulder.

Immediately he recognised the perfume that accompanied it. He turned. It was Nadine. His heart stopped.

'Allo Andy, I thought it was you,' she said, giving him a peck on the cheek. 'What are you doing in town? Mon cher.'

'The a...will reading was...a...today,' Andy replied, nervously looking towards the terrace.

'The will reading! I did not know. I was not told,' she said, tiny pink spots of anger flushing her cheeks.

'Look, can we…go somewhere…umm, into the reception area perhaps?' he said, hoping Helen wouldn't suddenly come out and see them together.

'Why? You have your wife with you?'

'Yes,' he said stiffly.

'Oh I see. You do not wish for your wife to see us. But it is OK, n'est pas. I 'ave already told 'er there was nothing between us. I already 'ad somebody.'

'Yes, I know. Even so, I…I'd prefer she didn't see us,' he said, holding her arm and steering her into an alcove of the huge entrance hall.

'The reading should not have occurred. I am contesting the will,' she said fixing him with a stare as they sat down. 'The Law firm knew of this and went ahead! Why, this is outrageous! I will call my Lawyer straight away,' she said reaching into her small clasp purse for her mobile.

Andy had never seen a diamond encrusted mobile phone before.

'Look. I think it's all 'done and dusted'. You're too late.'

'What do you mean 'done and dusted'? I do not understand,' she queried, now distracted from using her phone.

'The money has already been distributed.'

'Distributed! But how can this be? I was iz partner when he made some of iz money. I am entitled to some of 'iz estate.'

'I thought that you'd already received your Legacy.'

'A picture of a sunset! Pah! That is all he gave me. Zis is not a legacy. Zis is an insult for the love I gave him.'

'I think he'd decided that after you left him, while he was very ill, you had turned your back on him.'

'It was très difficile. I could not cope with iz illness,' she said self-consciously, wriggling in her chair. 'E was not the man I fell in love with.'

'Did you have a pre-nuptial agreement with him?'

'Non.'

Meanwhile, out on the terrace, Tim was still insisting on staying in Monaco.

'Oh come on Tim, don't spoil it,' Carrie pleaded.

'It's you that is going to spoil it. Look I can afford a bit of a flutter now,' he argued.

'So the money has gone straight to your head, as I thought it would. I knew it. As soon as you got the money, you'd want to spend it.'

'You don't tell me what to do Carrie. I'm my own man.' He slurred. 'I don't need you.'

'What?'

'You heard. I can do what I want, when I want. I don't need your permission.' Tim bellowed.

Carrie stared at him, disbelievingly. 'You ungrateful bastard. Just remember, if it hadn't been for me you would still be sitting in front of that X-Box playing games. I got you off your arse so you could earn this Legacy.'

'Bullshit, I did this because I wanted to. Not because you made me.

Anyway with that amount of money, I can even afford to lose a few grand at the tables.'

Embarrassed by the 'domestic' between Tim and Carrie, Helen excused herself and went to the entrance lobby to try and track Andy down, she was concerned that he might have a problem.

As she peered around the cavernous hall, she spotted Andy and Nadine in the alcove. Her hackles rising, she made a beeline straight to them, her heels telegraphing her anger across the polished marble.

'Andy what are you doing with this tart?' Helen demanded, surprising them. Andy stood up in shock.'

'No it's not what you think.' Andy said quickly, walking towards her.

'Do you think that I am so gullible that you can get away with flirting with this woman right under my nose?'

'I didn't...this wasn't arranged. Honest,' Andy pleaded.

'Don't lie to me. I've heard enough of your pathetic excuses. Kay persuaded me to give you a second chance and this is what you do with it...throw it in my face.'

'Please, let me explain.'

'There is nothing to explain It's obvious what you're up to,' Helen said, fixing Nadine with an icy stare.

'It's not what you think,' he pleaded.

'So you only went to the toilet did you? Well how come you're out here canoodling with this bitch?' she demanded.

'Who are you calling a bitch?' Nadine immediately stood up and glared at her.

'You...you...whore.' Helen's hatred for this woman overwhelmed her normally controlled manners. This woman had caused her so much angst, the remorseless tittle tattle of the school gate gossip.

'I will not stand for this. You insult me too much,' Nadine shouted, moving aggressively towards Helen. Her Latin blood boiling with rage.

'You two had this planned all along didn't you?' Helen screeched.

'No, honestly. We didn't.' Andy replied vehemently, positioning himself between the two ladies, hoping things didn't degenerate and become physical.

The shouting match had now attracted the attention of the Hotel Manager who walked briskly over to them, followed by two very large security people.

Standing between the two women he said calmly and politely, 'I think it is time for you all to leave, Monsieur, Mesdames. We do not wish to disturb the rest of our guests with all this noise do we?'

'I have never been so 'umiliated. You haven't heard the last of this,' Nadine threatened, walking quickly to the main entrance, shadowed discreetly by one of the security guards.

'We need to join our friends on the terrace and we will also leave,' Andy informed the Manager, embarrassed by the scene.

'But of course, please.' The manager gestured in the direction of the terrace and subserviently bowed from the waist.

Andy and Helen walked back quickly to rejoin the others, also shadowed discreetly by the other security guard.

'I have never been so embarrassed in my life,' Helen said under her breath. 'How dare you do this to me?'

'If you'd just listen with your ears and not your mouth, you'd know that this was not arranged,' Andy whispered, angrily.

'So now you try and wriggle out of it by insulting me? Well it won't work.' Helen hissed.

'She approached me,' Andy retorted, exasperated that he wasn't convincing his wife of his innocence. 'I didn't arrange anything. She was in the hotel already.'

'A likely story.'

'Why the hell would I want to mess up tonight's celebrations?'

'Who knows? Perhaps because you lied to me about the corridor incident in the first place, that's why.' Helen said through clenched teeth, conscious of the security guard.

'I didn't. Look, I want to end this pratting around with this frigging will and untangle myself from these guys as much as you do. But it looks like we've got another complication. She is contesting the will.'

They had arrived back at the table on the terrace just as Andy said it.

'Who's contesting the will?' Tim demanded, suddenly aware of the possible threat to his fortune.

'Nadine. I've just bumped into her.'

'Huh…bumped into her! My arse,' Helen retorted, angrily standing with her arms folded across her chest.

'Well that's it. I'm definitely going to go to the casino tonight,' Tim announced loudly, slamming his hand on the table and making all the glasses jump. 'I'm going to spend my share before she can get her hands on it.'

'Shhh, Tim. Quiet. Everybody is looking at us,' Carrie said in hushed tones, suddenly aware that they had become the centre of attention by the restaurant's clientele.

The Maître de was also looking uncomfortable wondering whether to intervene. He exchanged words with the security guard who had shadowed Andy and Helen, but was reassured that the matter would soon resolve itself.

'I don't care. Let them. I'm going to the Casino by myself, if necessary.' Tim told her.

'Fine, you go to the casino. We're going home, without you. So you'll have to find a hotel to stay at.' Carrie said angrily.

'That's OK, I can do that.' Tim replied furiously.

'Sorry about this...domestic,' Carrie apologised to the others. Glaring crossly at Tim, she stood up and marched away from the table.

The others followed as she strutted out of the restaurant leaving James to pick up the tab.

Tim sat and stubbornly finished off his drink, feeling the eyes of the restaurant clientele burning into the back of his neck.

Outside, the others found the stretch limousine waiting to take them back to Nice airport. Carrie climbed in and sat quietly in the back, deeply hurt by Tim's words. Helen sat next to her and squeezed her hand for reassurance.

'You OK? she asked quietly.

'Yes perfectly,' Carrie replied unconvincingly, putting on a brave face. 'I'm sorry if we embarrassed you.'

'Don't worry, these things happen, I can tell you,' Helen informed her, fixing Andy with an icy stare.

Ignoring Helen's obvious disdain, Andy asked, 'should we wait a few minutes? Do you think he'll change his mind?'

'No, please leave him. He isn't coming,' Carrie confirmed.

They drove to the airport in silence. The excitement of the day somewhat overshadowed by Tim's bloody minded insistence on staying on to gamble and Helen and Andy's row about Nadine.

While the others were making their way back to England, Tim had gone to the Casino as he'd intended.

Having been credit checked as a credible punter he was allowed into the back room normally barred to tourists.

He attracted the attention of several gorgeous young ladies to his side as he squandered his money. They egged him on to keep playing even when his own common-sense suggested he stopped.

In a hectic night of gambling, he had a roller coaster ride of success and failure, winning and losing.

The more he lost the more frustrated he became, swearing and cursing at his change of luck. He stopped short of accusing the casino of cheating. By the end of the evening he had reached the limit imposed by the Casino anyway. He was already one hundred thousand pounds lighter in his bank account.

Ignoring the croupier's advice to stop using expletives, the management eventually intervened.

DJ suited security guards then guided him unobtrusively to the door and wished him a Good Night.

Boasting that he had more money and would return the following night, he staggered back to his room that he'd booked in the Hotel de Paris and crashed out, his head spinning from the champagne and the amazing kaleidoscope of the day's events.

He had become a multi-millionaire. He had broken up with his girlfriend and business partner Carrie and he had now blown a hundred thousand pounds in the space of a few hours.

But what the hell! He could now get any woman he wanted. And the interest on the remaining millions would soon make up for some of his losses.

Indeed, with a few more lucky sessions at the tables he would possibly even increase his fortune.

With that thought in his mind he drifted off into an alcoholically induced sleep.

CHAPTER TWENTY EIGHT

As the privately chartered jet headed back to the UK, Andy noticed that Carrie was crying.

'Well, that's something I wasn't expecting from her,' he thought. 'The tough soldier has cracked. 'You OK, Carrie?' he asked gently, swivelling the white leather bucket seat to face her.

'Yes thanks,' she said dabbing her eyes and desperately trying to compose herself. 'I'm sorry again about the scene at the restaurant.'

'That's OK, these things happen.' Andy said, sympathetically.

'Still embarrassing though,' she giggled nervously and further emphasised her discomfort by a quick shrug of her shoulders.

'Yes, you have my sympathies.'

'Thanks.'

'Umm...this probably isn't the right time to ask... but I have to ask you while I think about it.'

'Go on.' She said, intrigued with what he was going to say.

'It might help to take your mind off things too.' Andy suggested.

'Go ahead. I'm alright, really,' she confirmed.

'Well, I wonder if you would like to help me on a Scout night hike.

'A what?' Carrie repeated his strange request. 'A night hike!'

'Yes I run one every year about this time for the scouts. And I'm short of somebody to man a checkpoint.' Andy informed her.

'Checkpoint?' Carrie echoed, surprised at the 'out of the blue' invitation.

'Yes on night hikes we set up checkpoints to ensure the kids follow the correct route. The thinking behind it is that if they get lost we, at least, know where they're likely to be. It obviously narrows the search area.'

'Sounds similar to Regiment selection hikes.' Carrie volunteered.

'Yes, probably. So you're obviously the right person to do the job. Each checkpoint has an activity base too.'

'What sort of activity is it?'

'The base I have in mind for you requires the scouts to put on a first aid sling and then you have to mark how well they do.'

'Why, yes that sounds great.' Carrie beamed, warming to the idea. 'Should be no problem. Part of my service training was as a first responder. You know, treating battlefield injuries.'

'Well hopefully we won't have any of them for you to treat. That's great then, thanks. Welcome aboard, we'll make final arrangements later in the week..'

'I'll look forward to it.'

Andy had been right, getting Carrie involved with something that she had 'professional' experience in had taken her mind off the row with Tim.

The group finally arrived back at Gloucestershire airport, tired from their exhilarating day and said their goodbyes before departing for their own homes.

Andy thanked the pilot and crew of the chartered jet and felt sad that his moment of glory organising the 'no expense spared' trips back to Monaco was finally over.

As they were about to drive out of the airport in the Merc, Carrie flagged them down.

'What's the matter? Battery flat?'

'No. I didn't bring the spare key for our motor. They're usually in the bottom of my bag.' Carrie said. 'And Tim has got the other set. Can I scrounge a lift home?"

'Yes, no problem. Jump in,' he directed, climbing out and lifting the driver's seat for her to get into the rear passenger seat.

'Can you take me home first Andy.' Helen asked stiffly. 'I told Kay we would be home earlier than this.'

'Please. If it's going to cause any problems, I'll get a taxi.' Carrie suggested.

'No, it's no problem Carrie, honest.' Andy reassured her.

The atmosphere in the car was 'tense' as Andy drove the white Mercedes back to his home. No-one spoke. Carrie sensed the tension between Andy and Helen and didn't attempt to make any small talk.

Helen got out and said good night to Carrie and hoped that her dispute with Tim would be resolved soon. Helen ignored Andy as she strutted to the front door.

'How was your trip?' Kay said, greeting Helen at the door.

'OK thanks.' Helen said politely.

'What no Andy?' she said looking around.

'No. He's doing a taxi service at the moment, Helen said stiffly. 'Have the kids been OK?'

'Yes they were fine, but it doesn't sound like you were though.'

'She was there.' Helen hissed.

'Who?' Kay asked, puzzled by Helen's demeanour.

'The corridor incident woman,' Helen said, avoiding using Nadine's name.

'Not at the will reading!' Kay said flabbergasted.

'No, I found Andy and her alone together having a cosy chat in the hotel lobby.' Helen's voice was tense as she recalled her discovery of them together.

'Oh dear. I'm sorry. I don't what to say Helen.' Kay said sensitively.

Helen led them in to the lounge.

'Of course, he came up with all the excuses. He hadn't arranged to meet her. She JUST happened to be at the hotel where we JUST happened to be eating.'

'She does live there though,' Kay suggested.

'Yeah. But not in the hotel,' Helen dismissed her suggestion.

'Some rich people do. They find it cheaper than running a house.' Kay enlarged her suggestion.

'Say what you like. There are just too many coincidences,' Helen said firmly.

'Yes I suppose so,' Kay conceded.

'You convinced me to give him a second chance and I did…and what does he do? He throws it back in my face.' Helen sat down as if to emphasise her upset.

'Sorry, I thought he was better than that.' Kay added, wondering if she had given Helen bad advice.

'So did I...and it's not over yet either.' Helen added.

'What do you mean?' Kay asked with growing concern.

'He's still involved making sure those Godsons spend their money correctly and what's worse,' Helen advised her. 'That Nadine is contesting the will.'

'Do you mean they haven't distributed Geoffery's estate then?'

'Oh yes. They've all got five million quid each.'

'Five million pounds! My word. Why, that's a fortune!' Kay exclaimed, sitting down.

'I thought Tim might have been in touch to tell you.' Helen suggested.

'No. As usual I've heard nothing from Tim about any of this.' Kay informed her.

'Well it's already causing problems.' Helen added.

'Oh?'

'Yes, I'm sorry to say but your Tim and Carrie had a big bust up in Monaco.'

'Oh really?' Kay sighed.

'Yes it was at the restaurant while we were celebrating.' Helen continued.

'I might have guessed. What's Tim done now?' Kay asked, sternly.

'After we'd had a lovely meal all he kept on about was going to the Casino to gamble some of his inheritance.'

'Sounds like Tim. On the rare occasions that he ever had money, he would always squander it on these dreaded slot machines. The damn fool. Money has always burnt a hole in his pocket.' Kay said, disgusted by her offspring's antics.

'Yes that was what Carrie and James were trying to tell him, but...'

'I know. He was too pig headed to listen.' Kay interrupted.

'Yes I'm afraid so.'

'What happened?'

'We left him there. He was determined to go to the Casino and we came home without him.' Helen explained, embarrassed to be telling tales.

'Pig headed little bugger,' Kay exploded. 'I blame those game consoles myself. He would spend hours on them. My efforts to get him to stop always fell on deaf ears. It was Geoffery's challenge and Carrie's persuasion that got him to put them down in the end,' Kay informed her.

'Well that's more or less what Carrie said. But he said he didn't need her. It might have been the booze talking but...'

'Was she upset?' Kay asked awkwardly.

'Surprisingly, yes. I didn't expect her to be so...so sensitive. It's especially strange when you come to think how aggressive she was sorting that Sue woman out.' Helen advised her. 'But yes she was very upset, so much so, that she was crying on the plane coming back.'

'That sounds like my son.' Kay tutted. 'The selfish little sod. I know emotionally Carrie's a bit sensitive since she started treatment for her PTSD problem.'

'But I thought I heard your Tim say that she was on the mend after her intensive sessions.' Helen queried.

'Well let's hope this row hasn't set her back.' Kay observed.

'I know what it's like when you're down,' Helen added, recalling her own depressive period.

'No. Lets' hope not. Anyway, enough of my heartless son. What are you and Andy going to do?' Kay asked.

'I'm not sure that I can trust him anymore, Kay. And to make matters worse, he doesn't seem to like spending time with us either.'

'What do you mean?'

'He spends more time with his Scouts and at work than he does with us...and now this will thing with Nadine.'

'Come on Helen. I think you're painting him to be worse than he is.' Kay counselled. 'As far as I can see, he's just one of those people who likes to be busy.'

'But not with his family. He just takes us for granted.'

'You're not thinking of ...of splitting up are you?' Kay asked, studying Helen's sad face.

'I don't know what to do Kay.' Helen admitted, sighing deeply. 'I wish I knew.'

'Would it help if he cut his hours again?' Kay asked.

'Well that's another thing, you see. When Geoffery was alive he worked casually for him for two days, so we saw a lot more of him. And he worked at the hospice for three days a week. But since Geoffery's death, Andy has gone back to full time working again.' Helen informed her.

'Mmm. Have you said anything to him?'

'Yes. But I think it's fallen on deaf ears. He did it for Geoffery. Why can't he do it for us?' Helen wondered. 'It's not that we can't afford it now after the generous payments we received from Geoffery.'

'It's just suddenly dawned on me.' Kay said. 'Who is Andy ferrying around?'

'Carrie.'

'Carrie! Why?' Kay wondered. 'Was she so upset that she couldn't drive herself?'

'No. Tim has their car keys. In the heat of the argument about him going gambling, apparently, she didn't think about the drive home until we landed back here.' Helen advised.

'You should have stayed with Andy.' Kay suggested. 'I would have been alright for a bit longer here.'

'No, I insisted he dropped me off first. It wasn't fair to you. As it was, we were already later than I was expecting.' Helen replied thoughtfully.

'You needn't have worried. I would have been OK.' Kay confirmed.

Just then they heard Andy's keys in the door.

'Do you want me to stay Helen?' Kay asked urgently.

'No, I'll be alright. We'll sort this out. Don't worry.'

'I hope you do. Not only for yourself but for your lovely children too. They need two loving parents.'

They heard Andy hang his coat up and then he came into the lounge. 'Oh hello Kay. I didn't think you'd still be here. Thanks for babysitting for us. Were the kids OK?'

'Yes they were fine. What about you two though.'

'Oh! What has Helen been saying?' he asked embarrassed. 'Look I'm sorry but you don't want to get involved with our marital problems.'

'I gather that that Nadine was…'Kay started to say.

'I'm sorry to be rude but this has nothing to do with you…this is between Helen and I.'

Andy turned on his heel and left leaving the two women flabbergasted.

CHAPTER TWENTY NINE

'I'll get it Ben,' Beth said, rushing to the front door. She opened it cautiously. Her heart sank. Her worst fears realised. Mike had returned.

'I told you the last time. You're not wanted here,' she said in hushed tones.

'I don't care what you want. I've come to see my son. Where is he?' Mike asked, raising his voice so that if Ben was in the house, he'd hear.

Mike's ploy worked. Overhearing the stilted conversation on the door step Ben's curiosity got the better of him and he joined Beth in the hallway.

'Mum, who is it?' he asked, concerned.

'Oh you must be Ben,' Mike said, stepping into the hallway uninvited.

'What if I am! Who are you?'

'Mike is...' Beth started to say, wondering how best to break the news '... umm...your ...'

'I'm your father,' Mike interjected. 'Hello Ben. Well look at you. What a good looking young man you are. Just like your old man here.'

Ben looked at the stranger in open mouthed astonishment.

'No this wasn't right,' Ben thought. 'This wasn't the tall, muscular, handsome, friendly man whom he dreamed about for so many years.

This man was skinny, shorter and older than his long held image. Worse still, he wore an earring and had a star tattoo on his neck. His dark hair was greased and 'spiked up'. He looked like a drug dealer. No. This wasn't right.'

Ben became, flustered. 'You! My Dad?' he uttered in disbelief. His utopian dreams of being part of a normal family, now, rapidly evaporating.

'Yes. Aren't you going to give me a big hug? After all, I haven't seen you…since… since you were…a baby.'

'Don't delude yourself. You didn't want to see him even then. Remember?' Beth hissed.

Ben's emotions were all over the place. Mechanically, he stepped forward and put his arms around this complete stranger. Mike hugged Ben awkwardly. It was an embarrassing moment for both of them. Ben's hugging was short lived. His senses overwhelmed by the smell of stale cigarettes on the other's clothes.

It didn't feel right. This wasn't the long dreamed of reunion embrace that Ben had anticipated for so many years.

'Well, aren't you going to invite me in?' Mike demanded, looking at Beth. 'I've got a lot of catching up to do with my son.'

'Yes, I suppose,' Beth begrudgingly agreed.

Ben didn't feel right about this man calling himself his Dad.

They walked into the lounge and after Beth had frantically cleared clothes, books and newspapers off the sofa Ben and Mike sat awkwardly next to each other.

'I'm very pleased to meet you Ben. I'm sorry it's taken until now to come back into your life. My other kids are really looking to meeting you.'

Ben was stunned by the news that he had brothers and sisters. As an only child he had always felt envious of his mates who had siblings. But having a ready-made family whom he didn't even know was somehow disconcerting.

'This isn't how I imagined you'd be ...Dad.' He found the word 'Dad' hard to say.

'Well son, I gather you've been looking for me.'

'Yeah, that's right.'

'Well now I'm here I want to be a part of your life. To be here, for you.'

'Thanks,' Ben said, unconvincingly.

'Excuse me while I go and be sick.' Beth said sceptically.

Ignoring Beth's jibe, Mike added, 'Gossip around here has it that your Mothers an alcoholic and...'

'Yes I'm an alcoholic,' Beth admitted, recalling the Clinic advice to recognise and admit her condition. 'But I'm having treatment for it.'

'Yes, so I hear. I gather your Millionaire friend was paying for it too. Well I reckon you must be loaded now, so how's it looking for a sub?' Mike laughed embarrassedly as if he was joking, but the intention was clear to all.

'I haven't got any money,' Beth was quick to say.

'Not the way I heard it. The boy...sorry, Ben's got a couple of very expensive bikes I see. All the kids around here are all talking about them. And your treatment must be costing a fair bit. It's only fair you share some of the money with me. After all I am Ben's father.' Mike became serious.

'Look! I keep telling you. There is no money,' she repeated.

'I understand social services are interested in you. Is that right?' Mike asked pointedly.

'No.' she said, trying to sound dismissive.

'I guess one word from an anonymous person and they'll take him away from you. Then he can come and live with me and his money will come to me anyway.'

'You're mad. I keep telling you there is no money. The bikes were a present from Mr Foster to thank Ben for helping him find his Godson James.'

'Come off it. I wasn't born yesterday. There's bound to be money. Don't try and blag me girl. Now what was that Social Services number?' Mike said, getting his mobile out.

'Oh don't be so stupid. Why won't you listen? There is NO MONEY.' Beth screeched.

Ben's long awaited euphoria at having his Dad back in his life was quickly disappearing in a cloud of despair.

'Will you two stop it?' Ben shouted in exasperation. 'As Mum said, there is no money.'

'Yes Beth, you're ruining my reunion with my son,' Mike was quick to pick up Ben's discomfort.

'I think you're doing a pretty good job of that yourself,' she said standing and walking to the window, arms crossed.

'I understand things haven't been going well here recently,' Mike suggested looking at Ben.

'We're getting on alright,' Ben lied.

'That's not what I'd heard.'

'Gossip, it's all gossip. They got nothing better to do than gossip round here.' Beth volunteered.

'Been missing school haven't you Ben? In trouble with the Police. setting fire to Scout huts, stealing

174

mobile phones. Not too perfect is it? Mike reeled off the list of Ben's issues.

"Don't believe everything you hear. Most of it is gossip,' Ben was quick to rubbish the list of misdemeanours.

'Son, clearly your Mother hasn't brought you up properly,' Mike suggested. 'You'd be much better off with me now.'

'You deserted us remember, you weren't around. I've done my best as a single parent,' Beth reminded him.

'Well it wasn't good enough was it? You're not a good role model for him are you?' Mike said, tightening his grip on Ben's shoulders. 'I can see he needs a man in his life.'

'Stop it, stop it,' Ben shouted, tears filling his eyes. 'You adults are all the same. Selfish and self-centred. When you two have finished arguing, what about what I want?' he asked.

Ben shrugged off Mike's arm and ran out of the room. His long anticipated reunion with his father ruined.

'Now look what you've done,' Mike accused Beth. 'You've upset the boy.' Although, at the same time he was thinking the kid was a bit of a wimp, running off crying.

'You're the intruder in our house. I think you should leave. Now.' Beth demanded.

'So shall I tell him to get his clothes ready?' Mike threatened, getting to his feet.

'No. He's not going anywhere. Especially with you,' Beth informed him..

'Oh is that right. Well we'll see about that shall we? Remember he was looking for me. He wanted to get away from you. You and your alcoholic ways,' Mike reminded her, cruelly.

'I'm trying to kick it,' Beth said, trying to keep a lid on her own emotions but starting to fill up.

'You're a worthless woman. Completely incapable of looking after yourself let alone our son,' he grunted, into her face.

Ben, who had been listening on the stairs, ran back into the lounge.

'No she isn't,' he shouted. 'She might have her problems. But she has brought me up alone, without you.'

'Come on Ben. You'd be better off with me.' Mike said walking towards him. 'I'd like you to meet your brothers and…'

'You don't want me for me…because I'm your son. You only want money. Well as Mum say's, there isn't any. So you might as well leave now.' Ben said angrily

'Son, you misunderstand me. All I want to do is to grow old with you by my side, 'Mike explained. 'To help you become a man. Let's face it, a boy needs a father to help him into manhood. There's certain things that you need to know about becoming a man that your mother can't tell you.'

'I don't need you. I've already got some people, some men who can help me. They want to help me because I am me. Not because they think I have money. I don't need you,' Ben heard himself say the words that destroyed his dream.

All his life he had been fantasising about having a father and now here he was telling him to go, to get out of his life. The dream had ended. He was devastated.

Mike started to protest, but instead, walked towards the front door.

'Nice bikes,' he said stroking the handlebar. 'And you say you haven't got any money? This isn't over Beth. Believe me. I'll get what's owed to me.'

'Get out!' Beth shouted.

'Goodbye Ben. Son.' Mike added, twisting the emotional knife in Ben's gut.

Ben bit his lip as Mike stepped out of the front door. Beth's prediction of the nightmare had come true.

CHAPTER THIRTY

The weekend following their return from Monaco, Andy drove a hired Minibus in to a clearing in the Forest of Dean near to the stunning tranquillity of the large lakes known as Soudley ponds. A large group of Andy's excited scouts disembarked noisily into the dark car park.

'Enjoy the trip Carrie?' Andy asked, as they stood waiting for the Scouts to sort their rucksacks out and don head torches.

'Yes. Lively lot aren't they? Reminds me of some noisy army exercises I've done in the past. Is Ben OK? He was a bit quiet on the way down. I couldn't get a word out of him.'

'Yes, I think so, Andy said, looking around to make sure Ben was out of earshot. 'He's had a bit of a disappointment.'

'Oh?'

'Yes you know he was looking for his father?' Andy checked her understanding.

'Yes, I heard James talking about it.'

'Well. His Dad came to Ben's house the other day... and things didn't go too well.' Andy said, keeping an eye out for Ben.

'Really! What happened?' Carrie asked intrigued.

'The bloke didn't match Ben's expectations and demanded money from them.'

'Money! What for? Protection money, blackmail?' Carrie whispered as a group of scouts walked by.

'No. A share of Ben's money that this bloke had heard Geoffery had given him. He threatened Ben's mother by all accounts.' Andy informed her.

'No wonder the kids quiet. I'd soon sort his father out.' Carrie added. 'Poor kid has a terrible life doesn't he?'

In the distance a volley of shots rang out. Andy was concerned that in Carrie's frail state of mind that the sound could trigger off another PTSD episode.

'You OK Carrie?'

'Yes, thanks. Why do you ask?'

'The gunfire isn't upsetting you at all?'

'No. I'm OK thanks. I'm used to it. I suppose that's the wild boar cull that I read about.'

'Yes. I gather their large numbers are creating a big problem around here.' Andy said looking around to see if the Scouts were ready.

'The article said the population problem started from a small number of boars being illegally dumped here in the forest.'

'Yeah, and it's exacerbated by the fact they breed so fast. They reckon a sow can give birth to as many as ten piglets a year.' Andy informed her.

'No wonder they've become a big nuisance.'

'Of course they've got no natural predators so the population just keeps growing. I assume that's the reason for the cull.' Andy concluded.

'So what's the problem?' Ben asked, joining them.

'Oh, hello Ben. It's the wild boar. They're wreaking havoc by digging up people's gardens, rugby and football pitches. They're even having a go at the grass verges by the side of the roads,' Andy informed him.

'I noticed lots of small piles of dirt by the side of the roads on the way down,' Carrie said. 'I wondered what it was.'

'What do they do?' Ben asked, feigning interest.

'They forage with their snouts. Apparently they're after fallen acorns and beech nuts.'

'Is that right they're nocturnal?' Ben asked, looking around.

'Yes, but the Scouts should be OK. Normally they run a mile when they see people.'

'Not if they have young. I gather, a bit like cows, they can be very protective and aggressive defending their young,' Carrie informed them. 'Lady we saw on one of our hikes in the Cotswolds said her dog had been attacked by a boar in the forest here. Cost her a fortune in vet's bills. So consequently they don't bring the dog down here anymore.'

'Well, so long as they stick to the route that I've given them they should be away from the culling area,' Andy added.

'I hope their map reading skills have improved then,' Ben observed. 'They usually get lost just going up Churchup Hill.'

Andy briefed them both. 'Right. So the plan is, that they are doing an eight mile circular incident hike with checkpoints approximately every two miles. I've already checked and the people came down early and are at their checkpoints and ready to receive the teams.'

'So how do you score them?' Carrie asked, fitting her head torch.

The teams who do it in the fastest time and success-fully complete the tasks at each checkpoint will win.'

'What happens if they get lost?' Carrie queried.

'They have an emergency envelope with instructions in it to tell them what to do. I've checked that at least one person in each team has a mobile phone. I've got a list of the numbers.'

Andy then split the scouts up into teams of three, gave each team a map and compass and told them to wait for Ben to set them off at five minute intervals.

'OK. Well, I'll be off to my checkpoint,' Carrie said, shouldering her rucksack. 'I gather I am the last one before they return back to here?'

'Yes that's right. If you take this path, you'll get to your checkpoint quickly. It's a short cut. The first team should arrive with you in about an hour after you've set up.'

'OK. See you later.' Carrie said, disappearing into the dark forest.

The night hike was going well. Two of the five groups had already been through Carrie's checkpoint on schedule and had successfully completed their first aid challenge.

She was waiting for the next group when she heard what she thought was a dog yelping in pain.

Carrie peered into the forest and shone her torch towards the source of the noise but couldn't see anything.

Shortly after, she heard something coming towards her along the path. She assumed that it was her next team but they were coming from the wrong direction.

As the noise got closer she could see that it was not the team but an individual approaching. The person was carrying a small bundle in their arms.

At that moment two GR4 tornado jets screamed overhead on a low level night exercise as a volley of gunshots echoed around the forest.

Carrie was immediately transported back to Afghanistan and the nightmare when she was staking out the suspected IED dig.

She felt the heat of the Afghan sun. She experienced the same helplessness as she saw the smoke trail of the missiles hurtling toward their target and the young girl carrying the bundle in her arms.

She found herself shouting 'abort, abort.' But this time she was able to run towards the figure.

She set off at a frantic pace, her prosthetic running gait laboured, animatedly waving her arms wildly and shouting, 'Stop, abort. It's a child, it's a child.'

As she got closer the image transformed. Instead of the girl from her nightmare. It was a boy. She couldn't understand the change. She stopped dead in her tracks.

As she stared at the figure, she realised that it was Ben.

He was carrying what appeared to be a small long haired terrier in his arms. There was blood. The animal was obviously hurt.

'Carrie are you alright?' Ben asked, frightened by her manic outburst.

Carrie shook her head to clear the nightmarish images. 'Yes. Yes I think so.' she said animatedly.

'Are you sure?' Ben asked again.

'Don't worry about me.' Carrie said and mentally confirmed she was back in the Forest of Dean 'What... what have you got there?'

'Are you sure you're OK, you went sort of...'

'Yes.' Carrie insisted, irritated with herself and the flashback. 'What have you got there?' she repeated again.

'It...It's a boar piglet. It's been shot. But it's not dead. Can you do something for it?' Ben asked, still confused by Carrie's behaviour.

'Put it down here,' Carrie directed, She realised she was shaking. Her head felt muzzy. She had to dispel the bad thoughts. But she had no time to 'box' her bad experience. 'Let me see.'

Carrie could see very quickly that the piglet had sustained a gunshot wound. It's fur was matted. There was blood and mud everywhere.

'Oh poor thing. It's in a very bad way.'

'You know all about gunshot wounds from the army though don't you?' Ben asked hopefully.

'Yes I do,' she confirmed, examining the animal in the beam of her head torch.

'So you can save it?' he wondered, watching her careful checking.

'If it was a human I would. But I think in this case the kindest thing is to put it down,' she announced, quietly.

'What do you mean? Kill it?' Ben said, surprised at her unsympathetic conclusion.

'That's why the guns are out tonight. If it doesn't die now they will hunt it down sooner or later,' Carrie counselled.

'No. If you can't do anything, we'll take to a vet. What if we use these as a bandage to help stop the bleeding?' Ben said desperately, picking up a sling.

Then they heard it. Something was moving noisily towards them.

'What's that?' Ben said his mouth dry with fear.

'Whatever it is, it sounds big,' Carrie said, shining her torch towards the source of the noise.

Suddenly through the undergrowth a huge wild boar appeared.

It was two feet across the shoulders, four feet nose to tail and had a shoulder height of over two foot six from its back to its trotters. Carrie estimated it to weigh about one hundred and fifty pounds.

It stopped momentarily when it saw them.

'Jesus!' Ben said, wondering what to do, where to run.

'Quick, get behind me,' Carrie instructed.

The sow regained its purpose and ran towards them, snorting loudly.

Ben picked up the piglet again and ran behind Carrie. She stood her ground and started frantically waving her arms, and at the same time shouting loudly.

The sow stopped at the sudden noise.

It raised its snout and sniffed. It could smell the piglet and resumed its charge, its lower tusks looking menacing as it hurtled towards them.

Carrie instinctively reached for the service dagger at her hip; the blade sheathed for quick extraction and the execution of its lethal purpose.

She maintained her position and braced herself as the sow continued its charge to retrieve its offspring.

In a blur of action and in spite of side stepping the charge, the boar caught a tusk in Carrie's trousers. Her legs buckled under her. The impact sent her flying backwards into Ben. He was sandwiched between her and a tree. The force of the collision knocked the wind out of him. He fell unconscious.

Fortunately, as she fell, her reflex action was to still direct the knife at its target across the charging animal's throat. The sow became the author of her own demise as the blade found its mark and slit its own throat.

The momentum of the dead boar carried it past them and it slammed into a tree where it slumped on to the ground and continued to twitch and convulse in its death throes.

'You OK Ben?' Carrie called, as she tried to stand, before realising that her prosthetic legs had been destroyed by the sow.

No reply.

'Ben. Ben can you hear me?'

Unable to stand, Carrie 'bum shuffled' over to Ben's prostrate figure.

'Christ, Ben's hurt. Shit, he's not breathing.' Carrie did a quick check looking for obvious signs of injury. She found none. Quickly she pulled his chin down to open his mouth and could see that his tongue had fallen back and was blocking his throat. He was effectively suffocating himself.

As Carrie hooked his tongue out of his airway she heard something moving towards them in the forest.

'Christ I hope it's not daddy pig,' she muttered, continuing to concentrate on her life saving task. 'Otherwise we might be in really big trouble this time.'

After pulling his head back to open his airway, she cupped her mouth over his and blew into it watching his chest rise.

The noise behind her was getting louder.

'Come on Ben. Don't make this difficult for me,' she implored, turning her attention to chest compressions, she started rhythmically pumping his chest.

The undergrowth moved and...Andy came into sight.

'Oh thank God it's you,' she said. 'We've got a little problem here. Ben swallowed his tongue, but I think he's just started breathing again.'

Within an instant, Andy was at Ben's side and targeted his neck to feel for a pulse.

'It's a bit quick, but yes, he's still with us. What the hell happened here?' he said looking around at the dead wild boars. 'Ok, I'll take over now,' he said, rolling Ben into the recovery position.

Carrie filled him in with the details as Ben slowly recovered.

'God, you gave us a bit of a shock there Ben.'

'What happened?' Ben said, holding his throat.

'You decided to choke yourself. Frightened the life out of me,' Carrie said, feeling relieved. 'You OK otherwise?'

'Yeah, I think so,' Ben said, sitting himself upright slowly. 'Although my throat hurts.' He grimaced, 'Oww and I think I've bruised my back,' he said, putting his right hand to the small of his back.

'I'm not surprised. You must have hit that tree quite heavily,' she said, concerned. 'Although I have to say you make a good cushion. You stopped me from damaging myself. Thanks.'

'Your legs. Oh my god, look at your legs.' Ben said, pointing at them. 'Your knees are pointing the wrong way.'

'Yes, that sow has got a lot to answer for. It's virtually demolished my prosthetics. But it's OK. At least I can get a quick replacement without too much trouble,' Carrie informed them, wiping the blood off her knife and sheathing it.

'What happened to the piglet?' Ben asked, looking around.

'It's dead too, I'm afraid,' Andy informed him.

'Sadly your errand of mercy failed,' Carrie added.

'Poor thing,' Ben said, looking sorrowfully at the blooded piglet.

'Well, it looks like we've got boar on the menu for Sunday roast for a few weeks,' Carrie said, insensitively, looking at the huge boar. 'She was looking for her baby, that's why she charged us Ben.'

'Sorry, I just felt sorry for the little thing.'

'You did the right thing. Don't worry.' She reassured him.

'I came to tell you that three teams have missed your checkpoint,.' Andy said. 'So we'll pack up here. Carrie it looks like I'll have to carry you back.'

'Fraid so. So if you two gentlemen would like to look the other way. I'll just slip my trousers down and remove these damaged legs. It'll make carrying me easier.'

'That'll give the kids something to talk about. I doubt that any of them realised you have prosthetics,' Andy said, discreetly looking away.

CHAPTER THIRTY ONE

Carrie hobbled slowly up the short incline, her replacement prosthetics hurting her bruised thighs, a painful reminder of the boar attack during the night hike.

She gripped the galvanised steel handrails that led from the gate to the house, the accumulated dust indicating their current redundancy. The disability handles either side of the door too, now no longer required by their intended user.

It was a mark of how things had progressed and reminded her of how she had helped make the change.

She knocked gently on the familiar door and waited with growing apprehension for it to open.

Eventually, after what seemed an age, she could see someone through the glass panel and the front door opened, cautiously.

Carrie had built herself up for this moment. She had expected a confrontation with Tim but, it was Kay, Tim's mother who opened the door.

'Kay...Oh, I umm...I a...' Carrie said, flustered.

'Oh. Hello Carrie, do come in.'

'Thanks,' she said, stepping into the hallway. 'Is Tim here?'

'Tim! No, why would he be?

'Kay closed the door, 'Come in and sit down,' she said, leading Carrie into the lounge. 'Pardon the mess. I've just started packing for my cruise.'

'I bet you're looking forward to it?' Carrie said, trying to sound interested.

'Oh, absolutely. Four months cruising the world! It really is a holiday of a lifetime. Geoffery, bless him, was so thoughtful to leave me that as a legacy in his will.

I shall go to the ship's rail at sunset, every night and as the sun slips below the horizon, I shall raise my glass to his memory. Mind you, on wet days I'll probably stay inside. Oh there's me chatting on. How are you doing?'

'Not feeling very good at the moment.'

'No I can see. You look a bit 'peaky'. Did I imagine it or were you limping?

'Yes. It's a long story.'

'Did Tim hurt you? Kay said, looking concerned. 'I know he's got a temper but...'

'No. Tim didn't hurt me. He wouldn't. I had a 'run-in' with a wild boar.'

'A wild boar!'

'Yes, but that's another story.'

'Oh, well. Is there anything I can do to help?' Kay asked sympathetically.

'I don't know... It's Tim, you see.' Carrie said awkwardly.

'Tim! Yes I've heard about his antics. What's the matter with him now?'

'I don't know...I don't know where he is.' Carrie revealed. 'We left him in Monaco over a week ago.'

'Have you two split up?' Kay asked cautiously. 'Are you still living together?'

'No, we haven't split up. As far as I'm concerned we're still living together... that is, we were.'

'Well, that's good at least.' Kay said relieved. 'So you mean you haven't heard from him at all?'

'No. Nothing since we left Monaco.'

'Well, as usual I haven't heard from him either. The last text I got from him was that you were both off to Monaco for the reading of the will and he was hoping to get his inheritance. But nothing since.'

'Oh we went alright and Tim got his money,' Carrie informed her, feeling uncomfortable with being Tim's messenger to his own mother. 'The Godsons each got five million pounds.'

'Yes I heard,' Kay said flatly. 'And I gather you two had a bit of a row too.'

'Yes...we did,' Carrie admitted, embarrassed at the revelation. 'But how did you know that?' And then the penny dropped. 'Oh, Helen and Andy. Of course!'

'I did try ringing him several times,' Kay added. 'But his phone is switched off.'

'Yes, I know. I've been ringing every day and leaving messages too, but get no response. I hope he's alright and nothing's happened to him.'

'Me too. He's out of his depth. With money in his pocket, he might attract the wrong attention.'

'Oh don't say that.' Carrie said alarmed at the thought. 'Perhaps I ought to fly out there and try and find him. To apologise.'

'Apologise for what?' Kay asked in disbelief.

'Well, after our celebratory meal, he kept 'banging on' about going to the casino and I said he shouldn't.' Carrie advised her.

'You obviously know him better than he knows himself.'

'He told me not to interfere and that he was fed up with me meddling in his life.'

'Oh that was unkind. Doesn't he realise what you've done for him?'

'He said that now he was a millionaire that he would do what the hell he wanted.'

'Typical. Straight to his head.'

'And then he said,' Carrie swallowed hard trying to control herself to say the words, 'he didn't want me anymore.'

'Oh Carrie, I'm so sorry.'

'I hoped he'd be back by now. But obviously not.'

'Well I suppose he could be. He doesn't have to come back here anymore.' Kay observed. 'If he's as 'loaded' as you say. He could be living anywhere now.'

'I miss him so much,' Carrie looked at Kay with doleful, puppy eyes.

Kay was taken aback by the transformation in Carrie. The distraught persona in front of her was a world away from the tough, quite violent person that she'd seen fighting Sue in Monaco.

'Oh I'm sure he didn't mean it,' she said, sympathetically holding Carrie's hand. 'It was probably only the booze talking.'

'After I lost my colleagues to that IED, I always promised myself I would never let anybody get emotionally close to me ever again. It just hurts too much when you lose somebody. They're gone forever.' Carrie dissolved into uncontrolled sobbing. 'I know he's been having a tough time with my PTSD episodes …and well I can't blame him.'

'Yes, he told me he was finding it difficult,' Kay volunteered. 'But I told him to stand by you. As you had done for him, when he was down.'

'He was being very supportive and I was starting to feel better about things...that intensive PTSD course and Cognitive Behaviour Therapy was really helping,' she said, dissolving again.

Kay took her in her arms and hugged her and held her while she wailed. 'Oh Carrie, what can I say?'

Eventually Carrie got control of her emotions again and dabbing her eyes she explained. 'I blocked out every emotion until Tim and I started getting on really well. I resisted any emotional involvement for a long time.

But eventuality I came to realise that I loved him. I let him into my head and heart. Now he has just cast me aside. I never thought I'd ever say this, but Kay, my heart is broken.' Carrie dissolved again.

'That's right, just let it all out,' Kay whispered sympathetically, still hugging her. 'You'll feel better for it.'

'I can't get him out of my mind. I think about him day and night. I can't eat. It's making me feel ill.'

'But you're a tough lady... coping with the terrible things you've seen.'

'Tough! Well yes I was...I used to be. Block out all emotions. That was all part of my coping mechanism during my service career. It can't hurt you if you don't let it in. But he overwhelmed my defences and got to me. I hate myself for being so vulnerable.'

'The trouble is, love makes fools of all of us.' Kay said, reflectively thinking about the illicit fling she'd had with Geoffery on her wedding day.

'Well it's certainly done that to me,' Carrie said, trying to compose herself.

'Perhaps the reasons you are so sensitive now is because the treatment for your PTSD has stripped back that veneer of toughness and undermined your emotional defences.'

'Yes, you're probably right.'

'It might sound difficult to believe now, but you'll get over it...the hurt eventually goes.'

'But I don't want to get over Tim. I love him.'

'I'm sure you do...I'm sure you do,' Kay said, gently stroking her hair. 'But the reality is, that Tim is a selfish individual.'

'Pardon?' Carrie said, stunned by Kay's observation.

'You might be surprised to hear me say that about my own son. But he's always been like that. I couldn't see it. I was blind to his faults but Geoffery Foster made me see the truth about him.' Kay confessed. 'Perhaps it was my fault. I should have been firmer with him. But I felt guilty about him losing his legs.

Then again Tim has always been...me...me...me.' Kay continued. 'That was, until you came along and he changed. You changed him. I couldn't believe the difference you made in him.' Kay informed her.

'Yes, I did see the change,' Carrie admitted.

'Well, sadly, it seems now he's got his money, he's reverted to type,' Kay concluded.

'And he's just pushed me out of his life.' Carrie sobbed. 'I don't want to let him go. I need him.'

'I guess when love comes along, we're all prisoners of our heart,' Kay reflected, thinking again back to her past intimate involvement with Geoffery.

'What can I do Kay, what can I do?' Carrie pleaded.

'It'll sort itself out I'm sure. Once he's got over the novelty of having money, he'll get bored and come back to you.'

'Are you sure?'

'If he loves you, he'll get in touch, believe me. I know it's a cliché, but love really does conquer all.' Kay added.

'Well at least he can't gamble it all away,' Carrie said, sitting up and wiping her eyes. 'Geoffery put a clause in the will that ring-fenced some of the money.

There is a large proportion that can only be used on our chosen project. So at least the walking company is safe. Although, I guess, I might have to find a new partner to help me run it.' Carrie concluded.

'Don't count Tim out too soon. As I say, I'm sure he'll come to his senses, believe me.' Kay advised.

'I'm not sure that I can wait. We have some walks programmed and a full take up of hikers.' Carrie informed her, blowing her nose.

'Oh dear. Well what about James? He's been helping you, hasn't he?'

'Yes, but James isn't physically fit. He will be trying to get his own project moving before he goes in to hospital. Don't forget, he's still waiting for his transplant.'

'Oh that's a point. What about his operation if Tim doesn't come back?'

Kay asked the question that Carrie had already been pondering.

'Not even Tim would be so cruel to go back on his promise, would he?'

'No, perhaps you're right.' Kay said, unconvincingly. 'No.'

'What about getting some help from Rupert?' Kay suggested.

'Well, Rupert has already designed the website for us. And he's got to get his own project off the ground too.

Don't forget he's a committed family man now. What with looking after baby Jeffery and Jo, as well, 'Carrie pointed out. 'Oh that reminds me.' She added, 'I nearly forgot.'

'What?'

'Some good news for them at last. Jo is going to the States to see a specialist in spinal injuries, hopefully for an operation to help her walk again.'

'Oh that's brilliant news.'

'So I think we can rule Rupert out of the equation. No, I'll just have to do it myself,' Carrie said resignedly.

'Perhaps being busy will help you get your mind off Tim.' Kay suggested.

'Yes perhaps you're right. I'm sorry to have bought my problems to you Kay.'

'That's alright. He's my son at the end of the day. We can sort this out together, I'm sure.' Kay said, optimistically.

'Thank you for listening. You were right. I do feel a lot better for getting that of my chest.' Carrie admitted, stuffing the tissue up her sleeve.

Carrie's demeanour had changed. It was as if she had stepped out of a Schizophrenic body double. She was now 'calm and collected'.

'He might have crushed me at the moment,' Carrie added. But I'm made of sterner tough. I'll get him back, you wait and see.'

'Good for you.' Kay said, amazed at Carrie's sudden metamorphosis.

'I must go. Things to organise,' Carrie said, standing stiffly holding her painful thighs.

'That's the girl. Don't let him grind you down,' Kay encouraged, leading her to the door. 'Don't forget, I'm here if you want me.'

Kay closed the door and made her way to the kitchen. 'Heavens what a mess! This calls for a cup of tea.'

CHAPTER THIRTY TWO

Ben had convinced his Mother that he needed time off school to recover from being knocked out during the night hike incident and was laying on the sofa watching TV when there was a knock on the door.

As Beth was out shopping he made his way gingerly to the door and opened it to see James on the door step.

'Just popped over to see how you are,' James said, taking up Ben's invitation to step in to the lounge. 'I heard about your run-in with that boar. That must have been frightening, old chap.'

'Yeah it was. I'm glad Carrie was there. She saved my life.'

'Yes, so I gather. Are you OK? Have you recovered yet?'

'My back keeps locking up, so I convinced Mother I needed to have some time off school.'

'Oh dear.'

'I've got some pills from the quack and hopefully I'll be OK for the big race.'

'Don't forget, I'm still quite happy to take you to the race, if you want?'

'Yeah, please if you don't mind.'

'OK, that's settled then. How's your Mum doing with her regime?'

'Regime?'

'You know, the plan that the lady from Young Carers created for you both.'

'Oh OK at the moment. She's been there to a couple of meetings with you and I haven't had to put her to bed again, yet. But she's very snappy. She goes 'off on one' a lot.'

'Yes, I know what that's like. The DTs are terrible. I've been there myself. But, if it's any consolation, she'll get better as her body adjusts to the lack of alcohol. It's a bit like a smoker giving up. It's the cravings that you go through, unless you experience it yourself, it's difficult to explain.' James informed him.

'Yeah, I suppose so. Are you feeling alright James? You look sort of...yellow...' Ben said peering closely at James' face.

'No, actually I'm not feeling that great, I have to admit. I've been a bit shivery and nauseous. My stomach has swollen too...Anyway, enough of me. Apart from wild boar baiting, what else is going on in your life?'

'Nothing, really,' Ben said, evasively.

'Come on now, I've known you long enough not to have to go through this act of trying to draw it out from you.'

'Well, if you must know. It's...it's... my Dad...he came to our house the other day.'

'Your Dad! Oh that's great news. That's what you've dreamed of all these years, isn't it?'

'Well...yes...but.'

''So why the long face? Surely your search is at an end?'

'Well, he wasn't exactly what I was expecting.' Ben informed him.

'Not what you were expecting? What do you mean?' James quizzed.

'He looked and sounded different from what I dreamed he'd be.' Ben said awkwardly, shifting his positon on the sofa.

'Why?'

'Well, you know there are some people you see and immediately don't like. Something about them that... you know...' Ben explained.

'Go on.' James encouraged.

'Well, if I saw him on the street...' Ben hesitated, wondering how to put it. 'He's the sort of person I'd avoid.'

'Oh dear. I see!' James sat back in his seat wondering what to say next.

'Yes. Well Mum did try and warn me and...'Ben added uncomfortably.

'Let's look at it another way.' James suggested. 'Imagine if you'd grown up with him all those years as one of his children.'

'OK.'

'You wouldn't know any different. He'd just be your Dad wouldn't he?'

'Yeah, I suppose.'

'If you give him a chance I'm sure you'll soon get used to him.'

'Do you reckon?'

'Yes of course. You heard of body chemistry between people?' James continued.

'No.'

'Well, it's all to do with the natural attraction between people. Anyway he's your Dad. You've got to give him a chance.' James concluded.

'It's not that simple, there's another thing. He was talking to Mum and there's some gossip going round the estate here, that we've got money.'

'Right.' James said, studying Ben's expression.

'I think that's why he turned up.' Ben expounded.

'Oh. I agree that doesn't sound good.' James confirmed.

'And he was threatening to tell Social Services about Mum's drinking problem so they'd take me away from her...unless...'

'Unless! Unless what?' James quizzed.

'Unless she gave him part of the money.' Ben added conspiratorially.

'Money! What money?' James asked, puzzled. 'Have you got a secret stash? Have you won the lottery?'

'No. He thinks Mr Foster gave me money.' Ben volunteered. 'But you know he didn't. He bought me the bikes instead and that was enough.'

'So what happened?' James asked, sitting forward.

'He was shouting at Mum...So I told him to leave.' Ben said, his voice choked.

'Oh Ben. I'm so sorry.' James said, putting a reassuring hand on Ben's arm.

'He was saying horrible things to her.' Ben continued. 'He just used her, made her pregnant and left her...left me. He didn't want to know me until now when he thought we had money.' Ben added tearfully.

'You must be gutted.'

'Yeah, I am. He even tried it on by saying my step brothers and sisters were going to be poor because he'd been made redundant. Mum reckons, he's never worked a day in his life. He's been on permanent benefits.'

'Oh he tried the guilt trip card did he?' James added knowledgeably.

'Yes. He was horrible.' Bed admitted realistically. 'Well, I guess in one way, it's nice to know I have brothers and sisters. I mean, to meet them would be cool. But I probably never will now.'

'Have you seen him around here before?' James asked.

'Yeah, but obviously didn't really take any notice of him. He was just somebody else on the estate.' Ben replied.

'Did he ever try and approach you before?'

'No.'

'Sounds like you're right then. He was only interested in you because of the rumour about the money.' James volunteered.

'I'm...gutted. I don't know what to do.' Ben said, helplessly.

'I can imagine.' James empathised. 'What's the families reputation like? Are they a...this is going to sound terribly snobbish but I don't know how to put it another way...Are they a reasonable family? Have they got a reputation for being troublemakers, do you know?'

'No, I don't know much about them. I gather they live on the other side of the estate.' Ben added.

'Well perhaps even if you don't want to know your Dad, perhaps it might be an idea to meet your step brothers and sisters?' James proposed.

'Why?'

'Well you might like them. I imagine it would be good to be part of a larger family.'

'Yeah but then, he'd be on the scene.' Ben added thoughtfully. 'No I don't think so.'

'Well think about it. There's no rush.' James suggested.

Suddenly James started clawing at his collar, a strange look came across his face. 'Errr...what were we talking about?' he said, his voice a whisper. 'I get... very confused these days.'

'James, James are you alright? You look kind of strange.'

James didn't reply, in response he fell forward off the chair and collapsed in a crumpled heap. Unconscious.

'Oh my God, James!'

Ben reached for his new mobile and rang for help.

CHAPTER THIRTY THREE

Thanks to Ben's swift action James was in hospital within fifteen minutes of collapsing at the house.

The doctors quickly checked his records and within a further thirty minutes he was being assessed by a substance abuse Specialist.

'Yes, as expected your cirrhosis has now reached a critical stage. The only option for us now is the transplant.'

'I thought you were going to say that,' James said weakly.

'However, before being considered for a liver transplant you need to sign an agreement not to drink in the future…and certainly no alcohol for three months.'

'That's no problem. I've already given up completely.'

'That's good news at least. However, I have to warn you that from time to time we conduct random alcohol tests and if you are found to be positive, we will take you off the transplant list.'

'Right. Yes I understand that.'

'I expect you know that we have a model here in the UK for assessing end-stage liver disease.'

'No. What is it?' James asked, desperately trying to focus.

'It is an assessment based on a scoring system for calculating the risk of a person dying if a transplant is not performed.'

'Scoring! Dying! Suddenly, the mention of dying hit home. How...how do you decide?'

'It's done on the average of four blood tests. The higher the score, the greater the risk of death. This is reflected by going higher up the waiting list.'

'Hence the blood tests,' James said, enlightened. 'I didn't realise their importance.'

'Yes. Your score now means that you are now considered to be urgent.'

'Heavens.'

'But you will be allowed to go home at this stage.'

'Thanks.'

'I believe your donor liver will be coming from an altruistic donor?'

'Sorry?'

'Your friend, the person who is prepared to donate part of his liver,' the specialist elaborated, 'is called an altruistic donor.'

'Oh Tim! Yes that's right.'

'So long as we have an acceptable blood and tissue match he will be an option for you. Otherwise we are waiting for someone carrying a donor card.'

'Yes I know. Someone who has passed away.'

'Clearly if that happens, we are in the lap of the gods, because any long delay will inevitably compromise your wellbeing.'

'You mean I might die before it becomes available?'

'Conceivably, yes. But we aren't in that situation yet are we? Your donor, I'm sure will be OK judging on the earlier tests.'

'Assuming that he is suitable, what can I expect after the operation?'

'Well, you're likely to experience a few challenges. It is a major operation after all. Your body has to cope with what it sees as a foreign object. The immune suppressants that you will have to be taking, potentially for the rest of your life, can cause side effects.'

'Such as?'

'In the worst case scenario it can cause high blood pressure, tremor, mood swings, occasionally mental health issues, weakness and weight gain to mention a few.'

'God, what am I letting myself in for?'

'To put it bluntly, the alternative is that you die. I appreciate it's a stark choice but you might be lucky and not have any side effects at all.'

'So what's the sequence? What happens during surgery?'

'Firstly we conduct the donor operation to ensure that the liver is healthy and suitable for transplant.'

'Right.'

'If OK, we remove part of their liver, it's called a lobe. Then we remove your diseased liver and transplant the donor lobe into your body.'

'Ok, I understand that, but will he be alright after the operation with part of his liver missing?' James asked, wondering whether he was asking too much of Tim.

'Yes, he should have no problems. The liver regenerates itself very quickly. So he will have normal function within a month of the operation, if not before.'

'How long am I going to be...'

'In hospital? Probably for two to three weeks, depending on how you cope with the operation.

You will be in the critical care ward for two to three days and then moved to a normal ward.'

'Critical care?'

'Yes. That's when we have someone with you day and night. You'll be on a ventilator and fed by a tube down your nose. If all is well, we'll take them out after a couple of days though.'

'How long will it take for me to get back to normal?'

'We're talking anything between three to six months during which time we'll keep an eye on you as an outpatient.'

'Ok thanks,' James said mechanically, his imagination already creating negative images fired by the detail of the proposed operative procedures.

'Right. We'll schedule the operation as soon as possible. But you have to realise, although you have a living donor, we still have to fit you into a schedule.'

'Yes, thanks.'

James left the hospital in a daze. He decided he could do with a drink to make him feel better. The temptation was so strong. Just one. Surely that wouldn't harm? Especially as he was getting rid of his damaged liver anyway.

CHAPTER THIRTY FOUR

Carrie really didn't have her mind on the task in hand. She had done one walk for service veterans by herself and cancelled another one for the general public.

So she decided to 'potter' in the office and looking at her Facebook account she found another message from the mysterious veteran.

SWS;

Sorry I was unable to join you on any hikes. But I am having a bad time at the moment with flashbacks. Thanks for your suggestion of joining a walk with others but I'm afraid walking in a group would remind me too much of a patrol that I was on when we lost two of my mates to IEDs. I understand why you are reluctant to do a One to One, but could you possibly reconsider doing it for me? I understand you were out there too and will understand what I'm going through. Please help me.

So in spite of what Tim had said about the financial viability of doing 'One to One' walks, Carrie decided she would go ahead and do it anyway. Here was a buddy asking for help. Tim wouldn't understand the unwritten bond that linked service people. She duly composed a reply:-

Carrie JDIW;

Sorry to hear about your mates. I, too, lost some very good friends as well as being blown up myself. OK, if you would prefer, I will do a 'one to one' walk for you; but I strongly recommend that you eventually need to start walking with others. Most have suffered like us, indeed I'm still undergoing treatment myself for PTSD.

Let me know your availability and I'll try and find a mutually convenient slot in the diary. Take Care.

'Anyway,' she rationalised, 'Tim isn't here to see what I'm doing. As far as I know he might never come back and I'll have to carry on the business by myself.'

Another worry for her was that the walking company bills were mounting and the cash flow was tight.

'Should I have words with Andy about the transfer of money from Tim's account into the business?' she wondered. 'Andy is supposed to be overseeing the projects. No,' she decided. 'That will only antagonise Tim even more.'

She had just sent the Facebook message off as the office door opened behind her.

'Tim?' she wondered, hopefully. But decided not to look and show him how much she'd missed him. No she was going to play it cool.

'Oh, this is looking very professional,' the voice said, admiring the precision and presentation of the brochures and maps lining the walls.

'I recognise that voice. Hello James. Thanks,' she said, swivelling her chair round to face him.

Carrie was shocked to see the substantial change in his pallor. James was not looking at all well. His condition had deteriorated significantly since she'd said goodbye to him on their return from Monaco.

'Not back yet then?' he said looking around.

'No, sorry James. I haven't heard from him either. His phone is still switched off.'

'Never mind. There's still time,' he said optimistically.

'Time?'

'You know, for him to come back to donate... for the liver transplant.'

'Oh yes. Sorry James, I had forgotten all about that.'

'Well that's perfectly understandable. You've got a lot on your mind at the moment. How are you getting on?'

'A bit down, you know.' Carrie volunteered.

Unsure what to say, he asked awkwardly. 'Can I make you a cup of tea?'

'No, let me make you one. Why don't you take a seat.'

'Thanks,' James said, sitting in Tim's vacant seat.

'Yes, a brew is always welcome anytime,' she said, clicking the kettle on.

'You don't think that Tim has changed his mind about...you know...donating his liver do you?' he asked awkwardly.

'I hope not,' Carrie said, failing to appreciate that a less than affirmative answer would cause James great anxiety.

James' spirits plummeted at her pessimistic reply, his face telegraphed his mood. He was crestfallen.

Seeing his reaction she quickly added, 'Well actually. No. I'm sure he hasn't.'

'Perhaps I should have stayed in Monaco when he asked me to.' James reflected. 'I could have given him an insight into the pit falls of gambling there.'

'No. You did the right thing backing us up.'

'I can understand...you know... if he has...changed his mind. I mean he's putting his own health at risk too by having the major operation. He's already been through a lot...what with the loss of his legs.'

'That was a long time ago though,' Carrie clarified. 'He probably never thinks about that now. No, I think he will come to his senses and will be back in time.'

'Yes, I'm sure he will. You're right of course.'

James hoped her optimism was well founded as he was starting to pass blood in his stools. Not a good sign.

CHAPTER THIRTY FIVE

Having spent nearly two weeks gambling and losing heavily in various Casinos, Tim finally came to his senses, chartered a plane and flew home.

Although he tried to convince himself that some of his lavish spending went on some very expensive hotel bills, in reality he had lost the majority at the tables. He was unsure what the overall bill for the self-indulgent two weeks was, but he estimated it to be in the order of half a million pounds. He shuddered at the thought of his extravagance and knew he would be hard pressed to explain his foolish spending to Carrie.

Consequently when the taxi arrived at the Gloucestershire airport to pick him up he directed the driver to take him to the five star Green Leaf hotel at the foot of the Cotswold escarpment rather than go home.

Eventually, after kicking his heels for a few days in the luxury 16th Century Elizabethan Manor house hotel, he decided to face the music and get in touch with his partner, Carrie.

He turned on his mobile for the first time since Monaco, when he'd given her the good news of his large inheritance.

His voicemail immediately alerted him to ten messages.

All but one had been left by Carrie, her messages getting more and more desperate as the days went on.

She had finally given up, obviously in great distress, several days before he switched his phone on again. Her last message was desperately heartbreaking. *'Tim, I am beside myself with worry. I can't sleep for fretting about you. 'Please, please just let me know that you're safe. I miss you so much it hurts.'* He heard her crying as she hung up.

The other message was left by Kay, his Mother, telling him to sort his life out. *'Tim, I don't know what you're up to but you have a lovely girl who is beside herself with worry. For God's sake get a grip and come home.'*

He rang Carrie's mobile and was answered instantly.

'Tim, Tim where are you? Are you OK?' she said in a rush.

'Yes…I'm nearby. Umm, do you want to come and see me?'

'Yes, yes of course. Tell me where you are and I'll come straight away.'

Tim told her which hotel he was staying at and paced up and down in the reception area until he saw the Walking Company minibus pull into the hotel car park.

It had barely stopped before Carrie was out and heading in his direction.

He walked down the hotel steps and into the car park towards her, looking to gauge her mood. He was shocked to see how tired she looked. Her hair was dishevelled, she had dark bags under her eyes.

She stopped three feet from him and looked deep into his eyes.

'Hi,' she croaked, her voice tired.

'Hi. Umm...do you want to come in for a coffee?' he asked, awkwardly.

'Coffee! Is that all you can say?'

'Well...I...umm.'

'By all rights, I should slap your face for being such a selfish bastard.'

'Yes I know and I'd deserve it,' he admitted.

'Well, how did it go? Did you win a fortune?' she demanded.

'No...I lost,' he mumbled, looking at the floor.'

'Is there any money left?' she demanded.

'Yes, of course,' he replied indignantly, hurt that she would think he'd be so rash as to squander all five million.

'How much did you lose?' she continued.

'Look, why don't you come in and we'll have that coffee?'

'Don't change the subject. How much did you lose?' she persisted.

'It's my money. I can do what the hell I like with it,' he said angrily. 'It's nothing to do with you.'

'No, you're right. It's nothing to do with me, unless you're jeopardising the walking company that we've worked so hard to set up. Which, you might recall, is the reason that you were able to get your hands on your legacy.'

'Carrie...look...I...'

'You what?'

'Oh nothing. Forget it.'

'So is that it? You disappear for several weeks and you think that's OK. It's nothing. Do you know what you have done to us?'

'So is there still an 'us' then?' he asked awkwardly.

'Why do you think I'm here, if I thought it was over.'

Tim moved towards her, he wanted desperately to hold her. To feel her soft body against his. For her to tell him he was forgiven.

Instead she backed away.

'Well perhaps I was wrong,' Carrie said tersely, 'because if you're not man enough to tell me. Then you can forget us. It's best we go our separate ways.'

'Half a million,' he croaked.

'Sorry, I didn't quite catch that,' she said sternly, knowing exactly what he'd said, but wanting him to repeat it, making him confess the scale of his stupidity and to humiliate himself.

'I won a lot and lost a lot,' he mumbled unhappily.

'How much?' she demanded again.

'Half a million.'

'Jesus, Tim. What the hell were you thinking of? Five hundred thousand pounds. Were you on drugs or just being stupid?'

'I got carried away.' Tim confessed, helplessly.

'I should think you did. The Casino obviously saw you coming.'

'I went into several to make sure they weren't cheating me.'

'I don't know what to say...I'm at a loss to understand why somebody would just throw all that money away. You might just as well have set fire to it.'

'It wasn't all losing. I won a lot too' he whined, hoping to sweeten the bitter pill of failure. 'You get a real buzz when you win. People congratulate you and there are smiles all around. You're the centre of attraction and...'

'Short lived though, wasn't it?' Carrie added, bursting his bubble of excitement. 'It's a mugs game and they saw you coming. Just think of all the good things you could have done with that money for some charities.'

'That was MY money,' he interjected, angrily. 'It was nothing to do with any bleeding charities.'

'You selfish bastard,' Carrie said finally. She turned on her heel and walked quickly back to the minibus.

Tim stood there for a second, mesmerised by her rebuff and watched her climb into the vehicle. This wasn't the reunion he had planned.

Shaking his head to break the spell of inactivity, he rushed over to the minibus as she fired up the engine.

'No Carrie, wait, please,' he pleaded.

Carrie dropped the driver's window.

'I didn't mean that,' Tim grovelled, 'I am just really pissed off with myself for losing all that money...and I...I've missed you.'

'You should have thought about that earlier.'

Carrie rammed the minibus into gear, revved the engine and steered around him, it's tyres squealing, leaving Tim in the middle of the empty car park open-mouthed.

She had not gone far before her anger quickly dissolved into tears.

'Stop it, you stupid bitch,' she berated herself. 'He's just not worth it. Forget him. Pull yourself together.'

But the pain in her chest meant her heart wasn't listening.

CHAPTER THIRTY SIX

Carrie drove back to the office struggling to see the road through her tears. Her throat hurt from her despair. The meeting with Tim hadn't gone the way she had planned. She castigated herself for letting her concern over the money get in the way of her need to be with Tim.

She unlocked the office door and sat in Tim's chair, stroking the arm rests to feel close to him.

'Come on, pull yourself together,' she told herself. 'Life goes on.'

She picked up the telephone and rang James.

He answered after the third ring.

'Hi, James.'

'Oh hello Carrie.'

'Good news, Tim's back.'

'Oh brilliant, thanks. Is he OK?' he asked, cautiously.

'He's in a bit of a foul mood at the moment, so I should leave it for a while if you're going to ring him,' she advised.

'Oh dear! Unfortunately I need to speak to him urgently. The hospital wants to do blood tests on us, so we need to make an appointment.' James revealed.

'OK. Well, best of luck.'

James rang Tim straight away. But an angry Tim rejected the first call. James called again. This time Tim reluctantly answered it.

'Yes,' he said bluntly.

'Hi Tim, it's me…umm…glad you're back home. I've just heard from the hospital. They want to do some tests on both of us before the operation. Umm… is that OK?'

'Why didn't you stay with me in Monaco? I lost half a million because of you,' Tim said vehemently.

'Oh heavens! No wonder Carrie was a bit short.'

'What's she been saying now?'

'Nothing. She just rang to tell me you were home. That's all.'

'That's a likely story. She's probably slagging me off.'

'No, she's not. Honest. So about these tests. How are you fixed for next week?'

'Sorry, I've had second thoughts,' Tim told him. 'I don't want to put myself through a lot of pain for a shit face that leaves me to lose a fortune.'

James' blood ran cold as he took in the implications of Tim's words.

'But I said I'd come back with you.' James stammered. 'It was just unfortunate that I couldn't stay with you in Monaco. Perhaps we can go back there after the operation?'

'Too late. You had your chance and you blew it.'

James' world collapsed. Tim had just sentenced him to death.

'Oh…OK,' he said hoarsely and devastated by Tim's decision, absentmindedly ended the call.

James sat there for a minute blankly staring at nothing and winced from a spasm of abdominal pain. It was almost as though his diseased liver had heard the conversation.

Then he decided that there was only one course of action open to him. Putting on his coat he went to the nearby Coop and bought himself two large bottles of cheap whisky.

'I might as well end it in alcoholic oblivion as carry on hoping for a miracle to happen. Tim has made his mind up. That's it. Finito!' he thought.

Carrie had also rung Andy to let him know that Tim was back.

'Oh, that's good. But you don't sound very happy about it.'

'We had a row. He has blown half a million quid gambling. Would you believe that? We need money in the walking company accounts because we're over-drawn. And he just throws money down the drain.'

'Perhaps I ought to speak to him. Where is he at the moment?'

'At the Green Leaf hotel. But he's on his mobile. Anyway, best of luck if you do. James was going to ring him too, said it was quite urgent.'

'Are you OK? Is there anything that we can do for you?'

'Not unless you can mend a broken heart. I'll just ring his Mum and let her know he's home.'

'OK, take care. I'm sure you'll sort things out.'

Carrie rang Kay to tell her of Tim's return.

'Kay speaking. Who's calling?'

'Kay, it's Carrie.'

'Oh, hi. How are you today? Do you feel better?'

'Well I did when I heard that Tim was home, until he told me he'd lost a fortune gambling.'

'Oh the silly idiot. I knew that would happen. Is he at your place? Can I speak to him?'

'No. He was too ashamed to face me. He's staying at a local hotel.'

'Have you seen him then?'

'Yes. We had an argument in the hotel car park.'

'Oh dear, I'm sorry to hear that. So what are you going to do?'

'It depends on him. I presume if the walking company folds then he will have to give his money back.'

'What about James and his operation?'

'Well he did threaten James that if he didn't stay with him in Monaco, he'd have second thoughts about donating his liver. I hope he isn't sticking to that threat.'

'I know he can be an arsehole sometimes but surely even he wouldn't sink to that level. Would he?'

'I don't know. He's in a hell of a mood at the moment. He might do.'

'Oh I hope not. Poor James. Tim is his only hope.'

'Yes I know.'

'Perhaps we ought to get Andy to talk some sense into Tim?'

'I think he's going to ring him anyway.'

'OK. Well don't get upsetting yourself about him. I'm sure things will turn out alright in the end.'

'I hope so,' Carrie said, ending the call.

Andy rang Tim's mobile. Tim looked at the caller id and was tempted to reject it, guessing that Carrie had alerted Andy to his return.

'Yes Andy?' his voice monosyllabic.

'Tim, nice to hear you're back. How's things?'

'I think you already know, if you've spoken to Carrie.'

'Yes I have. It sounds like lady luck deserted you didn't she?'

'You can say that again. If James had stayed, it might have turned out differently.'

'I shouldn't bank on it. Remember he lost all his money gambling too. Are you still OK with this transplant thing? James is now very ill. His symptoms are getting worse every day.'

'I...err...well actually no,' he confessed awkwardly.

'What do you mean? You're not comfortable with it or you're not going to go through with it?'

'I'm not going to go through with it.'

'Oh. That's not good. Sorry to sound melodramatic but you've probably sentenced him to death.'

'He's going to die anyway,' Tim added, dispassionately

'I can't believe you said that.'

'Well that's the truth isn't?'

'Yes but you gave him hope. And now you've smashed that to smithereens. Does he know?'

'Yes. I just spoke to him.'

'How did he take it?'

'That's a stupid question. How do you suppose he took it?'

'And you feel OK about that do you?' Andy probed.

'No. Not really. But he brought it on himself,' Tim said firmly.

'How do you fathom that out?'

'It was his fault I lost half a million.'

'No Tim. The only person to blame is the bloke who looks at you from the mirror.' Andy said tersely. 'James said he'd come back another time, but you couldn't wait could you? You were like a sulky spoilt kid. You wanted to do it there and then didn't you? Well, through your own impetuosity you got your comeuppance didn't you?' Andy said angrily.

'Don't lecture me. You sound like my bleeding Mother.' Tim shouted.

'It's about time you took responsibility for the repercussions' of your own actions.' Andy continued.

'Yeah, but I...' Tim tried to interrupt.

'And consider this,' Andy lectured, 'if you're going to take that course of action, you've got a big problem with your legacy.'

'Why? What do you mean? I've already got the money in my bank account. Well what's left of it, that is.'

'You heard Geoffery say that I had to ensure you all did what you promised to do?'

'So?'

'Well, you're reneging on the terms of receiving the legacy on two counts. One. You're not supporting the Walking Company and Two. Not doing something for your fellow man. i.e. James.'

'You can't touch my money.'

'I can instruct the Law firm to sue you for breach of contract.'

'What contract? We haven't got a contract.'

'Remember the form you signed in Monaco before we left? Tut, tut. Clearly you didn't read what you were signing.'

'This is blackmail.'

'No. This is a safety net that Geoffery built into the legacy process to guard against things like this happening. He obviously knew you better than you thought.'

'Bloody money has brought me nothing but grief.'

'Correction. Your own greed has brought this on you. So are we clear then? You either put much needed funds into the Walking Company bank account and go ahead with the liver transplant or you lose everything. It's your choice.'

'I guess I've got no option.' Tim admitted, sullenly.

'Yes you have two options. You can revert to being a miserable self-centred prick with no money. Or you can become a generous well respected benefactor. When you've got over your self-indulgent pity, you might also like to recognise that you are close to losing something even more precious.'

'What?'

'Carrie's love.'

'She doesn't love me. She stormed out of here and wouldn't let me explain.'

'Then you need to do some bridge building before you lose her altogether.'

'How?'

'By getting off your self-pitying arse and going to see her. And ask for forgiveness.'

'I'll think about it.'

'Don't think too long. Otherwise, it will be too late for both James and Carrie. Goodbye Tim.'

Andy hung up. He was annoyed with Geoffery that he had to continue to deal with the petulant Tim and angry that the money had already caused problems.

'God what's next? My divorce?

CHAPTER THIRTY SEVEN

Andy 'fired up' the white Mercedes and drove out of the estate. He was irritated by Tim's cavalier attitude and had decided to see Carrie to work out a strategy for getting the money from Tim.

The horrendous volume of traffic did nothing to lift his mood as he made his way in the sleek motor to the 'Just Do It' office.

At least the stop go traffic gave him time to think of an angle to persuade Tim to change his mind, somehow he had to ensure that the money would get in the walking company accounts. But how?

Although he was annoyed that Tim appeared to be going back on his promise to be an altruistic donor, donating his liver to James was a different matter altogether. This was a personal and potentially risky thing to do. And at the end of the day, only Tim could make that decision.

Finally, having come to no clear strategy, he pulled into the small business park and parked his car in the reserved JDIW customer parking place.

As he got out, a taxi pulled up next to him. Much to his surprise a sour faced Tim got out and thrust a handful of notes at the startled taxi driver who seemed delighted by the amount.

'Come to bankrupt me have you?' Tim demanded, standing uncomfortably close to Andy, invading his personal space.

'No I've come to help sort your mess out,' Andy replied, locking his car.

'I'm quite capable of…'

'Messing things up,' Andy interjected.

Andy led the way to the office. They walked in single file in silence.

Carrie, who was updating a wall calendar turned as they entered.

'Oh hello, what do you two want?' she asked, suspiciously moving towards her desk.

'Well I came to help you sort out the problems this man is creating for you,' Andy said, grabbing a chair and sitting down. 'Tim arrived at the same time as me. I don't know what he wants, but hopefully he's come to rectify things.'

'Tim?' Carrie asked, giving him a hard stare.

Tim stood next to the seated Andy. 'I…well. It's difficult with him here. We don't want to air our dirty washing in public do we?'

'He already knows most of it anyway. Sit down,' she commanded. 'We need to talk. It will be good to have Andy here to stop me throttling you,' Carrie said, sitting down herself.

Tim didn't move. 'You didn't give me a chance back at the hotel to say…say I was…sorry.'

'You're sorry? You're sorry? I've been out of my mind worrying about you…you selfish pig.

While you were having a good time over there playing the big I am, you didn't give a 'monkey's' about us, did you? As usual, you didn't think of anyone but yourself.' Carrie became animated, her angst causing her to breathe heavily. She banged the desk sending the meticulously arranged pens and paper clips into a disordered pile. 'You waste half a million pounds and all you can say is sorry?' she collapsed back into her chair.

'Well if James had stayed with me,' Tim whined.

'James came home because he is very ill.' Carrie informed him. 'He went against medical advice just to attend the will reading so you could get your grubby paws on the money. He didn't want to delay things for us or Jo's operation. He thought of other people, not like you, you selfish swine.'

'How was I to know? I thought he was being an ass' Tim pleaded in mitigation.

'No you're the ass. Feel good does it?' Carrie demanded, staring at him.

'So, are you still refusing to go ahead with the liver op then?' Andy interjected.

'What! What's this? You're not going to donate your...You heartless bastard. Get out of this office before I do something we'll all regret,' Carrie shrieked, jumping to her feet and staring menacingly at Tim.

Tim looked at the floor but didn't move.

'Did James ring you?' Carrie probed.

'Yes he rang me earlier. He said the hospital wanted to do some tests and when would I be available and...'

'And you said?'

'I said...I said I'd had second thoughts and I wouldn't do it.'

'Did you? Well you can jolly well get on that phone and ring him now and apologise.' She shrieked. 'This guy is dying. Do you understand that? Dying!' she thumped the desk and laboured the word to try to trigger his conscience. 'Without your liver, he's as good as dead. And of all the pathetic excuses you could come up with. *You won't do it because he didn't show you how to gamble.*' For Chrissake Tim, wake up to your responsibilities.

Andy, hold me back. I want to beat some sense into him,' Carrie pleaded.

'It's alright for you,' Tim added. 'You won't be having half your guts removed.'

'If I was compatible, I'd do it,' Carrie said looking intently at him. 'I didn't say I wouldn't be scared. But I'd do it because I was saving somebody's life.'

Tim turned away from her.

'Where do you think you're going?' Carrie screeched.

'Nowhere, I'm just trying to think. Just get off my back will you,' Tim demanded irritably.

Tim paced to and fro in the small office as the other two watched him trying to think of all the options open to him.

Finally he stopped pacing and looked her in the eyes.

'Alright…If I do it, will you…can we try and…make it up?'

She returned his gaze. 'Tim, you've wrung all the tender emotions out of me. I let you in to my heart once and you've ripped it apart. I don't want to go there again.'

'I'm sorry, I didn't realise. I…' Tim said sorrowfully, 'I'll make up for it. I'll…'

'I will stay for the business,' Carrie continued, 'and we'll see how things develop between us from there. That is, if you agree to get your act together. Is that a deal?'

'I suppose it's the best I can hope for,' Tim acknowledged begrudgingly.

'Right Tim, let's get you to comply with the terms of your contract,' Andy directed. 'First, phone James and secondly, let's get the money into the Walking company bank account.'

Tim stared at the phone and then at Andy. He had a great apprehension about the operation, he felt the knot of anxiety in his stomach returning. He looked at Carrie, the anger still visible on her cheeks.

Unsure what to say he lifted the receiver and dialled the number he knew well.

James' phone rang out for some time and was answered just before the voicemail was about to click in. A very depressed sounding James answered.

'Yes?'

'James...James it's me Tim.'

'Yes,' James replied flatly.

'Listen... I...errr...This Monaco thing. I didn't know about you having to get back for a hospital appointment. I thought you were being...you know, awkward. I'd had a bit of booze too so...Listen...look what I'm trying to say is...I'll go ahead with the operation. I'll donate part of my liver.'

'Do you mean that?' James asked suspiciously. 'You're not just saying that, because I can't take any more false hopes. I feel absolutely awful now.'

'No, this is genuine. Cross my heart.' Tim looked at Carrie, she gave him a faint smile and nod of approval.

'Thank you Tim.' There was no spark of joy in his voice. Clearly he had come to the end of his health tether.

'I'm sorry I messed you around. We'll go for those tests anytime you want. How about tomorrow?'

'Yeah, the sooner the better really. I'll ring the hospital and see if they can fit us in. I'll make the appointment and let you know. Thank you Tim. I owe you my life,' James said, rallying slightly.

'S'alright,' Tim croaked, filling up, suddenly realising the devastating impact of his proposed withdrawal from the operation 'Speak to you soon then.'

Tim ended the call, 'Shit. He sounded terrible.

Meanwhile, in his flat, James screwed the top back on the whisky bottle and poured the untouched glass of scotch down the sink.

'That was close,' he said, relieved that he'd resisted drinking the alcohol for as long as he had. Had he touched a drop, that would have been the downward spiral. He would have been removed from the transplant list and consigned himself to certain agonising death.

'Thank you Tim, I appreciate how hard that was for you to agree. But you really are the last chance he has.' Andy said, patting him on the shoulder.

'I'll do an instant money transfer to sort out the walking company finances.'

All this time Carrie had been studying Tim, her anger now abated. She was almost at the point where she liked him again.

The following day, Tim collected James and drove them to the Birmingham Liver Transplant Unit.

They were subjected to all the usual pre-operative tests and James was breathalysed too.

James heaved a sigh of relief, nobody knew how close he had been to drowning his sorrows in a bottle of whisky. Ironically he had nearly sabotaged his own liver transplant.

The consultant examined James thoroughly and confirmed his earlier diagnosis; that the transplant was now the only course of action open, to save his life.

Turning to Tim, he said. 'You'll recall our earlier discussions Mr Springfield about your operation. We are going to remove the left lobe of your liver. We normally only use the left lobe, the smaller of the two lobes, for children, but because Mr Charles is so slight, we believe this will be adequate for his continued survival.'

'What about me without the lobe thing?' Tim asked, seeking reassurance that he wasn't going to shorten his own life.

'Your liver will recover very quickly. We would expect it to regrow by 85% within the first week. You shouldn't notice any difference in your own health after the post-operative recovery period. You will be provided with a full dietary list of what you can and can't drink during that time.'

'OK. Thanks for that. But what about James?'

'Oh Mr Charles should be OK,' he said, looking at James to reassure him. 'The procedure is one I have conducted many times before. Basically, we have to remove his damaged liver and transplant the lobe from yourself into the gap.'

'Will it be OK? I mean, what about the rejection phases?' James asked, his mouth drying in trepidation.

'We anticipate that the anti-rejection medication will be quite effective. Don't worry. We have every hope for a successful outcome.'

'What's the long term looking like for him?' Tim asked the question James feared to ask.

'To be blunt, there are a fair few hurdles to overcome because we are suppressing his immune system. But the bottom line is, there is no other option open to us.

It is this transplant or nothing. The liver is too badly damaged and as you are experiencing, Mr Charles, this is causing you other associated problems.

'OK Doc, the sooner the better as far as I'm concerned,' James said quietly.

'As a result of a cancellation, I have you on my list for next week. Do you think you can keep going until then? the consultant said, trying to make light of it.

'I'll do my best,' said James hopefully.

CHAPTER THIRTY EIGHT

James was frightened. The visit to the liver transplant consultant had brought home the dire reality of his health issues.

The apprehension was making him extremely tense. If the operation and recovery went well, he would be able to get on with his life. However, if things went wrong...he could die.

Death was an outcome he tried not to think about. But even if the operation was successful, the recovery itself was going to call on all his mental stamina. And then of course there were the side effects of the drugs.

The simple freedom of going for walk or a drive in the countryside when he wanted, might disappear. The possible life changing consequences were getting to him. He needed some 'air' to calm himself down.

Consequently, he drove his car out of town and headed off for a drive around the Cotswolds, but due to a navigational mistake he ended up in a no through road at the end of a narrow lane.

He stopped the car and took in his surroundings. He had parked facing the large wrought iron entrance gates of a 17th Century manor house. Supporting the gates were two tall square limestone gate piers on top of which were carved urns, an apparent symbol of wealth.

Behind the gates the imposing two storey limestone building showed Tudor design influence and a round arched doorway enhanced with stylish architrave which would have impressed guests arriving for lavish banquets. Large mullioned windows gave natural light into the depths of the large building.

Close to the grand Country house he spotted an ancient church and feeling tired from driving and spiritually weak he decided that the 11th century church of St Mary Edgeworth might provide him with physical rest and a moral prop for his psyche.

But entry into the church was far from easy, for the porch entrance was protected by large floor to ceiling metal mesh gates used to stop birds flying into the ancient place of worship. Undaunted by the barrier, he eventually mastered the locking mechanism and entered, carefully closing the gate behind him.

Beyond the ancient oak church door, which was already open, he could see on the far wall a crucifix and a picture of what he assumed was Mary and at her side a small child.

Nearby he studied documentation referring to a 14th century stained glass window thought to be displaying the image of St Thomas a Beckett.

Fascinated by antiquity, he read about a miracle linked to the locale when an Edgeworth man, suffering from leprosy, was cured after he kissed the sepulchre of St. Thomas.

James thought, 'Perhaps there are such things as miracles after all, he hoped so, he felt he needed one himself.'

Although not particularly religious, he nevertheless slipped into a pew, clasped his hands together and said a quiet prayer, asking to be given strength to deal with his forthcoming ordeal.

After a few moments of quiet contemplation he left the church and made his way back through the ancient graveyard feeling rather light headed. 'Was this a sign?' he wondered.

As he stepped back on to the road, he spotted two mountain bikes coming towards him at speed, so he quickly stepped back on to the grass verge and waited for them to pass. Instead they pulled up in front of him. It was Ben and Janie.

'I thought I recognised the car,' Ben said, smiling.

'Hello Ben, Janie. Sorry I didn't recognise you. You all look the same with your helmet and sunglasses on. What are you doing out here?'

'It's one of our training rides for the Malvern race,' Ben said, removing his water bottle out of the bottle cage and taking a swig.

'We could ask you the same,' Janie ventured,

'Just having a ride round before I go in for my operation.'

'When you going in?' Ben asked, concerned.

'Tim and I went to Birmingham yesterday and they've got a cancelled slot in the schedule, so it's going to be next week.'

'Scary stuff, I bet you'll be glad when that's over,' Ben suggested.

'Yes, I will. Anyway, how is your back Ben?'

'Oh he keeps moaning about it,' Janie said quickly before Ben could reply.

'Yeah, well, it's alright for you. It just suddenly locks up.'

'That's your excuse for me matching your pace,' Janie added smirking.

'So your training is going OK then?'

'Yes it's nice and hilly around here. We need to build up our strength and stamina for the race.'

'James, you OK?'

'I feel a bit faint actually.'

'Quick sit down before you fall down,' Ben said getting off his bike and rushing towards the ashen faced James.

James started to sit as directed but his body gave out just before Ben could get to him and he collapsed backwards on to the grass.

'Oh God is he OK?' Janie asked, joining Ben.

'No I don't think so. Let's get him into the recovery position and we'll ring for help. Have you got your mobile?'

'No.'

'Damn, neither have I. I left mine at home charging.'

'I wonder if James has got his!'

'Yeah. Good thinking,' Ben said, starting to check James' pockets and eventually finding it in his trouser pocket.

Just as he pulled the phone out of James' pocket, two elderly ladies walking their dogs were passing by and saw what they thought was a robbery taking place.

'Oh my God, look at those young people. They've knocked that man out and they're robbing him. We should call the police,'

'Don't let them see us. They might attack us too.'

The two ladies quickly back tracked along their route and called the emergency services on their own mobile.

Meanwhile Ben was relieved to find that James' phone was not password protected and he telephoned for an ambulance.

'What's the name of this place Janie?'

'Edgeworth. We're by Edgeworth Manor.' Janie said re-checking the map.

'Ben repeated the information and hung up, turning his attention back to the prostrate James.

After a few minutes they heard the sound of a vehicle travelling very fast coming towards them, with an occasional blast of an emergency vehicle siren.

'Blimey, they were quick,' Janie said looking along the road. 'Oh, it's a Police car.'

'What they doing here? I asked for an ambulance.' Ben said, looking at the approaching car.

'Perhaps they got the message as well,' Janie suggested as the police car screeched to a halt in front of them. It was single crewed, the driver leapt out as soon it stopped.

'Right. What's going on here?' the policeman demanded looking at Ben who was still kneeling beside James.

'He's collapsed.' I've called for an ambulance.'

At that moment the dog walkers re-emerged and said, 'That's them officer. They were robbing him. Is he dead?'

'What!' Ben said incredulously.

'OK son. Step away from the man please,' the policeman ordered, reaching for his handcuffs from his equipment belt.

'He's my friend. He's collapsed. I've rung for an ambulance,' Ben said, ignoring the order to move.

'Move away and put your arms out,' the policeman repeated firmly, moving towards Ben.

'He's telling the truth,' Janie said. 'Our friend James has just collapsed.'

'See what I mean Janie, these coppers have got it in for me.'

'Ah now I recognise the face. Its Ben Bird isn't it? I might have guessed. Stand up or I'll …'

Just as he was reaching for his pepper spray a paramedic fast response vehicle arrived in a screech of tyres.

'See, I told you,' Ben said, still crouching by James.

The female paramedic was quickly by Ben's side.

'So what's the problem sweetheart?' she asked, quickly checking James' pulse. 'Do you know what happened?'

'Yes, he's waiting for a liver transplant. It's supposed to happen next week.'

'What's his name?'

'James.'

'James. James can you hear me,' she called loudly, gently shaking him.

James didn't respond. 'Ok. Well he certainly doesn't look too good, does he?' Quickly she checked his temperature and blood pressure and put on a fingertip pulse oximeter on his index finger to monitor his blood oxygen level and pulse rate.

Unhappy with what she was seeing, she said. 'Right, he needs to get to hospital straight away.'

She immediately radioed her control to confirm the need of an ambulance.

Meanwhile, the policeman had stepped away from James, Ben and the paramedic to talk to the dog walkers, but they had gone.

They had overheard the conversation with the paramedic and realised they had read the situation incorrectly and had wandered off very red-faced.

The ambulance wasn't long coming and James was quickly loaded into it.

'Where will they take him?' Ben quizzed the paramedic as she packed away her equipment.

'Gloucester Hospital, the A & E department.'

'OK thanks. I'll ring Andy and let him know,' Ben told Janie.

The policeman waited until the ambulance was leaving and apologised to Ben and Janie. 'Sorry about the misunderstanding, but I had a report of a robbery taking place and as I was in the area, I was tasked to come and sort it.'

'That's alright,' Ben replied, despondently. 'I'm used to being blamed for something I hadn't done.'

Ben called Andy and was fortunate to get him before he started his shift at the hospice.

'Hello James, 'Andy answered, the name appearing on his screen. 'Everything alright?'

'Andy, it's me Ben.'

'Ben! why aren't you using your own phone?'

'It's a long story, but we just bumped in to James up at ...what was the name of this place Janie?'

'Edgeworth.'

'Yeah, we're at Edgeworth and James has collapsed.'

'Have you called an ambulance?'

'Yes, he's on his way to Gloucester A & E now.'

'OK, I'll see if I can get some time off and go and see what's happening. Is he in a bad way?'

'Yeah, I think so.'

'Let's hope it's not a problem with his liver. He's not due for his transplant until next week. Are you two both OK?'

'Yeah, it looks like we arrived just at the right time.'

'Good for you. Now don't worry I'm sure he'll be alright. I'll call you when I've found out anything.'

'OK thanks.'

Ben hung up and he and Janie cut short their ride and headed for home fearing the worse for James.

CHAPTER THIRTY NINE

Following his collapse James was urgently assessed at Gloucester Royal hospital A & E department, where his condition was classified as critical.

Within hours he was airlifted by helicopter ambulance to the Birmingham Liver Transplant Unit. Time was critical, as James' condition worsened considerably threatening irreversible major organ failure.

Andy was unable to leave work immediately following Ben's call but as he neared the hospital he witnessed the helicopter taking off from the helipad, unaware that its passenger was James.

After feeding the street parking meter, he dashed over to the hospital and made enquiries at the reception desk only to be informed that James had been taken to Birmingham.

Coincidentally the consultant who had examined James arrived at the desk and took Andy aside into a relative's room nearby.

'I gather I've just missed my friend,' Andy said, sitting next to the Doctor.

'Yes. I'm afraid he is in a critical condition. We had to get him to the Liver Team as soon as possible, hence the helicopter.'

'But the transplant date is still a week away?'

'I'm afraid the Transplant Hepatologist had obviously been too optimistic in his assessment. Mr

Charles' sudden deterioration has taken us by surprise, unfortunately.'

'Presumably they'll operate as soon as possible?'

'Yes I'm afraid we're into emergency surgery now.'

'But what about his donor?'

'The transplant hospital will deal with that. I gather he has an altruistic donor?'

'Yes that's right. A sort of friend of his.'

'Well let's hope they get him to Birmingham in time.' The doctor's pager sounded. 'You'll excuse me,' the doctor said studying the screen of his bleeper.

'Yes, of course. I can see you're a busy man. Thanks for your help with James.'

Andy went back to his car wondering his best course of action. He wondered whether to ring Tim and warn him to expect a call, but decided that it might get in the way of a call from the Transplant Team. Instead he sent a text message.

'*Tim, James very ill. Expect a call from hospital to go urgently to Birmingham.*'

He tapped the send icon and waited for the recipient confirmation bleep, it didn't come.

'Damn, he's either out of range or he's got his phone off.'

He tried to re-send it with the same negative result.

He then rang Carrie's mobile which immediately diverted to voicemail. He tried the office number which cut into the answer machine, he left a brief message.

'*Carrie, Tim when you get this message call me urgently. James needs an urgent transplant now.*'

He rattled his brain to think of other places where Tim was likely to be. He rang Tim's mother, Kay.

'Kay. Is Tim there?'

'No. Has he gone off again?'

'No, it's James he's critically ill and needs the transplant urgently.'

'Oh dear. Poor James.'

'I've rung Carrie and the office with no success. If you speak to him get him to call me urgently.'

'OK. I hope James will be alright.'

'So do I, so do I.' Andy knew from experience that once major organ failure started it was usually a one way street. It was unlikely that they could reverse the damage.

In a final attempt to track Tim down he rang the Green Leaf hotel only to be told that Tim was no longer a guest there.

In the meantime, having been alerted to the crisis, the Birmingham based Transplant Team were also trying desperately to contact Tim. But, as Andy had experienced, Tim wasn't answering his phone, it kept reverting to his voicemail as did the 'Just Do It Walking Company' works mobile. These were the only two contact numbers the team had on file.

In desperation they called the Gloucestershire Police and explained the desperate nature of their quest. The police had no further contact details but sent a patrol car to the walking company offices. On arrival they found that the office was empty.

Andy too had decided to visit the offices, having already gone round to discover they were not at Carrie's house either.

He advised the Police of his own activities and reluctantly went back to work.

The Police made enquiries with other companies on the Business park and discovered that Tim and Carrie, had gone off in the walking company's minibus together, but nobody knew where.

Having updated their control with the lack of success the Police crew were instructed to go back on patrol and to keep an eye out for the liveried minibus.

The Police control duly informed the transplant team of the lack of success. In a desperate last ditch attempt the Transplant Team then asked the local radio station to put a 'life and death' appeal out for Tim to contact them urgently.

Then they sat back and waited.

All the while, time was running out for James.

Coincidentally, on nearby Cleeve Common, a small group of radio hams from the local Radio Amateur's Emergency Network, RAYNET, were doing some transmission path mapping for a forthcoming event.

One of the members was listening to the local radio station as he was driving his specially authorised 4 x 4 over the Common to his appointed radio 'mapping' location and heard the appeal on the local BBC radio station.

'Blimey, something must be up for them to put an appeal out on the radio.'

'I missed it. What were they saying?' his grey hair colleague asked.

'They're appealing for anybody who has seen a bloke called Tim Springfield. They think he's driving a minibus for a walking company.'

'What was the name of the company?'

'Was it, 'Just do It'…something like that?' the driver replied.

'I saw a white minibus in the quarry car park. I wonder if that's the one?'

'Might be worth checking out.'

The driver turned the vehicle around and went back to the quarry. As soon as they spotted the vehicle they confirmed that it was the walking company minibus. Unfortunately it was empty and there was nobody in sight.

'So the bloke they're after might be around here somewhere.'

'Better give control a call. With three of us positioned over the Common one of us might see him.'

'Glos Raynet 2 to Control, receiving over?'

'Go ahead Raynet 2.'

'Don't' know if you caught the local radio appeal for a guy they need to contact urgently. A bloke from a walking company. We've just spotted his minibus. So he might be around on the common.'

'Glos Raynet 3, relevant.'

'Go ahead Glos Raynet 3'

'Yes, Glos Raynet 3, I've just been watching a couple of people at the bottom of Postlip Warren. It looks like they're setting up an orienteering course or something. Over.'

'Control, Glos Raynet 2. I've just spoken to the radio station and apparently they've tried calling him but they're not getting any response from his mobile.'

'Glos Raynet 3, that's quite likely, it's a mobile black spot down there. I've been stationed down there before and it's useless for mobiles. What do they want him for? Did they say not to approach him?' Over.'

'No, they're talking about a life or death appeal.'

'Control, three; Any chance you could pop down there and check them out?'

'Yes, Roger. I knew this 4 X 4 would come into its own, one day. I'll give you a call when I've spoken to them. Glos Raynet 3 out.'

The 4 x 4 bounced its way cautiously down the steep rutted limestone track until he got to the pair.

'Excuse me. Sorry for bothering you. I'm looking for a Tim Springfield.'

'Yes,' Tim replied, walking over to the vehicle. 'That's me. What do you want? We've got permission from the Common Conservators to be here,' he added defensively.

'Don't know anything about that, but we've just heard on local radio that they appealing for you to contact them urgently. Apparently it's a matter of life or death.'

'Life or death?' Tim repeated, puzzled.

Carrie joined him. 'What's up?'

'Apparently, they're looking for me. It's a matter of life or death.'

'My phone hasn't rung.' Carrie looked at her mobile. 'I've got no signal. Has something happened to your Mum, I wonder?'

Tim quickly checked his too. 'No signal either.'

'I wonder if it's James,' Carrie suggested.

'His...our, operation isn't booked until next week.'

'Perhaps he's had a problem.'

'I'll let my control know that I've found you. What do you want to do?'

'Well as soon as I've got a signal...I get in touch with whoever wants me.'

'Would you like me to take you back up to your minibus?'

'Yes, that would be a good start, thanks.'

Carrie and Tim quickly gathered their stuff together and climbed into the 4 X 4.

'Control, this is Raynet 3, receiving over?'

'Yes go ahead, three.'

'I've found the gentleman and I'm taking him back to his minibus. He will call whoever wants him as soon as he has a signal on his mobile. Understood? Over.'

As the vehicle bounced its way back towards the minibus the Controller called back.

'Raynet 3, this is Control.'

'Go ahead.'

'I have just spoken to the Police. They are sending a helicopter to your location. Can you take the gentleman to the Golf course Clubhouse? They will pick him up from there. Over.'

'Yes understood. Over.'

'Blimey it must be something serious if they're sending a helicopter to get you,' Carrie said looking at Tim, who was now starting to look apprehensive.

'Hell yes.'

Coincidentally, both Tim and Carrie's mobile rang as they got back into signal range. Tim was first to get the message.

'It's the Birmingham Transplant hospital. James has collapsed and they need me there immediately. And I've got a text from Andy too.'

'Oh dear. Poor James,' Carrie whispered, grabbing Tim's hand. 'Are you OK?

Suddenly the gravity of what he had agreed to do hit Tim. 'Shit. I think so.'

At the hospice Andy was relieved to hear the beep of confirmation that Tim had at last got his text message. He just hoped he would be in time.

CHAPTER FORTY

As the blue and yellow police Eurocopter settled gently on to its skids on the hospital's rooftop helipad, the reality of what he was about to undergo suddenly hit home to Tim.

The change in the emotional pressure had been extreme, one minute he was enjoying the tranquillity of the Cotswolds and the next he was overwhelmed by this frantic and unexpected whirlwind of urgency.

His anxiety had 'ratcheted up' since his 'discovery' on the common by RAYNET.

He had been inundated by a stream of panicky 'life and death' messages and then the gusty wind conspired to making the helicopter pick-up difficult, the pilot had to make several attempts to land to get him on board. And then, in only his second time in a helicopter, he was subjected to a bumpy flight to Birmingham.

He felt so helpless and totally out of control.

The desperate urgency continued as Tim was whisked down from the roof to the transplant ward where the surgical team were waiting for him.

After changing out of his day clothes and undergoing preparatory checks, Tim was immediately prep'd for the operation. He was surprised that his blood pressure was acceptable as his hammering heart felt as if was going to beat itself out of his chest.

The medical team were, however, taken aback when he revealed his prosthetic legs.

'There is no mention in your notes about any prosthesis,' the nurse preparing him said, re-checking the medical notes.

'Is that a problem?' Tim asked, hoping that he wouldn't have to undergo the operation after all.

'No, it's not a problem, unless there is undeclared medication that you're taking.'

'No, nothing.'

'That's OK then.'

Tim's hopes were dashed. He was going to have to go through with it after all.

Meanwhile Carrie, who had had been unable to fly with him in the Police helicopter, returned home and got a bag of Tim's personal stuff together. She then drove round and collected a shocked Kay and was on her way to Birmingham within an hour.

When they arrived at the hospital they were directed to a ward where Tim was already gowned up and about to be taken to the theatre for his operation.

'How long will it take?' Carrie asked the nurse accompanying him.

'It normally takes about three to four hours,' she said, busily helping to manoeuvre his bed out of the ward.

'But they won't do James' operation until they've checked that my liver is OK to give him,' Tim added.

'I'm very proud of you Tim,' Kay said, tearfully holding his hand. 'Best of luck son.'

'I'll be here for you too. I love you,' Carrie said, surprising herself by her public declaration. It was the first time she'd expressed her feelings since giving him the 'cold-shoulder' for his gambling faux pas.

'I'm sorry. We have to go,' the nurse said gently, pushing the bed towards the operating theatre.

'Love you too,' Tim said, feeling scared, unable to grasp Carrie's renewed declaration of love for him.

Carrie and Kay waited until Tim was put into the lift then they went to try to find James.

After making their way through a labyrinth of corridors, following vague signs, they eventually found the intensive care ward where he had been taken on his arrival.

A kind faced nurse led them from the nursing station to his bed.

As they approached him, they were taken aback by how dreadful he looked. He was naked to the waist; camped on his chest was a multi-coloured medical octopus of wires and sensors.

They were shocked to see how painfully thin his body was, his bony frame showed through his jaundiced skin and his breathing was so shallow that at first they thought he was already dead but the heart monitor indicated he was still alive.

A doctor at his bedside was checking his condition.

'Is he going to be strong enough to undergo the operation?' Carrie asked, concerned.

At the sound of Carrie's voice James tried to open his eyes but it resulted only in a flutter behind his eyelids, as if he was dreaming in the REM phase of sleep.

'If he isn't strong enough, you need to stop Tim's operation, now,' Kay said urgently.

'It's going to be touch and go. But the transplant is his only chance now.' The Registrar advised them.

'Oh my God! What a dilemma,' Kay said, putting her arm around Carrie. 'I'm sure it'll be OK. He's in safe hands. They know what they're doing,' she said, looking at the Doctor for confirmation that her faith was well placed.

'I hope you're right Kay. Otherwise my poor Tim will go through the operation for nothing. I'm sorry I don't mean to sound callous.'

'No that's a perfectly understandable concern. But rest assured, we wouldn't be going ahead if we thought it was going to be unsuccessful.' The doctor assured her.

Carrie was having a crisis of conscience herself as they were ushered into the relative's waiting room.

'What if Tim dies? It will be my fault for pressurising him to undergo the operation,' she chided herself.

'Don't think like that. We need to be strong for both of them.' Kay said firmly.

'Yes, sorry.'

'Let's look on the bright side and be positive. Everything will be OK, right?'

'Yes…yes of course.'

As they entered the waiting room, Kay saw an opportunity to change the subject and get their minds off the operation.

'Oh this is nice,' she said, looking at their surroundings. 'I like the décor in here. It's very tasteful. Much better than the usual drab hospital waiting rooms that I've wasted many hours in. Isn't it?' Kay added.

'Yes. Yes it is.' Carrie said distantly, her thoughts still firmly immersed on the man she loved.

As she took in their surroundings, Carrie was relieved to see that they were the only occupants.

The room was light and airy and decorated in a restful pastel pink.

A small wooden table in the centre of the room held a pile of magazines, surprisingly new. Not the usual 'dog eared' collection.

Positioned around the walls were ten large wooden recliner chairs, each chair within easy reaching distance of the short centre table.

In one corner, a small drinks dispenser vended a variety of hot and cold drinks.

'I could murder a cup of tea,' Kay said, walking over to the machine and read the instructions. 'Do you want one Carrie?'

'Yes please, I'll have a black coffee.'

Kay busied herself with the machine as Carrie sat down.

After a few wrong selections, Kay finally produced the desired beverages and sat beside Carrie.

They started their vigil by foraging through the magazines, picking one up after another and absent-mindedly turning the pages without reading anything.

They punctuated their page turning by pacing around the table countless times and drinking endless cups of tea and coffee - anything to 'run the clock down'.

Considering Carrie's former service life and her ability to remain static for endless hours, she found this to be purgatory. It was the longest three and a half hours of her life.

Eventually the door opened and a theatre gowned surgeon stepped in.

Both of them stood and studied the visitor's face, trying to detect any signs of bad news that he might be delivering.

'Are you Tim Springfield's relatives?' he asked, quietly.

'Yes', they answered in unison.

'Well you'll be pleased to know that everything went according to the book. We took a small part of Mr Springfield's liver as planned and now he's in the Critical Care Unit.

'Can we see him?'

'Of course. He is still heavily sedated so don't expect any conversation. Don't be alarmed by what you see. He has wires and tubes plumbed in to him at the moment.'

'How long will he be...unconscious?' Carrie asked, wringing her hands.

'He will continue to be sedated for some hours yet. Perhaps even until tomorrow morning. But we will be monitoring him closely.

Then, we will wake him up by slowly withdrawing the sedation. When he's fully conscious and we're happy with his recovery, we'll move him onto a normal ward.'

'And what about James? ...Mr Charles. Is he strong enough to have his operation?' Carrie asked.

'Mr Charles is already in the operating theatre. As soon as we saw the excellent condition of the donor's liver, we had another team start his operation immediately.'

'Will they be alright?'

'Mr Springfield should be OK, but it's going to be a challenge for Mr Charles. Unfortunately, the level of toxins that have built up over a period of time has made him very poorly. We'll do our best. But it'll be down to him now.'

'Thank you doctor. We're very grateful.'

'My pleasure,' the surgeon said and left the relieved couple.

'Oh, thank God for that,' Kay said, hugging Carrie. 'He'll be OK I'm sure.'

'So what are you going to do now? Stay here or go home? Apparently they've got some relative's bedrooms here if we want to stay.'

'I'd like to be here when Tim comes round and James doesn't have anybody either really.'

'Yeah, me too and I suppose we could doze off in these recliners if we want.'

'Shall we go and see him?' Carrie said nervously.

'Of course.' Kay grabbed Carrie's hand. 'I don't like hospitals any longer, although it doesn't smell of disinfectant like it used to.' Kay said, leading them into the corridor.

'They don't bother me anymore,' Carrie said, looking for the signs to the CCU.

'I guess after your incident in Afghanistan you're used to all this hospital paraphernalia. But it's a long time since I used to travel back and forth to hospital after Tim's operation on his legs. I've put it all to the back of my mind.'

After walking through a maze of corridors they eventually found the CCU.

The pair were apprehensive as they were directed to see the unconscious patient.

Like James, Tim too was bare chested, lying in a bed linked up to various electronic gadgets. A tube up his nose, another down his throat, a catheter draining his urine and a cannula in his arm linked to several IV drips. On his abdomen a large sterile pad covered the operation site. They squeezed each other's hands as they gazed at him.

Like every other patient in the CCU, a nurse sat by his bedside monitoring him closely, watching him for any signs of distress. Nearby a doctor moved between patients constantly checking.

Occasionally alarms would sound and disturb the ordered calm of the unit. The buzzers galvanised practitioner activity around one patient or another.

They were reassured when they saw that Tim appeared to be peacefully asleep, his breathing normal, the heart monitor displaying regular peaks and troughs.

And, after a few minutes gazing at his unconscious form, they returned to the waiting room and 'clock watched' over the next four hours during James' surgery.

To break the boredom they occasionally wandered back and forth to see the unconscious Tim.

At last a surgeon came to see them.

'Are you waiting for news about James Charles?'

'Yes.'

'Well, everything went well. I think we were just in time. Although had we delayed an hour longer, the outcome would not have been so positive.

'You mean it might have been too late?' Kay observed unnecessarily.

'Yes. However, I'm pleased to say that the new liver is functioning well and performing properly. His jaundiced skin colour changed almost immediately the clamps were removed. The next few days are going to be critical while it gets rid of all the toxins that have built up in Mr Charles system.'

'Thank you Doctor,' Carrie said, shaking the surgeon's hand.

As the surgeon left, Kay made her way to the drinks dispenser. 'I think a cup of tea to celebrate is required and then perhaps we might be able to have a doze,' she said, manipulating the buttons on the machine.

'I don't think I'll ever sleep again with all this caffeine,' Carrie volunteered.

'Oh, I just remembered. I told Andy I'd let him know as soon as I heard anything about James.'

'I'll text him if you like,' Carrie said, taking her phone out of her pocket.

'Yes, you'll be quicker than me,' Kay admitted.' I prefer to actually speak to people. Not your fancy texting.'

Carrie chuckled at Kay's confession as she texted Andy.

'I gather Ben and his girlfriend were there when James collapsed and had to call the ambulance.' Kay continued.

'Well, Andy will be able to put Ben's mind at rest hopefully. Carrie added.

'Poor kid must be beside himself.'

'Anyway well done to Ben, I'm not so sure I'd have been able to cope at his age,' Kay admitted.

Carrie's phone bleeped, she quickly looked at it. 'Andy's got my message and says fingers crossed for both their recoveries.'

'Final trip to see Tim and James before we try and get some sleep?'

'Yes, why not.'

Together they headed off down the corridor, tired but happy from their long vigils.

CHAPTER FORTY ONE

Tim was moved out from Critical Care the following morning, having shown no signs of any problems after the liver lobe removal.

When Carrie and Kay went in to see him, they were surprised to see him sitting in a chair, still connected to wires and tubes.

'Blimey, they don't hang around do they? I thought you'd still be in bed,' Kay said surprised.

'No. They insist on getting you out as soon as possible. They reckon it aids a faster recovery.'

'Where's your legs?'

'Over there,' he said pointing. 'It was too difficult to fit my legs with all these tubes in. So they just lifted me out.'

'How do you feel Tim?' Carrie said, kneeling beside him and hugging him gently, whilst also desperately trying to avoid getting entangled with the tubes and wires.

'A bit sore. But the pain treatment seems to be doing its job OK.'

'Oh, good.'

'I think the worst part was when that sadist of a physiotherapist made me cough. He said it was to get rid of the anaesthetic out my lungs. Can you imagine it? I thought at any moment my stitches would burst and my entrails would pop out. God it hurt.'

'Yeah, they did exactly the same to me when …after my incident. Although I didn't have stitches in my guts,' Carrie said, squeezing Tim's hand gently.

'I'm glad to hear that my sacrifice wasn't in vain then, I gather that James survived the operation too.' Tim said.

'Yes, it was a bit touch and go as he was so ill. We've been to see him and he's holding his own, although the next few days are critical.'

'Yes.'

'Who was that lot who found us on the common?' Tim quizzed. 'I didn't understand who or what they were.'

'Raynet,' Carrie answered. 'I've done some exercises with some of them when I was in the army. They're radio Hams. They use their radios to supplement the rescue services comms.'

'What Tony Hancock and all that?' Tim added, flippantly.

'No, don't you let them hear you say that. This is all serious stuff. They've been going since some Amateurs used their radios to help rescue people in the1953 floods.' Carrie continued.

'Whoever they were, they were certainly in the right place at the right time, otherwise, I reckon, it would have been too late for James.' Kay observed.

'Yeah. It was a miracle that they found us.' Tim suggested.

'Somebody was looking after him that day.' Kay added.

After ten minutes they could see Tim was flagging. 'The nurse said we weren't to wear you out,' Carrie said, kissing him. 'See you later. Love you.'

'Love you too.' Tim said quietly.

'Well I don't know what you've done to him,' Kay said, as they headed for the car, 'I've never heard him so...so love struck.'

'Perhaps, it's the drugs he's on,' Carrie said, smiling joyfully feeling happy and relieved that at last things were starting to go right for them.

The following day, after school, Andy drove Ben and Beth to the Birmingham hospital to see James.

Ben had been upset by James sudden deterioration and the long hours waiting to hear progress reports following the operation. Consequently, he was looking forward to seeing him, to erase the mental image of the desperately ill James being loaded into the ambulance.

Although Beth disliked hospitals, Ben had persuaded her to go anyway.

James had spent an additional day and night in the CCU because he was gravely ill when they operated. But the transplant was working well.

'Hi James. You look a lot better than the last time I saw you. How are you?' Ben said, excited to see that James was awake.

'I'm fine,' he said, weakly. 'I believe I have to thank you once again for coming to my rescue Ben.'

'That's Ok. Janie helped too. But promise you won't do it again.'

'Well hopefully with my newly functioning liver, that sort of thing is past history.

'I've made you a 'Get Well' card.' Ben said, thrusting the card forward. 'I hope you don't laugh too much and split your stitches.'

James took the card and carefully opened the envelope.

'Now let's see what we have here. Oh it's a cartoon drawing. Yes it's a doctor. Ah, he has a brief case. Oh I see he's a transplant surgeon and he's asking his wife what's for dinner? '*Liver and onions*' she's said. '*I think I'll pass*' he says.'

James smiled, 'I daren't laugh, it hurts too much. But thank you Ben, I appreciate that,' and extended his hand and gave Ben a 'high five'.

James suddenly started shivering.

'Are you cold James?' Andy asked.

'I...feel a bit...strange, actually,' James replied.

'What's the matter with him?' Ben asked, concerned.

'It sometimes happens after major surgery,' the Critical Care nurse said.

But the shivering changed to uncontrolled shaking so the Nurse suggested they stepped outside while she called a doctor.

The emergency medical team were quickly by his bedside. 'It looks like he's got an infection,' the registrar quickly diagnosed. 'We need to get some antibiotics into him urgently. I think it's got in through the incision for the tube in his neck.'

Carefully he removed the suspect tube and connected an antibiotic drip to his cannula.

'Andy you're a nurse. What's going on?' Beth asked, horrified at seeing the drama unfold. The incident confirmed her dislike of hospitals and sick people.

'I'm not sure, but it could be some sort of infection. The doctors will treat it. They know what they're doing.'

'Could it kill him?' Ben asked, pointedly, his earlier elation now turning to dread.

'Let's hope not. Although, hospital acquired infections can be potentially fatal.'

'You mean like C-diff and MRSA?' Beth said, feeling uneasy.

'They're the ones we most commonly hear about, but there are others.'

'That's awful though isn't it? He's survived the operation and now he might die from an infection. Will he be alright Andy?' Ben said, crossing his fingers.

'It's difficult to say. The trouble is, he's on anti-rejection medication so his immune system is suppressed which makes him very susceptible to infection.'

'Blimey,' Beth said, starting to feel queasy.

'Whatever it is, it's going to set back his recovery from the operation.'

'Poor James.'

The Registrar came to see them.

'Are you Mr Charles relatives?'

'Friends.'

'OK. Well Mr Charles appears to have picked up a serious infection. We are giving him very strong medication and we will be sedating him again shortly. There is nothing you can do here. I suggest you go home and call for a progress update later.

Following his advice the trio left the hospital without going back to see James.

Fortunately, within a couple of days, James' infection was brought under control and when his condition stabilised he was moved into a normal ward next to Tim.

The consultant came with an entourage of other medical staff to see James. 'How do you feel now Mr Charles? You gave us quite a shock there.'

'A bit sore, but a lot better than I've felt for a long time.'

'Good, that's excellent news. Now over the next few weeks you will be a bit up and down. But don't be downhearted. Stick with it. The signs are looking good.'

'How long before I'm fully recovered?'

'I don't want to build your hopes up too soon. There's a long way to go yet for any certainty. We could be looking at anything between three to six months.'

'Thanks for your honesty. I'll do my best to make it three.'

'That's the way. We find that a positive mental attitude helps the healing process no end.'

Ben and Beth arrived again with Andy at the weekend to see the patients, only to find that Tim was packing his bag ready to go home.

'Wow that was a quick recovery,' Andy said, watching him stuffing the last bit into his small travel bag.

'Yeah. Always was a fast healer according to Mum. Anyway my op was minor compared to James. I got rid of a bit of my guts. Poor James has got to get used to having a bit of me inside him. Poor sod. Right that's it I'm off.'

'Tim, what can I say? Thank you just seems so inadequate for what you've done for me. I owe you my life. Thank you a million times.' James said, sandwiching the other's hand between his own before trying to give him a tearful hug.

But the drains and tubes, to which he was still attached, restricted his movement.

Embarrassed by James' show of emotion, Tim quickly said, 'Just do me a favour.'

'Anything.'

'Stay off the booze and look after my liver. I might need it myself one day.'

'Yes of course.'

'Good man. And one other thing.'

'Yes?'

'Keep doing the paperwork for the walking company, so I don't have to do it. That will be thanks enough,' Tim added.

Carrie bent and kissed James. 'Look after yourself. As Tim says, we need you back in the office shortly.'

A much relieved Tim followed Carrie out of the ward and carefully got in the passenger seat of their car and headed for home.

'Thank Christ that's over,' he said happily, as they drove out of the hospital car park.

'Well you did it Tim,' she said, glancing over at him. 'I'm proud of you.'

'Does that mean we're OK again?' Tim said hopefully, putting his hand on her thigh.

'Of course,' she said, taking her hand off the steering wheel and covering his hand with hers.

Tim had finally vindicated himself. He allowed himself a self-indulgent smile.

After saying their goodbyes to Tim and Carrie, Ben said anxiously, 'James you aren't going to give us any more frights are you?'

'Sorry Ben, I keep doing that to you, don't I?'

'Yes. Enough's enough now James,' Andy said smiling. 'I think he's passed his first aid badge now.'

They laughed.

Ben, Beth and Andy stayed with James for a short while after Tim had left but could see he was pretty exhausted by the effort to hold a conversation so they made their excuses and left.

As they walked back to Andy's car Ben said, 'See Mum. If you keep on drinking, that's how you'll end up too.'

Beth looked horrified and vowed, 'I'll never drink again if that's what happens to you.'

Sceptically Ben thought. 'If only.'

PART THREE

A new beginning

CHAPTER FORTY TWO

Tim had been home from hospital a week and was feeling well enough to go into the office. He was finishing off hike planning paperwork as Carrie returned home early to start preparing a special romantic meal for them now that their relationship had improved.

She had put her car keys on the hook in the hallway and was heading past the lounge door towards the kitchen when she stopped in her tracks.

Her heart froze. She did a double take hoping she was seeing things.

But there, lying on the floor was her precious miniature treasure chest.

Quickly she rushed into the lounge.

'Oh, my god, somebody's opened it,' she said as she knelt and picked it up gently, her hands shaking. The lid had clearly been prised open

This was the secure box where she 'imprisoned' her nightmares and bad thoughts, the method she used to control her PTSD episodes.

She was fearful at the possible consequences. All those bad thoughts were now loose, unconfined. It felt like some ethereal gunman was waiting to ambush her, pointing a blunderbuss of evil at her head. But she didn't know when or where he would strike.

She recalled the conversation with the Psychologist when she started using the 'box' technique.

'Just imagine you are putting your bad thoughts and dreams in the box. Once they are in there, then they will not come back to trouble you.

When you start using the technique you will feel better. And keeping the contents of the box locked away from your mind becomes easier and easier as you regain control over your imagination.

It's a one way trip. You will become reliant on it once you realise that it works.'

'But, what's to stop the bad thoughts coming back to hurt me?' she'd asked.

'You. You have to believe that once they are in there, they are gone forever. Do not think of them again.'

'But if I do?'

'If you stop believing in your ability to control them, conceivably they might 'escape' and cause you some significant psychological trauma.'

'What sort of problem?' she'd asked and was haunted by his response.

'Imagine disturbing a swarm of bees. What happens? They attack you. Psychologically this is what you might experience. It might lead to a breakdown.'

'The box was empty. The nightmares were loose. What would happen to her now?' she wondered, frightened. She closed the box lid quickly and illogically looked around, wild eyed, to see if she could see any bad thoughts.

There were no signs of a break-in. so Tim must have done it. That was the only explanation. Tim had been to outpatients for a regular check-up after the liver operation before he went to the office.

'He's been irritable since the operation. Perhaps the medication he is taking is making him paranoid,' she thought.

At that moment she heard the door open and Tim came in.

'Why did you damage my box?' she demanded, almost hysterically, walking aggressively towards him.

'Tim looked at her surprised by the pitch of her voice, I...errr.'

'Don't try to deny it. I know it was you.'

'I...I wanted to find out...' he cleared his throat, apprehension clamping his vocal chords. 'Umm...what the big mystery was about the box...and who you were two timing me with, while I was in Monaco.'

'Two timing!' she said in disbelief, her voice now falsetto. 'I wasn't two timing you. I told you the box was purely a metaphorical way of controlling my nightmares.'

'Yeah, but...'

'It's a coping mechanism that they recommended for managing my PTSD episodes. I thought you understood that.'

Tim looked shamefaced at her angry outburst.

'Well. Did you find what you were looking for?' she probed.

'No of course not,' he said, slumping heavily into a chair. 'There were a few pieces of paper that had some odd words on but nothing else.'

'Do you realise what you've done could have serious consequences on my mental well-being?'

'Oh don't talk a load of bullshit,' he shouted.

'Tim, I let you into my heart again. So why do you continue to hurt me? Why? Why do you need to do that?' The psychiatrist said that...'

'I don't want to hear any more of your mumbo jumbo.'

'Why are you such an arsehole?' she said, cradling the box protectively to her chest.

'Look, the lid's been off the box all day.' Tim pointed out. 'And nothing bad has happened to you, has it? You didn't even know it was open until now.'

'That's not the point. It might. The nightmares might come back. Don't you understand?'

'Hell, I understand what you've been through when you were in the services...and to be honest if it had been me, I would probably have topped myself by now. You are a strong person...when you go off on one of your episodes; it frightens the shit out of me.

I'm scared that you'll become a nutter and I will lose you altogether. Now do you understand? I guess what I'm getting around to saying is... I need you. There, now I've said it.'

Carrie looked at him in amazement. 'You need me?' she said, unsure that she heard correctly.

'You heard, I can't say it again,' he said, looking embarrassed.

Carrie put the box down and walked over to him. She looked deep into his eyes. He held her gaze. He was telling the truth.

'Why do you always have to make life difficult for me?' she said sitting on his lap.

'I don't know, I guess it just happens.'

'And so does this,' she said, planting her lips on his.

CHAPTER FORTY THREE

They say the path of true love never runs smooth but Carrie and Tim's emotional roller coaster was running very well, following the incident of Carrie's nightmare box.

The pair had become romantically closer. Tim had even bought Carrie a dozen red roses to apologise for upsetting her.

Both of them realised that they were worrying about each other. Carrie about Tim's recovery from the operation and Tim about Carrie's PTSD episodes.

Although he didn't want to say anything to her, Tim had noticed the frequency of her disturbed nights had dropped dramatically since the Scouts night hike.

Consequently, as they'd had their minds on other each other, they had not been servicing the walking company email regularly.

So when Carrie logged into her computer she saw that there was a week old notification for her from Facebook.

She clicked on the link and saw that it was a message from the Veteran. 'Christ I forgot about this guy, I see they haven't given up.'

SWS;

Thank you for your understanding about my desire not to walk in a group of strangers. I appreciate you

*have commercial targets to meet, but at the moment
I am a bit down on my luck. However I will pay for
your services. My diary is a bit difficult to predict at the
moment, so please come up with a date and I will see if
I'm available. Of course I'll give you directions. I would
prefer to do a late evening walk, when it's dark. I don't
like being seen as I'm camped on private grounds.*

'I suppose I can still do this one by myself. So she
scanned her schedule and chose a suitable date and
replied.

Carrie JDIW
*That's an unusual request to do a night hike but
I don't want to compromise your hiding place, so happy
to comply. I suggest 20th August at 2200hrs. Hope
that's OK. Please send me directions. A grid reference or
postcode would be helpful. Looking forward to walking
with you.*

Carrie sent the Facebook message and continued with
other paperwork when the phone rang,
'Just Do It Walking. Carrie speaking. How may
I help?'
'Carrie, it's Andy.'
'Hello Andy. Want to book your Scouts in for a
walk?'
'No thanks. We couldn't afford it.'
'I could do you preferential rates.'
'As tempting as it is, the answer's still no. Anyway
I've rung to tell you that that awful woman is being
sentenced at Crown Court tomorrow. Did you and Tim
want to come and cheer for when she's incarcerated?'

'No. Sorry Andy. As much as I'd love to see her 'banged up', we've just got so much to do here. But give her my love, I don't think.' She added sarcastically.

'Oh that's a pity. But never mind. Rupert and I are going, so we'll let you know what sentence she gets.'

'The longer the better. For everybody's sake.'

'Hurrah to that,' Andy said enthusiastically.

'Incidentally, as we didn't have a chance to chat at the hospital, presumably Ben is OK now after the night hike incident?' Carrie enquired.

'Yes, he's resumed training for the bike race. But he's still complaining about his back.'

'I hope he'll be fit enough. He'll be really disappointed if he isn't.'

'He's been looking forward to the competition at Eastnor for months now. James and I have heard nothing else from him.'

'He's a nice kid. He deserves to do well. Hopefully win.'

'It's thanks to you that he's around to enter it, let alone contemplate winning.'

'Well I wasn't expecting to have to use my service training for battlefield response though on a scout night hike.'

'Clearly your quick action saved his life.'

'Well in the heat of battle you have to be able to think on your feet. Although in this case, I had to think on my bum. That boar put me down on my ass.'

Andy chuckled. 'But were you OK? The impact must have bruised your thighs.'

'They were a bit sore for a few days, but as expected, my prosthetics were completely wrecked.'

'Did you have any problems getting them replaced?'

'The workshop who normally repair them wouldn't believe I'd had an encounter with a wild boar. They had to bin them.'

'It's just as well they were artificial otherwise you would have lost a leg for real I reckon. That sow was a bit steamed up wasn't she?'

'Yeah, I don't think Ben will be trying to rescue anymore injured piglets for a while.'

'Incidentally how was your Sunday roast?'

'Very nice, thanks. The freezer is well stocked. We'll be having wild boar dinners for a few weeks yet. These survival course techniques certainly come in handy.

Anyway I must get back to the paperwork. Ask the Judge to lock her away for life.'

'Fraid there's no chance of that, but at least Rupert will have some peace of mind for some time, knowing she'll be locked up.'

CHAPTER FORTY FOUR

The white van was travelling at 80 mph as it headed north up the M5, the passengers on board had been subjected to an uncomfortable ride as the driver ignored the speed limit and wove in and out of the rush hour traffic.

'You went to a lap dancing club? The driver said looking at his mate half in admiration and half in disbelief. 'You never did!'

'Yes I did, and paid forty quid for the pleasure of admiring a young lady at close quarters.'

'You mean her close quarters? Why you dirty little sod. Wait til I tell the others.'

The driver was stunned by his mate's revelation. This was the guy who wouldn't normally say 'boo to a goose'. And now his mild mannered mate was boasting of going to a seedy lap dancing club.

'Go on, you're having me on,' he added, calling the others bluff.

Wanting to prove the validity of his risqué adventure and improve his 'street cred', the driver's mate dug into his pocket and presented the tickets to the driver.

'Here look, if you don't believe me,' he said.

Just then a VW Passat joining the motorway shot down the slip road and dived straight out into the inside lane and into the path of the speeding prison van.

The driver, who was checking the validity of his mates lap dance club tickets didn't see the speeding car until alerted by his companion shouting a warning.

'Look out.' But the warning came too late.

The prison van 'clipped' the back of the Passat and the van driver's reaction over compensated putting his speeding vehicle into an unrecoverable 'tank slapper'.

The swaying vehicle went into a high speed sideways skid. As the tyres on the offside gripped the tarmac, the unstabilised van went beyond its centre of gravity and toppled with a heavy impact onto its side.

The mobile cells slid in a cacophony of noise along the motorway until the cab impacted heavily with the concrete wall separating north and southbound carriageways.

Cars and lorries following behind the van slammed on their brakes and skidded to a halt in clouds of tyre smoke. Drivers battled desperately to try to avoid colliding with each other and the overturned vehicle.

The occupants of the van were deafened by the scraping noise as it slid along the tarmac.

Bruised but not seriously injured, they started kicking at the doors in panic, banging on the walls, shouting to be let out. What if it caught fire? They were trapped. Locked in their cells. Unable to escape, claustrophobic fear replaced shock.

In the cab, the driver lay unconscious. His shocked mate suspended by his seat belt was desperately trying to release himself.

Within a few minutes other motorists caught up in the chaos, surrounded the cab fearing the worst, but were relieved to see the driver's mate struggling to get out. An off duty policeman, a veteran of many crashes, came armed with a big tyre lever and quickly assessed the situation.

Telling everybody to stand back, he started raining blows at the windscreen, eventually smashing his way into the crushed cab.

Stepping carefully inside, glass crunching under his feet, he released the seat belt suspending the driver's mate and carefully helped him out before turning his attention to the driver.

He was relieved to see that he was still breathing and as there were no signs of major bleeding, he knelt by the man just to keep an eye on him.

Within a short period he could hear the sirens of emergency service vehicles racing to the scene.

The shocked drivers mate stuck his head back into the cab. 'How is he?'

'It looks like he's just been knocked out. Hopefully nothing serious.'

'Thank Christ for that.'

'How do we release your passengers?' the policeman asked.

'Umm, let me think,' he said, clearly in shock. 'There's something about a security procedure I got to follow.'

'Bloody hell, it can't be that hard. Have you got keys? Is there a switch?' the policeman asked, exasperated by the vague response.

'You can't, unless there is a risk to life. They are not to be released,' the driver's mate recalled. 'I've got to call for a replacement vehicle.'

'How long is that likely to be?'

'Don't know. Probably an hour or so. The prisoners must stay in there until it arrives.'

'Don't be daft. They could be hurt.'

'Sorry. But that's what I've been told. Otherwise you could have cons escaping left right and centre.'

Just then a fast response paramedic arrived and stuck his head into the cab. 'Thanks goodness you're here,' the policeman said, standing up. 'Let me get out of your way. He's breathing OK, I can't see any signs of obvious injuries.'

'Thanks.'

'Now what's the story about your passengers?' the off duty policeman demanded

'They are not restrained and they might abscond. They are convicted prisoners on their way to court for sentencing.'

'Well that might be. But I have a duty to save lives. Let me have words with your control.'

All the time other ambulances and police cars were battling their way through the gridlocked traffic and arriving on scene.

Eventually, after a long debate with the Security firm's control, a paramedic was allowed to go into the back of the vehicle and assess the occupants for injuries, opening their cells one at a time, the additional police officers, standing guard while the paramedic did his assessments.

Sue was one of the occupants of the overturned vehicle. The irony of the crash escaped her. Here she was on the same motorway as the fatal crash which she had caused and for which she was now incarcerated.

She complained that she'd 'blacked out' in the crash after banging her head as the van tipped over, she also whinged that the incident had aggravated her neck injury which occurred in the original fatal motorway crash.

'We'll have to take you to A&E to check you out for concussion,' the paramedic said, gently putting a neck brace on her.

She was carefully removed from the van and loaded in to an ambulance, where in spite of her protestations; she was handcuffed to a policeman and taken to Cheltenham hospital A & E.

As a precaution it was decided that all the other occupants of the cells, each similarly accompanied by a policeman, should be checked over in hospital, so a fleet of ambulances took them to various hospitals as part of the major incident procedure.

Having been alerted to the RTC and a major incident having been declared the hospital security and medical staff were waiting for the casualties.

On arrival, the prisoners and escorts were chaperoned to an isolated area within the Accident and Emergency department.

A large team had been galvanised to treat the injured and a well-rehearsed process snapped into action.

The A &E consultant did a quick check of all of the patients as they arrived and insisted Sue's handcuffs were removed before she could be treated effectively.

Reluctantly, the policeman escorting her removed them and was invited to leave the cubicle while a nurse set about Sue's clothes with a pair of scissors. Sue protested vigorously as they were cut off.

'If you'd have asked, I could have taken them off myself rather than you ruining perfectly good clothes,' she moaned.

'I'm sorry, but we can't be too careful. You might have severe spinal injuries; the minimal amount of moving you around, the better.'

They covered her modesty with a blanket and the team gently turned her on her side while a doctor checked her spine carefully for any obvious signs of injury. Satisfied that there were no injuries to her back, she was helped into a gown while they checked her all over for any other injuries.

Satisfied that there were no signs of concussion either, the nursing staff left her in order to deal with other casualties from the crash.

In the next cubicle to hers, she could hear that one of her fellow prisoners was arguing with the medical staff and had become aggressive. The policeman and security team were having difficulties restraining him.

She listened with growing concern about the battle going on, hoping she wouldn't get embroiled in the fracas.

Eventually, she heard the policeman who had been stationed outside her cubicle, going to his colleague's assistance, leaving her unguarded.

Sue lay there for a while listening to the commotion and decided she didn't like the idea of spending several years locked up with violent criminals.

Instead, she assessed her chances of making a dash for freedom.

Peering around the cubicle curtains she could see that everyone was focussed on the battle going on next door.

So in spite of a throbbing head and severe neck ache, she decided that now was her chance to try to escape.

But first she needed something to wear as, thanks to the nurse with the scissors, her own clothes were useless rags. Clearly she couldn't wander the streets as she was, wearing only a gaping hospital gown.

She slipped out of her cubicle away from her noisy neighbour and made her way gingerly past a line of other curtained cubicles into a short empty corridor. She spotted a door labelled 'Private Staff only'. Her luck was in, it was partially open.

The keypad by the side of the door meant that normally access was protected by a key code but someone had failed to close the door properly.

She gently pushed the door and decided, if there was anyone inside, she would say she was looking for the toilet.

However she was in luck. There was no-one there. It was a cloakroom with several sets of women's clothes neatly hung on coat hangers.

She closed the door and quickly checked out the small room.

She spotted that some trusting soul had even left her handbag in there. Quickly she rummaged through it and found a purse. She would need money to help her escape. She took all the notes, an estimated £70 and put them on a chair while she turned her attention to the line of clothes.

None of the clothes were what she would normally wear but 'beggars can't be choosers,' she thought.

Mindful that at any minute someone might come in, she quickly chose a pair of black slacks that were slightly too long for her short legs and a white blouse from another hanger. A long brown coat from somebody else also went to complement her escape kit.

She slipped off the hospital gown and put on her new wardrobe, feeling uncomfortable without a bra and knickers underneath.

She took the cash from the chair, cautiously opened the door and peered out. The corridor was empty. She stepped out and looked for the exit signs.

'Damn,' she muttered, seeing the direction she needed to go.

Unfortunately the signs indicated that she would have to go past the cubicle where she had been examined.

'Oh well, here goes,' she said quietly, to reassure herself. She pulled the coat collar up and made her way towards the exit.

She was relieved to see that everyone was still focussed on the disturbance with the prisoner still shouting and struggling.

Clearly she still hadn't been missed, so she walked casually out of the entrance of the hospital in to the fresh air without being challenged. She had made it.

Sue was free.

CHAPTER FORTY FIVE

Rupert joined Andy outside Gloucester Crown court as agreed. The usual crowd of smokers littered the steps of the ancient court house as they made their way in.

Rupert was experiencing a mix of emotions; Pleasure at the thought of seeing Sue's face when she was incarcerated for many years. But apprehension that she would have found some way to manipulate the judiciary system to get a lesser sentence.

Rupert reflected on the build-up to today's sentencing, for the original hearing had been somewhat of a trial for him too.

It had taken him a long time to summon up the courage to attend court in the first place, let alone give evidence against her.

However, in the end, he was pleased with himself. He felt he had acquitted himself well. Especially when facing hostile questioning from the defence barrister.

Perhaps, as horrific as it was, the experience was what he needed to initiate a change to his personality. He felt he had become a stronger, more confident person. Certainly the responsibilities of fatherhood had broadened his horizons and kept him busy.

Since Sue had been remanded he'd felt able to relax a little, he wasn't constantly stressed wondering when she would reappear to make his life hell again. He found it difficult to explain to Jo about the gut wrenching terror he lived with during every waking hour, always fearful of Sue's sudden arrival. The dreadful anticipation of something else she would do to hurt him, physically or emotionally.

But Jo had been kind and understanding when he was on the verge of a nervous breakdown. That was where their relationship started after she found him blubbing in a meeting room at work. She had been his life saver. He owed so much to her for rescuing him from Sue's evil clutches.

But she too had fallen foul of Sue's demonic evil, the accident that Sue caused had robbed Jo of the ability to walk, but hopefully the American neurosurgeon could reverse her malevolence.

Perhaps after Jo's operation they could even emigrate to New Zealand, so Sue wouldn't blight their life ever again.

He felt sure that his considerable IT qualifications and experience would earn him sufficient points to put them quite high on the required skills list of the immigration ladder.

But as they waited in the crowded court corridor, prior to going to the public gallery, the black gowned Usher arrived and called an informal meeting.

'Could I have your attention please?' she called over the noisy hubbub. 'I have to inform you that the prison van bringing prisoners to court today has been involved in a crash on the motorway.'

Her audience gasped at her news.

'Although there are no fatalities, several prisoners and the guards had been injured and have been taken to hospital.' She continued. 'Consequently, the sentencing will be rescheduled for some time in the future. I have no further information for you, thank you.' And she walked away leaving the corridor filled with noisy concern.

'I hope Sue's hurt. I hope she suffers like she made Jo and I suffer. How ironic,' Rupert observed, 'that she has been involved in a crash on a motorway.'

'It certainly sounds as if she got a taste of her own medicine,' Andy said, smiling.

'I wouldn't put it past that, evil, conniving, bitch to somehow have caused it to get a lesser sentence,' Rupert said bitterly.

'Who knows? You might be right.'

'Oh well, no point hanging around here then,' Rupert said finally.

''Do you have to dash off anywhere?' Andy asked.

'No, I was expecting to be here all morning.' Rupert replied. 'Why'd you ask?'

'OK. In that case, how about going for a coffee then?'

'Yes, I suppose we might as well,' Rupert replied, feeling somewhat cheated that he wouldn't see Sue squirm at receiving a custodial sentence.

They went to a coffee shop in Gloucester Quays and in the end the pair extended the coffee break to include a lunchtime meal.

After the meal Rupert said his goodbyes to Andy. And, as he was in the vicinity, he decided he would pick up some of his clothes from his former marital home.

So it was not until the early afternoon that he drove to his old address.

As he turned the corner he nearly collided with a Police car which was driving slowly in the middle of the road going the opposite way.

'I suppose if I'd crashed in to him it would have been my fault.' Rupert thought to himself.

Thinking no more about it, he parked the car in the road outside his house and made his way along the short path to the familiar front door.

As he did so, he felt the anxiety returning. He experienced the familiar knot in the pit of his stomach again that he hadn't felt since the trial.

His imagination conjured up all the spectres of his former unhappy, painful relationship with Sue. This was her domain. He was frightened.

He stopped in his tracks, gazing at the front door, half expecting it to open and her face to appear haranguing him. He had endured so many years of abuse here.

His heart raced. He felt weak kneed. All the positive resolve that he had felt at the Court house had just drained away.

Finally, taking a deep breath, he forced himself to put his key in the lock and gingerly pushed the door open.

Initially, it resisted through lack of use and squeaked as it moved a fraction. The noise made him jump. Nothing happened. He chided himself for being so stupid.

He pushed it open further and was surprised not to feel the resistance from a mountain of junk mail blocking its movement. But there was none.

Perhaps Sue had frightened off the junk mail people too.

The house still smelt of her. Fear grabbed his bowels as he recalled the dreadful humiliating life that he used to have here. It was difficult to comprehend that it was now all a thing of the past. Just a passing nightmare. He closed the door behind him.

He took another deep breath and calmed himself. He summoned up his courage and bounded upstairs to their former bedroom. He opened the door with great apprehension, as if she might be there too.

But it was empty. No shouting or berating. Just an uninhabited room in its usual, ordered, house proud state. Another one of her many obsessions.

The bed was pristine. The pillows pumped up and in line. The duvet laid out inch perfect either side of the bed.

Her dressing table ordered. Everything symmetrically arranged. It was as though she had just popped out to do her shopping.

He went to the wardrobe and pulled open the door on his side expecting to see the familiar line of his suits and trousers. It was empty.

'What the...'he said under his breath. 'The bitch... she's got rid of my stuff.'

Behind him the floorboards creaked. He turned.

Sue was there, smirking. His heart froze. His mouth dried.

'The charity shop was very grateful for your clothes,' she said, leaning casually against the door frame.

'What the...what are you doing here? You're supposed to be in the hospital or in custody,' he said, stepping further away from her.

'Oh, I escaped and I needed some clothes and...well the Gods are really smiling on me today aren't they?

Escape from prison and an unexpected bonus to see you here too. I told you I would come and get you didn't I? And I always keep my word.' She smiled evilly.

Rupert stepped back into the corner of the room as he spotted the baseball bat in her hand.

'You thought you were being so brave didn't you? Standing up in court telling them all our secrets?

Look at you now. You haven't even got that bitch Carrie to protect you either, have you?

You'll regret ever setting her against me. I will deal with her later. Then I'll come back and you'll really suffer for what you've done.'

'How did you get in? I closed the door.'

'I always kept a spare back door key under a brick in the back garden,' she said, advancing menacingly towards him, patting the baseball bat against the palm of her other hand. 'I was here when you arrived.'

Summoning up his new found courage, Rupert moved towards her, surprising her.

'Oh, what's this? So you want to fight do you?' she said, ferociously swinging the bat at him at waist height. 'You think you're man enough do you?' she taunted.

Rupert stepped back to avoid the blow and tried to grab it as it whistled past his stomach, but failed.

Sue recovered from the unsuccessful attempt and changed tactics this time thrusting the wide end of the bat into his stomach instead. It connected just above his navel and winded him, forcing him backwards.

As he stumbled back he managed to grab the bat and held on tightly.

She tried to yank it out of his grip by twisting it around. But he was now determined that she wasn't going to get the better of him ever again.

For, he reminded himself, that he had changed. He was no longer her punch bag. He was going to stand up for himself.

They wrestled viciously for the ownership of the bat. She fought dirty and used her elbows, fists, head and teeth but finally Rupert prised it out of her hands and yanked it from her.

'Right, so now you've got it, what are you going to do with it? You haven't got the guts to hit me,' she goaded.

Rupert raised the bat over his shoulder.

'Go on, just try it,' she sneered, stepping towards him.

'I'm warning you,' Rupert said. 'Don't come any closer or I will.'

Out of the corner of his eye Rupert saw a Police car drive past. The penny dropped.

'So, that's why they were out there. They're looking for you, aren't they?' he said, flexing his arm.

'Even if they get me, they won't keep me inside. I shall stalk you forever.'

Much to Sue's surprise, Rupert brought the bat down and jabbed her in the chest with it, pushing her off balance. She sat down painfully on to her bottom, jarring her already painful back.

'You stupid bastard, you'll regret that,' she said viciously and started to stand.

'Stay down there. You're going back to jail where you belong,' he said, a mixture of fear and exhilaration filling his head.

The adrenalin had dried his mouth. His heart was pounding and he had surprised himself, yet again. He had never hit anyone before, let alone her.

'The Police car will be back any second. They're closing in on you,' he said looking out the window.

Unfortunately his moment of distraction allowed Sue to deliver her usual male incapacitating 'coup de grace' as she lifted herself off the floor and kicked him in between the legs.

The effect was immediate. As Rupert yelped in agony, pain exploding in his stomach, he crumpled to the floor holding himself. She grabbed the bat and stood up.

'I told you not to be so disrespectful, didn't I? Now you'll regret it,' she said, swinging the bat from over her shoulder aiming at his head.

Through his tear filled eyes Rupert saw the blow coming and managed to jerk his head out of the way, just in time.

Sue continued to rain blows down at him, most of which he blocked with his forearms whilst desperately trying to grab the bat.

The frantic conflict continued with him squirming around the room on his back, dodging the line of blows until he stunned himself by banging his head against the bed base.

This gave her the opportunity to better target him. Fortunately for Rupert, in her excitement to finish him off she miscalculated the strike and only delivered a glancing blow. It was enough to render him unconscious.

'Got you, you pathetic excuse of a man. Now I'll send you back to your girlfriend so she won't recognise you.' Sue raised the bat again as the Police car stopped outside.

'Damn it. It'll have to wait. But you know I always keep my promises,' she said, stepping over his unconscious body. 'We'll meet again.'

Sue quickly made her way to the back door as the Policeman knocked on the front.

'There's a parked car outside but no sign of forced entry,' he said into his radio. 'There's no reply from the front door either. I can't get down the back because the side entry door appears to be locked and bolted. Have a look on Google maps to see what the back garden looks like.'

Sue knew the back way very well and knew that none of her neighbours would be home from work either. So she could make her escape unseen.

She picked up the bag that she'd prepared before Rupert arrived, containing clothes, a rarely used credit card and money from her hidden stash.

A sudden thought struck her as she was about to leave. She dashed back and picked up a hidden memory stick upon which was a copy of the compromising video and photos of Andy and Nadine.

'He'll regret not paying my ransom,' she thought, as she locked the door. Within moments she had disappeared off the scene.

CHAPTER FORTY SIX

After lunching with Rupert, Andy was home in time to
see Helen just setting off to pick Amy up from school.

'I'll come with you,' Andy said, unlocking the car.

'Please yourself,' Helen said coldly. His 'so called'
bumping into Nadine was still causing tensions in their
relationship.

'We'll drive there if you like,' he said.

'No.'

'Why not?'

'By the time we get the baby in the car we could have
walked there.'

'Please yourself.'

'Anyway we've got to try and keep the peace.'

'Peace! What do you mean?'

'The people living in the street next to the school are
moaning about the parking. The school has written to
all parents about it.'

'Oh I saw the letter on the side. I wondered what it
was all about. OK.' Andy said, locking the Mercedes.

Together they headed off towards the school, Helen
pushing baby Molly in the pushchair.

'Well. How did it go? How many years did she get?'

'She didn't.'

'What!' Helen stopped and looked at him. 'Surely
you don't mean she got away with it?'

'No. The prison van bringing her to court crashed and they've postponed the sentencing for some time in the future.'

'Was she hurt?'

'We don't know.'

'Anybody killed?

'No, we don't think there were any fatalities, but several prisoners and the guards were taken to hospital.

'Oh, that's a bit of a coincidence. There was something on the local radio about a prisoner escaping from the hospital, but I didn't hear it all. They didn't give out any details either.'

'I wonder if it's one of them from the prison van?'

'Well, let's hope it wasn't that woman.'

'No. That would really freak poor old Rupert out. Probably send him right over the edge, if it was her.'

'Well enough about him and her. What about us?' Helen said firmly. 'It's about time you started thinking of our family now that your involvement with the Godsons is nearly over.'

'I'm still going to work at the hospice, if that's what you mean?'

'Yes. So you keep saying. But you don't need to, do you? I mean, Geoffery was very generous. We've got a fair bit in the bank now and...'

'Yes, but it won't last long,' Andy reposted quickly.

'It's nearly ten years salary. What do you mean it won't last long?'

'Well you want to move to a new house don't you?' Andy reminded her.

'Yes. But it isn't going to take all the money.'

'No, but it'll take a significant amount.'

'I thought perhaps you could take some time off and be at home with us a bit more.' Helen suggested, looking at him to see his reaction.

'Yeah but…You know I love my job there. I feel that I'm in the right place.'

'What about being in the right place, at home, with us?' She quizzed.

'It's different.'

'How is it different?'

'It's a very special privilege to look after a dying person.' Andy explained quietly. 'Although I have to admit, no matter how you steel yourself for the inevitable, it sometimes breaks your heart when you lose a patient. To feel that you are doing something worthwhile is absolutely brilliant.' He added enthusiastically.

'Yes I know, and what about me bringing up our children?' Helen demanded.

'You're doing a great job too.' He said trying to placate her.

'But I need you to help me from time to time.'

'I do things when you ask me.'

'I shouldn't need to ask. You should know.' She reminded him.

Andy didn't say anything. He knew he was 'skating on thin ice'.

'What about spending time with us, your family?' Helen continued.

'It's somehow different. And you do a brilliant job for the girls.' He flattered. 'I'd only be in the way. Anyway, you aren't ill.'

Helen's angry look made him quickly reconsider his words.

'Yes I know you had a bad time recovering from the baby blues but...physically, I mean you don't have a medical condition. That's what I meant.' Andy grovelled.

'I think you'd better stop there before you dig yourself a bigger hole.' Helen said sternly. 'I still needed help though. Thank goodness for Kay's help.'

'Yes Kay was brilliant wasn't she?' Andy admitted.

'That's more than I can say for you.'

'I was there. I was keeping an eye on you.' He added in mitigation.

'Well it wasn't that sort of help I needed though, was it?'

Andy could see he was 'batting on a losing wicket' and went back to his original thoughts about his job at the hospice.

'I mean, people deserve a dignified and peaceful death and I only get one chance to get it right,' Andy continued passionately. 'You can't always understand what people are going through when they are dying, but I reckon I can 'walk' with them and support them on their journey.'

'How about supporting us, your family, on our journey?' Helen persisted.

'Don't belittle what I'm saying.' Andy snapped. 'We're talking about people near the end of their life. They obviously realise that I can't make them better, but at least I can give them a reasonable quality of life while they are here.'

'There's always an excuse isn't there. You've always got answer for everything. I don't know why I bother.' She added, resigned to not being able to change Andy's mind.

'Anyway, I've got to ensure that Geoffery's legacy to the hospice is correctly administered.'

'Why are you making excuses for not wanting to be with me...us?' She demanded.

'I'm not... it's just that...I'd be off my head in a few days if I wasn't at work.'

'Well thanks. Thanks very much.' She said, hurt by his insensitivity. 'My company would be that boring would it?'

'No that's not what I meant.'

'So what do you mean?'

'I'd miss all the excitement of work.'

'And I'd miss you coming home carrying the weight of the world on your shoulders when things aren't going well.' She pointed out.

'That's not fair.'

'Well, why don't you cut your hours to three days a week? You did when you were working for Geoffery.'

'Look, let's change the subject shall we?' Andy said battered by her constant demands.

'Would you prefer to talk about you and that Nadine in Monaco and the shame that you've brought on us all?' Helen said viciously.

'No.'

'I gave you a second chance when you came back shame-faced from the first trip. Then we had the newspaper story and then you have another fling with her under my very nose. Do you understand why I'm asking you to think about us for a change?' Andy noticed Helen's anger reflected by her white knuckled grip on the pushchair. 'You have to make your mind up.' She continued vehemently. 'It's either us or your job. It's your choice.'

Helen walked away from him leaving Andy gobsmacked. Then he noticed the school gate gossips pointing at him, giggling to each other as they arrived in the playground.

'God, this is a nightmare,' he thought, striding after Helen.

CHAPTER FORTY SEVEN

Rupert came round. His head was pounding. He couldn't focus his eyes. He couldn't get his bearings.

There was a loud banging. He couldn't understand where the noise was coming from.

He put his hands to his head and felt the large bump on the one side and something sticky on the other side.

As his sight returned he looked at the fingers that had touched the sticky stuff. It was blood. His blood.

Then his focus became clearer. He recognised the lampshade in the middle of the ceiling.

It all flooded back to him. He was in his old home.

'Oh my god,' he said under his breath. 'She's here.'

Anxiously he looked around expecting any minute to hear her voice shrieking at him and to see her evil leering face. He was fully expecting that she'd launch another attack with the baseball bat.

But nothing happened.

He heard the banging again. It was coming from downstairs.

Perhaps she was leaving. He had to move. His groin was hurting as he rolled over onto his knees. He couldn't lift his head, it was pounding so much.

The banging downstairs changed to a splintering noise and there was a lot of shouting and footsteps running upstairs and more shouting.

He felt a knee going into his back. He was forced flat and his face was pushed down to the carpet. Somebody was shouting at him.

He couldn't understand what they were saying. Something metal was being put on his wrists. It was cold.

Then there were more footsteps. Urgent footsteps. And then someone saying. 'All clear. She's not here. Although she has been, there are clothes, matching the description of the stolen ones, in a dustbin.'

'So she's definitely been here,' the voice holding him said.

Somebody was telling Rupert something and sitting him up. Pushing his back against the bed.

He could see the blue crash helmet. It had the word 'Police' written across the top of the visor. The man was wearing black body armour. Then he lifted the visor and shouted for a paramedic.

'OK fella, it's OK. We'll get somebody to sort your head out. That looks like a nasty gash you've got there.'

'Gash!' Rupert repeated trying to understand what the word meant.

'Where is she?'

Rupert's mind was still woozy.

'Where's who?'

'The woman who lives here? Williams Screen. She was spotted coming here.'

'I don't know. She hit me. Must have knocked me out.'

'That's a convenient story.'

'What, what do you mean? Story!' Rupert's head was pulsating. 'It's the truth,' he struggled to say.

'Who are you?'

Rupert thought about it for a minute. Things were starting to become clearer, the cotton wool filling his brain was vanishing.

'I'm unfortunate enough to be her husband.'

'Husband?' The officer said surprised.

'Yes. We're separated though,' Rupert added quickly.

'So what are you doing here?'

'It's my house.' Rupert said astonished at the question.

'Yes I appreciate it's your house.'

'I came to get some of my clothes.' Rupert explained.

'Not to help your wife escape?' The policeman suggested.

'No, of course not. Rupert replied indignantly. 'Why would I want to help her escape? She's been abusing me for years. I've just given evidence against her.'

'Is that your car outside?' The other continued probing.

'Yes.'

'You weren't planning to spirit her away in it then?' His interrogator enquired.

'Of course not.' Rupert said irritated by the line of questioning.

'Bit of a coincidence that you are both in the house at the same time though!'

'I didn't even know she was free until she confronted me with a baseball bat.'

Another person entered the bedroom and said. 'I can confirm his story. I arrested her in the first place.'

Graham Fredericks said walking towards Rupert. 'He's telling the truth.'

Rupert remembered the voice, but his pounding head wouldn't recall the name of its owner.

'Looks like you have been in the wars again Mr Screen, doesn't it?' he said. 'Right. Let's get these cuffs off you.'

As he removed the handcuffs, the policeman who had been questioning Rupert summoned the paramedic who had been waiting by the bedroom door.

After a quick check of Rupert's injuries he said, 'You look OK, but I think you ought to go to hospital for a check-up anyway. That gash could do with some stitches too.'

'Do you know why she came here?'

'She said she was getting some clothes.'

'What clothes was she wearing?'

'To be honest I was concentrating more on where she was swinging that baseball bat than on her clothes.'

'Is there anything missing that will help us spot her...a hat, a scarf, an umbrella?

'I don't know. I've not been out of the bedroom since she attacked me. I'm sorry.'

'What about money. Do you have a joint account?'

'No. She kept her hands on the money. But I had an account she didn't know about.'

'Well I think we owe you an apology for letting her slip through our fingers. Where do you think your Missus is likely to go?'

'Don't know unless...oh my God! She might be on her way to my partner's house. Can you get somebody down there to protect her and my baby?'

'Just give me the details and we'll get somebody there immediately.'

'I need to call her. To warn her.'

'Just leave that to us. Don't worry.'

Rupert summoned up his thoughts and gave the Policeman all the details. 'Thanks. Now let's get you to hospital.'

Rupert's head was throbbing. He didn't have the strength to argue. He just gave in to the Policeman's direction.

CHAPTER FORTY EIGHT

Janie was sitting on one of the big green communications boxes swinging her legs. Her bulging school bag lay in a crumpled heap by the side of it.

Ben had been looking forward all day to meeting her after school. But when he saw her, he wasn't so sure she wanted to see him. She was unsmiling as he approached.

'Hi,' he said, eagerly.

'Hi,' Janie responded, flatly.

'What's up? You don't look very happy to see me,' Ben said, immediately thinking she was going to dump him. Although they weren't 'going out' together, they had been getting on well in spite of the vodka bottle incident.

'Nothing.'

'Oh, OK!' Is there something you want to say?' he asked awkwardly. Hoping she wasn't going to say it was over between them.

'Well if you really want to know…'

Ben held his breath.

'An old bloke told me off this morning for dropping some paper.'

Ben immediately relaxed.

'He did what?'

'Yeah! We was on our way to school. It was only a small piece of paper off my sausage roll.'

'What you doing eating a sausage roll at that time of the morning.'

'God, you sound just like my mother. Dur! It was my breakfast, dummy.'

'Breakfast!'

'Yeah and what's wrong with that? I get one every morning.'

'Oh, right.' Ben said, thinking it was a strange start to the day.

'Don't look at me like that, weirdo. My friend Clair and I always go to the bakers and get one.'

'Sorry.'

'Well I didn't even know that I dropped the paper, like.'

'So what happened? Did he shout at you?' Ben asked, moving towards her.

'No, but he asked me to pick it up.'

'What did you do?'

'I gave him a 'one finger face look' and ignored him. Clair and I carried on to school.'

'So what you looking so miserable about?'

'He reported me to the school.'

'What! Over a bit of paper!'

'Yeah.'

'How did he know which school?'

'Dur!' Janie gave him a sneer, suggesting he was being thick.

'...your blazer of course.' Ben took the hint.

'He was stood at reception talking to Mrs whatever-her-name-is when I walked past to my next lesson.'

'That was bad luck.'

'Yeah.'

'So what happened?'

'Well he spotted me didn't he?'

'Yeah, so what did Mrs whats-her-name say?'

'She called me over to her desk and asked him if it was definitely me.' Janie said agitated, kicking her heels against the green box. 'Course he said yes.'

'The miserable old git.' Ben said, giving her a sympathetic look.

'She thanked him for being 'public spirited'. Then she gave me a detention.'

'That's not fair. It wasn't even on school property.'

'So it means I can't go training with you tomorrow.' Janie said woefully. 'Sorry.'

'Oh that's a bummer. Never mind we'll change it to another day.' Ben suggested quickly. 'What about Friday?'

'Yeah, don't think I'm doing anything. But I need to check if Mum's friend will look after Mum for me. Hopefully it should be OK,' Janie confirmed.

'Yeah, great,' Ben beamed.

Ben was relieved. He really liked this girl and always looked forward to their training rides together.

'I'll tell you something that will make you smile.'

'You can try,' Janie invited.

'You know Mr Young the exam invigilator?' Ben quizzed.

'Yeah, I like him, he's a nice bloke.' Janie confirmed.

'Well he brought an exam to a halt the other day.'

'Why?'

'He slipped over on a wet bit of floor and he went flying.'

'Why was it wet? Somebody pee themselves?'

'No. A kid had stepped in some dog poo and brought it into the hall.'

'Ugh, that's revolting. You'd think they'd know wouldn't you?'

Anyway they got it mopped up.'

'I should think so too.'

'Course the floor was wet. And he slipped over on it.

'Oh my god! Was he alright?'

'Yeah, although he banged his ribs and bruised his knee.' Ben added dramatically. 'Course he was embarrassed.'

'What happened to the kids taking the exam?'

'Well after everybody got over the initial shock, they all burst out laughing.

'Oh, poor Mr Young.' Janie said sympathetically.

'Course everybody took the 'mick' as they were leaving the hall, pretending to trip.'

Janie brightened up as Ben picked her school bag off the floor.

'Come on, I'll walk home with you,' he said offering his hand so she could get down from the box.

Janie took Ben's proffered hand and jumped down landing immediately in front of him, almost touching his chest. They stood like that for a second, looked into each other's eyes and embarrassed, turned away. She let go of his hand.

'Want to give me my bag? she asked quietly.

'No, it's OK, I'll carry it for you,' and instead he took her hand and together they walked to her home feeling good in each other's company.

CHAPTER FORTY NINE

Rupert had been taken to hospital by ambulance, but insisted on ringing Joanne before he was stitched up.

'Jo, hi it's me.'

'Hello Rupert. Well, what did she get?' she asked expectantly.

'She didn't.' Rupert said frustrated. 'The prison van crashed and she was taken to hospital.'

'Serves the bitch right.' Jo said uncharacteristically vengeful.

'Trouble is she escaped.' Rupert added.

'Oh my God!' Jo put her hand to her mouth in alarm.

'Now don't worry.' Rupert reassured her. 'She...I... went to my old house to get some more of my clothes and she was there.'

'Oh Rupert. What happened?' Jo asked nervously.

'She attacked me...and...'

'Oh dear, are you alright?'

'Yes. Nothing to worry about.' Rupert said calmly trying to downplay the whole event. 'Just a few bruises and a bit of a cut to my head. I'm being checked over at the hospital now.'

'The hospital!' Jo shrieked.

'Yes, just routine that's all.' He reassured her. 'But I want you to make sure that you don't answer the door.'

'Why?' Joanne asked, now feeling very vulnerable

'She's still on the loose.'

'Oh my God.' Jo was starting to panic and illogically looked towards the door.

'Don't worry. The police will be guarding us until she's recaptured.' He sought to console her.

'But she doesn't know where we live.' She said, trying to calm herself.

'I wouldn't count on that. There is so much published on the internet now. She'll know, believe me.' Rupert immediately regretted adding to her angst.

'When will you be home?' Jo asked fearfully.

'As soon as they have finished checking me over, I shall be on my way. OK?'

'How long will that be Rupert?' She asked, wheeling herself to the front door and dropping the catch.

'Not long. Don't worry. I'll see you shortly and remember, don't answer the door, unless it's the police. OK?

'OK, but hurry please.' She demanded, 'I miss you.'

'I miss you too.' Rupert said, a knot of anxiety in his stomach as he ended the call.

As soon as he had rung off from Joanne, Rupert quickly rang Andy.

'Andy, it's me, Rupert.'

'You OK? You sound a bit strange.' Andy asked.

'Sue's out.' Rupert said bluntly.

'What?' Andy couldn't believe his ears. 'What do you out?'

'She's escaped. She was at our old house.' Rupert advised him 'When I got there, she clobbered me.'

'God, are you alright?' Andy asked, shocked that she had not only escaped but had been able to get to Rupert.

'I'm at the hospital getting some treatment.' Rupert said, in a matter-of-fact way. Not feeling at all scared, but quite the contrary, feeling strangely under control.

'Are you badly hurt?' the other quizzed.

'No, but I've got a gash on my head, so they're checking me for concussion. Oh, I see I've got a few bruises to my arms,' he said, quickly examining himself. 'But otherwise I'm OK.'

'What actually happened when she…?'

'She took a baseball bat to me, but I managed to fend off most of her attack. Rupert relayed. 'Fortunately the Police arrived just in the nick of time, before she could do any real damage.'

'Have they recaptured her yet?' Andy asked, wondering if he should be taking precautions too.

'No she escaped again. They've got a manhunt going. They're trying to find her now.'

'What about Jo and the baby?'

'I've just spoken to her, she's OK. The police are going to stake out Jo's house and they'll probably stay until they find that frigging maniac wife of mine.'

Andy was surprised by Rupert's choice of words. He had never heard him swear before.

'Are you OK otherwise? It must have been quite frightening.'

'Yes it was pretty scary, but I'm fine. Honest. I even managed to give the bitch a taste of her own medicine. I've never hit her before and I have to confess to have quite enjoyed putting her down.' Rupert said joyfully.

'Good for you.' Andy said, encouraged by his positivity.

'I wasn't the pushover she was expecting. I've moved on Andy, I just realised that.'

'The Lion looking for courage eh? Good old Geoffery,' Andy reflected quietly.

'Sorry Andy I didn't hear that. There's a lot of noise here.'

'Nothing Rupert, I was just talking to myself.'

'As soon as they've finished with me here, I shall be back to Bristol. I might even ring Carrie to see if her mates are available to do their security screen like they did when we were in Frenchay.'

'Why do you want to do that if the police are going to do it?'

'Just in case the police drop their presence. You never know what impact these cuts are having do you?' Rupert observed. 'Best to be safe than sorry.'

'If there's anything I can do, just give me a call.' Andy added going straight to lock his own door.

'Thanks Andy.'

Rupert immediately rang Carrie and repeated the story.

'Are you sure you're OK?' Carrie asked sympathetically.

'Yes, thanks. But I'm after a favour.'

'Go on.' She prompted.

'Can you get your army mates to do the security thing for me at our house please. Rupert asked. 'This time we've got some pennies from Geoffery's will so we can pay them properly.' He added.

'Yes, no problem.' She confirmed. 'Mind you the police gave them a bit of a hard time the last time at Frenchay...something about being vigilantes.'

'I don't care what they're called. So long as they keep us safe.' Rupert added.

CHAPTER FIFTY

Suitably clad in his riding gear Ben rode his new mountain bike to Janie's house and was pleased to see she was already outside on hers waiting for him. She looked every bit a mountain biker.

She was wearing a stylish pink and black short sleeve cycle top, black lycra shorts and a white cycle helmet completed the ensemble. On her hands she wore black fingerless mitts.

'Wow, look at you,' Ben said 'parking' next to her. 'You're dressed up. But can you ride as good as you look?'

'Cheeky sod. You know I can. I'll show you,' Janie said, giving his arm a playful punch.

'What about somebody to look after your Mum.'

'Yeah. Our Mum's friend's already here. She said she'd come over every day while I'm training for Eastnor Park.'

'Great. The weather forecast says it's going to be dry.'

'Good. I've been looking forward to it all day.' Janie said enthusiastically.

'Come on then. Let's make some dust,' Ben said, cycling off.

'Where're we going Ben?'

'I got a nice tough route for us,' he said, pedalling ahead.

'Well I hope it's not so tough that we end up pushing our bikes. What about your back?' she called, trying to match his pace.

'Oh, it's OK at the moment.'

They cycled up along several busy roads and entered a narrow lane.

Ben's route took them up a six hundred foot climb on to the Cotswold escarpment via a green lane that ran past the Green Leaf Hotel. This was the place where Geoffery's wake had been held. He still had vivid and painful memories of all the incidents that had surrounded it.

Ben shuddered as they cycled past and he put on an extra spurt to leave it and the memories quickly behind them.

As the ascent started, the track conditions got tougher too.

Centuries of rain had eroded the soil so that the track was nearly six feet lower than the fields either side. Consequently, the lane was littered with small limestone rocks that had been washed down over the years by countless streams and rivulets running off the escarpment. This made it difficult to ride.

The steep banks either side of the track were populated with hawthorn, holly and blackthorn bushes which clung perilously to the rocky ground. The sharp prickles and leaves a hazard for the impetuous rider who wavered off course.

Several trees, casualties of the forces of nature and the shallow root space, had succumbed to gravity and lay rotting alongside the green lane. Some had clearly fallen across the track at some stage and had been sawn up and dragged unceremoniously out of the way.

As they got further up the climb, they entered a tunnel like area where the trees bordering the track intertwined overhead.

The track got steeper and steeper Ben was in the lowest gear and was standing on his pedals to maintain momentum. He was impressed that Janie was still matching his pace.

Eventually, the track gave way to a narrow tarmacked road serving a few remote houses and then it levelled off. The pair stopped to catch their breath as they entered some woods.

'God, that was a bit steep,' Janie panted, out of breath.

'Yeah, well, you didn't do too bad I suppose,' Ben said ungenerously.

'Well I reckon I did pretty good to keep up with you,' she puffed.

'It's only because my back's playing up. It slowed me down. Otherwise you wouldn't have seen me for dust.'

'Yeah, any excuse. Just because I kept up with you.'

'You know I hurt it trying to save that piglet,' he said, indignantly.

'Yes I know. You keep going on about it.' Janie said now getting bored by his whinging.

'Well, it's really playing up today,' he whined, putting his hand on his sweat soaked back.

'Anyway, I think you were ever so brave trying to save that little baby boar.'

'I expect you'd have done the same.' He suggested generously.

'Oh, I'm not so sure. It was bleeding wasn't it? I'm not too good with blood,' Janie admitted.

'Although, like Carrie said, it probably wouldn't have survived anyway. It was bleeding quite badly.'

'God you must have been scared when it's mother came looking for it.'

'Yeah, too true. You should have seen the size of that sow! It was like a miniature hippo.'

'Why did it charge you?'

'Carrie reckoned she was trying to protect her baby.'

'Like any mother would I suppose.' Janie said, reflectively.

'Yeah. well I did what I thought was right, it's a shame it died though.' Ben said still holding his back.

'I didn't realise you had a soft spot for animals.'

'Well you know. I even fancied being a vegetarian once.'

'Do you mean a veterinarian?' Janie joked.

'Ha ha. Very funny,' Ben said, lightening up.

'I thought so too, dull boy.'

'Anyway, my mother said she couldn't afford to buy all the veggie stuff. It was just a passing fad.'

'I thought of becoming a veggie myself but I couldn't give up my Sunday roast. My Mum does,' Janie corrected herself, 'used to, cook a great roast.'

'Mind you it's pretty barbaric breeding animals just to kill and eat them though isn't it?' Ben added.

'What about that boar then?'

'Well, Carrie had to kill the boar, otherwise I might not be here today,' Ben said reflectively.

'Yeah. Good job she was there then, I suppose.' Janie agreed reluctantly

'She was great. She saved my life stopping the sow from attacking us.'

'Yeah, so you've said,' Janie said, now getting tetchy about hearing Carrie's name so often.

'Anyway, I nearly died. I swallowed my tongue.'

'You can't swallow your tongue. It's impossible.' Janie insisted.

'No it isn't.'

'Yes it is. It's connected to the back of your throat.'

'Look, I ought to know. It was my tongue. Carrie had to hook it out of my throat.'

'Ugh, fancy messing with somebody's tongue.' Janie shuddered at the thought.

'It was blocking my windpipe. What else could she do?'

'Did she give you... mouth to mouth?' Janie asked, suspiciously

''Yeah, I suppose so. Why?'

'She kissed you then?' Janie enquired, trying to sound nonchalant

'Yeah. But it wasn't like kissing, kissing.'

'Oh!'

'Why? Are you jealous?' Ben taunted her.

'Well no. Of course not.' Janie protested modestly.

'You are aren't you?' He continued.

'She's a grown woman. I mean you're a kid.' Janie said disgustedly.

'So! It was first aid.' Ben reassured her.

'It's a bit...you know, kinky though, isn't it?' Janie suggested.

'She had to do it to save my life.' Ben said frustrated at Janie's questioning.

'Yeah, I suppose. Anyway are we training or what? Come on. Let's ride, 'Janie said, moving off.

'You are jealous aren't you?' Ben said catching up with her. 'She was saving my life that was all.'

'It could have been worse. Imagine if it was Andy!'

'Yuck! It doesn't bear thinking about.'

Ben suddenly stopped.

'Come on,' Janie shouted as she disappeared into the tree line.

But Ben was in pain. His back had suddenly locked. He slowly and painfully got off his bike and leant against a tree. He broke out in a sweat and thought he was going to pass out. After a few minutes the pain eased.

Janie came back to see where he'd got to.

'You OK?' she asked, looking concerned. 'Your face is ever so white.'

'It's my back,' Ben said, giving up the idea of remounting his bike. 'I've been having muscle spasms and my back suddenly seized up.'

'Perhaps we ought to go back and forget about training,' she said sympathetically.

'Yeah. That's a good idea. As much as I need the practice for Eastnor, I don't think I can ride anymore today.'

'I hope you'll be OK for the race.'

'So do I,' he said pushing his bike back towards the road. 'I've been dreaming about this race for ages.'

'Are you sure you're going to be alright to ride back?' Janie asked with genuine concern.

'Yeah I think so.'

'At least it's downhill most of the way.'

'If I can't ride back, I'll have to ask James to come and pick me up I guess.'

'James!'

'Yeah, he's been staying at my house.' Ben informed her. 'It's mutual aid.'

'Mutual what?' She puzzled.

'Mutual aid. Well, he's still recovering from his operation so my Mum is fussing around him. And he's keeping an eye on Mum.'

'Why's he doing that? Does he fancy her or something?'

'No, it's not like that. It's so she doesn't stray back to the booze. I'm surprised they get on so well.'

Painfully, Ben remounted his bike and gingerly started for home followed by a concerned Janie.

CHAPTER FIFTY ONE

The letter had been tempting her all day. It was addressed to Andy.

Normally they opened up each other's mail, as they had agreed never to have any secrets from each other.

But this letter was different. The writing on the envelope was a woman's handwriting. The postmark and stamp was Monaco and she could smell a faint perfume.

It was obviously from Nadine.

She tried to ignore it by keeping busy but it was there, tantalising her staring at her every time she went into the kitchen. The apprehension of knowing its contents was consuming her.

Andy was at work and wouldn't be home until much later.

Finally she decided to call Kay and get her guidance.

After a few rings, Kay answered and recognised the callers ID, 'Hi Helen,' she said. 'To what do I owe the pleasure of your call?'

'Kay, I want the benefit of your advice.'

'Well if I can be of help. I'm more than happy to listen.'

'Andy has just received a letter. I think it's from Nadine.'

'Oh dear. What's in it?' Kay asked conspiratorially.

'I don't know. Although we don't have any hang-ups about opening each other's mail, I'm not sure I want to see what's in this one and he's at work at the moment.' Helen informed her.

'What time is he due home?'

'Not for another few hours and I'm trying to ignore it... but it's getting to me.'

'Well why don't you open it then?' Kay encouraged.

'Suppose it's a love letter? or, they are thinking of eloping?'

'Well unless you open it you won't know will you?'

'No I suppose not.'

'Go on. Take the bull by the horns and open it.' Kay egged her on.

'I'm scared.'

'What are you scared of?'

'In case this is the end of my marriage.' Helen confessed nervously.

'Well if he's going to run off with the woman, whether you open it or he opens it, it's neither here nor there. He'll be off.' Kay pointed out logically.

'Perhaps I ought to ring him and tell him it's here,' Helen said, at last feeling she had solved her own dilemma. 'Yes, that's probably the best idea. If he says it's ok to open it, I can read it to him.'

'There you go. See, you've answered your own query.' Kay said. 'Do it straight away and put yourself out of your misery. Let me know how you get on.'

'Ok, will do. Thanks for your help.'

'I didn't do anything.'

'You were there. That was enough. I'll call you later, bye.'

Helen hung up. She went into the kitchen and gingerly picked up the letter. A faint waft of perfume pervaded her senses. She winced at the smell. After getting the letter in front of her she rang the hospice.

'Can I speak to Andy Spider please.'

'Is that Helen?'

'Yes.'

'Hi.'

'Hi Sharon,' she said, recognising the receptionist's voice.

'I'll see if I can track him down for you. Please hold.'

'Thanks.'

After a few minutes listening to classical music, Andy came on the line.

'Hi, anything wrong?'

'Well no, not really. It's just that you've got a letter here.'

'You know you can open it. You don't need to ask.'

'Only it's from Monaco and the handwriting looks like a woman's,' she said dramatically.

'I wasn't expecting anything from the law firm. They usually type my name anyway,' he said pondering what it was likely to be.

'The letter smells of perfume. I think its Nadine's.'

'Oh…well as I told you before there is nothing going on between us. You had better open it and read it to me.' He directed.

Helen slid her finger along the flap of the envelope and nervously removed the folded paper. Her eyes scanned it to quickly identify the sender.

'Yes, it's from her alright.' She confirmed. 'Are you sure your want me to read it?'

'Yes of course. I keep on telling you.' He said, irritated by her reluctance. 'I've got nothing to hide.'

She read:

Dear Andy, it was a pleasant surprise to bump into you at the Hotel de Paris.

Thank you for letting me know about the will reading, I was shocked to hear that it had gone ahead as I had instructed my Lawyer to contest it.

However, as the will has now been read and Geoffery's estate has been distributed, I now have to find another strategy to obtain what is rightly mine.

I wonder if you can help me get justice in the matter of Geoffery's will.

Clearly he wrote it when he was ill and confused, therefore he was not of sound mind. I would like to call you as a witness if my appeal goes to court.

As you know Geoffery and I were very much in love and I'm sure he confided in you about our relationship during his stay in the hospice.

Your statement could help me prove my case.'

'Well, there's no chance of that happening,' Andy said firmly. 'I've had enough. Does she say anything else?'

'Yes. Just a bit more.'

Helen read on:-

I am sorry for the anger between your wife and I. She is obviously very protective of her love for you. I hope you recognise it.

However, she insulted me greatly and slandered me at the hotel when she called me a whore! I have taken legal advice to sue her. But I have asked my lawyers not to proceed at the moment.

'Ouch! That could be costly if she does go ahead with it,' Andy said quietly.

Helen made no comment and continued to read

'Thank you for your sympathetic kindness whilst I was grieving.

I am sorry if your thoughtfulness has caused you any marital difficulties.

In return for helping me to resolve the unfairness of being excluded from Geoffery's estate, I will of course drop my slander action.

I will be in touch again when my plans are formalised.
Love Nadine.

'The conniving bitch,' Andy said angrily. 'See. I told you nothing was going on. Now do you believe me?'

'You've got to admit it was all a bit suspicious though wasn't it? Can you blame me?' Helen responded defensively.

'Not if you'd trusted me.' He said bluntly.

'Yeah, well. How do I know that you didn't get her to write it?' Helen said.

'Oh, please! I need to get back to work now,' he said abruptly. 'I'll see you later.' Andy hung up.

Helen rang Kay back immediately.

'Well, how did you get on?' Kay asked, foregoing any pleasantries.

'Yes. As I suspected, it was from her and unless he got her to write it, she confirms that there was nothing going on.' Helen informed her, relieved.

'Well there you go then. See, you had nothing to worry about did you?'

'No I suppose not.'

'But surely she didn't write the letter just to say that there was 'nothing going on', otherwise, I too, would be suspicious. Was there anything else in it?'

'Yes. She wants him to give evidence in court because she's contesting Geoffery's will.' Helen advised her.

'Oh, and what did he say?'

'No chance. He wants to finish with all the peripheral crap surrounding the will. There is just one thing that might upset the apple cart.'

'Yes and what's that?' Kay enquired suspiciously.

'I called her a whore in the lobby of the hotel.' Helen admitted, embarrassed at her confession.

'Good for you.' Kay said heartily.

'The trouble is, she is threatening to sue me for slander, unless Andy helps her get money from Geoffery's will.'

'Oh heavens.' Kay said shocked. 'What will he do?'

'I don't know because she isn't sure herself what she's going to do next.'

'Oh dear!'

'Well thanks again for being my sounding board.' Helen said sincerely.

'Don't worry, I'm sure it'll turn out OK.' Kay assured her.

'Thanks. I hope you're right.'

After Helen had hung up she sat in the kitchen staring at the note wondering what would happen next. She wished that Geoffery Foster had never chosen Andy's hospice to see out his last days. The money had brought nothing but stress and tension to their marriage. She started filling up, feeling sorry for herself but just then little Molly started crying, it was a welcome diversion. She lost herself in being a doting Mum.

CHAPTER FIFTY TWO

Following the acrimonious discussion with Helen about his working hours, Andy had done nothing to change anything.

Uncharacteristically, he was undecided. The debate was all about his work life balance.

The issue of whether he should give up work altogether to be with his family more often just wouldn't go away. But his marriage might.

So he had to make a decision. One way or the other. Family or work.

'Surely,' he thought 'there has to be a 'middle of the road' solution.'

Normally, he could see both sides of any argument but now, because he was personally involved, he couldn't distance himself from it.

One of his patients was Cyril, a seventy five year old former GPO engineer who had nursed his wife through a long and debilitating illness. Sadly, within a few months after her death, he too was diagnosed with a terminal illness.

The doctors thought that looking after his wife had kept his own symptoms repressed, but after she'd gone, the grief exacerbated the advance of his own illness.

In a rare moment of openness Andy had talked to him about Helen's ultimatum of 'Job or Us'. He explained how difficult the decision was.

'What will you do if your wife says she has had enough and takes the children.'

'I don't know.'

'Then you will have lost out. You won't see anything of your children. You won't have a home to go to. Chances are you will become depressed and won't be able to do your job either. Who's won? Nobody!' Cyril pointed out.

'Guess you're right.' Andy agreed.

'Sometimes you have to compromise to be able to move forward.' The old man advised. 'Let's face it at the moment you are not your usual happy self. In fact, I'd go so far as to say you're a bit of a grump. Just think, if you do change, we will all be winners. OK, we won't see you so often, but when we do we'll see your smiling face again and we'll feel good having a happy nurse.' He continued. 'Your children will see more of you and you'll be a better husband too.

Remember, the children grow up so quickly. As they get more independent they won't need you to the same extent so you can change your working pattern back again. This doesn't need to be a one off decision.'

'No I suppose not.'

'Do you love your wife?' Cyril probed, taking Andy by surprise.

'Yes, I think so.'

'Think so! Oh dear! That sounds like you're already thinking of ditching the family unity for something else.' The old man observed. 'With your wife you can provide a stable home for your children.'

'Yes I appreciate all that but I enjoy my job.' Andy said wearily.

'The decision is yours but a work life balance is important. I gather you can afford to do it. Remember what I said.' Cyril reminded him. 'Appreciate what you have now. It might be gone tomorrow.'

'Thanks, I'll think about what you said.' Andy said tidying the old man's bed clothes.

'But no decision?'

'Not yet. No.'

Sadly Cyril passed away the next night.

Andy resisted the temptation to heed Cyril's words out of a false sense of moral guilt.

CHAPTER FIFTY THREE

The stretch limo pulled up outside Carrie's and Tim's new abode and James pressed the intercom button for their flat. He was quickly answered by Carrie who as usual was punctual and ready.

'Hi, who's there?' She asked.

'Carrie, it's me, James. Your carriage awaits.'

'Great. We'll be down shortly.'

Tim had bought the new executive flat to try to placate Carrie for his reckless squandering of half a million pounds in Monaco and it was doing the trick, their relationship was as strong as ever and they both loved the penthouse.

James had arranged the trip to the restaurant to express his special thanks to Tim for saving his life.

Considering the major surgery involved, Tim's recovery had been going well. His trips to out-patients were now becoming few and far between.

Whereas James had had a few setbacks and the immunosuppressive medications were causing him various side effects including mood swings and headaches.

The hired limousine took them out of the city to a small restaurant in a vineyard near Newent.

'What's the name of this place?' Tim asked as they entered into the small building.

'Three choirs vineyard,' James replied.

'Three choirs vineyard. Tim repeated thoughtfully. 'Isn't there a walk around here called the Three Choirs walk? We should add that to our walk portfolio.' He suggested to Carrie.

'I think it's called the Three Choirs Way, it's a reference to the choirs of Gloucester, Hereford and Worcester cathedrals. But it's not around here though.' James informed them. 'Part of the route goes the other side of Newent.'

They were shown to their table situated by a large picture window through which they had a panoramic view of the vineyards.

'Oh this is nice isn't it?' Carrie said gorging herself on the view.

She studied the symmetrical lines of neatly tended vines which stretched away to the horizon in the rolling fields. The gnarled vine trunks, which were barely three foot high, each sprouted vibrant green tentacles along taut supporting wires.

The layout of the hundreds of the vines arranged in ordered groups caught Carrie's imagination.

'The vineyard reminds me of ancient armies lined up in regimental formations ready for a battle to begin,' she suggested, whimsically.' One army facing another.'

'Blimey, what have you been taking? Tim asked, sceptically. 'Where's that come from?'

'It's just so lovely, though isn't it?' she added.

'The red Marl soil here reminds me of an enormous red fruit bowl overflowing with grapes,' James added poetically.

'You two are on a different planet,' Tim declared, shaking his head. 'It's just some fields with vines in as far as I can see.'

'I read somewhere that vines planted in this type of fertile soil normally ripen later than in other soil types. I think it adds acidity to the wine too.' James continued, ignoring Tim's cynical assessment of their comments.

'Listen to that. Not only do we have a free meal, but we get educated as well,' Tim added, sarcastically.

'Tim,' Carrie's tone of voice conveyed her displeasure. 'Remember where you are. You promised to be on your best behaviour.' Carrie instructed him.

'What? I only said... Oh never mind,' he replied, picking up the wine list.

'I think all the wine is made and bottled here.' James said, attracting the attention of a waitress.

'Could you bring us a bottle of your best Three Choirs red wine and a bottle of Elderflower cordial for myself, please?'

While they waited, James took in the quiet ambience of the restaurant with its plumb coloured walls, naked brick and terracotta friezes. Discreet lighting was provided by wall mounted uplighters and natural light through the large picture windows. Each window was framed tastefully with large floral curtains and matching material pelmets.

The tables were generously spaced so that each party had privacy where conversations could not be overheard by their neighbours. Gentle piped music played in the background.

James' review of the restaurant was interrupted by the wine waiter who arrived carrying a bottle and showed him the label for his approval.

'If, that's the best, that's what we'll have,' James said.

'Would you like to taste it, Sir? the waiter asked.

'No thanks, I'm 'tea-total' but I'm sure it will be OK. Please pour it out for my friends. Mine is the Elderflower.'

When their glasses were filled, James proposed a toast to Tim.

'To my very good friend and lifesaver, Tim. Thank you so much for giving me the precious gift of life.' They chinked glasses.

'Cheers,' they chorused.

'What are your plans for the walking company now?' James asked.

'You might have heard us say that we are planning to extend it across the country.'

'Expansion, eh? What's the thinking behind that?'

'It's so that our clients, who are mainly service people, don't have to travel long distances just to go for a relatively short walk,' Tim informed him.

'That sounds like a good business strategy.'

'We believe we have a brand that we can franchise out. Thanks to you and Rupert,' Carrie added.

'Even better,' Tim added enthusiastically. 'We are getting a brand new Land Rover Discovery. I'll be getting it modified for Carrie and I.'

'You mean with hand controls?'

'Yes that's right. And we've designed a brilliant livery for it too.'

'What about you James?' Carrie asked.

'Oh, the charity is all go. I have a board meeting next week and we hope to finalise a deal for a new shelter in London.

The sooner the better, as far as I'm concerned. It's quite alarming to hear the number of young people who run away from home every day'

'Did I hear young Ben say that you were thinking of buying a house too.'

'Yes, I was going to ask for your advice, if you don't mind.'

'You're more than welcome, for what it's worth. What have you got in mind?'

'I'm buying a large house in Churchup and I'm thinking of inviting Ben and his mother Beth to live there with me as well. What do you think?'

'Why?' Tim said bluntly.

'You aren't getting involved… with Beth are you?' Carrie asked cautiously.

'Well, yes and no. At my time of life I don't think a leopard can change his spots. But I am quite fond of them both. To be honest, I feel sorry for Ben having to constantly pick up the pieces of his mother's addiction.'

'Yeah, so do we but…'

'As you know, from donating part of yourself to me Tim, I have had my moments with alcohol abuse in the past and I can empathise with the struggle that Beth is going through. It really is so very hard to break the cycle. She needs something positive to help change her lifestyle.'

'Yes, I can understand that,' Carrie agreed.

'Personally, I think that's a dumb idea,' Tim said insensitively.

'I'm surprised at you Tim. I would have thought having gambled away almost half a million pounds you would be more sympathetic to people who have weaknesses,' Carrie hissed, glaring at him.

'No…well…that was different. I don't gamble all the time.'

'Only because you know I'd nag you to death. Go on James. Why do you think it's a good idea.' Carrie asked.

'Sorry, I didn't want to cause a 'domestic'. This is a night of celebration. Perhaps we ought to change the subject?'

'No, it's fine. Tim and I are OK now. We have an understanding don't we Tim?'

'Yes...yes we do.' Tim confirmed, more hesitantly than Carrie liked.

'OK, if you're happy for me to carry on.'

'Yes, perfectly, aren't we Tim?' Carrie hinted, kicking him under the table.

'Yes.'

'Thanks. Well, I think I could give her some moral support...and more importantly get her away from bad company. Her so called 'friends' are the main cause of her lapsing back on to the drink.'

'Do you think she would want that? I mean, her friends are her friends, good or bad. Surely you can't possibly fill that gap. Especially as you say there is no romantic attachment involved.'

'No, but call me naïve if you like. A good solid friendship can be almost of fulfilling as a romantic one. Can't it?'

'You mean a platonic friendship?'

'Yes.'

'Do you think you've got that sort of relationship with her?' Carrie quizzed.

'Well it might not be there yet. But there are signs. Positive signs.' James divulged.

'I think you're being a bit ambitious,' Tim suggested.

'Ben and I get on well too...and following his disappointment when he met his father...well I thought... perhaps...' James added, self-consciously.

'What! That you'd become his Dad? You mean adopt him?' Tim blurted.

'Well, the kid is so uptight about being taken in to care and if his mother continues to blot her copybook... well, I'd be there so they wouldn't be able to take him away, would they?'

'I see where you're coming from,' Carrie acknowledged. 'But surely you would have to marry his mother for the legalities to make you his guardian?'

'I don't know to be honest, but I wanted to discuss my thoughts with somebody before I went any further.' James explained.

'I think you're bloody mad taking on a delinquent kid and an alcoholic woman,' Tim said tactlessly.

'No James, I think you should carry on and do some more investigations. The theory sounds good and so are your intentions. But be careful, that's all I would say,' Carrie advised.

'Ok, thanks Carrie. I appreciate you letting me get it off my chest. Anyway, I'm keeping you from eating.'

'Yeah, my guts are starting to protest.' Tim grumbled.

'Oh I see they've got your favourite on the menu Carrie.' James said smiling mischievously.

'My favourite?' Carrie asked, puzzled, looking again at the menu.

'Wild boar,' James said and laughed.

CHAPTER FIFTY FOUR

After being interrupted in her ferocious attack on Rupert, Sue had evaded the massive 'manhunt' that swung into place to recapture her.

Luck was on her side as she fled. Heavy rain and low cloud had 'grounded' the Police helicopter and although Police dogs were deployed, they soon lost the trail in the wet conditions.

Police were posted at bus and train stations and both foot and mobile patrols were increased.

Sue took advantage of the rain and shielded her face from the multitude of CCTV cameras under an umbrella, which she'd picked up from home.

She knew that someone would be given the unenviable job of checking scores of monitor screens and their recordings to see if they could spot her.

As she splashed her way past a multiscreen cinema she had a sudden thought. She could 'lay low' in its darkened interior for several hours while the search was at its most energetic.

Consequently, she bought a ticket for a random movie from an automatic ticket machine in the foyer and duly took a wall seat in one of the multiscreens.

During the screening of the movie she racked her brains for what to do next. Eventually, she decided that the police would probably be scrutinising all forms of public transport. However, the last place they would look was right under their noses, so she decided to stay in the city and find a local B & B.

At the end of the movie she went in to the toilets and changed her clothes in case somebody had spotted her earlier on CCTV and would be looking to recognise her by what she was wearing. Fortunately she had also included an anorak waterproof coat in her bag.

She was relieved to see that it was still raining as she left the cinema so again had the perfect cover of her umbrella from the myriad cameras that covered the area around the cinema.

Finally having splashed around for an hour looking at suitable places she booked in to a run-down looking Bed & Breakfast.

The owner, a friendly lady in her late seventies, was surprised by her request for lodgings at that time of the evening.

'Yes, I have a vacancy. In fact you'll be the only one staying. What brings you to this area?' she enquired kindly.

Oh, just visiting relatives,' Sue lied.

Leaving the hood of her anorak up and wearing a pair of reading glasses, Sue registered using a false name.

'That's nice. Well you're the only one I have booked in so you can have your breakfast anytime from eight o'clock.

The old lady showed her to the room. It was clean. The furnishings were a bit twee and the window showed signs of neglect with the wind rippling the net curtain as it blew through the rotting frame.

Sue stayed in her bedroom for several days saying that she was not feeling well. Indeed the prison van crash had actually exacerbated her neck and back problem and she was taking pain killers.

The old lady was concerned and provided her with an evening meal in her room.

After a few days, Sue felt confident enough to venture out and find an internet café.

Her vitriol and desire to wreak revenge on Andy occupied her waking hours and it had galvanised her into a spiteful course of action.

She planned to distribute copies of the compromising photograph of Nadine and Andy to several newspapers, radio stations and TV channels along with a brief article documenting the scandal.

As she made her way to the front door she saw the local newspaper in the hallway and picked it up. The front page was still full of her escape.

Escaped prisoner still on the run.

Police today said the injured prisoner who escaped from hospital is still at large. Convicted felon, Susan Williams Screen, was on her way to Crown Court for sentencing when the prison van she was travelling in was involved in a road traffic collision on the M5 motorway.

Along with all other occupants of the prison van Williams Screen was transferred in a fleet of ambulances to hospital where she made her escape.

An inquiry is to be held to establish how the prisoner escaped from her police guard.

Police said;" While we do not believe that Williams-Screen poses a risk to the public at large, anyone who sees her should not approach her, but should call 999 immediately."

Fortunately, for her, there was no picture associated with the article.

She was just debating whether to continue with her plans or return to her room when the old lady came out in to the hallway.

'Oh hello dear. Feeling better?' The Landlady asked studying her face with genuine concern.' Just going out are we?'

'Thanks. Umm, yes I am.'

'Oh well done, the fresh air will do you good. You see.' She encouraged.

Sue's mind was made up for her. Wearing her anorak with its hood up and her reading glasses, which she hoped would provide her with some anonymity, she left quickly and headed back into town.

After wandering around for a while constantly on edge, fearful of discovery, she eventually found the 'Byte' internet cafe.

As she'd never used one before, she had to ask at the counter what she needed to do.

The owner duly took her over to a station and showed her the process.

Having been shown how to log in to the pc she surfed the internet to get all the various media contact details to whom she was going to send the compromising pictures of Andy's indiscretion with Nadine.

Nervously she kept an eye on the entrance as she worked, all the while concerned that she might be discovered by a curious policeman.

Finally, after hastily typing up a 'public have a right to know letter' and printing off multiple copies of both letter and pictures, she quickly left the café to buy envelopes and stamps.

However, in her haste to complete her vicious mission and get back to her 'hiding' place, she absentmindedly left her memory stick in the pc station.

Fortunately, the owner of the café spotted it and quickly dashed out to see if he could catch her but she was nowhere in sight.

So, he put the memory stick under the counter to await her return when she realised her oversight.

As she hadn't returned after thirty minutes and business was slack, he decided to see if he could find any ownership details on Sue's memory stick.

He interrogated 'the stick' and listed the files on the device, on finding a word document, he opened it.

It was a letter which Sue had written to the local council complaining about the dustbin men. It contained her name and her home telephone number, so he decided to ring it.

He dialled the number and after a few rings it was answered.

'Hello, can I speak to…' he studied the letter again…'A Mrs Williams Screen please?'

'Who's calling?'

'It's the Byte internet Café.'

'Can I ask what it's about?' The voice asked.

'Yeah. She's just been in here and printed off some stuff but left her memory stick in the pc.'

Fortuitously, the police had just arrived at her house with a Scenes of Crime Officer (SOCO) to see if they could get any clues to where she was likely to be hiding out.

'Right, this is Graham Fredericks, Gloucestershire Constabulary, here. I want you to hang on to that until we get there. If she comes back in, please stall her.'

'Why? What's she done?'

'It's OK. She's not dangerous. I'll tell you when we get there.'

At last, this was the lead the Police were looking for.

In the meantime Sue had realised she had left the memory stick in the café and, in a panic, decided to collect it on her way to post the letters.

Back at the café she rushed over to where she had been working and was dismayed at not finding it still in the machine.

Quickly she went to the counter and waited impatiently while the owner's assistant dealt with another customer.

Eventually he became free and she interrogated him about the whereabouts of this 'very important' memory stick.

Unfortunately, the owner, who had been directed by the police to delay her, had just popped out to get some sandwiches and failed to pass the message on to his assistant about stalling her.

Consequently, the assistant looked under the counter and found the memory stick, which he immediately handed over to Sue.

Relieved to have reclaimed her vital blackmailing tool, she left the café.

It was only a matter of a few minutes later that Graham Fredericks arrived and flashed his warrant card.

'Where's the memory stick?' he demanded.

'Memory stick?' the assistant replied blankly.

'Yes. I told you to hang on to it and stall the lady.'

'Not me mate.'

'You spoke to me on the telephone,' the Policeman said exasperated.

'No. It was probably the boss.' The assistant replied defensively. 'Anyway the woman has just been back in here and I've given it her.'

'How long ago?' the policeman demanded.

'Oh, probably a minute.'

'Damn it. What was she wearing?' He barked, irritated by the lapse in communications.

The assistant gave him a shrug. 'Search me mate.'

'Thanks for nothing. What about CCTV?' The Detective asked spotting the camera.

'It's waiting to be repaired.'

Incensed, the policeman turned on his heel and radioed that Sue was in the area and for the 'boots on the ground' to keep their eyes open for her.

Sue had spotted the increased police activity and realised they were looking for her. She pulled the anorak hood further down over her face and made her way towards the post office, desperate to post the bundle of letters.

Sue saw them coming, the blue hats swivelling around clearly looking for her.

The letter box was tantalisingly close, the other side of the square but a policeman stood in her way.

She thought she'd evade them by finding another box. However as she stepped back to leave, she bumped into somebody and was just about to castigate them, when a voice she recognised said, 'Going somewhere?' the detective asked. 'I think that's it now. You've had your fun. You're nicked, Screen.'

'Don't call me that,' she said angrily, 'My name is Williams Screen as well you know, having interrogated me several times. I have rights. So just be careful.'

'So have your victims, Screen,' he said grabbing her hand to handcuff her.

'Careful of my back,' she said, resisting as he put handcuffs around her wrist.

'Hurt it hitting your husband did we? You should be more careful.'

'I just need to post these letters first please.'

'Sorry, you won't be posting anything for a long time. Escaping from custody will add a nice bit to your sentence. The judges don't like being messed around.

Someone cuffed her other wrist while Graham Fredericks took the envelopes from her.

Let's have a look in here shall we?' he said, opening one of the envelopes addressed to the local paper. 'What were you so desperate to post?'

'That's my private property.' She protested vigorously. 'You have no right to be looking in there.'

'So you were telling the judge you were only having fun when you had these extortion photos on your computer.' Graham Fredericks said, studying the letter. 'I don't think he'll share your sense of humour, especially when he sees what you've written. Take her away.'

Sue was loaded into a custody van and taken to the Police station.

Later, Rupert had the call he'd been hoping for from Graham Fredericks.

'We've got her. You can relax.' He said with an air of satisfaction. 'She's definitely back behind bars now where she deserves to be.'

'Oh great news. Many thanks.' Rupert breathed a sigh of relief. 'Let's hope she can't get out again.'

'No. I don't like having to chase felons after we've already sent them inside.' The detective said vociferously.' We catch them, they keep them. That's the name of the game.'

Rupert quickly told Jo that Sue was back inside.

'Oh, thank God for that.' She said tearfully. 'I don't think I could go through that awful anticipation again.'

'Don't cry sweetheart,' Rupert said, kneeling by her 'chair. 'I'll protect you.' He added tenderly, wrapping his arms around her.

Rupert rapidly passed the news on to the others.

'I've just heard from the police that bitch of an ex-wife of mine has been recaptured,' Rupert gleefully informed Carrie.

'About time too. Let's hope they hang on to her this time.' Carrie exploded, annoyed that the justice system had let Rupert down again.

'Yes, we've been on tenterhooks since her escape.' Rupert admitted. 'Anyway I've thanked your army mates and paid them as well. Let's hope we don't need them again.'

'Yes, you can sleep easy in your bed tonight.' Carrie reassured him.

'Yeah, hopefully.'

CHAPTER FIFTY FIVE

James had been recovering well from the transplant. He had impressed the doctors with the speed of his return to good health after just three and a half months since the major surgery.

Although the anti-rejection medication was still giving him a few side effects, he was generally feeling on top of the world.

Therefore, he kept his promise to take Ben to the mountain bike race that both Ben and Janie had been training for over several months. However, their journey was dogged by the sheer volume of traffic through the winding country roads and consequently they were running late.

'Look at this queue,' James said, also anxiously looking out for signage to the event.

Ben checked his watch. 'Damn. I think we've missed Janie's race now.'

'Sorry about that. I didn't realise the traffic was going to be so bad, otherwise we could have left earlier or hired a helicopter.'

'James, how do you know if you're gay or not?' Ben asked suddenly.

'Blimey, where did that come from?' James said, glancing across at him.

'Only, I've been wondering because I...I like being around you and Andy.'

'Doesn't mean to say you're gay. It's probably because you have no father...' James corrected himself quickly. 'It's probably because you look at us as a father figure that's all.'

'Yeah, I suppose.'

'Anyway, here's what we're looking for,' he said, spotting the heavy six bar agricultural entrance gate which was already open, and relieved to be changing the subject he added. 'Let's hope we're in time.'

Lycra clad bikers on their way to or from their races impatiently weaved in front of him as he drove slowly along the muddy track.

'I didn't realise it was so organised and well supported,' James said peering around as he threaded his car through the hundreds of others already parked on the rolling fields. 'It looks like the whole of the mountain biking fraternity are here, they're everywhere, like an occupying army.'

'This is a mountain biker's heaven, 'Ben said excitedly, looking around. 'All the big named bikes will be here. Names like Specialized, Cannondale, Mongoose. Each bike is worth thousands of pounds.'

'Really, I didn't realise they were so expensive,' James said in amazement.

'My own bike cost Geoffery over three thousand quid and that's under half the price of the most expensive ones.' Ben revealed.

'Heavens!'

'This will be the first real test of my lightweight carbon fibre frame. It's got full suspension and the drive train has got a Shimano ten speed cassette.' Ben informed James knowledgeably.

'Well, I don't know what that means but I'm sure you know what you're talking about. Let's hope it proves its worth and gives you a good race then.'

'There's a parking place over there,' Ben indicated, stretching his arm under James' nose.

Barely had James pulled into the space than Ben leaped out and undid his precious mountain bike from the bike rack attached to the boot.

'I know you're anxious about racing here, but If we've already missed Janie's race, why the rush now?' James asked, switching off the engine.

As the sound of the engine died, James could hear an indistinct commentary and 'pop' music playing continually over the PA.

'My race is due to start in thirty minutes and I don't know where to go.'

'Oh I see. I didn't realise. Is there anything I can help you with?' James offered

'No, I just need to get my stuff on and my head together.' Ben said, his voice betraying his nervous anxiety.

Ben was already wearing the brand new mountain bike clothes that James had bought him for his birthday. He had been training with Janie on the various dirt tracks around his home for some time and had done some minor races.

Janie had talked him into doing the race over the Malvern Hills at Eastnor Park, the biggest one he had ever entered.

He was excited but nervous about it. He knew a few other riders from his school who were racing there too.

'Crikey, this is a 'big' event isn't it?' James said looking around at the steep Malvern Hills. The craggy outline of the ridge looked like a miniature mountain range reminiscent of some of the uplands he'd seen in west Wales.

'Yes, it's part of a National mountain bike race series. Riders come from all over the country,' Ben said, continuing to check his bike out. 'There's lots of different races and categories.'

James' eye was attracted to a rider on a distant hill facing them. 'Look at that guy coming down that hill. If he falls off he'll kill himself,' he said concerned.

'That'll be one of the downhill bikers. Don't worry. They wear body armour.'

They watched in awe as the biker hurtled at breakneck speed through the tree line onto an open area of hillside opposite them, skilfully jumping over unseen obstacles and slewing the bike around at an incredible pace.

'The idea is to be the fastest down to win,' Ben added. 'Have you seen my race numbers? I need to put one on the frame and one on my jersey.'

'Yes, here they are,' James said, producing them from the glove compartment. Here are the cable ties I promised you too,' he said, giving him the black plastic straps.

Ben hastily attached the one number to his bike while James watched open mouthed as one racer after another hurtled down the hillside opposite.

'Wow! Look at them go.'

'I reckon he's a works team rider. You know, sponsored by the bike manufacturer,' Ben said, without looking up from his preparations. 'That's what I want to become, a 'works rider'. Would you mind pinning my race number on my jersey please?' Ben asked, at the same time slipping into his sidi cycling shoes.

'Yes, no problem.' James said, taking the safety pins from him and carefully securing the plastic race number to the back of Ben's jersey.

'Thanks. I'd love to give that downhill racing a crack, some day.'

'Well, you've got to dream.'

Ben climbed on to his bike, clipped his shoes into the pedals and after a few unsteady wobbles started riding his way back up on the track heading for where he hoped the start line was.

'Be careful and good luck,' James called. 'If I don't see you before, I'll see you back here after the race.'

'OK, thanks,' Ben shouted, without turning around and then he suddenly stopped.

'Whats the matter?' James asked concerned, walking quickly towards him.

'It's my back. The muscle's gone in to spasm. Oh shit, that hurts,' he said unclipping his feet and taking James proffered hand to climb off.

'Perhaps you ought to forget racing,' James suggested, looking at Ben's ashen face. 'Perhaps it was the ride in the car that exacerbated it?' he suggested.

'No chance. I've been training hard for this. I shall be OK in a minute.'

'Do you want some painkillers?'

'Yes please. In my bag,' Ben said, pained.

Ben leant on his bike while James dashed back to the car and found the tablets.

'Here,' he said giving Ben two. Have you got some water?

'Yes,' he said as he swallowed the tablets and lifted a water bottle out of the cage on his bike. 'How we doing for time?'

'Don't worry about that. Just catch your breath. Make sure you're OK first.'

After a few minutes Ben's colour returned as the painkillers took effect.

'I've got to go or I'll miss the start,' he said, climbing stiffly back on to his bike.

'Are you sure you should be racing?'

'Yes. I'll be OK.' Ben insisted.

James pushed him to give him forward momentum and Ben was soon lost to sight as he disappeared into a mass of other adrenalin pumped up riders.

On his way along the track Ben passed other riders some of whom were warming up 'pulling wheelies' and doing 'bunny hops' on their way to the start line.

Checking first that it was his race he was joining, Ben merged into a multi-coloured army of fashion conscious bikers already waiting on their equally expensive bikes in the Start/Finish area.

Each rider was similarly clad in a bright cycling top and wore the, comfort essential, padded lycra shorts with its vital chamois leather inner.

The biker's fashion statement was completed by a mandatory helmet, also in a myriad of colours, complimented with a pair of 'designer' sunglasses.

A very enthusiastic DJ was giving an excitable commentary over the top of loud pop music, creating an 'electric' atmosphere, further hyping up the high spirits of the massive crowd of spectators.

There was an air of tense excitement as Ben stiffly scooted his bike slowly through the others towards the front of the pack and managed to get to the sixth row from the start gate, exchanging some friendly banter as he moved forward.

'Oi...oi, Ben, over here.' Ben recognised Janie's voice.

He turned to see her at the front of the crowd barrier waving to him. She was wearing her bright yellow cycling kit she had worn in her race.

Unwilling to lose his place near the start gate he asked one of the other riders, 'Would you mind hanging on to my bike for me. I got to see the girlfriend.'

'No, that's OK,' the other said, grabbing the handlebars.

'Thanks, I won't be long,' Ben said, fighting his way over to her

'Hi,' she said, smiling.

'Sorry I missed your race. We got stuck in traffic. How did it go?'

'Not too bad. I finished about tenth out of fifty, I think.' She said pleased with herself.

'Oh well done.' He said enthusiastically. 'See. All that training was worthwhile.'

'Yes it was.' She agreed. 'Anyway how do you feel? You OK?'

'Yes, bit nervous,' he confessed. 'But I'll do my best.'

'How's your back feeling?'

'Ok at the moment,' he lied. 'Hope it lasts the race.'

'Well I've bought you a lucky charm to help you win,' she said and as she leant forward to secure a necklace around the back of his neck, she kissed him gently on the cheek.

Ben was taken aback by the show of affection. After all, although they had walked hand in hand, they had never kissed before.

Embarrassed, he desperately struggled to find some cool words to say but only came up with a pathetic, "I think I'll stay with you instead.'

Janie pushed him playfully away. 'Go on, but hurry back and I'll...'

The PA interrupted her. '*Five minutes to go Competitors, Five minutes.*'

'And best of luck,' she added.

As Ben made his way back to his bike, the riders started 'shuffling' up towards the start line.

The banter from the excited crowd diminished as the competitors started psyching themselves up to make a fast get away.

Ben kissed the necklace and looked across at Janie. Behind her, he saw that James had just arrived from the car park and was standing next to her.

'Pity Mum couldn't make it,' he thought, 'still I've got two supporters.'

'*Right riders, don't forget, this is a three lap race. Best of luck,'* the Commentator announced.

Ben subconsciously checked his helmet. He became focussed, determined to get a good start. He clipped one foot into a pedal and positioned it to the top of the chainset for maximum leverage.

The PA burst into life again. '*Five, four, three, two, one. GO*'. A horn sounded and they were away.

A brightly coloured avalanche charged across the start line and immediately hit a bottleneck as the start gate exit funnelled down from six wide into a maximum of two abreast. A few riders at the front of the pack collided and were inevitably unseated. Ben weaved his way through the fallen bikes and to his surprise dropped in to fourth place.

The Commentator was quick to inform the excited crowd; 'There is a collision on the start line. That's put the cat among the pigeons, as some of the favourites are down.'

Janie and James started shouting in excited unison 'COME ON BEN, COME ON.'

The spectators lost sight of the riders as they disappeared into the tree line, but reappeared at various places around the hilly route. The multi-coloured pack left a dust cloud in their wake as they charged around the drying track.

The course required 'technical' as well as physical abilities as it meandered uphill, through 'bomb holes' and over obstacles. Soon the demands of the course started stretching the line of riders out.

In the distance Janie could see that Ben still looked 'comfortable' in fourth place, his yellow jersey making him easily identifiable.

After a further fifteen minutes the riders had completed one circuit. The crescendo of support from the crowd of spectators increased as the leaders' streamed through the start finish area going flat out. A cowbell was rung repeatedly, hooters sounded as the excited crowd showed their support.

The Marshall changed the 'laps to go' board from three to two.

The Commentator informed the enthusiastic crowd. 'As the leaders go through for the first time John Hazelnut from Banana Sport is just in front of Roger Orange from Team Mad Panic; behind him Ian Hunt from HPP followed by an unsponsored rider Ben Bird.'

Janie and James add their voice to the supporters. 'COME ON BEN.'

'He's doing well isn't he?' James said, watching him disappear into the tree line.

'Yes.' Janie said, her stomach full of nervous butterflies.

'How did your race go?' James asked, his eyes still firmly on Ben's yellow jersey.

'Oh, very good thanks. I was pleased with my results. Anyway how are you now?' She enquired. 'The last time I saw you, you were being loaded into the back of an ambulance.'

'OK now, thanks.' He replied, 'I'm a lot better than I was. Let's hope things continue the way they're going.'

'I'm pleased to hear that.'

'I'm sorry for giving you such a fright.' James apologised.

'It wasn't your fault. These things happen. Ben told me about your operation and things. It sounded horrible.'

'Fortunately I didn't know too much about it. In fact it's because of Ben that I'm alive today.' He revealed.

'Really? He didn't tell me that.' Janie said looking at him, surprised.

'No, well Ben and I met in London in very strange circumstances and... well he helped me off the booze,' James volunteered. 'He's a really good friend. He could do with some luck.' James added quietly, thinking about all the issues in Ben's life. 'I hope his back holds out.'

'Why is it playing up again?' Janie asked, surprised at the news after Ben had assured her he was OK.

'Yes. He had to have two painkillers before he left the car park.' James informed her.

'Oh. He said it was OK.' Janie said, concerned.

They watched with increasing excitement and concern as the riders' streamed around the course.

The crowd noise increased, cowbells rang, hooters sounded as they hurtled through the Start/Finish again

At the end of the second lap Ben had dropped back to eighth place. He looked to be in pain.

'Oh dear! It looks like his back isn't going to last after all.' James said seeing Ben's pained expression. Nevertheless, he joined Janie shouting encouragement.

'COME ON BEN. YOU CAN DO IT' Janie and James chorused.

The laps to go board was changed to 'One'.

The field was well strung out now as the leaders headed towards the tree line.

'Oh come on Ben,' Janie whispered into her cupped hands, a knot of concern filling her stomach.

Suddenly, the leader jumped off his bike and looked despondently at his rear wheel. He kicked it in a desperate attempt to resolve whatever mechanical failure had caused him to stop.

The Commentator was quick to observe, '*Disaster. It looks like Hazelnut has punctured. That's going to make for an interesting result.*'

The former leader put his bike over his shoulder and started running around the course with it as the other riders' streamed past him.

As the riders emerged from the woods Ben appeared to have overcome his temporary setback and had fought his way back through the field towards the leading group.

'COME ON BEN,' Janie shouted, excitedly bouncing up and down.

The Commentator now echoed the excitement of the crowd as he announced *'It's up hill for the final time. This time the new first place man Roger Orange is being closed down by Ian Hunt. As the leaders approach the finish line, Hunt makes an audacious move on Orange. It's bound to end in disaster.*

Oh no, the two riders have collided and have taken each other off.

There's going to be words over that, but that gives third place Bird a chance to take the victory.'

Ben saw his opportunity and went hell for leather crossing the finish line first.

'Bird wins followed by Nolan and Harroway.'

James and Janie are both elated at Ben's victory, leaping up and down and hugging each other.

'Meanwhile, Orange and Hunt have picked them-selves up and are pushing their bikes over to finish fourth and fifth.'

James and Janie manoeuvred around dozens of dusty bikes and exhausted riders and quickly chased down a delighted Ben.

'Wow, that was exciting. I feel sorry for the others, but that's the name of the game, I won...I won.' Ben said emotionally, hugging both of them. A beaming smile filling his face.

'Congratulations Ben, that was brilliant. I was keeping my fingers crossed for you all the way round. I feel quite exhausted just watching,' James admitted.

'And your back? Janie asked conspiratorially, giving him an 'old fashioned look'.

'Yeah it started playing up after the first lap. But it was OK in the end'

'It wasn't OK before the start then was it?' Janie said chiding him.

'No.' Ben conceded, 'James told you then?'

'You're OK, that's the main thing. And you W O N too,' she said excitedly hugging the sweating Ben and putting her head on his shoulder.

'God that last lap, I tell you… my thighs were burning. But I did it, I did it.' And he kissed the top of Janie's head in his jubilation.

'Yes, you did. I'm so pleased for you,' James said smiling.

'Let's go to the stage for the prize giving,' Ben beamed, picking up his bike.

A large crowd of spectators were already gathered around the small stage when they arrived.

Janie kept her arm around Ben as they waited.

'Pity your Mum's not here, I know she would be very proud of you,' James said, breaking the silence.

'Yeah, well, another time perhaps!' Ben shrugged

The commentator climbed up on to the platform and said, '*And now after what has been a great day of racing. We have prizes for the final race of the day. In third place we have Paul Harroway.*'

The crowd applauded as the beaming rider climbed on to the podium and made a 'yes, I've done it gesture'.

'*The second place goes to Terry Nolan*'

The second place rider joined the other on the podium as the crowd applauded and he shook hands with the third place rider.

'*And finally,*' the commentator continued; '*The lucky winner of today's Fun race. Ladies and gentlemen, put your hands together for a brilliant ride by Ben Bird.*'

Janie and Ben untwined from each other as a smiling Ben headed towards the stage.

The crowd responded as before when Ben climbed jubilantly onto the podium and did a high five with the other two. He then grabbed their hands and raised them victoriously.

After Ben was presented with his trophy by one of the organisers, he stepped forward, kissed it and raised it triumphantly in the air.

James 'filled up' as he watched the prizewinning Ben beaming from 'ear to ear'.

The happy trio made their way back to James' car with Janie and Ben walking hand in hand, Janie carrying the Trophy in her free hand while Ben pushed his bike single handed.

'How did you get here Janie? Do you want a lift home?' James asked.

'No, it's OK. I came with my friend's Dad. But thanks.'

'Am I going to see you later?' Ben asked her, hopefully.

'I'm not sure. My Mum's respite carer will be going home after tea,' Janie said, unhappily. 'I need to be there for her.'

'Oh, OK. Never mind,' Ben sighed, disappointed.

Reading the signs, James discreetly busied himself in the car while Ben and Janie made their goodbyes.

CHAPTER FIFTY SIX

James took an excited Ben back home. On the journey, James said, 'with reference to our earlier discussion about recognising if you're gay or not. Judging by your farewell with Janie, I think you've just answered your own question.'

James pulled up outside Ben's house and helped him carry his trophy, bike and bag.

'OK Ben. Well done. I'm sure your Mum will be very proud of you.'

'Do you want to come in for a cuppa?'

'That would be nice. I'm in no rush. Yes OK. My new house is a bit empty at the moment.'

Ben stored his bike in its usual place in the hall and surprised that Beth hadn't greeted him, he opened the door of the lounge.

Beth was slumped on the sofa, an empty bottle of vodka by her feet. There was blood on the carpet. There were cuts on her forearms.

'Oh God, Mum!' Ben shouted in alarm. 'James come quick, Mum's bleeding.'

James rushed into the lounge and saw Beth.

'Oh Beth, what have you done?' He said to the unconscious woman. 'All that good work keeping away from the temptation and now you do this! You silly, silly woman!'

James quickly checked her arms and could see the injuries weren't serious.

'It's OK Ben. Don't worry. I think the cuts are superficial. We can sort this out without getting anybody else involved.' James said calmly.

Ben slumped down on a chair distraught, the euphoria of his win rapidly draining away.

After cleaning the cuts and putting some large plasters over the site of Beth's injuries, James set about the task of sobering her up.

With large measures of sympathy and copious quantities of black coffee he eventually managed to get some sense out of her.

'Did you hurt yourself?' James asked quietly, already sure that she had self-harmed.

'Yes.'

'Why would you do that?'

'Because I let you and Ben down,' she wailed. I said I would keep off the booze and I failed again. I had to punish myself. Oh I'm so sorry,'

'Sorry! You don't know the meaning of the word.' Ben said coldly. 'In spite of what you promised me at the hospital and after you saw what James had gone through because of the booze.'

'I know, I know,' Beth replied tearfully.

'What was the point of getting help from the young carer's people? What about your plan to quit? Oh you're hopeless.' Ben walked the window in disgust and stared out, unseeing.

'Not that you're probably interested, but I won my race, Mum,' Ben said quietly.

'Yes you should be proud of your son. He rode a brilliant race and won.' James added proudly. 'Anyway, why didn't you come with us today Beth?' he asked gently.

'I was going to, but Jenny persuaded me to have a nice 'girly' session with her while Ben was away playing on his bike. So we could have some fun like we used to.' She sobbed.

Ben felt gutted. His Mother had demeaned his glorious victory as 'playing'.

'Who's Jenny?' James asked.

One of her pathetic friends,' Ben replied angrily. 'She's been the cause of a lot of Mum's problems.'

'I was doing OK …I resisted the booze to start off with but then your father came,' she said looking at Ben tearfully, 'and started demanding money again.'

Ben looked at her horrified, feeling guilty that in looking for his father he'd started something he now had no control over.

'Anyway after we'd had a shouting match on the doorstep,' Beth continued, 'he left with his tail between his legs.' Beth looked at Ben imploringly, 'I told you it would be a nightmare if you went looking for him didn't I, Ben?'

'That's right make excuses.' Ben said already feeling guilty. 'Blame me.'

'My nerves were all over the place, after so long without touching a single drop. Then Jenny persuaded me that a little glass wouldn't hurt; that it would be alright. Well it wasn't was it? I got drunk.'

'But why did you cut yourself?' James asked.

'I'm so weak willed,' she wailed, 'I'm sorry. After Jenny left I realised what I'd done. I had to punish myself for letting you both down. I'm so sorry Ben… James. You must hate me?' she wailed.

Ben ran out of the room and sat on the bottom of the stairs and cried. His brilliant day had descended into a nightmare.

'Perhaps she's right,' he thought. 'Perhaps it is my fault. If I hadn't tried to find my Dad.'

His emotions were all over the place, winning the race had been so wonderful, but his mother's behaviour had negated all the pleasure from it.

James gave him a few moments by himself then came out and sat on the stairs by his side.

'Ben, I am so sorry that you have to continue to deal with your mother's problems. But believe me, there is a light at the end of the tunnel.'

'Yeah? I can't see it. All I see is her ending up like you. I'm sorry I didn't mean to…'

'No, you're absolutely right. If she carries on, she will. The worse thing is that she will also lose the person who loves her most, too. Won't she?'

'It was my fault that Dad came. Perhaps I am to blame for her going back on the booze?' Ben repeated his guilty thoughts.

'No. You mustn't blame yourself. You did what any kid would do. Looking for a parent.'

'But it went wrong.'

'You weren't to know that,' James comforted.

'I just can't take any more of this.' Ben said tearfully.

'I know, I know. But you don't have to cope with this alone anymore.'

'What do you mean?'

'I have made a decision to invite you both to live with me in my new house in Churchup.'

'What? Live with you! Why would you do that?'

'This will move your Mum away from all the bad influences around here and hopefully give you both a fresh start. Possibly a new circle of friends. And your Dad wouldn't bother you either, I'll see to that.'

'No way mother would agree. She won't leave here.'

'She will. She said she'd be willing to do anything to stop you running away again.'

'Yeah! Just another one of her false promises. I don't believe any of them anymore.'

'You will have your own side of the house,' James continued, ignoring Ben's protestations. 'So we aren't getting in each other's way...and I have a double garage where you can lock your bikes up, do training, whatever you want.'

Ben looked James to see if he was being sincere. 'Do you mean it?' he asked, a small bubble of excitement building in his stomach.

'Yes. I think you know you can trust my word.' James said. 'I can also keep an eye on your Mother too. Hopefully, together, we can help to keep her on the straight and narrow.'

Ben was starting to warm to the idea when there was a knock on the door.

'I hope it's not my Dad, otherwise he'll get a mouthful from me,' Ben said angrily, running to the door.

He yanked it open ready to 'let fire', but it was Janie standing there, smiling at him.

'Hi. My Mum said she was OK for a couple of hours. So I thought I'd come and help you celebrate your win.'

Ben rushed forward and enveloped her in his arms and gave her a great big hug.

'You've made my day. Thank you,' Ben said, welling up.

CHAPTER FIFTY SEVEN

Carrie unlocked the office door and automatically switched on the electric kettle for the first 'brew' of the day. She checked her watch. It was six o'clock.

'Good,' she thought. She had kept to her schedule.

Getting by on a few hours' sleep a night and then getting up early was ingrained into her metabolism by her years of military service. She had developed the ability to sleep with half an eye open always ready to leap into action at any time of the night.

Unlike Tim, who had difficulties getting out of his bed at any time of the day.

She had established a regular routine - kettle then computer, while both electric devices 'warmed up' and remembered their purpose in life. She would cover her desk with mail trays, files, pens - the detritus of a busy office. When she left at night it was all spirited away into a cupboard. Maintaining order and a strict clear desk policy was part of her logical, disciplined mind.

Finally, she placed her small treasure chest, which she'd nicknamed 'Pandora's box', precisely in its usual place by the right hand side of her keyboard. Initially, she had kept it at home, but since Tim had prised it open and invaded her privacy, she now carried it with her at all times.

Their plans to expand the 'Just Do It Walking Company' business right across the country as well as their schedule of local walks, was keeping Carrie busy.

Frustratingly, Tim was still waiting to take delivery of their new Land Rover Discovery and making arrangements to get it specially modified.

So she had forgotten about the random messages they had been getting from the reclusive Veteran.

However this morning, when she 'logged on' to her email, there was notification from Facebook about another message. She clicked on the link and read.

SWS;

Yes the date and time is fine. I'm sorry but I don't have a Grid Ref or Postcode. The location you are heading for is near Falfield. From Gloucester direction follow A38 towards Bristol. Go through Falfield until you see the signs for the Eastwood Park. Turn up the drive, go past the entrance to the training centre and park in a small layby. Flash your lights three times, then switch your engine off. Walk along the track and I will meet you.

'Whoops I had forgotten about you, matey. I hope the date is still free.' She checked her diary.

Satisfied that she could still make it she replied:-

Carrie JDIW

I see you haven't lost any of the precision of your military training, all very clandestine. The directions are fine thanks. I should be able to find that location from Google maps etc.

I'll bring all the necessary equipment for a night hike. I don't know what you've got by way of walking gear, so I will bring a selection for you. I'll work out a suitable route. You'll be the first to do an overnight hike. Perhaps we'll start a new trend for night hikes. OK, I look forward to seeing you there.

Carrie looked at 'Pandora's box' and wondered what state of mind she would find the person in. Perhaps she could help whoever it was to contact 'Combat Stress' and get them back into society, if that was what they wanted.

Whether it was psychosomatic or not, she certainly felt easier in her mind having the box to 'prop her up.'

CHAPTER FIFTY EIGHT

The Law firm had identified the majority of outstanding bills associated with Geoffery's estate and had sent Andy a notification of the amount of money that would be given to the Dorothy and Tom hospice.

Andy duly took the letter to the chief hospice administrator Ann Place, who was surprised and delighted to receive it.

'Mr Foster said he'd leave us a legacy in his will, but three million pounds is far in excess of what I was expecting. It will go a long way to helping us to add more facilities to the hospice,' she gushed.

'Yes. See. It was worth my while working for him wasn't it?' Andy said, recalling all the angst that he had received from her during the time he was working part time for Geoffery.

She ignored his 'dig'.

After completing the windfall delivery, Andy started his shift.

Unusually, the hospice had a special wing for young children. Andy loved working there in spite of the heartbreak of seeing young ones so gravely ill.

He tried to stop comparing his young patients to his own children but it was hard not to see the similarities and recognise that these children would miss out so much when their young lives would be cut, so cruelly short.

One of his patients was a pretty young girl called Angelina. She had lovely piercing blue eyes which, in spite of her illness, stayed bright and alert. She'd arrived at the hospice with beautiful shoulder length hair, but unfortunately, her golden locks had been an early victim of the aggressive chemotherapy she had bravely undergone. Her pale skin was almost transparent but her spirit was awe inspiring.

She was about the same age as his own five year old daughter.

'Andy? Do you think my Daddy will be sad when I die?' she asked quietly.

'Why, yes of course he will. Why do you ask?'

'My Daddy is a soldier in the army, so he doesn't see me very often.'

'Oh that is sad. But sometimes grownups have to do things that they don't want to do, to earn money for the family. For instance, I spend a lot of time at the hospice here looking after people who are unwell. So my family don't see too much of me either.'

'Do your children miss you?'

'Yes, I'm sure they do but their Mummy looks after them really well.'

'I think my Daddy will be sad because he hasn't seen me grow up.'

'Sure, I expect he will. But I bet he thinks about you every night...and I guess he's got your picture stuck up where he can see it too.'

'I've got his picture on my cupboard here,' the little girl said, pointing at the picture of a smiling soldier in full desert camouflage gear.

'Oh yes, I can see it. He looks like a nice man.'

'I kiss his picture before I go to sleep every night.'

'That's good. And I see you have a pretty dolly too.'

'Her name is Misha. My daddy brought it for me from abroad.'

'That's nice.'

'I tell my Dad on the phone not to worry about me, that I'm OK...and he tells me not to worry about him because he drives a big armour covered lorry so he is safe.

I feel sorry for my Mum because she worries about both of us.'

'Yes, I'm sure she does. Well I think it's time for you to go to sleep now, don't you?'

'I need to say my prayers first to ask baby Jesus to look after my mummy and especially my daddy.'

'Ok.'

'Do your children say their prayers too, Andy?'

'Yes I think Amy does. Molly is still too little.' In reality Andy didn't know. He hadn't put them to bed for a long time.

Andy watched the frail youngster hold her hands together and say her prayers. He had a tear in his eye as he watched.

Here she was, desperately ill and instead of bemoaning her own fate, she was thinking of the pain of others.

What a wonderful compassionate person she would have grown up to be if she had not been struck down by leukaemia.

It made him think about his interaction with his own children. He realised that he wasn't engaging with them as much as he should do. He didn't even know which cartoons Amy liked or what music she preferred.

On the other hand, he felt he was doing a good job for his patients and the scouts. But this was other people's kids. So why was he abandoning his own children? It didn't make sense, he had to admit.

What if one of his children contracted a life threatening illness? It would be too late to be a good parent then.

Andy heard her say 'And god bless Andy and his children too. Amen.'

Angelina picked up the picture of her father and kissed it. 'Goodnight Daddy. Be safe.'

Andy ensured the little girl was comfortable. 'Good night Angelina' he said before moving on to another patient.

At the end of his shift, Andy went home. Helen was already in bed.

In the kitchen, stuck to the wall, he noticed a new picture that Amy had done.

It was of two stick people holding hands painted with crude child-like brush strokes.

She had written the words 'Daddy and Mummy' in random sized multicolour letters across the bottom of the page.

He could almost imagine her concentration as she copied the words given to her by her teacher.

Each letter successfully completed would have brought a smile, a sense of achievement.

She would have been so eager to show her Mother how clever she was when she came to collect her.

'Her Mother.' Andy dwelled on the thought.' Her Mother. Not me.'

He reached out and touched the painting. Gazing at the sloping letters which ran off the edge of the page, a 'lump' formed in his throat.

'What do I have to do to get my family back? Or was it already too late? Has Amy already relegated me from her heart? Am I now just the bread winner with no emotional ties?' he wondered.

On his way to bed Andy opened Amy's bedroom door a chink and looked at the sleeping child.

Unlike Angelina, her long tousled hair cushioned her head, a few wisps stuck to her rosy cheeks. She had no tubes or cannulas restricting her freedom.

His heart told him what to do. The decision was made.

CHAPTER FIFTY NINE

Carrie came off the M5 at junction 13 and headed south on the A38 towards Bristol.

The veteran had expressly requested for Carrie to come alone for a one to one walk. Carrie empathised with the request, for, as a troubled veteran herself, she appreciated the problem of interacting with others.

Although Tim was concerned about her going by herself, Carrie insisted that she would be alright.

In spite of the weather forecast of continued thundery showers Carrie had decided to go ahead with the walk anyway.

She recalled the directions in the Facebook posting:-
The location you are heading for is near Falfield. Follow A38 towards Bristol go through Falfield until you see the signs for the Eastwood Park.

'Ah, here it is. Right. I have to go up the drive and past the entrance to the training centre. Right now, where's this small layby?' she said peering into the night. 'Oh yes, I see it.'

Carrie steered the new Land Rover Discovery into the small layby and flashed the headlights as directed.

She turned the engine off, got out and stopped by the side of her car while her eyes got used to the dark.

It was a warm humid evening. The rain showers had finally stopped. There was a freshness in the air. She could smell the aroma of freshly mown grass.

'Well, someone obviously took advantage of the break in the rain to do some gardening,' she thought.

She decided not to use her head torch as the intermittent starlight was sufficient to find her way. Silently, she started walking along the small muddy track.

'Somewhere along here is our mysterious veteran. Although, I'm surprised they chose this place, it's not the remotest of locations,' she thought, looking at the lights from nearby houses.

Her senses were heightened as she soundlessly moved along the track. Her night vision was giving her the confidence of where she was placing her feet. It was as if she was back on patrol.

She was listening carefully to her surroundings. In the distance she could hear the roar of traffic on the motorway, nearby a faint hubbub of voices, but in the woods it was quiet. Too quiet, she thought. It was odd that there was no bird song. Unusual, for the robin is quite often one of the nocturnal songsters.

A sudden rustling behind her made her stop midstride. She was about to turn to see the source of the noise, but too late. She felt a blow to the back of her head, followed by an excruciating pain. She blacked out.

Carrie slowly regained consciousness. She could hear a car engine and felt movement. She was obviously being driven somewhere by somebody.

She tried to open her heavy eyelids, but they refused to budge. Her head ached. Her mind was confused. Her mouth felt as though it was full of cotton wool.

Was she dreaming? Was this one of her nightmares? But normally she didn't feel pain. Now the back of her head hurt and she felt like she'd been stung by a bee in her buttocks.

She tried to lift her head but it felt too heavy.

By her side, a voice said.

'Come back to the land of the living have we? Shit ! That's a pity.'

Carrie struggled to recognise the voice or recall the name of the owner.

'That injection was supposed to have knocked you out for longer than this. That amount of sodium thiopental was supposed to have been enough to keep you under until it was over. Another five minutes would have done it. Sod it! I shall have to have words with my contact in the prison pharmacy.'

Carrie slowly lifted her heavy head, opening her reluctant eyelids. Then she remembered to whom the voice belonged. It was that awful woman Sue.

But it couldn't be. She had been recaptured. She was in prison.

'I must be imagining it,' Carrie thought. 'Perhaps she was dreaming after all. What did she say about an injection?'

'I've been waiting a long time to get back at you. You bitch. Now it's your turn to feel fear,' Sue screeched.

'What...what the hell's going on?' Carrie had difficulty getting her lips to form the words. 'Where... what the...' Slowly the fog in her mind was clearing. 'I...I was supposed to meet somebody.'

'Yes, I know. Marvellous this social media stuff isn't it? Anybody can pretend to be who they want to be.'

Carrie swivelled her head and looked across at the face beside her. She had to keep blinking her eyes to clear a misty film which seemed to cover them. Desperately she tried to focus. Then, as if a veil had been drawn aside, she could see that it really was Sue.

'Pretend to be...' Carrie said, running the words through her sluggish brain. 'So It was you. You are SWS?'

'Of course it's me. I can't believe that you were so thick not to recognise the link SWS – Sue Williams Screen. I just had to tantalise you with that,' Sue said gleefully.

As her level of consciousness increased Carrie realised she was in her own car. She could smell the newness of the Discovery. She recognised that they were travelling at speed. 'I thought you were in prison?'

'I was transferred to an open prison at Falfield and was assessed as a harmless and model prisoner. I told them what they wanted to hear so that categorised me at the lowest level. I'm even allowed some privileges, including use of the internet. So tonight I went for a little walk, just to see you. I hope you're grateful.'

'They'll lock you up again.'

'I shall be back before they know I'm missing. It'll all be over within an hour. We're only half an hour from the prison. Anyway, being in prison is the perfect alibi for me, if they even suspect foul play. Which they shouldn't.'

'Foul play! What will be over in an hour?'

'Oh I don't want to spoil the surprise. You'll find out soon enough. Anyway if they do find out it's going to be worth it to get my revenge on you. It's the only thing that's kept me going over the last year.'

As the fog in her mind cleared further, Carrie suddenly realised that her trousers and prosthetic legs had been removed. 'Where are my legs?'

'They're safe in the car. It was easier to carry you without them. So I removed them. Don't worry you'll soon be reunited with them. Anyway, you won't need those plastic things where you're going.

By the way, nice knickers. Does your boyfriend Tim like lacy ones?'

'Cow! You'll pay for this,' Carrie said, uncharacteristically losing her cool.

As she attempted to move, she realised her hands were tied behind her back and the seat belt was jammed tight across her chest.

'I don't think so.' Sue said confidently. 'You'll find those cable ties will cut into your wrists if you struggle. Now be a good girl and sit still.'

'Where are we going?'

'You'll find out soon enough.'

Through the rain swept windscreen Carrie could see that they were driving through a housing estate.

'You were obviously impressed by my military training? It evidently fooled you,' Sue said smirking.

'You've never been in the military in your life.'

'Well that's where you're wrong.

'Do you mean you were in the services too?' Carrie asked, in surprise.

'It was going to be my lifeline, my escape from my violent father and shitty family life.'

'What happened?' Carrie asked, feigning interest, trying to win some time.

'He was in the services himself. He couldn't cope with civvy life after being in action on the beaches in the

Dunkirk. I suppose these days they would call it Post Traumatic Stress.

He was a selfish, evil bastard, who used to spend the family allowance on booze. When he was thrown out of the pub, he'd come home and beat up our Mother.' Sue said angrily. 'I couldn't wait to get away from him and leave home. Eventually I joined the army to escape him.'

'Now I understand why you're like you are.'

'What's it to you? In my neighbourhood, you had to be tough to survive.'

'No wonder you are such a violent person.' Carrie observed.

'Oh, I was tough enough for the army. But they thought I was too aggressive.'

'I can understand that.'

Sue continued her revelations while Carrie was desperately trying to hatch a plan to escape.

'Nobody got the better of me. I could have been in the Regiment too. Unfortunately one of the instructors pushed me too far and I 'chinned him.' I was returned to my unit and subsequently charged with assault, court marshalled and sent to Colchester to serve my sentence. Then they gave me a dishonourable discharge. It was the end of my dreams. I never forgave the army. The bastards.'

'Sorry about that, but you've got the wrong idea about me.'

'You're a soldier, an assassin. Isn't that what you were trained to do?'

'Not now. Now I'm a civilian.'

'The only difference between us is that you used to get paid for your anger and I got jailed for mine.'

'Anger doesn't come in to it. It's all about being in control. I was doing my duty, serving my country.'

'Bullshit, you were serving yourself and getting all the commendations for doing it.'

Carrie could see that they had passed the housing estate and were now in the countryside driving parallel to a river. Caught in the headlights, she could see that the river level was nearly bank high following two weeks of thundery rain.

Sue took her eyes off the road for a second and fumbled in the driver's door looking for something.

'Well enough conversation about the services. I think it's time we put you back to sleep with another little jab. Hopefully you'll never wake up again this time,' she said, removing a hypodermic syringe from the door pocket.

'If they find your body, they'll put it down to an accident; lost control whilst driving along the banks of the swollen River Severn. What a shame,' she mocked.

'You'll never get away with it.'

'You ought to know me better than that. I always achieve what I set out to do. Now just keep still and it will all be over shortly.'

Sue swopped the syringe to her left hand and raised it like a dagger to jab into Carrie's foreshortened thigh.

But as Sue returned her gaze to the road and concentrated on taking a bend, Carrie twisted her body sideways and was able to release the seat belt catch with her tied hands.

'Oh no you don't!' Sue said, elbowing Carrie in the chest, the blow pushing her back in to her seat.

Sue dropped the syringe which fell on to the carpeted floor on the passenger side.

'Shit,' she said, trying to see where it had fallen.

Carrie saw her chance. Her desire to escape gave her extra strength and she swung herself over to the driver's seat head butting Sue on the side of her temple.

The car veered from side to side in the narrow country lane as they fought, the brand new Land Rover Discovery bouncing off small saplings and scraping paintwork off on sharp hawthorn bushes bordering the narrow lane. Foolishly Sue did not ease up on the accelerator as they battled.

Distracted by the conflict, she failed to see another sharp bend coming and the car crashed straight through a small copse at speed.

Such was the velocity of the out of control vehicle that its trajectory carried it twenty feet from the bank in to the swollen river, where it landed with an almighty splash.

The Discovery was rapidly spun around by the strong current and straightaway it started taking in water. The heavy weight of the engine forcing the front of the car down and quickly submerging the bonnet. As the water flooded the electrics, the lights went out.

With all thoughts of drugging Carrie now gone, Sue's mind switched to self-preservation.

She grabbed the door handle and tried to push it open. It refused to move. She remembered that she had locked all the doors to stop Carrie escaping.

She pushed the central locking buttons but nothing happened. There was no reassuring clunk as the solenoids released the locks. The buttons weren't responding.

Frantically she jabbed at the electric windows switch too. Nothing moved.

Then the truth dawned on her. The river water had killed all the cars electrics, rendering all the switches ineffective.

They were helplessly trapped. Escape was impossible.

'You stupid bitch. Now you've killed both of us,' Sue shouted as she stood up on her seat and started kicking at the windscreen.

She was now panicking as the cold muddy brown water invaded their space and quickly rose up in the car.

'Undo my hands and I'll get us out of here,' Carrie shouted over the sound of rushing water.

'What? So you can escape and leave me to drown? Think again.'

'Why are you such a stupid vicious bitch?' Carrie asked, trying to twist her now wet wrists out of her restraints.

'You're not the only one to have had a shitty life,' Sue shouted, still vainly kicking at the windscreen.

'I never said I had a bad life. Until I lost my legs, it was a great life in the army,' Carrie said desperately trying to think of a plan as the freezing water ran into the seat swab. Time was running out

'Look, untie me and I'll get us out.'

'Oh yeah. What are you going to do? Kick the windscreen in with your stumps?' Sue said mockingly, retrieving a sheath knife out of the door pocket.

'Undo me or we're going to die.'

'At least we'll die together. I've got a knife, perhaps I should finish you off now.' Sue said malevolently.

Carrie thought quickly to persuade her otherwise. 'Look. Cut these plasticuffs and I'll get both of us out of here,' Carrie suggested.

'Yeah, and kill me into the bargain. You've got to be joking,' Sue said, still vainly kicking at the windscreen. The water was rising at an alarming rate and now up to the bottom of the dashboard.

'Look, I know how to get us out of here. I've been trained in escaping from a sinking car. The boffins have figured out a method on this type of car. Just undo me. I reckon by the rate that the water is coming in, we've only got about 30 seconds before the car sinks altogether.'

'I've got a better idea, you tell me and I'll do it.'

'And leave me here! Come on, I wasn't born yesterday. It's either both of us or neither of us.'

'I suppose this was all part of your specialist training. Well, they wouldn't train me, the bastards.'

'Sorry I can't help that. But we're both going to be part of the past unless we get out of here.'

The water had now risen to cover the top of the dashboard. The buoyancy of the water was lifting Carrie out of her seat; they were being forced together, shoulder to shoulder. The small air pocket was reducing at an alarming rate.

'OK, turn around,' Sue instructed. Carrie did as she was bid quickly. Sue ran her hands down Carries submerged arms, found the plastic cable ties and cut them.

Quickly Carrie grabbed hold of Sue's arm.

'Give me the knife,' she demanded.

'What, so you can kill me?'

Suddenly there was a loud bang on the outside of the car.

'What the hell?' Sue said, frantically looking around.

Unexpectedly the car tilted, forcing the bonnet further down. Water now covered the whole of the windscreen forcing them to move backwards to the air pocket over the boot.

Outside, the large tree which had impacted with the back of the car was pushing it along in the strong current.

'No, you fool. I'm going to cut the windscreen seal,' Carrie said breathlessly, the water now lapping her chin.

Reluctantly Sue gave her the knife fully expecting to feel the point of it going into her chest. Instead, Carrie took a deep breath and ducked her head underwater and went to work on the rubber seal she had been told was a weak point, she hoped they were right.

Tracing the line of the windscreen with her fingers she found the spot and jabbed at the rubber, thrusting the knife between the metal and the glass. Success! The knife penetrated the rubber. Running out of breath she surfaced into the small air pocket where Sue was now spluttering.

'Done it?' Sue demanded.

'Not yet.'

Carrie gulped another lungful of air and disappeared again to work on the seal.

She quickly found the knife again jammed in the frame and twisted it to lever the windscreen. Her fingers sought to find the edge of the seal and desperately she tried to pull the rubber to unravel it from around the periphery of the glass. It refused to move.

Her lungs bursting, she was forced to surface again. Gasping, she bobbed up into the air pocket face to face with Sue.

Realising time had run out she shouted at Sue. 'I need your help. Take a deep breath and we're going to pull the seal out and go out through the windscreen without coming back up here OK?'

'OK,' Sue said, breathlessly.

'On my count. One, two, three.'

Together they ducked under. Suddenly the car spun around as the tree was caught again by the current and was carried off down river.

Carrie was briefly disorientated by the movement but quickly regained her bearings. Holding Sue's hand she led her to the small piece of protruding rubber.

Together they pulled at it. Nothing moved. Their fingers kept slipping off the rubber. Sue pushed Carrie's hand out of the way and now, able to grasp more of the seal, pulled it partly away from the frame.

She placed Carrie's hand on the glass which now moved slightly. Carrie used all her strength, her lungs bursting.

Quickly Carrie squeezed through the small gap that opened between screen and frame and kicked her way up to the surface away from the sinking car.

After what seemed a lifetime, her head finally broke through in to the cold night air, she gorged herself on the elixir of life, taking great gulps to fill her aching lungs. Her head felt woozy from hyperventilating, oxygen starvation and the knockout drug.

She trod water and waited for Sue to bob to the surface. But Sue did not appear.

CHAPTER SIXTY

Andy's head was reeling from the emotions of the day. Talking to Angelina and seeing Amy's picture had made him rethink his life.

Coupled with the visit to the school with Helen he realised the embarrassment that she was experiencing daily from the tongues of the school gate gossips.

Although he had only once experienced the sly comments and giggling innuendo, Helen had to undergo this several times a day whilst walking through the wagging tongues.

'Oh, that was horrible,' he thought. 'I had no idea what she has been going through. Poor Helen.'

The thoughts disturbed his sleep so he got up in the early hours and decided to write a letter to himself to clarify his thoughts.

As he got out of bed he disturbed the light sleeping Helen.

'Is it one of the girls?' Helen croaked, her voice full of sleep.

'No,' he whispered. 'It's alright. Go back to sleep.'

'What time is it?'

'Half past three. I can't sleep.'

Helen turned over and went back to sleep while Andy went downstairs. He found a notepad and pen. He poured out his thoughts and wrote for an hour.

Satisfied he had unburdened himself, although he hadn't actually come up with a solution, he dozed off in the chair.

Helen was unsettled by his absence and concerned when he hadn't returned to bed. So she crept downstairs only to find Andy asleep, the notepad and pen by his side.

She picked up the notepad and read the letter he had headed 'A letter, never meaning to send.'

My Dearest Darling Helen,

A part of my heart died today-that is the emotional bit not the biological side of me. So don't get worried or rush to check out the Life insurance policy just yet.

She smiled at his attempted humour.

I realised at last (you'll be pleased to know) just what a self-centred fool I have been, concentrating on my own aims and not our family.

I realise I have been living in a bubble of my own self-glorification and not appreciating what you have been doing by building and cementing the family base from which I can do the things I want to do.

The other day I ran the gauntlet in the school playground of wagging tongues just once and it hurt. Heavens knows how you put up with it day after day.

I am sorry that I have put you in this dilemma through my thoughtless, but innocent actions.

Although I have done nothing to be ashamed of, I realise that the circumstances of the events have stretched the credibility of the truth.

Thanks to you, I have been able to do my demanding job. You have been my rock, my confidante, my sounding board. Somebody I could off load my troubles to *when sadness overtakes me from the death of a special patient.*

You have allowed me the opportunity to do my Scouting and help turn around the lives of disadvantaged young people.

I felt good about feeling good, confident in my personal achievements.

But I realise that while I have been focussed on my own rewarding interests I have taken my eye off the most important part that gave structure to my life and allow me to do what I do - MY family.

How could I have been so blind to the dangerous desertion of my own family whilst climbing up my own 'pyramid of needs'.

Please forgive my short-sightedness. How can I ever vindicate myself? Or make you feel proud of me again – or is that me, just being self-indulgent again?

I used to think that all the good deeds I did as a Scout Leader and Hospice nurse made me a pillar of society. I realise now my vanity has actually resulted in my being a pillock not a pillar.

Helen smiled.

I know you do not ask for much, but I will do my best to meet your simple request of spending more time with you and the girls.

Hopefully, that will make you and the girls closer to me and restore my 'boasting' rights of being an all-round 'good egg' Oh dear, there I go again.

Finally let me assure you that you have no love rivals – apart from work and scouts. You are my only mistress.

Deepest Love Andy

Helen woke him. At first he thought he was dreaming. He struggled to open his heavy eyes. Helen stood in front of him with the notepad in her hand.

'Andy, what's this?'

'Oh heavens! You weren't supposed to see it. Sorry I...just...was going to rip it up...It's a bit soppy isn't it?'

'I'd say tender was a better way to describe it. Do you really mean this?'

'Yes, but I didn't have the guts to say it.'

'Oh Andy. Why do you make life so difficult?'

She knelt in front of him and enfolded him in her arms.

He pulled back from the embrace and studied her face. He looked deep into her eyes and saw the spark of love that he had been looking for. They kissed passionately like young lovers. Their love renewed.

CHAPTER SIXTY ONE

'Oh God where is she?'

Carrie frantically looked around her to see if Sue had surfaced somewhere else. But there was no sign of her. No frightened face staring back at her in the dark.

'Oh shit, I'm going to have to find her.'

Quickly she ducked back down to look. But the current had swept her away from the submerged car.

Desperately she surfaced again and estimated where the car was likely to be. She swam against the strong current until she found it after a few yards.

Finding the roof first she traced it around to the front of the car and the windscreen.

She ducked under water again and felt around the edges of the glass. She quickly discovered that Sue's hand was jammed in the partially displaced windscreen.

'The pressure of the water had obviously sprung it back in place preventing Sue from following me through,' Carrie thought.

Using all the strength she could muster Carrie kicked purposefully at the windscreen. But to no avail. Her stumps just slid sideways across the glass.

Changing tactics she jammed her fingers in to the edge of the glass and pulled. She was relieved to feel the screen move and finally dislodge.

Running out of air again she frantically grabbed the unconscious Sue's hand and struck out for the surface.

The trip seemed to take an age. Her lungs were hurting and bright stars filled her head. At last she surfaced and quickly pulled the lifeless Sue's face clear of the water.

Now on the surface the current was creating waves, the turbulence bouncing them around in the water, threatening to drown them again.

Carrie was very doubtful that she could continue to tread water long enough to keep both of their heads above the water.

Debris brought down by the flood was knocking into them. Trees and bushes raced past them in the strong current.

Carrie thrust her arm out hoping to grab hold of a tree or branch to help them. Instead her fingers found something soft and woolly. It was the fleece of a drowned and very bloated sheep.

She did not care about the fetid smell coming from the rotting corpse. She was just grateful that the gases that inflated it's stomach was adequate to provide sufficient buoyancy to keep them afloat as they were carried further along the river.

Conscious that unless she did something quickly Sue would die in her arms. Carrie clamped her mouth around her limp lips and blew, hoping at least that some air would get into her lungs. Carrie continued this operation as often as her own tired lungs allowed.

The trio - Sue, Carrie and the sheep, were eventually spat out by the current on a bend in the river and swept towards the shore.

Reluctantly letting go of their fleecy life raft, Carrie grabbed hold of a tree branch as they were swept towards the muddy bank. The sheep was quickly caught up again by the current and disappeared into the night.

Without her prosthetic legs Carrie was at a great disadvantage on land. However by doing a 'bum shuffle' she was able to drag Sue partially out of the water.

Wasting no time, she straddled the unconscious woman and started CPR.

Although completely exhausted by her escape and rescue efforts, Carrie nevertheless carried on pumping her patient's chest and blowing air into her lungs for ten minutes with no sign of life.

'Come on you bitch,' she shouted, thumping Sue's chest.' Breathe.'

Suddenly Sue coughed. A fountain of water gushed out of her mouth.

Carrie quickly rolled her over on to her side just in time for Sue to vomit more river water.

Carrie rolled off her, exhausted by her efforts and lay on her back listening to Sue gagging and sucking in lungful's of air.

All the while, the water was tugging at Carrie's stumps, trying to grab her mud covered body back to a watery grave.

It was only now that Carrie started to feel chilly. She put her cold hands up behind her neck to open her lungs and felt her muddy hair plastered to her it.

Carrie was surprised to hear Sue get up, after a few minutes, and slowly squelch her way along the muddy bank.

Shattered by her life saving efforts Carrie just lay there prostrate, her eyes closed.

After a short period Carrie heard Sue sluggishly returning, splashing her way back along the muddy river bank towards her.

'You OK?' Carrie managed to croak.

In return Carrie felt something hard being pushed firmly against her throat.

She opened her eyes in surprise to see Sue stood in front of her with a six foot long aluminium boathook.

'Look what the river sent me. Something to finish off the job I started. Right bitch. Now I shall keep my promise,' Sue said, with great malevolence.

'What!...what are you on about?' Carrie said in disbelief. 'I just saved your life.'

'You don't expect me to say thank you do you?' Sue sneered. 'Now I can finish off what I began.'

'What the...' Carrie croaked, shocked by the pressure on her windpipe.

'This doesn't change anything. I still intend to kill you,' Sue said viciously.

'So isn't it ironic? Now I've got you where I want you. In the river where I planned to get you all along.'

'You'll never get away with it,' Carrie struggled to say as Sue leant on the boathook putting more pressure on her windpipe restricting her breathing.

Carrie tried in vain to remove the weapon but her cold mud covered fingers just kept sliding down the shaft.

'Oh no you don't! Remember the hotel room in Monaco when you tried to throttle me? Now it's your turn. You don't like it do you? I said I'd get you back, didn't I? Well tonight is judgement night.'

Carrie grabbed hold of the vee of the boathook that was squashing her throat, only to be rewarded by Sue stomping on her stomach.

'Don't try it or I'll end it now.'

'Carrie reluctantly pulled her hands away, her mind in overdrive as she planned her next move.

'That's better.'

'I should have realised that a leopard doesn't change its spots,' Carrie muttered, realising now that saving Sue's life had been a stupid idea.

Sue had set out to kill her. Nothing had changed.

Suddenly Sue lifted the boathook off Carrie's throat and rapidly swung it down again aiming at Carrie's head.

Carrie reacted like lightning. She twisted away from the blow by spinning her legless body along the muddy embankment.

'Oh great. This is going to be good fun,' Sue smiled evilly. 'Hit the whirling woman.' She swung again. Carrie managed to spin away again, the boathook missing her head by inches.

Predicting where the next blow was likely to land, Carrie swung back the opposite way, and wrong footed Sue.

All the while Carrie was desperately thinking of a way to arm herself.

'Damn you,' Sue screamed. 'You aren't going anywhere. You might as well get it over with.' Thus saying she swung the boat hook again and glanced the side of Carrie's temple.

'Got you!' Sue said maliciously.

Carrie spun away again, at the same time trying to grab the boathook, the downward force of which had sunk it into the mud.

There was a brief tug of war between the two but the mud on Carrie's hands meant she could not maintain her grip.

Sue raised the boathook again. Carrie twisted away but crashed into a tree trunk which had been swept up the bank by the flood.

'Now what are you going to do?' Sue said smiling evilly, moving around to prevent Carrie twisting away again.

'You'll never get away with it,' Carrie shouted, still trying to look for some means to defend herself.

'Won't I?' Sue said, raising the boathook as high as she could to get as much downward force as possible.

Suddenly Sue stopped and twitched. Sparks flew from the top of the boathook. Molten aluminium rained down and hissed into the muddy river bank. Carrie shielded her eyes as the firework display continued briefly.

Sue had accidentally hit a fallen power line which had been brought down by the storm.

The surge of power through her body caused her muscles to go into spasm, her body dancing like an uncontrolled marionette.

She had a surprised look on her vengeful face. Her eyes bulged wide open, disbelieving and staring trying to comprehend. Sparks came from her hands and feet. Carrie could smell the sickly aroma of burnt flesh in the cold air.

Finally Sue fell backwards into the river, still clutching the boathook- a victim of her own aggression.

The strong current quickly stole her body and despatched it into the night.

Carrie sat mesmerised, the bright electrical sparks burnt into her night vision.

Finally, she slumped back onto the muddy bank, relieved that her ordeal had at last ended.

Complete exhaustion and relief overwhelmed her.

'Goodbye Sue, you've got your comeuppance at last,' she whispered.

Suddenly a torch beam broke the darkness. 'Police. Anybody there?'

'Yes, over here,' Carrie croaked. 'God, where were you when I needed you?' Relieved to have been found, her body finally gave in and she lost consciousness.

The Police had been alerted by a passing motorist who had seen the lights of the car in the river before the electrics failed.

The policeman had been searching along the shoreline beyond where the car had left the road and saw the fireworks as Sue hit the electricity cable

'Where are you?' he called.

Carrie was now unconscious and her mud covered body blended in to the muddy river bank making his task more difficult.

'Oh shit, Sorry I nearly stepped on you there. Are you alright?'

No reply.

The Policeman shone his torch on her and was distressed to find a legless survivor.

'Bloody hell, she's lost her legs.' He said in alarm.

Obviously unaware that Carrie was an amputee, he feared the worse and called for a helicopter ambulance to evacuate her. Although he was surprised that there was no blood for such a traumatic injury, he assumed the mud had somehow staunched the bleeding.

CHAPTER SIXTY TWO

As a result of her long exposure in the cold river water, Carrie's body temperature had dropped dramatically.

The paramedic who arrived within ten minutes of the Policeman's call had mentally prepared himself to treat a severely injured woman who had lost both legs, with the associated blood loss and trauma.

He was therefore much relieved to discover that she was actually a long-term amputee.

However, he quickly recognised that she was suffering from severe hypothermia and therefore seriously ill. Her vital signs had deteriorated to a critical point. Her core temperature had dropped to a dangerous life threatening phase below 28 degrees. She was no longer shivering. The body's natural defence against the cold had stopped. Her shallow breathing also confirmed his diagnosis.

Immediately he sprang into action and cocooned her in a thermal blanket to prevent her body temperature falling any lower.

'Hi, can you hear me?' he asked, gently shaking her by the shoulder. 'I'm Alex. What's your name?'

No response.

'Hello can you hear me?' he repeated. 'What's your name?'

Somewhere deep inside her Carrie heard the request and forced herself to respond.

'C…C…C…Carrie,' she said, almost imperceptibly.

The paramedic strained to hear her. Finally, he grasped the name.

'Ok Carrie. Don't worry. We'll soon have you somewhere nice and warm.'

Carrie was falling in and out of consciousness as the helicopter ambulance circled above her. A nearby small grass paddock had been selected for a landing site for it.

Several police cars were repositioned to shine their headlights on the field, their flashing blue lights creating a homing beacon for the incoming helicopter.

As well as the headlight illumination, the pilots also wore night vision goggles to identify any power cables that would compromise the landing site.

In spite of her confused state, somewhere deep in Carrie's psyche, she heard the helicopter and her finely honed military instinct suddenly kicked in and alerted her.

'Must secure landing area for the incoming flight,' she said, overcoming her fatigue and sitting up, surprising the paramedic.

'Need to set up a security cordon,' she uttered.

'It's OK Carrie. Alex coaxed calmly. 'Just lie still for me. We'll soon have you in hospital.'

'Clear sector A,' she called.

'It's just a helicopter. Your taxi to the hospital,' he said, comfortingly.

'The dust! I can't see it,' she croaked, trying to wipe the caked mud away from her eyes.

'Don't worry it's just a bit of muck. I'll tell you what. Let's get it off your face shall we? We don't want you looking less than glamorous do we?'

Gently he wiped the thick mud away from her eyes with an antiseptic wipe. 'You'll soon be in hospital. Just relax.'

Her muddled mind distorted the sound of the single engine Eurocopter to the lazy comforting double beat of the Medevac Chinook.

She was too exhausted to struggle any more. She gave way to the hands gently pushing her back onto the stretcher.

As the helicopter was still settling on its skids, the air ambulance doctor leapt out and ran to where the police indicated.

He quickly came to the same conclusion as the paramedic and agreed that she was seriously ill.

Her dangerously low body temperature would potentially mean she'd need a cardio-pulmonary bypass to warm her blood.

She was strapped to another stretcher and, with the aid of the policemen and paramedic, was hastily loaded into the helicopter.

Unlike the last helicopter trip in Monaco, which uncharacteristically had caused her great distress, this time she was too ill to care.

While the concerned doctor watched her vital signs on the monitors attached to her, the helicopter flew over the city of Gloucester and within eight minutes it touched down at the Gloucester Royal Hospital.

Carrie was rapidly transferred into A & E from the helipad where she was quickly assessed by a Consultant who agreed with the other's diagnosis.

The team used a technique seldom practised in rural Gloucestershire, where hypothermia cases are rare.

Her muddy body was gently washed in a bed bath. They had to avoid the temptation to use external warmth that could potentially dilate the blood vessels in her limbs. Any deviation in following this clinical procedure could cause catastrophic blood pressure failure leading to other major problems.

But while arrangements were being made to implement blood warming with a heart-lung machine, Carrie surprised the doctors.

Her vital signs improved very quickly and within two hours she was showing almost normal readings. The medical team were astounded by her speedy recovery.

She was then treated for a list of minor injuries, including the head wound when Sue knocked her out, the bump on her temple as the car shot into the river and the pin prick where Sue had injected her with the knock out drug sodium pentothal.

She was also given a tetanus injection to ward against any infections from immersion in the river water.

Initially the police had only Carrie's tee shirt logo to identify her as she was not really well enough to be questioned to track down her 'nearest and dearest', but as her condition improved, the hospital were able to get a contact name from her.

Consequently, Tim received a call from the hospital and rushed there to see her. He was understandably upset as he was ushered into the cubicle.

'Oh my God. Carrie are you OK?' he said, grabbing her hand.

'Feeling a lot better now than I did,' she said wearily.

What happened? All the hospital would say was that you'd been involved in an accident.'

'That veteran I went to meet.' Carrie said quietly.

'Yes?' Tim said suspiciously.

'It was no other than that evil woman Sue.' Carrie revealed, looking at Tim.

'I knew it! I knew I shouldn't have allowed you to go alone,' he exploded. 'What happened?'

'She knocked me out at the rendezvous. She was going to dump me in the river. But we had a fight and we ended up crashing in to the Severn.' Carrie related, her mind reliving each frightening moment of the incident.

'Jesus!'

'We were trapped in the sinking car, but I managed to escape.' She added, squeezing his hand. 'She was trapped and I went back and got her out. I saved her life and then she still tried to kill me.' Carrie said still disbelieving Sue's ingratitude.

'The bitch. Where is she now? Have the police got her?' Tim demanded horrified.

'No. She's dead.' Carrie said coldly.

'You didn't kill her did you?' he probed, horrified by the thought that Carrie might be charged with her murder.

'No, she was trying to kill me, but she accidentally electrocuted herself on a fallen power line.'

'Oh, thank God you didn't kill her.' Tim said, relieved.

'No she did that herself. Her evil ways got her punished at last.' Carrie said calmly.

'But she's dead. She's out of our life forever.' Tim beamed, assessing the implications. 'Thank goodness.'

'Yes, she's gone.' Carrie confirmed, looking at Tim. 'Rupert's rid of her at last.'

'He'll be 'over the moon' about that.' Tim added.

'I'm sorry but we've lost the new car.' Carrie suddenly remembered. 'The Land Rover is at the bottom of the river.'

'Don't worry about the car. It was insured.' Tim reassured her. 'We can replace that. We can't replace you though.' He added, tenderly stroking her face.

'After all your hard work getting it modified too.'

'Forget it. You're OK, that's the main thing. I don't know what I'd do if you'd...not made it,' he said, filling up.

'Oh Tim, don't cry. I'm a tough old bird.' Carrie said holding his hand to her cheek. 'Nobody will get the better of me.'

'Look, I don't know how to say this...' Tim said clearing his throat. 'I know you've got some reservations about...marriage...but I realise how much I need you. I couldn't bear it if you....'

'What! Are you...are you...?' Carrie asked incredulously, amazed at what she thought he was getting around to saying.

'Proposing? Yes. 'Tim confirmed. 'This probably isn't the right time or place but...will you marry me?' He asked gazing romantically in to her eyes.

'You're not just saying that because you're feeling sorry for me?' Carrie queried, testing his sincerity.

'No...I love you.' He said holding her gaze.

'Oh Tim. I didn't realise you had it in you.' Carrie said bringing the moment 'back to earth'.

'Well?' he demanded earnestly.

'Yes, yes. Of course I will.' She replied, pulling his head down and sealing her acceptance with a lingering kiss.

A loud cheer went up from all the doctors and nursing staff in the vicinity who had been eavesdropping on the conversation.

CHAPTER SIXTY THREE

Andy received a call from a very emotional Tim.

'Andy. You'll never believe it but that bitch tried to murder Carrie.' Tim said hurriedly his words an almost incomprehensible jumble.

'You what?' Andy asked, unsure what Tim's rant was about.

'Rupert's missus kidnapped Carrie and tried to drown her.' Tim said taking a deep breath and talking slower.

'But I thought Sue was back in prison?

'She was.' Tim confirmed. 'But it's a low security one and she escaped.'

'What! Again! I don't believe it,' Andy said, stunned by the news, his blood running cold. Quickly regaining his composure, he asked. 'Is Carrie OK?'

'She's in hospital suffering from hypothermia, but she's recovering OK, which is more than can be said for that bloody woman.'

'Has Sue been recaptured then?' Andy demanded.

'No.'

'Oh God, not again,' Andy groaned, the knot of fear returning in his stomach. Quickly he went to the front door and ensured it was locked.

'Don't worry,' Tim continued, 'apparently she electrocuted herself and...

'What? Electrocuted herself?' Andy repeated, puzzled. 'How?'

'Yes, she was trying to hit Carrie with a metal boathook when she got entangled in a power line.'

'Poetic justice,' Andy observed, suddenly feeling relieved.

'They haven't found her body yet though.' Tim added. 'She fell into the river and it got swept away.'

'Serves the bitch right.' Andy said vehemently. 'Thanks for letting me know. Does Rupert know?'

'No I haven't spoken to him, I thought I'd leave that to you.'

'Ok, I'll give him a call and tell him, especially if the media get hold of the story and start hassling him. Give Carrie my love and take care.' Andy said hanging up, still reeling from the news.

Andy rang Rupert straight away. The phone rang for a few minutes before he answered.

'Rupert is that you?'

'Yes. Sorry for the delay, I was putting Jeffery in his cot.'

'It's me Andy.' He said unnecessarily, pondering how to tell him about Sue. 'I have some good news for you.'

'Go on.' Rupert invited, wondering what possible news Andy could have.

'It's your estranged wife, Sue.' Andy blurted.

Rupert's skin crawled at the mention of her name. 'Have they locked her up and thrown away the key?' he asked hopefully.

'No, it's better than that.'

'Better than that!' Rupert questioned. 'What could be better than that?'

'She's dead.' Andy declared dramatically.

There was a momentary silence as Rupert absorbed the information. 'Dead? What do you mean dead?'

'Well, long story short. She kidnapped Carrie and...'

'Kidnapped her?' Rupert interrupted. 'How? She was in prison. Did she escape again?' he quizzed.

'Apparently.'

Rupert thumped the table in frustration. 'What the hell's wrong with the prison service allowing somebody like her out.'

'Makes you wonder doesn't it?

'And I dispensed with the services of those security pals of Carrie, too. She could have come down here and murdered us in our beds,' Rupert said, starting to get wound up.

'Yeah, but she didn't did she? Now, just calm down.' Andy soothed.

'Oh my God, Did Carrie kill her?' Rupert surmised.

'No, she didn't. Apparently Sue killed herself.' Andy revealed.

'What suicide?' Rupert said dismissively. 'There's no way she would 'top herself'. She was too cock sure of herself to do anything like that.'

'No. She was trying to kill Carrie and she accidentally electrocuted herself.'

'Electrocuted herself!' Rupert repeated, trying to rationalise the information. 'How?'

'Apparently she hit a fallen power line.' Andy said, with a hint of joy in his voice.

'There is a God after all.' Rupert smiled. 'At last I'm free.'

'Great isn't it?' Andy couldn't help suppressing his delight that another link of his involvement with the Godsons had also come to an end.

'Well I for one won't be going to her funeral.' Rupert said, gleefully.

'It doesn't look like there's going to be one anyway.' Andy said quickly.

'Oh! Why's that?'

'She fell into the river.' Andy added. 'They can't find her body.'

'The devil has probably taken her home,' Rupert suggested, flatly.

After an overnight stay in hospital under observation, Carrie felt well enough to leave.

She was interviewed by the Police and was able to tell them about her abduction by Sue who had absconded from the Prison.

The prison authorities were quickly able to confirm that Sue was indeed missing.

The following day a missing persons ('Misper') search was conducted by the police and several voluntary rescue groups including the Severn Area Rescue Association (SARA), Cave Rescue and Mountain Rescue. Their search, directed and coordinated by SARA, to try to find Sue's body, included a search in the River Severn itself and scouring the river banks and, in case she'd survived, the adjoining fields.

The searchers were split into small Teams and each given an area to search.

Regular status reports of the progress of their search and team welfare was checked every thirty minutes by radio links coordinated by RAYNET.

No trace of Sue's body was found. After a few fruitless days, the search was called off.

'Her body has probably snagged on a tree root. It'll come up some time.' Rupert was told.

'She means nothing to me anymore,' he said, happily contemplating a future free of looking over his shoulder.

CHAPTER SIXTY FOUR

It was a bright sunny afternoon as the christening party cars arrived at the Church on the Hill and disgorged their occupants all dressed in their Sunday best.

Rupert and Jo liked the quaint, ancient Church sitting on a small hillock on top of the 500 foot Churchup hill.

Its elevated position gave it pride of place, made it special; as did the ancient architectural design of its small castellated tower, the long knave, stone arched windows and the wide stone buttress.

They also liked the history of the place and decided that baby Jeffery would be christened there in the 14th century font, to become part of a special heritage.

Since his own Godfather, Geoffery Foster, had appeared on the scene, twelve months previously, Rupert had met and grown close to his fellow 'Godsons'. Consequently, he had invited two of them, Tim and James, to be the baby's Godparents.

Amongst the other guests the proud parents shared the occasion with Andy, who had also been asked to be a Godparent, and he had brought Helen with their two children.

Carrie and Tim's Mum, Kay, were there too along with Beth, who had become James' good friend.

Ben, of course, came with the package and he had brought his young lady friend, Janie.

Rupert lifted Joanne's wheelchair out of the boot of the car and helped her into it. It was her first real outing since returning from the States following her spinal surgery.

The minimally invasive key-hole surgery by the world renowned specialist was deemed to have been successful, but it was too early to assess what level of mobility Jo would regain.

Jo wheeled herself to the back of the car and lifted the baby out of his backward facing car seat and gently wrapped him in a white crocheted blanket.

Jeffery was dressed in a cute white romper suit and soon gained the 'oohs and ahhs' of all the ladies in the party.

He had been born preterm at 24 weeks by caesarean section following the accident that had crippled Jo. But in spite of the shaky start, Jeffery had made up for it and was now a seven month old bonny baby who seemed happy and contented.

Along with the other ladies, Carrie came to admire the baby.

'Oh hello Carrie. Sorry to hear about your ordeal with that horrible woman. It must have been absolutely awful.' Joanne said.

'Yes it was.' Carrie said shuddering at the recollection of her ordeal.

'However, I believe congratulations are in order. Let me have a look at your engagement ring,' Joanne said, cradling the baby.

'Oh thank you,' Carrie said feeling slightly uncomfortable at doing an un-macho 'girly' thing.

Nevertheless she presented her left hand and proudly displayed the beautiful diamond ring that Tim had bought her.

Oh, that's really beautiful. Look at it sparkle. Well done you. Congrats Tim,' she shouted. Tim turned at the sound of his name. He was standing with a group of the others nearby and acknowledged the compliment.

James noticed that Ben and Janie were standing away from the others and looking a bit uncomfortable as they waited.

Leaving Beth talking to Helen he went over and spoke to them.

'You OK Ben?'

'Yes.' Ben said flatly.

'I can understand why you feel a bit uncomfortable being back here.'

'Yeah, brings back a few bad memories.' Ben admitted.

'Yes I know. But time will help. Believe me.'

'Hope you're right.'

'It's OK to feel apprehensive after what happened here in the Churchyard. But one thing's for sure. That wretched woman isn't going to be bothering you ever again. And you've got Janie to help erase those memories too.'

Janie intertwined her hand with Ben to reassure him.

Anyway you're not allowed to be sad today. A christening is a celebration.'

Andy had been watching the discussions but resisted the temptation to go over and join in. He was holding Amy's hand and repeated his new mantra 'Family first'. He had vowed to spend more time with his own family having now reduced his working week to three days.

Helen, too, saw what was going on with James and Ben and was expecting Andy to join them any minute.

But when he didn't she was impressed. Perhaps Andy was changing after all and becoming the new family man he had promised to be.

Led by Rupert, the little group meandered their way along the narrow pathway to the ancient church. Their journey took them through the old graveyard where they circumnavigated the tall grave stones that stuck out at rakish angles from the short grass.

Andy had volunteered to push Jo's wheelchair up the steep path to the church while Rupert carried their precious baby.

'I'd quite forgotten how tough the push up here was,' Andy said, puffing.

As they made their way up the steep meandering path Andy was transported back to when the whole saga had begun.

On that occasion he was pushing Geoffery Foster up to the church for his own daughter's christening.

Geoffery's collapse during the service had triggered the old man's quest to track down his own Godsons and Andy had been 'coerced' into helping him.

'God, there's been a lot of water gone under the bridge since then,' he thought.

Andy was brought back to the present as they arrived at the ancient Oak door. He remembered to duck his head as he pushed Jo through the low doorway.

A grey haired lady in clerical gowns was waiting for them.

'Hello Vicar,' Rupert said.

He recognised the kindly face. It was the same lady Vicar that conducted Geoffery's funeral service.

'Good morning. This must be little Jeffery. He looks a handsome little chap, don't you darling?' the Vicar said, bending to address the baby. Jeffery smiled.

'Hello Mum,' she said, addressing Joanne. 'He certainly is a lovely baby isn't he?'

'Thank you. Yes he is. But then again I'm biased. He's not a tearful baby and thankfully he's good at night too. Having said that, I hope he'll be OK during the christening.'

The group gathered around the ancient stone font and to everyone's surprise Jo stood up. The others gasped in amazement. There was a ripple of applause as she walked a few hesitant steps towards the font holding on to Rupert's arm.

'Wow. Well done you,' Kay said, full of admiration.

The vicar was puzzled.

'It's OK vicar. As much as I'd like to tell you that a miracle has happened...the one that made the lame to walk. This is down to the skills of an American neurosurgeon and hours of physio sessions at home,' Jo said, pleased with herself, wobbling slightly.

'Yes. She was determined to stand at the font today,' Rupert told them all. 'That was her goal. This is the first time Joanne had stood since our accident.'

'I have to thank Carrie for keeping my secret too,' Jo added. I have had surreptitious discussions with her about how she had motivated herself to get walking again.'

The vicar smiled. 'Now I understand the reason for your jubilation. So today you are really celebrating two great events.

Well I suppose we ought to get on with the Christening, especially as this is my last one,' she informed them. 'I am retiring next week.'

'Oh that's a pity,' Kay said quietly to Carrie. 'She is a lovely lady, very personable. It's easy to see why everybody loves her.'

Andy took baby Jeffery from Rupert.

He smiled at the baby and Jeffery smiled back.

'Who are the Godparents?' the Vicar asked.

Andy, Tim and James stepped forward.

'*As Jeffery's parents and godparents, you have the prime responsibility for guiding and helping him in his early years. This is a demanding task for which you will need the help and grace of God. Therefore let us now pray for grace in guiding this child in the way of faith*'.

Andy handed the baby to the Vicar who duly baptized him. Jeffery just smiled as she poured the holy water over his head made the sign of the cross on the baby's forehead.

Handing the little one back to Andy, the Vicar lit a candle from the altar for Jeffery.

'*God has delivered us from the dominion of darkness and has given us a place with the saints in light.*

You have received the light of Christ; walk in this light all the days of your life'.

'*Shine as a light in the world to the glory of God the Father*'.

The vicar concluded.

'You may take photos now that the ceremony is over. If you would like, I'll borrow a camera and take one of the whole group if you wish,' she said.

They all duly posed for several photos around the ancient font and Rupert even persuaded the vicar to have her photo taken with the Godparents and baby Jeffery.

After the photo session Jeffery's proud Dad went to the smiling Vicar.

'We are going to a local community centre for a small buffet. We'd be delighted if you could come and join us Vicar.' Rupert asked.

'Oh that's very kind. Yes, I will pop in for a few moments and join you for a cup of tea.'

'We have a lovely christening cake that Helen made,' Jo added. 'Jeffery has been so lucky to receive lots of cards and little presents.'

With the ceremony over and at Andy's suggestion, the christening party made their way down the steep path and into the nearby burial ground to see Geoffery's grave.

Andy dashed back to his car and got twelve red roses out of the boot. He re-joined the group and gave one to each of them.

Andy addressed the group standing around the grave and said, 'I thought while we were all here it would be nice to come and pay our respects to Geoffery Foster. Without him and his quest to seek out his Godsons, all our lives would be totally different.

He was a man of many talents. A very determined person right to the end.

I think that you, his Godsons, have all benefited not only financially but are now stronger characters for his brief involvement in your lives. Indeed, we all owe him a lot.'

Then at his direction they all laid the flowers on Geoffery's grave.

Ben was upset as he gazed tearfully at the grave. Janie squeezed his hand and whispered. 'Is this the man that Foster Lodge is named after?'

'Yes. He was a very nice man,' Ben said quietly. 'He bought the Scout hut for us and my bikes too.'

'He was obviously a very generous person too.' Janie observed.

'Because of him my life is now so different.' Ben added.

'What do you mean, different?' Janie asked, puzzled.

'My new bike helped me win that trophy. I've got a new Mum, he paid for the 'drying out clinic'. Hopefully she'll now continue to be alcohol free. I've got a new house we're sharing with James and my new friend James.'

'Is that all?' Janie asked expectantly.

Ben thought for a second and looked at her. 'No, I've got a lovely girlfriend too.' He said and gave her a gentle kiss. 'How much luckier can anyone be?'

Janie blushed at Ben's public show of affection.

Andy studied the group gathered around the grave and finally said. 'Well I think you'll agree that we have all changed and moved on. I guess you can say we're living up to Geoffery's motto.

IT'S NEVER TOO LATE TO BE WHO YOU COULD HAVE BEEN.

As the Christening party returned to their cars a distant figure left their concealed vantage point and quickly drove off, unseen.

END

Godsons readers comments

- *Only read at bedtime – I found myself going to bed earlier and earlier to read the book to find out what happened next.*
- *I like the format, quick punchy chapters.*
- *I can't wait for the next book in the series.*
- *I went home from the book launch of 'The Godsons Legacy' and read the complete book all night.*
- *The characters are so real.*